THE DURABLE FIRE

BOOKS BY HOWARD SWIGGETT

NOVELS

The Power and the Prize

The Strongbox

The Durable Fire

ADVENTURE AND ESPIONAGE

The Stairs Lead Nowhere

Most Secret, Most Immediate

The Hidden and the Hunted

NON-FICTION

Forgotten Leaders of the Revolution

The Great Man: George Washington As a Human Being

The Extraordinary Mr. Morris: A Life of Gouverneur Morris

War Out of Niagara: Walter Butler and the Tory Rangers

The Rebel Raider: A Life of John Hunt Morgan

Diary of a Rebel War Clerk: J. B. Jones (edited with notes)

March or Die: A History of the French Foreign Legion

The Pinkerton Story (with James D. Horan)

THE DURABLE FIRE

HOWARD SWIGGETT

HOUGHTON MIFFLIN COMPANY BOSTON

The Riverside Press Cambridge

 • Library of Congress catalogue card number: 56-11576

PRINTED IN THE U.S.A.

To Leonard Outhwaite

Forty years ago in my youth at . . .

But true love is a durable fire,
In the mind ever burning,
Never sick, never dead, never cold,
From itself never turning.

Sir Walter Ralegh: "As ye
came from the Holy Land"

THE DURABLE FIRE

1

THE LAST AFTERNOON OF THE YEAR WAS FADING over the Hudson and there was utter quiet in the empty offices of Continental Industries Corporation in Rockefeller City. It was time set aside every year by Edward Rutledge, the chairman, to examine the personal financial statements of his principal officers. The officers themselves made them up and delivered them to him for his sole consideration. If what they owned and owed was unexceptionable, he destroyed the statements forthwith. Two or three were ordinarily locked away for discussion after the New Year. The purpose of it was to satisfy him that "no one in a responsible post was in any sort of a jam, or under unusual pressure." Sometimes a word of caution against getting overextended followed and in rare cases he had even had to warn against parsimony. His highly paid men were expected to live commensurately.

At sixty-five, Rutledge himself was a desirable combination of trustee and entrepreneur. "Has this fellow got a vision of the unbounded future of industrial America? Does he think in terms of new products, new techniques, new machinery, higher standards of living for all?" were his main standards for judging men. So spoke the entrepreneur. As a trustee his test question was, "Is he a man you'd allow to loan money for you?"

2

Of course, in his position life was enormously cushioned in minor ways but in the great final decisions of business, those of expansion or retrenchment, when to move and when to wait, above all the selection of men, he carried the heaviest responsibility and was the captain of his ship. He was an essentially kind and modest man, attributing the power and wealth that was his largely to the fact that "I have been fortunate," and he felt the best advice he could give young men was what had been given him—get in a fundamental industry and work up.

He had made this year-end rite into a symbol. He was at his desk when all were gone, the last man to leave the ship, the man who thought of everything. "Now let's see if we can't all remember this fall to put the lights out when we leave," he always told the office manager the Monday morning after daylight-saving ended. "I'll always remember the shock it was to the late James A. Farrell in 1930 to find that U. S. Steel was spending $500,000 a year on office equipment. It's very easy to get complacent."

By right of seniority Harold Titcomb, the head of the mail room, a veteran of fifty years with the corporation, took over the reception desk when Mr. Rutledge returned from lunch on New Year's Eve and the rest of the staff went off to the revels. It was not a hardship. On leaving, the chairman said, "Happy New Year, Harold," and shook hands with him, and Titcomb always found a fifty-dollar bill in his hand. It was a gift from friend to friend. He then put out the last light and went to meet his wife. They had a fine dinner and "took in a show." He was a few years older than Rutledge and past retirement age but at fifty he had married a woman twenty years younger. She was very pretty and he was proud of her, and, as he said, she gave him young ideas. He often wondered who there was among the younger men fit to take over the sentry post when he did retire. Too many of them were just "damn specialists," good enough on a postage meter, say, but no good with a comptometer, hopeless on a PBX board, wholly unable to wrap a package and of course not on friendly terms with Mr. Rutledge's florist. Some of them were "nuts on electronics."

3

As the hour drew close to four, Rutledge was about through. In general the statements were very satisfactory. He was particularly pleased by the number of farm investments among the senior officers. Even if they did not pay out in the first year or so, there was nothing like a stake in the land, that is to say in cows or poultry or that well-bred flock of sheep Hewitt had up in Vermont where the skiing was so famous. He made a note to ask Evans whether, as he supposed, his large increase in common stock holdings was the result of an inheritance—just as well to let them all know he kept informed.

Well, that was about it and he tore up all the statements except James Peale's. How in the world did Jim happen to have $500 of overdue bills? Well, must be an oversight and listed out of that meticulous rectitude characteristic of Peale.

Titcomb knocked as he was locking the statement in his private-file drawer. He said Mr. Lowry had arrived.

Rutledge had never met Lowry. Earlier in the month there had been a board decision to bring in an outsider as vice-president in charge of foreign operations and casting around for an exceptional man a number of Rutledge's friends had strongly recommended Stephen Lowry, a man about forty who was just leaving government service abroad. He had arrived from Europe only a few days before.

Titcomb ushered him in. He was a good-looking fellow with easy agreeable manners and was unmistakably a person, but his appearance was somewhat startling to Rutledge. It was cold, almost bitter, outside. Lowry apparently had neither hat nor coat, and his face, neck and hands were red as a tramp's with the cold. He wore flannel slacks, a rather old but very expensive tweed jacket, a soft shirt and a gray knitted tie. Now in the summer Rutledge worked in his shirtsleeves as often as any man could in an air-conditioned office and, moving with the times, enjoyed jokes about the Brooks Brothers type. But he did hope there was some sensible reason for this unconventional attire in a job hunter, even a very high level one. And he had the feeling that Lowry's slightly amused look was not wholly in keeping.

It was a little disturbing. A corporation office is not a country club or a college campus. He wondered what Titcomb would think of an officer dressed this way. Titcomb was under no difficulty. He took Lowry to be the new herd master, a title which impressed him, at Rutledge's large Long Island "dairy farm." He told his wife at dinner there was nothing like a farm of your own. When he did finally retire he was going to get them a little place upstate where they could raise chickens. "You get yourself a chicken farm and you've got something," he told her. "Can you imagine what it would be like to have a little house with cross-ventilation?"

"Very cold," she said.

"Well, Mr. Lowry," Rutledge began after the first greetings. "We've been hearing very good things about you, very good things indeed. I didn't think Alec Channing thought highly of anyone. I hope you're going to want to come with us. We're looking for a foreign specialist with vision and administrative ability. When I say 'we' I mean not only the directors but all of my associates. Our president, Mr. Johnson, was sorry not to be here this afternoon. There's not one iota of opposition to the plan. All my associates knew about it from the start. All approve. We're building a new managing team of younger men which will be good for twenty years. There is no problem about pension or participation rights or seniority rights which we have not thought out and settled. A cordial and even fraternal welcome awaits the right man and I can safely say I don't know a place in any major industry with such opportunities. Is it the sort of thing that appeals to you?"

"Oh very much so," Lowry replied. He did not think it necessary at that moment to say he was not interested in a "managing team" after the next ten years. By that time he hoped to have made enough money to retire to something more interesting than business.

Rutledge continued. "You probably know that our original unit, the rolling mill, began as the century did. Their annual sales were about seventy-five thousand dollars. This year our whole operation isn't a great deal less than several thousand times that in fifty countries. Yet in another sense we've always remained a small company. We've grown, if I may say so, like a tree from our own strength."

This last firmly held article of faith was not wholly true. The growth had of course come largely from consolidations with and purchases of other companies, yet, in the sense Rutledge intended, it was true. The founder had been a man of deep social consciousness, aware, as few of his generation had been, of responsibilities toward the community for the safety of its labor at work and for every man's right to better himself.

"You'll find us very conservative about the way to do business and you'll find us as daring as a pure scientist about new ways to improve a product or reduce a cost or junk an obsolete machine. I'd like to add this about company politics. I honestly do not believe we have any. Everyone knows who'll succeed me when I retire. I happen to have been at M.I.T. and my successor to have started as a steel puddler, but our own mothers couldn't tell us apart, as they used to say of a Harvard gentleman and a Yale drunk. Oh, you're Yale, put it the other way," he said with a laugh. "What I want to make clear is that it would be the same man whether our labor or our management or our directors selected him. And what he thinks should go for dividends, and what should be plowed back is what I think and what my predecessor learned from the founder. If, as I suppose, you have investigated us as we have you, you may feel our policies haven't been too unsuccessful." He said it with a pleased and almost boyish smile. "Now do this for me if you will. I have been rather curious about it. Just sketch for me the sort of business day, I mean a typical day, in your government position."

"Well, I arrive at the office a little before nine and read the cables from Washington."

"Now what would they be about? I'm not asking for government secrets."

"I've served in six European and Near East countries since

nineteen-forty-six and of course the cables vary according to the host country, as we call it. But they follow a general pattern. Washington will cable authority to let the host country purchase hand pumps for an environmental sanitation project, provided bidding is open to U.S. suppliers and that procurement procedure follows agreed-upon standards, something which we will already have told them has been agreed. The next will tell us that the program recommendations for next year must be ready in a week. This will be in reply to a question from us asking for policy guidelines, which of course they will disregard."

"You mean that sort of thing happens under the present administration? I can understand it under the old one."

"They're much alike," Lowry said.

"That's very interesting, very. Go on, tell me more."

Lowry smiled. "Well, the bombs really start bursting in air when one says that a constituent of a senator, from any state you like, has written him about personally seeing U.S. fertilizer soaking up rain in an open freight car in the middle of a famine area. We are ordered to see the Minister of Agriculture forthwith, direct him to cease and desist from wasting fertilizer and to reply in such form that the cable can be shown the senator."

"How'd you ever get anything accomplished? Do you mean to say the government has no confidence in its men in the field?"

"Oh sure, lots of confidence, but those are some of the limitations of the democratic process."

Rutledge shook his head. "Do you see much of the, of the uh—host-country politicians?"

"Oh sure, one from some remote part is announced. He wants, as he tells you, to 'deal direct' and bypass his moribund central government. He wants a grant for vocational training of high-school-age boys in his locality, which is likely otherwise to go Communist. You explain the central channels through which you must work. This affects him very adversely. He had supposed two things: one, that American know-how cut red tape and, second, that the U.S. was against Communism. Since it is evident neither is true, he will bid you good day. You glance at your appointments. At six you have your telephone talk with Washington and at six-thirty you're to confer with the Economic Counselor. You have to dress for dinner at the Turkish Embassy at eight. You ask your visitor to do you the honor of having a drink with you at seven-fifteen. He accepts on behalf of himself, his wife and a few relatives of hers living in the capital."

Rutledge frowned slightly. The note of levity in Lowry's voice annoyed him a little. "What would the conference with the Economic Counselor deal with?"

"Oh, his analysis, or hers, as happened when I was in Paris, of estimates, current foreign exchange trends. Perhaps most often the probable foreign exchange shortages a year or so ahead."

"Your friends tell me you're a terrific worker, Mr. Lowry," Rutledge said.

"Well, I have a good deal of health and energy."

"I think I can promise you that there would not be such frustrations as you describe with us."

"Then it may not be as much fun," Lowry replied blandly.

Though by no means a grim fellow, Rutledge did not like the word fun applied to business. He thought he had better say so. "If business were fun, children could handle it," he observed. "Tell me, did you ever hear of Raymond Fosdick?"

"Yes."

"About thirty-five years ago Fosdick shocked some of us by saying it was an educated man's duty to work against the idea that business was the be-all and end-all of life. What's your answer to that?"

Before Lowry replied there was a knock on the door. Rutledge turned in evident surprise and said, "Come in." Titcomb entered, looking very annoyed, and closed the door behind him.

"Excuse my interrupting you, Mr. Rutledge. I just didn't know what to do. Mr. Cramer's outside and says he just dropped in for a minute to pay his respects. I did my best to explain . . ."

"Oh bring him in, bring him in," Rutledge said getting up. "You'll forgive my breaking off a moment?"

"Certainly, would you like me to wait in another room?" Lowry replied.

"No, no, want you to meet him. It'll just be a minute. Well,

Mr. Cramer, delighted to see you," Rutledge said as Titcomb showed him in with some asperity. "This is Mr. Lowry, I think I mentioned to you, Mr. Lowry, our good friend Mr. Cramer. Thought you were in Chicago."

Cramer, a stocky man about fifty-five, well bundled up against the weather in belted camel's-hair coat and muffler, beamed at them from behind his spectacles, and shook hands. His manner was modest and slightly apologetic.

"Just stopped for a moment to pay my respects and wish you a happy and prosperous New Year," he said. His voice was very low, its tone flat but unusually distinct. In spite of his snappy camel's-hair coat, he made Lowry think of an old-fashioned, small-town druggist.

"Very glad you did," Rutledge said heartily. "Mrs. Cramer with you?"

"No, Mother decided not to come on from the West at this time. Our boy is just back from Korea and I'll be with them for New Year's in the morning. Great joy to us to have him back safely."

"I know it must be," Rutledge said. "Want to talk to you about John very soon. We'll have to get him in harness."

Cramer smiled and said he must get to his train, and after he had shaken hands again with Mr. Lowry, Rutledge walked to the door with him.

"Awfully nice of you, awfully nice to stop in this way. I do appreciate it. My love to your family and new successes in the New Year," Rutledge said and, when Cramer had gone, turned back to Lowry to say, "Now that was a characteristical nice thing of Cramer. He's a remarkable man. He may strike you as small-town, but that fellow has the respect of more important men in New York than anyone I know."

"Is he in the company?"

"No, we met him oh twenty years ago when his firm was our auditors, and then in the thirties the Founders Trust put him in a variety of shaky situations, all of which he got back on their feet; made a great reputation. We got him for our engine company in Illinois at one time. He's an industrial adviser to a number of important banks and corporations, but it's never gone to his head. Just as nice as he can be, simple, unaffected. I don't know another man who could refer to his wife as 'Mother' without its embarrassing me."

He glanced at his watch. There was a great deal more he wanted to ask Lowry. He was still troubled by the note of levity in some of the things Lowry had said. Certainly he had not been dynamic, but a "managing team" such as he was building needed variety. There were plenty of dynamos on it now. Perhaps this fellow would act as a balance wheel. As a matter of fact, the absence of "pressure" from him, so rare in a job seeker, was most gratifying.

"Tell me," Rutledge said. "You went in the Army in nineteen-forty, I understand, and from there straight into Foreign Service?"

"Yes."

"What did you do before that? I've got some record of it, but just refresh my memory."

"I graduated from college in 'thirty-four and did various things for five years, none of them very well."

"What were they?"

"You will recall," Lowry replied, "that it was a little hard at the time to get any job, much less settle on your lifework?"

"I do," Rutledge said with a smile. "There's been quite a change. I understand now that 'leading industrialists' sit at 'round tables' over 'the problem of *attracting* the bright young men who will become the business leaders of tomorrow.' I haven't come to that but we're always interested in talent. However, about you. Who attracted you?"

"I was in a publisher's for a year. I drove a truck for the Loyalist Relief in Spain for two years and I was in the foreign department of the Founders Trust just before I went into the Army."

"I see," Rutledge said. Well it could have been worse, but offhand it was not very impressive. Still, let's see—three years out, a boy of, say twenty-five or so, he did see the light and went in a bank. St. Paul was older than that before he saw it on the road to Damascus. Henry Ford was a failure for a good many years. Washington himself didn't really settle down until his marriage. "By the way, you're married as I recall?"

"Oh yes, three children."

Despite some reservations, Rutledge was inclined to go ahead. Unquestionably Lowry would broaden the organization and Rutledge was aware that uniformity was as dangerous in a business as complacency. And he must essentially be the right man or there would not be a folder of letters from important men saying that he was. And it was getting late.

"I haven't told you very much of what you'd do here, don't think it's necessary. We simply want our whole foreign operation headed up. I suppose we'd both better think it over but I'd say I'm ninety-nine per cent ready to go ahead. How do you feel?"

"I'd like to know something more about the general setup and the other men at what would be my level."

"Good question," Rutledge said, getting up and going over to draw an organization chart down from a rack on the wall. "Our subsidiaries are almost entirely autonomous except for foreign sales. Their financial supervision, as you see, is under Charley Curtis, our treasurer and senior vice-president. Operations under Calvin Hewitt. Leslie Evans has engineering—in broad terms—design, plants, new models, this thing automation they're talking so much about. An outstanding man. There, as you see, Jim Peale has been spread too thin—an eye on the foreign business as well as P and D, progress and development. Expansion, in other words. New fields, diversification. All of them men you'll like. That enough?"

"Yes, for the moment."

"The assistant vice-presidents you'll get to know. The new head of our foreign business will be on the same level as these other men. The Board set thirty-five thousand as his start-off salary. Henry Dennison told me he explained the management pool to you and our stock-option plan. We haven't made a lot of millionaires here but on the other hand, well, a man can make a decent living and have something to look forward to."

They both smiled at the magnificent understatement.

"Right now," Rutledge went on, "some of the men who have been with us as little as five years have a very handsome paper profit in their options, though of course you never know how the market will turn. Oh, there are two small formalities: physical examination, and I know you won't take this other one amiss, but we ask a man coming in at your level to give us a complete statement of his affairs. I'm the only one, literally the only one to see it. All officers make such a report to me at the year's end. You can see the reason for doing it at the start. We took a man on once, whom we had all known and done business with for years, and after he had been here a week he told us he had to have a major operation and all his teeth out and asked us to advance the cost of it. Very embarrassing of course. I'm not suggesting—well, you see what I mean?"

Lowry said he did and would be glad to comply. Rutledge went over to his closet for his hat and coat.

"You leave your things at the door?" he asked.

"I didn't have any," Lowry said.

The thing is not as absolutely clear-cut as I'd like it to be, Rutledge thought. There was one person on whose judgment of men he had come greatly to rely. "Look here," he said, "Mrs. Rutledge is waiting for me in the car downstairs and we're going to the Waldorf for a drink. It's an annual practice of ours and there's a story connected with it may interest you. We went there, just by chance, a New Year's Eve afternoon in the late thirties. As it happened, one of the Austrian Rothschilds had landed here as a refugee that morning and as we were having our drink he came in with two gorillas if I ever saw them."

He had turned to face Lowry and suddenly stopped dead in the story. "Well, no matter," he said in evident embarrassment.

Lowry, puzzled, said, "Oh come, tell me the rest."

"No, no, just forget it. What I was going to suggest was that you come along with us."

"Are you still suggesting it?" Lowry asked with a grin.

"Yes, I'd like you to meet Mrs. Rutledge," he said and then began to laugh. "Oh dammit, I'll have to tell you. The fact is I've had great confidence in her opinions since that day—in business, I mean, always had it in other things. Rothschild sat down at a table with these gorillas and they proceeded to go to work on him. He was pale, droopy and exhausted. You could just see these two confidence men taking him over and I said to my wife, 'That's a pathetic sight.' 'It certainly is,' she said. 'In an hour Rothschild'll have the shirts off their backs.' I want to see what she thinks of you. Mind?"

Lowry laughed. "I'll be delighted, but my wife's also waiting for me."

"Well, fine, we'll pick her up too. Where are you?" He hung on the answer.

"The Pierre."

Rutledge felt considerable relief. He had been afraid of something incommensurate like those hotels you passed west of Sixth Avenue when you went to the theater.

"Couldn't Mrs. Rutledge and you come to us? They've given us a sitting room. Why don't you do that, unless Rothschild's waiting for you?" Lowry asked.

It was not a bad idea. Seeing Mrs. Lowry as hostess, even in a Pierre sitting room, Mrs. Rutledge could make a very clear assessment. They went down to the car after leaving greetings and a handclasp with Titcomb, who sprinted ahead to relieve Rutledge of the need of ringing for an elevator.

Mrs. Rutledge, bundled in furs and smelling of flowers, was waiting in a Cadillac.

"Susan," Rutledge said, poking his head in the door, "this is Mr. Lowry I told you about and he's asked us to go up to the Pierre where they're staying for a drink and I said we'd love to. Mrs. Lowry is there. Is that all right?"

"Why darling, of course, how delightful. Get in next to me, Mr. Lowry, before you freeze. Here, take half the robe. What would your mother say if she saw you without a coat in this weather?"

2

ROSALIE LOWRY, THE WATER RUNNING FOR HER bath, did not hear the telephone ring when her husband called from the Pierre lobby to tell her he had arrived and that Mr. and Mrs. Rutledge were with him.

He took them up to what Mrs. Rutledge thought was a very homelike sitting room for a hotel. There was domestic amenity—two vases of flowers and a half-dozen new books on the table and desk; a leather traveling-frame with pictures of two young boys and a younger sister; the framed photograph of a handsome man, another evidently of the hostess, sun bathing on a beach. But a pleasant disorder went with it—a pile of laundered shirts and some shopping items half opened; letters and cards, some still unopened. He put away their coats, settled them comfortably, went into the bedroom, and as he closed the door behind him they heard a shower running.

The sight of his wife unclothed or clothed had continuously waylaid Lowry for almost twelve years. He stared appreciatively at her standing in the tub as she gasped with surprise and cold water, and turned her back.

" 'Good afternoon, sir,' " Lowry said. "The Rutledges are outside waiting for a drink."

"Oh good," she said, turning off the water and stepping out. "Then it went well? You think it's settled?"

"Oh I think so. How long will you be?"

She took off her shower cap and shook out her pale bronze hair.

"Just a few minutes. Be careful, you'll get all wet. Is she silks or tweeds?"

"Silks."

"That blue thing be all right?"

"Perfect. Do you object to champagne, in view of the season of the year?"

"No, go order. I'll hurry. What's he like?"

"Very nice. Earnest but nice about it."

"My wife will be here in just a moment. She's delighted you could come," Lowry said to the Rutledges as he asked the operator for room service.

"Is this your wife?" Mrs. Rutledge asked, picking up the photograph of the barely covered sun bather. Her husband had spotted it as soon as Lowry had left the room. He had been of two minds about it—that Mrs. Lowry, having no warning of their arrival, had had no chance to put it away. But it was not the sort of picture anyway which in his view you left around for waiters and bellhops to gape at.

Lowry nodded as he ordered some champagne.

"How perfectly lovely she is. And these are the children? Are they here?"

"No, they're in school abroad."

"Mrs. Lowry an American girl?" Rutledge asked.

"No, Estonian."

Rutledge looked again at the picture.

When Lowry crossed the room to admit the waiter, his wife entered from the bedroom. She wore a blue velvet hostess gown and her actual looks startled Rutledge more than the picture had. She was beautiful, rather tall, with a manner all easy cordiality.

"We were admiring your lovely children," Mrs. Rutledge said. "When are they joining you?"

"Not until summer. They're in school in Switzerland. My

brother," she pointed to the photograph of the handsome man, "and his wife are having an eye on them. We felt that, much as we'd miss them, getting a place to live would be so difficult, to say nothing of the right schools, they'd better stay."

"We also thought it would be fun to be alone for a while," Lowry said.

There was that word fun again, Rutledge thought. At the same time he assessed the large sapphire ring and diamond clip his hostess was wearing and they gave him a comfortable feeling that Lowry had private means.

"You've been in America before of course," he said to Mrs. Lowry.

"No, I haven't. Stephen has been back frequently but the difficulty and expense of moving young children about led me to stay with them."

"I'm curious, Lowry, as to why you stayed so long in Europe. You'd more than paid the debt we all owe our country several years ago, I should have thought." Actually he was a little more than curious. He was a little troubled lest Lowry might be one of those voluntary expatriates who did not think the American scene cultured enough for them. He was not looking for a man like that.

"I sometimes think it was because of the flowers," Rosalie said.

If he had heard correctly, Mrs. Lowry had now said something which really disturbed him. Of course he was fond of flowers, himself. Annual flower-show prizes to him were proof of that.

"I think that's the most delightful reason," Mrs. Rutledge said, "and I know exactly what you mean."

"In my view," Rutledge said, "the street corner vendors of flowers you see all over Europe are the direct result of the general low standard of living and the general obsolescence of their industry. You'd agree with me on that, Lowry? Look at our wage scales. Compare the poorest of them with the take of thousands of people in Europe selling flowers."

"I'd agree that the product of flower sales won't buy many cars, or TV's," Lowry said.

"You didn't have any trouble finding a place to buy these flowers, did you?"

"No trouble, no, but quite an expense."

"Well, it all adds up to the creation of incentive."

"I think the rainfall and climate of Western Europe has a good deal to do with it," Mrs. Lowry said.

"Do you like New York, Mrs. Lowry?" Rutledge asked her.

"It's very exciting. The great office buildings around Rockefeller City make me speechless with awe. Please don't think I'm being critical of my new country when I say the lack of trees and parks also makes me speechless for another reason."

"Oh come, we have parks. Look out your window," Rutledge said. "Lots of trees, leafless this season of year, of course. Gramercy is a nice little place."

"There's only one of it. I made Stephen take me around. We saw Washington and Stuyvesant Squares, and we saw Gramercy–but–" She shook her head. "They are not as beautiful as they should be."

"Well, we have a very mixed population in New York, lots of vandalism in the parks. They come out in droves in the spring and tear down my dogwoods and lilacs."

"They wouldn't," Mrs. Lowry replied, "if New York had city parks like those not only in Paris or London or Rome but in all the little countries, like my own along the Baltic."

Rutledge had had to deal with a wide variety of difficulties raised by wives of new associates. If they came from the Middle West their frequent complaint about New York was that people there did not realize who they were at home where Dad "owned" the bank and the largest factory. If from the South, they were a descendant of a Signer, through Grandfather or his wife, as well as of one of General Washington's "most trusted officers."

Both types, however, were American and their attitudes natural and comprehensible to an American. But there was something disturbingly foreign about a woman making an issue of flowers and parks. At the same time she seemed to be a sensible enough woman. Mrs. Rutledge was asking her about the capitals Lowry had been posted to and she was talking freely and easily and without any name-dropping. Rutledge very much disliked name-dropping, except as he himself used it to point out that so-and-so had been at M.I.T. with him, or was "a neighbor in the country" or was on the President's Economic Advisory Council with him, or a fellow trustee of the world's largest life insurance company.

"We're a rather closely knit family at C.I.C.," he heard his wife saying, "and I'm sure you'll like most of the wives."

"I can only hope they'll like me," Mrs. Lowry replied so modestly that Rutledge forgot about parks and flowers. Obviously she intended to "enter in." He realized that the long training in tact and adjustment which she had had as the wife of a government official would be most valuable.

"Well," he said half banteringly as Lowry filled his glass, "I'll concede the flowers and parks. Maybe we should have more. But, Mrs. Lowry, you'll concede, won't you, there's an air of efficiency, of vigor here that makes up for a lot of flowers? Europeans laugh at our gadgets but I've found they're glad to use them."

"They have a wonderful little gadget in Europe too. Waiters carry keys. When you order morning coffee in bed, that's where they bring it. They let themselves in. Here you have to bound out and let them in and then crawl back into your bed."

It seemed to Rutledge this was not only put most indelicately but the very idea of C.I.C. officials having coffee in bed was displeasing. He turned the conversation deftly away from such decadence. "New York is the most friendly city in the world," he said, "that's what you'll find."

Mrs. Lowry half turned her head. "In Paris," she said, "the gendarmes shake hands when they meet. The bus drivers lean out to shake hands when they pull up beside each other. Small children shake hands when they're through playing in the parks. Concierges—"

"That's not real friendliness. That's affectation," Rutledge replied. "Have you any clubs, Lowry?"

"Only Yale nonresident, I'm afraid."

"Well, we'll take care of that. We don't make a point of such things, of course, but I will say there's not a decent club in or around New York—I'll not go that far, though it's true and of course you have your own friends to propose you. The University and The Hounds are the natural places for you at present, and I'm a governor of one and Jim Peale of the other."

Lowry smiled. "Jim Peale is my oldest friend."

"Now I never knew that. Why in the world didn't he say something? He knows all about this."

"I asked him not to," Lowry replied. "There's a rule my father taught me, 'Make friends through business but don't go in business with your friends.' "

"That's very well put, very. What did your father do?" Rutledge asked. He was very pleased. This was a man with his head on the right way.

"He had the Lowry Equipment Company in Ohio."

"Oh of course, I remember."

The telephone rang and Lowry said, "I think that's the Peales now. They're dining with us."

"I'm actually shaking," Mrs. Lowry said to Mrs. Rutledge. "I've never met either of them."

"You'll like them."

Lowry hung up the telephone and hurried out to the elevator to receive them. His wife stood anxiously waiting, hoping, almost praying, that she would find favor in the eyes of the man, reunion with whom meant so much to her husband. They had been like brothers through school and college and now in the prime of their lives, after long separation, there could be a renewal, a deepening of all the ties of comradeship. She would "like" Peale whatever he was, if only he "liked" her and did not feel that Lowry had thrown away his life by his illogical, impetuous marriage to her.

Then her husband and the Peales blew in with gay greetings and Peale came straight to her, arms extended. She was aware of his good looks, his athletic figure, perhaps a trifle too straight and erect, and an appeal at once austere and passionate in his dark face.

"I should have been there to have done this at your wedding," he said, kissing her. She laughed and kissed him.

"Oh I'm so glad," she said.

"Lucky man," Mrs. Rutledge said.

"It's our wedding anniversary," Lowry told her.

"How do you like him, Edward?" Peale asked Rutledge.

"How can he help it?" Evelyn Peale asked, looking up at Lowry. She was dark and slight, tired-looking but effusive, as befitted the occasion.

"Don't know about him. Like his wife. That's enough. Well, all good things come to an end, and we must be off," Rutledge said.

Down in the elevator, out to their car and in it, Mrs. Rutledge was bubbling with enthusiasm over the Lowrys. Rutledge had fallen silent.

"Darling, what's the matter?" she asked. "The champagne wearing off? Why didn't you kiss your hostess? You were the best-looking man there."

He took her ungloved hand under the robe.

"I don't know," he said. "I suddenly feel rather depressed."

"Why, dear, how unlike you. What is it? You liked them, didn't you?"

"Yes, I like them very much."

"Don't be depressed tonight and don't think about the business until after New Year's."

"I always think about it," he said.

3

WHEN ROSALIE LOWRY HAD TOLD THE RUTLEDGES that she was actually shaking because of the Peales' arrival it had been quite true and arose from even more than anxiety over the first meeting with her husband's closest friend. In spite of all her social experience as Lowry's wife, the prospect of America was frightening to her. In Europe Lowry had been hers in a special way—Europe was not his country as it was hers. There were aspects of life there, nuances of experience which she understood at times better than he did. In general, the people they met were as new to him as they were to her, and he did not know people like Jim Peale, who had been important to him before she had. The large figure of her brother, Armas Lainvee, was always in the background. She knew what Foreign Aid was meant to accomplish and understood and was proud of what her husband's part in it was.

She was in complete agreement with him that he must return to and make his way in his own country and that their children should be American in outlook and education. But she felt a great unease about American life. She was sure its influences on Stephen would be centrifugal—above all the demands of Big Business, which she only vaguely understood; the relations with his mother, his sister, his wayward brother, Dahlgren; his feeling about Yale and the renewal of all the ties with the men who had been there with him, especially Jim Peale. Although long and widely separated, Peale and he wrote to each other a great deal—seldom long letters, but anecdotes, comedies, coincidences, small encounters, discoveries.

Now Lowry would need her less. There would be little in their new life, so she felt, on which her opinion would be useful. Their great mutual project, Principal Errors, might slip away and she had the fear that her hold on him might become mainly the physical passion they had for each other. Vivid as it was in Europe it was there only a part of a whole unity or mutuality of interests and behavior in which they complemented each other.

Yet, as the year went to its wine-bright end in laughter and reminiscence and midnight kisses, she had more and more the feeling that the Peale she was with was not the friend, closer than a brother, whom Lowry had described to her. She could not put her finger on it. She supposed it was natural for Peale, during dinner, to talk quite a bit about C.I.C., but she could see that at the time, C.I.C. and all its assets meant nothing to Stephen, gay and exuberant with a hundred things he had been going to tell, and she thought Peale's reference to some great party in Sutton Place they "had gotten out of" to be with the Lowrys seemed rather unnecessary. Peale made a ponderous observation on the political situation and Lowry, gulping down more champagne, said, "Jim, what a judicious remark from you. He's not getting judicious, is he, Evelyn? He was once, though, to great effect. I've never forgotten. It was when he told me you were engaged. I knew you were seeing a lot of each other but I had no idea that it was at that stage, and I said, 'Isn't this rather sudden?' And Jim, in that wonderful superior way of his, said, 'As Proust has well said, *Everyone who is not in love imagines that one chooses the person one loves after endless deliberation.*' Have I got it right, Jim?"

"Substantially," Peale replied.

"I proceeded on the same lines with Rosalie," Lowry said.

It seemed to Rosalie that Evelyn Peale might have replied, but she sat silent.

"Oh I must tell you," Lowry went on. "This afternoon Rutledge had just asked me what I thought of a statement by one of the Fosdicks to the effect that educated men should resist the idea of business as the be-all and end-all of life, and I was about to launch into a hearty affirmative with a discourse on Corinthians and Epicureans, when we were interrupted, and he forgot to come back to it."

"Just as well you didn't," Peale said. "I don't think he would have liked it."

But all this judicious propriety was certainly not the whole of Peale. He seemed to talk to her more easily than to Stephen and did so absorbedly and even gaily. He made some reference to being tired after the strain of a hard autumn's work and she thought sympathetically that after all, Stephen and she had been on holidays for three weeks and had had a wonderful crossing of the Atlantic by ship from Lisbon to invigorate them.

He said something else, about wishing he could get away from immensities, so sadly that for a moment her heart went out to him and she found herself touching his hand and saying comforting little things to him as she did to her children. He told her she was very stirring and she tried to draw her hand away, not having meant to be that at all. He kept her hand in his but spoke of having met and liked her brother Armas in Paris three years before, while she was away. Told her how devoted he himself had always been to Lowry's mother—both his parents had died before he entered Yale—and to his sister, and what a charming scamp Dahlgren, Stephen's older brother was. And he talked a good deal about his eighty-five-foot auxiliary schooner and what fun they would all have on it next summer.

Sometime after eleven o'clock, Evelyn, talking away across the room with Stephen, called to her. "Rosalie, if I do two card tricks will you do your Spanish dance I'm hearing about?"

"I can't. The costume has disappeared."

"Do it in that," Peale urged.

"Not a Spanish dance in this."

"Well, some dance in something," Evelyn said.

"Or nothing," Peale said, trying to find music on the radio. "There, won't that do? Sounds like 'Bolero.'"

She hesitated a moment, rose, felt the rhythm sweep around her, took the glass Stephen handed her and began to dance. She had the feeling it was the unwisest thing she could do, but a happy year was almost at its end and who knew the future, and it was fun to please, and she danced well, her robe swirling in great spirals around her. Then glancing at Peale's rapt face, she sank to the floor in obeisance and held out her hand to Lowry to lift her to her feet.

"Oh," she said, "I never thought. We haven't any cards."

"And the trick's only for children," Evelyn said. "And it's ten of twelve and we must dance the New Year in." She switched the dial to a dance band and turned to Stephen. Peale pushed a table aside.

"Fill the glasses for midnight," Rosalie said to him.

"Come, there's no time," he said, trying to put his arms around her. She took the bottle herself and slowly charged the glasses, anxious lest Stephen leave her with him at the hour. They danced a moment, Peale holding her too close, the seconds ticking away. Then the dance tune dwindled away into "Auld Lang Syne." Stephen stopped beside them. "I forget how it goes, that wonderful passage: 'They stood in the noon of that strange and solemn splendor as if it were the light that shall unite all who belong to one another.'" He handed Evelyn to her husband and took Rosalie in his arms.

"Forever?" he whispered as he kissed her.

"Everything," she answered.

Then they joined the singing coming over the air and drained their glasses to each other.

An hour later when the Peales left, after more kisses and laughter, Lowry asked her eagerly how she liked them.

"Darling," she said, "I have drunk so much champagne that I can't think of anyone I don't like. Come to bed, tell me how much you love me and tell me everything you first thought about me."

Lowry, loosening his tie, looked at her with happily drunken gravity.

"I want to kiss you," he said.

"I am not opposed to anything."

"Well," he said, "then I have to shave, lest I mar that magnolia skin."

"That's very thoughtful of you," she replied, kicking her slippers across the room. "I'll watch you shave. Do you remember the first time I did?"

Late in 1942, Captain Stephen Lowry, an American officer, on duty in London, was somewhat mutinous at having missed the landings in North Africa and at being refused combat duty there on grounds of "greater usefulness where you are." In the course of his duties he had learned of Operation Sardine, a two-man mission to the Norwegian Resistance, and volunteered for it.

In mid-December he was called before his C.O. regarding his application.

Colonel Channing, in peacetime the senior partner of a stock exchange firm, regarded our foreign enemies as morally lower than the Exchange and Securities Commission and considerably less intelligent. Inside his handsome head and underneath a manner of intolerable contempt for most of mankind an almost first-class brain was sleeplessly at work. His plans were at once audacious and thorough to the last detail and his record of success impressive. His young officers regarded him with a mixture of distant awe and hero worship.

He now looked at the well-built, well-uniformed Lowry affably, which was to say that he appeared to have some pity for a man so badly put together in such an atrocious uniform.

"What do you regard as your special qualifications for Sardine? I presume you speak Norwegian?" he asked.

"No sir. My main qualification is my high rating in the cold-climate tests."

"Well if that were the most important we could send an Eskimo. I presume you are really animated by the spirit of adventure, the desire to travel at government expense, meet new people, take advantage of your opportunities. And I suppose it's pure coincidence that you apply just as Colonel Nedberg asks for you?"

"Not entirely, sir. I suggested to him that the Norwegians—"

" 'The splendid Norwegians' is the correct term, just as we say 'the sturdy Dutch.' "

"The splendid Norwegians might like to see they have other allies than the British."

" 'Indomitable British.' In short it is not a desire for a posthumous Medal of Honor? You don't have the death-wish?"

"Oh no sir."

"You're just all healthy mind in healthy body."

"Well, yes sir, though I shouldn't have put it that way."

"Good, that's the type I like to see made expendable. By the way, you have no allergy to fish, have you?"

"No sir."

"Very fortunate, as there are likely to be a great many fish about. But the splendid Norwegians cook them before eating so you are not likely to get leprosy." He glanced at his wrist watch. "You will report to Colonel Nedberg in ten minutes and after a twenty minutes' talk you will both come back here and give me a detailed outline of *how* you will carry out this mission. Assuming that it does not overtax you mentally or physically, this is what you will do: land on the Norwegian coast at the Resistance Rendezvous Twenty-Seven, where the local clergy, Pastor Larsen, will receive you. Nedberg will proceed to the neighborhood of Ordmark and prepare or be supplied with a report of the extent of sabotage at the heavy-water plant. This will be in terms comprehensible to the scientists. You will bring it out three days later. In Nedberg's absence you will select and bring out with you that Resistance officer who impresses you as being most likely to be of value to the monitoring and broadcasting people. The officer must speak, in addition to a Scandinavian language, Russian and German. More if possible. If your choice is a poor one you will return to your native land on a slow boat for assignment to Motor Transport."

There were four men in the room of the Norwegian fisherman's log hut—Lowry, Colonel Norodd Nedberg from the Norwegian Forces in London, a Lutheran pastor named Larsen, the head of the local Underground, and another Resistance officer. The room was warm but Lowry and Nedberg, stripped of their soaking clothes, were being briskly toweled by the other two and, whether from immersion or nerves, were still shaking. The room smelled of fish and wet clothes. On the table two oil silk packages were open. In one were a dozen cigarette cases and in the other twenty vials of Benzedrine tablets.

Outside the hut the moonless night was silent except as the snow itself creaked with the cold.

The door to the hut's other room opened slowly and an unseen hand dropped their dried clothes inside and closed the door. Lowry and Nedberg got into them. The warmth was slowly restoring their souls, and Nedberg, a signal officer, picking up one of the cigarette cases, opened it and began to explain in rapid Norwegian the workings of the wireless receiving sets inside them. It seemed incredible to Lowry's ears that the sing-song baby-talk of the Norwegian language, as it sounded to him, could possibly possess the technical vocabulary necessary. The Resistance officer, haggard and drawn, glanced at his wrist watch and helped himself to a Benzedrine tablet. Then he apparently began to repeat back to Nedberg the instruction he had received. Several times Nedberg stopped and corrected him. The Pastor followed each word spoken by either.

Then over their shoulders Lowry saw the door slowly open again and around the corner of it peered what he was sure was the loveliest face he would ever see, and staring straight at him its owner smiled. It was a face of beauty and of ancient courtly race, he thought—like that of one of the young grand duchesses of the last czar. The cheekbones were high and far enough apart to give ample space for the wide dark blue eyes. The nose was tip-tilted in the slightest degree and the lips were full but decorous. The girl's short hair was a pale bronze color.

She asked the Pastor something. An assent rumbled out of his vast beard and she withdrew.

When the rubber boat that had brought Nedberg and him in from the British submarine tipped them into the icy fjord, Lowry had considered what a misbegotten sense of duty and patriotism had led him to volunteer for the mission. Now he could plainly see the hand of God had been in the affair. This was a face worth going through great perils and deep waters to see.

Its owner reappeared with some mugs of tea and four glasses of schnapps.

The Pastor said in English she was Officer Lainvee of their group and she shook hands with both newcomers. She wore stained pants, rough sweater and fisherman boots to the knee. As the men drank, whatever was feminine about her seemed to dissolve and her attitude was as grave, soldierly and alert as theirs.

Nedberg, putting down his glass began in rapid Norwegian what Lowry understood was a fill-in on the North African landings and the successes there. Dropping an occasional explanatory line in English to Lowry, he continued as to the objective of their mission. Captain Lowry would return to London, as he had come, taking with him a technical report on the Nazis' heavy-water plant near Ordmark, which the Resistance had just sabotaged. Nedberg would proceed to the neighborhood of Ordmark to secure it. They said it was already in preparation. After Lowry's departure Nedberg would remain with them. London wanted an officer brought back with Lowry, familiar with the terrain and the extent of Resistance operations, but who was also a fluent Russo-German-Baltic linguist.

The last provoked a long argument which Lowry could not follow. Nedberg said there was difficulty in producing those requirements. They all laughed at something that was said and Nedberg told him only the herring-gutter had the qualifications.

"Who's the herring-gutter?" Lowry asked.

"Lainvee."

"She guts herring?"

"Yes, that is her ancient fishlike smell."

"What's her first name?" Nedberg asked.

"Rosalie," he said. "She's an Estonian, escaped in June, 'forty, in a boat to Sweden and came over the mountains alone."

The talk went on as to Nedberg's move to Ordmark.

"They have thought it best, having regard to dangerous elements, to confine the knowledge of our presence to themselves. They consider it best that I go alone to Ordmark. Meanwhile your own movements will be confined to this and the other cottage. The Pastor will give you as full a briefing on operations here as possible and what he can, without scientific knowledge, of the heavy water. If I do not return you will go off as provided and tell them what you can."

"With Miss Lainvee?"

"She cannot be spared. Oh, in event of the Nazis arriving here, the Pastor will shoot you."

"I see," Lowry said. "I'd rather be shot by her."

"Oh, I think she would make no difficulty about that. However, let us hope it does not become necessary."

"Doesn't Officer Lainvee speak English?"

"Very limited, I understand. Perhaps you can give her a lesson or so. The command is now to sleep. Larsen and she go on guard."

The herring-gutter helped herself to the Benzedrine, and went out with the Pastor.

Nedberg left in the early morning darkness and when he was gone the Pastor began his nontechnical account to Lowry of what had happened at Ordmark. The mutual limitations of knowledge led the Pastor to say he should have thought a scientist would have been sent. Lowry told him no scientist could be spared. Lowry was an expendable courier. He ventured to ask what would be done about the linguist wanted by London. The Pastor said Lainvee would see what was possible after she had had some sleep, and proceeded with a briefing on details of Resistance plans.

It was not until late afternoon that Lowry saw the herring-gutter when she appeared with a loaf of bread and proceeded to make tea for them. Communication was difficult not only across the language barrier—though he had the feeling she spoke and understood more English than she pretended—but because it was difficult to talk about what he wanted to.

The peril they were in and in which she continuously lived, the cold silence without and within the room—so that the slightest sound was like a tocsin—anxiety for Nedberg perhaps appearing closely pursued, the dread responsibility for meeting the scheduled submarine, fear that he himself might not play his part as he wished, all this in the presence of such stirring appeal as he had never faced, disguised though it was by her fisherman attire—all made it difficult to speak.

She asked him how much German he spoke. He said he knew a good many words and constructions but understood only if someone spoke slowly enough for him to think out the meaning.

"It is so that I am the same in English," she replied.

"Where have you studied?" he asked her.

"At University in Tallinn, and I was some in Vienna a little."

"I have heard that in Estonia there is much education."

"Then who told you does not know Estonia. Until nineteen-seventeen there was almost none. Then maybe too much of a kind. All wish to go to University. So when they do, afterwards there is no work they can do."

"Do you mind my asking what your father did?"

"What does that mean?"

"What was your father?"

"He was lawyer. His life was very hard. He must work for years by himself to get education because the Russians would not let us go to the University then—"

"What did his father do?"

"Do? He was peasant like all Estonians."

From pantomine and what he always insisted to her later was his extrasensory perception of language, he acquired during the next hour a considerable knowledge of Estonia and of Rosalie. It was only, he understood, by great exception that she, born in the upsurge of nationalism after the Bolshevik Revolution, should have "international name" and not an Estonian one like Inge. Somehow from her voice, face and gesture he began to get a picture of life in Estonia, not as he had supposed hers to have been in ancient castles of the Teutonic knights, of whom he had read in Keyserling, but on the farm of her grandfather, in her father's apartment in Tallinn and her family's small summer house on the Baltic dunes, where at midsummer you could read the epic *Kalevipoeg* until midnight or sing around the fires on St. John's Eve as the flames were fed so that the flax would grow long. Once she sang a bar of one of the songs in a deep contralto, and years after found the English words for him:

> "Wild wailing winds of misfortune and sorrow,
> Wizards from Finland, ride by on the blast."

It conveyed to him as nothing ever had the tragic pathos of the little countries marvelously establishing during the few years of her life their previously forbidden culture and language, asking only to be let alone and, without resources or experience, opening a new room of civilization, a little world that was not a factory or a mine.

They were interrupted by the Pastor coming to summon her to record reports from Resistance officers who had come. Left alone with the Pastor, Lowry questioned him about her. The Pastor said her history was not an unusual one. On the terrible fourteenth of June the Red forces had entered Tallinn and by night found and arrested the Estonian leaders. The men, her father among them, were packed in cattle cars for Siberia in the morning. Her brother had got away. She had no idea where. Her mother and older sister had been jailed. Their fate was unknown. As for Rosalie with her beauty there had, he supposed, been the inevitable fate. He had not asked her about it. She had not spoken directly of it. Like most Estonians her hatred of Russians and Nazis was equal. A woman of the Norwegian Resistance had told him Lainvee had suffered greatly, but where all suffered, who was to say which was the greatest? In time the Omnipotent, in whose hand even the monster Hitler stood, dealt with such matters.

After supper Lowry insisted on taking the night picket on the Ordmark road by himself. The exhausted three agreed reluctantly and after Hansen had briefed him on signals and directions, the Pastor took him aside. Rosalie was already asleep in her clothes.

"I have watched you," the Pastor said, "as we ate and talked. I remind you that the safety of us all and many of our comrades may depend on your alertness. The moon will be up. Think not of the moon but of our enemies."

All the frozen lonely night Lowry kept his wits and senses at the trigger for the enemy, but underneath them he was powerless to keep his mind away from Officer Lainvee. Duty and desire fought inside him. Certainly she met the requirements for the Resistance officer to return with them, or at least Channing had not made maleness one of them. But to bring her out only to lose her in the great complex of London was intolerable. While no one could apply to him what Hector said to Paris, "thou gaper after girls"—at least not fairly apply it—was he better than Paris, enamored of a beautiful face?

He had accepted the discipline, the loss of individuality in the Army with good cheer and acted effectively under it. Now the whole damn war seemed like an intrusion on his private life.

His relief came out at seven o'clock, and back in the hut he found Officer Lainvee getting breakfast.

"You have not found an officer to go to London?" he asked.

She shook her head.

"My orders are to bring out the best choice I can make. The Government in Exile has given the same to Colonel Nedberg. Therefore, I assume you will go with me."

"I will not go. It is too easy," she replied, pouring some coffee.

"It is not a matter for your decision. But there is another side to it. May I talk to you about it?"

"So then talk," she said, handing him a plate of smoking herring and a piece of bread.

He was ravenously hungry and began simultaneously on the herring and a labored exposition of his feelings, during which to his own astonishment he found himself saying he wished them to go as man and wife.

"Such are the orders?" she demanded.

"No," he said, trying to set forth the depth and tenderness of his feeling for her.

"It is so that you wish me simply to go to bed with you?" she asked angrily. "One of them has told you I wish to go to America. You think I will do that to go?"

"No, no, I don't mean that. I desire to protect you in London because—"

She burst into a torrent of polyglottery, at the close of which she spat on the floor. "That is what peasants do," she told him. It was done, he thought, with the grace of a grand duchess. She grabbed her coat and left the hut and he did not see her alone again that day. Pastor Larsen told him she was seeking an officer to go to London.

The next afternoon about dusk Nedberg arrived from the neighborhood of Ordmark. Lowry, waiting on the snowy road, saw the skier come over the brow of the hill and swoop down. He ran to him and found a man close to final exhaustion. Nedberg gasped out that he had the detailed report on the sabotage of the heavy-water installation, and that all was well. Lowry gave him a drink from his thermos of coffee and schnapps, and with Nedberg leaning heavily on him, stopping at intervals with exhaustion and drowsiness, made a slow way back to the hut. They stripped him and the Pastor massaged him with warm fish oil, rolled him in blankets and left him to sleep.

He was awake at ten the next morning, seeming fully restored and Lowry restlessly paced the room as he breakfasted. When finally he lit his pipe and sat back with a contented grunt, Lowry felt he could speak of what with him now ranked with, if slightly after, winning of the war.

"Norodd," he said, "I should like to talk to you about a personal matter."

"So then, talk about it," Nedberg replied.

"I don't know just how to put it to you. I need your help."

"So you have my help."

"It is my desire to marry Rosalie Lainvee."

"So then ask her."

"I have tried to do so and there is considerable language barrier. Will you see what you can do? I would like the Pastor to marry us at once."

"She is disinclined to you?"

"I don't know. I'm afraid so. I expect nothing.'

"That may be the trouble."

"I desire only to love and serve her."

"That, my comrade, has little appeal to women. But how has all this come about?"

"My God, you've seen her face, you've—"

"Well, I have seen many faces and it is so she has a nice one. Has she said no?"

"I think so. I can't leave her here."

"I have it in mind to speak to her then, but I don't know whether I will have success. Where is she?"

Lowry glanced at his watch. "She's monitoring until eleven."

"In the other house? What time is it now?"

"Yes, it's ten before eleven."

Nedberg got up and knocked out his pipe. "I go," he said.

Half an hour later he returned with Rosalie, looking annoyed but grand-ducal in her herring-gutter clothes. The nod she gave Lowry was a jerk of the head.

"Many problems," Nedberg said. "First it must be said that Officer Lainvee has found no suitable officer to go to London. It therefore appears that if you carry out your orders to bring out the most suitable officer available, she must go with you. That should end the matter."

"It does not wholly end it, since I desire to marry her. If she will do that she will be able to go to America, whatever happens to me. I will change my will and my insurance and everything else."

"Do you understand?" Nedberg asked Rosalie.

"I did not understand and I did not listen."

"You mean marriage?" Nedberg asked Lowry. "That is, marriage legal and binding, not going to bed? There has maybe been misunderstanding."

"I mean it, for better for worse, till death do us part."

"Hum, expressive. Is it original?" Nedberg asked, looking at the ceiling and then translating for Rosalie.

At that a torrent of words poured out of her in a long declaration.

"What she is saying is she doesn't love you. That is in effect. At the same time it doesn't seem wholly hopeless, since she hates Russia and Germany, the invaders of Estonia, and would like to live in America after the war. There is more to do with the general problem of eight centuries of oppression but not, I think, very relevant. I myself did not understand all, as she spoke a great deal in Estonian. Wait, she is beginning again. Hum, yes,—you see, you seem to think she is aristocrat. She is not aristocrat but of peasant stock like all Estonians. She would, let me see, maybe ruin her face rather than look like a grand duchess, well words to that effect, maybe not important, almost certainly not true. You know women. Now she wants to know how old you are, how many brothers and sisters you have and are your parents living. Maybe this is progress. No, she says never mind, but she is born May, nineteen-eighteen."

"December, nineteen-thirteen. Please ask if I am repulsive to her."

"Oh we needn't ask that. Quite foolish. She is now saying you're just dreamer."

"Dreamer or not, what is her answer?"

"You desire me to put the direct question?"

"Yes."

Nedberg did so and as Rosalie began her reply, he said to Lowry, "We had better sit down, this will be a long speech."

"I prefer to stand," Lowry replied and did so at excessive attention.

Nedberg started to fill his pipe, and then with a gesture of despair reached for a pencil and paper and made occasional notes. Her voice rose and fell in cadence and volume but there was no break in the flood of words. It stopped at last in a gesture of seeming defiance, after which her hands clasped her breasts.

"Well, now," Nedberg said, glancing at his notes, "whether you are well advised to marry a woman of so many words, I do not know. Still, time and circumstances may alter that. It is so that under many restrictions, mainly having little to do, so it seems to me, with reality she will marry you. Oh yes, are you Lutheran?"

"Something like that."

Nedberg informed her and she nodded.

"There is no implication of permanence. It is for her a means of escape. However, she will not disgrace you. She will have to be married in these herring-gutter clothes, not very nice for either of you. All that peasant business is repeated. Also you must understand, rather difficult to interpret, she had, well, an unpleasant time when the Red Army entered Tallinn."

"I understand."

"She also has doubts about the official situation."

"I was to bring out a Russo-German-Baltic-speaking officer. She is both."

"Yes, they did not tell us to bring a woman or command you to marry her. Furthermore, if in the getaway she is wounded or lost, you are to carry out your duty as to the Ordmark report as though she were a male comrade. That is indispensable to her and I may say, as your senior officer to me."

"I accept it."

"She is just saying that you have no obligation to go ahead with this just because you began it. She is content to leave matters as they were."

To a degree Pastor Larsen proved more difficult than Rosalie. He became completely the Lutheran clergyman, concerned with illegalities and the absence of orthodox procedure. He did not believe the plan was proposed soberly, advisedly and in the fear of God.

"I do not know whether my vows and the laws of church permit this. I do not know the legalities. It may be I should merely be giving a sanction to cohabitation. Waiving the question of banns, serious enough in themselves, there will have been no registry. I do not think I can pronounce you man and wife."

"The situation is also difficult for me," Lowry replied. "Under the regulations of our army I cannot marry without my Commanding Officer's permission. I will ask it at once on arriving in London. I believe my record and this mission will make him grant it at once on compassionate grounds."

"Then why not wait for that?"

"Because I do not wish to take her away under the promise of marriage."

"She is going as a polylingual Resistance officer."

"If she goes only as that not only may I lose her but I cannot give her the protection I would wish."

"But if your Commanding Officer refuses?"

"Then I desire to be able to say we are married and pay the penalty."

"What would it be?"

"Loss of my commission and drafting into the Army."

"I must think about this," the Pastor said, "and talk to Colonel Nedberg. But is he not your Commanding Officer? Is not that a solution?"

"I'm afraid not."

The massive bearded man shrugged like a Frenchman.

"I suggest this to you, Pastor," Lowry said. "However much the world is changed, marriage is still for the protection of women. I suggest you can compromise some of your scruples to allow me to protect her."

"From what I know of her, what you have just said would be intolerable to Rosalie Lainvee."

"Of course it would. You know how women have to be protected from themselves, the poor little things."

"There is something I might do," the Pastor replied. "I must ask Divine guidance about it after I have talked with Colonel Nedberg."

Later in the day the Pastor talked again with Lowry. "Norway," he said, "is a wild country of lonely isolated saeters, the hill farms. Sometimes roads become impassable with snow and ice and a spring wedding must consecrate a union already consummated. In our folk ways a betrothal, before witnesses, has the solemnity of marriage, carrying with it binding rights and privileges. Perhaps I could betroth you before God. More than that I cannot, since you tell me you are not of your own will allowed to take final vows."

"Will she not think it a subterfuge of mine?"

"No, she will understand quite well, as would any Nordic maiden."

After the ceremony and a meager feast it was evident that whether Rosalie was bride or betrothed, Pastor Larsen, Nedberg and Rosalie herself expected that Lowry would spend the night alone. His heart had been touched to the quick when Rosalie, shed of her fisherman clothes, had come in with Pastor Larsen in a white dress. She had made her faint responses in Norwegian and he, as the questions and vows were translated for him, in English. Somewhere Nedberg had found an old-fashioned gold ring, too large for her thin finger, which she had had to clutch to hold the ring.

In his exultation, he had no doubts about the wisdom or rightness of what he had done. And if ahead there were months or even years of being a guardian and not a lover or husband, he was keyed up to accept them. What concerned him was that she should understand he really meant what he said and recognized that she was to be won, if at all, only by waiting. But he tried to lighten the shadowy room and her sorrowful face with his own high spirits.

Whatever their private emotions, sleep itself was nothing to be trifled with at a Resistance point. Their own and many other lives depended on that great nourishment.

He took two blankets from the five in the bunk, spread them on the floor, and indicated he would sleep on them and she in the bunk.

"No, no," she said firmly in an Anglo-German dialect. "It is so you are betrothed bridegroom and now you have rights." She indicated by speech and gesture she knew what was expected of a bride and would not be something else. They wrestled linguistically over what the something was and she finally tried "*object de pitié, charité, l'on qui ne fait pas son devoir.* I know men are pre-date-ory animals at wedding," she concluded in English.

"Predatory? I'm not predatory."

"You will be cold," she said pointing to the floor.

"It doesn't matter."

"It matters. I now have responsibility. *Sie können in dem Bett schlafen ohne mit mir schlafen.*"

"Certainly not before we're at least using *Du*," he said, pleased at having caught the *Sie*. He had heard but not fully believed there was a way of learning a language better than any Berlitz school.

"*Nach Du sind wir nicht, sondern Sie können nun Ihres Rechts nehmen.* I am not *chicaneuse.*"

He removed his boots and socks and rolled up in the blanket. It was certainly very cold. He heard her moving around for a minute or so and then she blew out the candle.

"Goodnight," he said. "Sleep well."

After a long pause she said goodnight.

He was not sure how much time had passed when she spoke to him again. He had been unable to sleep, less because of desire than the problems and anxieties thronging through his mind.

"It is *schrecklich* cold," she said. "I need those blankets. Get in this bed before we die."

He obeyed at once, bringing the blankets with him. She was lying with her face to the wall in her fisherman clothes but her icy feet touched his as he lay down.

"I am sorry it all smells of herring, but I was so cold. I thank you very much."

In the morning, though she sat on the edge of the bunk gravely watching him shave, she made no reference to them or their situation and was as much a Resistance officer alone with him as when they were joined, after a discreet knock, by Nedberg, looking amused, and the Pastor, looking very dour. And the final hours of waiting for night and the submarine were too full of anxiety for her to be anything else.

Lowry wished he had something he could give these devoted

men he was leaving behind, and did bring the Pastor to accept his wrist watch.

"Have you any of your own money with you?" Rosalie asked him in a moment during the afternoon when they were alone.

"Plenty, what would you like?"

"I would like to give the old woman, who went a long distance in the snow to borrow her daughter's wedding dress, a present."

"Of course, what about a hundred dollars? I have plenty."

"No, no far too much. Would you please give me twenty-five? What kind of money is it?"

"Swedish kroner."

"Oh good, thank you. I will be back in plenty of time. Oh, *wir sind nach Du*, as Resistance people say, if you like."

He felt really married as he gave her the first of what he hoped would be a great deal of money. Nedberg came in and observed him with quizzical amusement, plainly stopped only by being a gentleman from demanding news of the previous night.

They purposely supped late, the Pastor with them, so that the wait before going down to the shore would be as brief as possible. Half an hour before the moment fixed the Pastor, looking at Lowry's watch on his wrist, asked them to kneel while he invoked the protection of God for them all. Kneeling in the dim candlelight, head bowed, Lowry felt Rosalie's cold fingers reach for his and then her hand firmly clasping his. It was the closest physical contact there had been between them, and he felt, as Amen was said, a consecration he was sure would be with him forever.

4

FROM THE SUBMARINE'S BASE IN THE ORKNEYS they were flown late the next night to London, and Colonel Channing, having left orders to be awakened, received them at his flat at three in the morning. At that hour he was freshly shaved and in uniform and gave the impression of having just breakfasted well on fresh eggs and grilled bacon. He looked at the unkempt arrivals with some distaste.

"Sir," Lowry said, "this is Officer Lainvee of the Norwegian Resistance. This is Colonel Nedberg's report on the heavy-water plant." Rosalie clicked the heels of her fisherman's boots and stared straight ahead while Channing glanced at the report. As Rosalie was in the midst of an uncovered yawn, Channing, without looking up, asked, "Is the officer fatigued, Lowry?" As he asked it, Rosalie toppled over on the floor in a faint.

Lowry, shedding a borrowed British Warm, knelt, picked her up and put her in a chair with head between her knees.

"The officer, sir, is a very brave woman who has not eaten or slept in some time," Lowry replied wishing that striking a superior officer did not incur the penalty it did.

"Lowry, I am very sorry. I really didn't notice. I'll get some brandy," Channing said. He came back with it and, to Lowry's astonishment, was as considerate and helpful as a woman. Rosalie opened her eyes, a little dazed, tried to apologize and get to her feet.

"She must get right to bed," Channing said. "My God, what a beauty. She can stay here. I'll send for a nurse."

"There is a friend I can stay with, Colonel Channing," she said. "You must not think me weakling."

"Would you like some tea? What would you like?"

"To give you my papers and to tell you I shall do my best in any duty you give me," she said, then added, "sir."

"Call the motor pool and have a car sent at once, Lowry. I think I'd better get you some breakfast."

"I could not eat, thank you. I will be all right in a very few hours. Will you please read my leader's notes on me?" Rosalie asked.

Channing looked carefully at the paper in Pastor Larsen's writing. "You seem to have chosen well," he said.

"Thank you very much, sir. We were very fortunate."

"Shall we say two o'clock at my office? No, I'm afraid it must be no later than noon. Can you both report then?"

"Yes sir."

"Good. Help yourself to anything there is until the car comes." He picked up the telephone and asked for the Duty Officer at the Scientific Office.

The car took them through the now early morning to his two-room-and-bath flat off Russell Square, Rosalie dozing during the drive.

"When will shops be open?" she asked. "I need many things."

"Some by nine-thirty. We can sleep till then. Or you can go on sleeping. Make a list of what you want."

"Have you anything to eat?"

"Lots. What about canned orange juice, canned chicken, powdered cream and coffee?"

"Um," she said. "I will have it ready when you come back."

They walked up the stairs to the small ugly rooms.

"Were you ashamed I fainted? I was. Oh a bed and sheets," she said as he put on the lights. "Close the door until I call you."

When she did, her clothes were on the floor and she in bed "Please take them to the cats. I am sure there are many fishes heads in them. Is there soap I can wash my hair with and any scissors for manicure? And any sweet powder, even if I am a peasant? Have you a robe? Wake me when you go out. Bring me slacks and *tricot*. Lipstick, it may be you can. Thank you," she said drowsily and was asleep.

He set the alarm for nine-thirty and lay down in the other room. Wrapped in his robe, she wakened him just before the alarm went off.

"I'm all rested and have bathed and washed my hair. And put out the things for breakfast. Where is cloth for—" she asked, running a finger along a grimy tabletop.

"Dust?"

"I think so."

"I don't know of any," he said softly. "Take an old shirt. I'll have a quick shave and shower and get in a uniform."

In the sub, at the Orkneys, in the plane and until she fainted at Colonel Channing's, her speech and manner had been undistinguishable from that of any officer returning from a mission. Toward him she had been reserved and largely unsmiling. He sensed her troubled feelings in wanting to do what was expected of her, and was so touched by it he almost told her, "Look, we needn't stay married if you can't stand it. Your happiness is all I want." But what real "happiness" was she likely to find in a war-torn capital in the midst of a war far from won? With him she had some measure of protection. He realized that he was saying really the most offensive of masculine offensiveness—I am a gentleman and she can trust me and she might get in with someone who wasn't.

"Well, I'll hurry," he said and closed the bedroom door after him. When he came out, dark hair wet and brushed after the shower, dressed in a custom-made uniform, she looked at him in amazement and made a very guttural remark.

"What did you say?" he asked.

"I said *Sa Puha Jumal*, an exclamation in Estonia meaning 'Thou Holy God.' It's compliment."

"I see," he replied, looking in the mirror. "Now forgive my saying this, but I am to bring you new slacks and *tricot* and presumably you'll get a uniform this afternoon. But won't you need something to wear under them?"

"Again please?"

"Lingerie," he said straightening his tie. "Because of the fish."

"I will buy later."

"I see, all right, just want to be helpful."

He returned in an hour with a small gold wedding ring engraved S.L. to R.L. He showed it to her.

"How is possible?" she asked.

"I stood with pistol to the engraver's head. It took twenty minutes. May I put it on?"

She nodded and held out her finger. His hope for a kiss came to naught. He had a small bunch of flowers in an old newspaper and slacks and jersey from the PX in extravagant American wrapping. And a trench coat lined with wool. She shook her head over them all rather ominously, he thought, and then looked up at him.

"There is nothing different?" she asked.

"What do you mean?"

She gave two deep sniffs and stood with her nose in the air. "I bathed again after you went out. You can't tell after all the soap, it is still fish?"

"Oh no, it's lovely."

"Thank you. I have thought so. Any lipstick?"

He handed it to her.

"I come," she said, going in the bedroom with the slacks and jersey.

"The right size?" he called in a moment.

"You will see soon."

The door opened and he turned to see her looking like a page from *Vogue*.

"Never will I touch any fishes again," she said.

"You're wonderfully beautiful."

"Thank you, you may kiss me, if you like. You are very good to me."

He took her in his arms eagerly but she only brushed his lips with hers, and then leaning back her head said, "Don't be angry or laugh but it is a little embarrassing for me and breakfast is ready."

To have the descendant of Estonian peasants, the herring-gutter, the Resistance officer and the *Vogue* model before him all in one was marvelously exciting and romantic, but as she found tablemats and china he didn't know he had, and set the table and served the orange juice and the creamed chicken and poured his coffee it came over him, in a great wave of revelation, that though he had gone a long way to do it he had really married the well-brought-up little girl next door whom he had known all his life. The Lord had indeed made of one blood all the nations of the earth.

At noon they reported to Colonel Channing. He saw Rosalie first, alone, while Lowry waited nervously in the anteroom. It was after one when she appeared, looking somewhat drawn and anxious.

"It is all right, I think," she said quickly to Lowry. "This is where I go." She showed him a pass to the Ministry of Information. "For monitoring. I wish I could speak a moment but I am ordered to go immediately. I will meet you at five today, other days very late."

"At home?"

She nodded and went down the stairs. Channing motioned Lowry to come in. The ensuing interrogation was long and searching but made no reference to Rosalie. When it was completed Channing told him he was to go to Norwegian Headquarters and repeat the report. He gave no indication of the degree of his own satisfaction with what Lowry had said.

Lowry, rising to leave, asked if he might speak to the Colonel as man to man. Channing nodded coldly. Lowry asked whether the Colonel felt the mission had been satisfactorily accomplished. Channing said the answer would depend in part on the value placed on his information by the Norwegian Headquarters. As to the Ordmark report, the answer was yes, but he had not expected an officer of his would make a hash of a simple job.

Subject then, Lowry said, to how the Norwegians viewed his report, he desired the Colonel's permission to marry Officer Lainvee immediately.

"Then," asked Channing, "you do not regard the ceremony performed by Pastor Larsen as sufficient? Or are you trying to evade the penalty of what you have done?"

Lowry, startled and shaken, realized that Channing could only have learned of it from Rosalie, and why she had suddenly decided to do so distressed him. Or had Channing in questioning her caught the scent of it and then caught her? Or had she seen a way to be rid of him? He told Channing that he regarded himself as bound by the betrothal ceremony and that while he had no desire to evade the consequences of his behavior, he hoped that circumstances and compassion would justify permission to marry.

"Before you went on Sardine, you applied for combat duty in northwest Africa. The application has been approved and your E.T.D. is five days off. I take it that disposes of this other whimsey," Channing replied.

The assignment he had so earnestly sought for the moment lost some of its attraction. He expressed his thanks but said it made the permission more vital to him.

"You will be informed of the decision in due course," Channing said.

"But sir—I have only five days. I implore you to agree. It means everything to me."

"Is it more important to you than winning the war?"

"Sir, it is another universe of discourse. They are not commensurable cases."

"Dismissed," Channing said and Lowry left the room.

Three Norwegian officers questioned him for over an hour and he had the feeling as he left that their report to Channing would be a commendation, even a high one. But he made his way to his rooms a prey to the most gloomy emotions.

He found Rosalie already there, poring over an English grammar. She looked up at him with obvious concern.

"Are you angry with me? Please don't be."

"Of course not. What happened with Channing?"

"I am very sorry, but he is like a devil in some ways. He was examining me in most minute fashion. Everything, everything you said or did in Norway. He had a sheet of paper with hours marked on it and he made notes as I answered him. Then he said, 'Now let us go back to Colonel Nedberg's return from Ordmark. What did he do?' I told him and he kept changing from day to day and hour to hour and then he said very quietly, 'Now cast your mind back to the night before you left, not the night you left. What time did the three of you separate?' and I answered, 'After the betrothal. Captain Lowry and I went to the other hut.' "

"Oh my God," Lowry blurted out.

"I know. I could die. What have I done to you?"

"I don't know. It doesn't matter if you will only marry me."

"I have married you already."

"What more did Channing say?"

"I tried to explain and I could not say why I had done it. I did say I was willing to leave Norway because it was not my country. I was only in a sense a refugee there. And I said I would do anything asked of me for the Allied Cause."

"I asked him for permission to marry you and he would give no answer except to say that I am to rejoin my regiment in North Africa in five days. I had asked to do that before I went to Norway."

"Five days?" she gasped, getting to her feet. Then she said, "Whatever will be, I am bound to you if you want me to be."

"By love?"

"No, I cannot say that, but by promise and duty. You may think you love me but it is not, I am sure."

"Do you want it to be?"

She made a gesture of what he regarded as unnecessarily cruel indifference. He said he would take her to dine at the Savoy as soon as he had washed. He closed the bedroom door behind him and noticed the twin beds had been freshly made and when he opened his shirt drawer he found that lying neatly beside his shirts were stockings and underclothes of hers and two pairs of pajamas. In the bathroom the shelf had been neatened to make room for a modest array of her new toilet articles. He was examining them all with consuming interest when she knocked gently on the door.

"Yes," he said, opening it.

She held out an official envelope. He tore it open, glanced at the signature, "Alexander Channing, U.S.A., Commanding . . ." and saw the words, "Permission to marry is granted . . ."

"Oh my God, it's all right."

"I guessed. Look," she said holding out a personal card of Colonel Channing's on which he had written, *The brave deserve the fair. Floreat Estonia!* "It came with a bottle of champagne."

"No caviar?"

"Please do not speak even of the eggs of fishes," she said.

"Are you happy?" he demanded. "For God's sake, say so."

"I am not happy that you go to Africa. But this minute I am."

"Happy, say it."

"It is so."

To blow into the Savoy, flown with wine, beside a beautiful girl with bronze-gold hair, the observed of all observers, whom he scarcely knew but who was his somewhat unlawful wife was really, he thought, the splendor and crown of life.

In the soft luxury of the broad Pierre bed in New York they talked about it, their recollections supplementing each other's, asking and answering questions as they had scores of times.

"Do you remember," she asked, "that when you came back after the first day in London, you found me studying an English grammar? I was so smart to do that. I knew I must quickly speak good, fluent English."

"I thought your dialect was enchanting," he said.

"You would have been exasperated by it in a short time. I can hear you, 'For God's sake speak correctly. Can't you ever learn?' "

"What made it happen that night? We were still strangers," he asked.

"Estonians are realists. I thought we should either sleep as sensible married people or I should go away."

"So it wasn't love?"

"Of course not. As now, I was a little drunk, but it was logic and realism."

"You were very serious at dinner. Why?"

"You're mean. You know why. I was half in love with you, you had such nice manners and habits and I hadn't planned to fall in love and you made me forget every unhappy thing and I felt deliciously wicked and more than acquiescent, oh much more."

"You talked about being faithful, do you remember?"

"Of course. We both swore we would be, which was utter madness at the time. How could we know? You made a big to-do about my being free but that I must promise not to be unfaithful when I was angry or lonely or because I pitied somebody. What a time I had understanding all the words. But promising those three things left no way to be unfaithful."

"I didn't forbid it if you fell in love."

"Oh 'fell in love'—you were already beginning to be dominant and I knew I wouldn't dare fall in love or you might throw me out a window."

"You confessed to being without physical modesty."

"That is an absolute lie. I never said such a thing, and it wasn't that night besides. I said all Nordic people, especially Balts, loved sun and air all over them and—" *Connais tu le pays wo die citronen blühn*, she sang. "You see, I am still polyglot and you were never to think because I took all my clothes off it meant anything else at all. But I never said that at the Savoy, Mr. Long-Remember."

He remembered how she awoke laughing, that divine morning, and how ever after in the weal or woe of their life she had been *riante* with him. He remembered when he first discovered the full beauty of the word. After the triumphal entry into Tunis, his General had taken him and a number of younger officers who had distinguished themselves to be presented to the frock-coated Bey. They had all been astonished by "the democratic manners and Western ways" of the potentate, and at one point the

General had asked him if he would not like some American cigarettes. The Bey said he did not smoke but that one of his wives would like some very much. There was a stir among the young Americans. It was as though the Secrets of the Harem were known. Through all their young minds went visions of veiled beauties and the dark-eyed daughters of the Bul-Bul Emir. As they emptied their pockets, promising cartons by truck "toute suite," Lowry saw an old thick red book on the table. It was a Larousse dictionary and, as what they assumed were eunuchs came in with champagne, he opened it to *Riante.* It might, he thought, have been the definition of Rosalie:

Qui annonce de la gaieté . . . agréable à la vue . . . agréable à l'esprit.

In September, 1943, while he was fighting in southern Italy a son was born to Rosalie in London. Lowry was of course tremendously pleased and proud, but when at the end of the year, after being wounded, he was yanked from his outfit to go with the Overlord planners to London, he felt for the moment a most unworthy jealousy of his small son, whose mother he had so briefly known. His feelings horrified himself.

Two weeks after his birth, Rosalie had reported for duty at the Ministry, to be told it was felt best that she not return. In reply to her normal surprised questions there had been assurances of high satisfaction with her work, but she was told she could not cable her husband about it or refer to it in a letter, except as being her own decision.

"But he will think me a quitter, a weakling, if I say that," she protested.

The D.D.G., to whom she was talking said, "There can be small doubt that the Nazi forces in Estonia are trapped and will be taken or slain by the Red Army. Our ally will occupy the whole Baltic. You are known to be anti-Russian—"

"Anti-Russian. God in Heaven, my father, my mother, my sister, I—"

"I know, but there is a great desire in high quarters to keep the Russians happy. The Nazi forces were welcomed with flowers in Estonia—"

"And in many parts of Russia and in Estonia for only a fortnight. Does no one understand that there is no difference in evil between these two terrible peoples? Does this mean Estonia will never be free? Is that what the war is for?"

"It may, though never is a long time. But the Russians list your name among undesirables, and reviewing your case it is felt no real hardship is involved in pleasing them and it is desired to please them. I have ventured to say that in pleasing them 'the last case of the man will be worse than the first,' but one man or woman matters little."

Her dark-lashed blue eyes filled with tears.

"That is true if one individual is sacrificed to save many. This will save no one. There is nothing I can do?" she asked after a moment.

"Nothing," he said, "except to regard it as nothing."

She knew of course only approximately when Stephen would arrive. It was in a moonlight week and the thought of his flight across Biscay filled her with terror. It took a moment, whenever door or telephone bell rang before she could speak. Absurd alarms filled her mind—that he had the wrong address or that the house would be bombed just before he came and he never be able to find them. Or that on meeting one or the other would feel a sudden overwhelming revulsion toward the other. The only letters she had ever written to him had first to be read by someone else. Their time together had been too short for any lovers' cipher. There was not even a basis for such a cipher. They had had no time to learn what images, what precious secrets, what assurances, what transports they sought words or symbols for.

Toward the small son they would stand more as godparents than authors of his being. If the warrior-father came back and expected she was ready to go to bed with him as a matter of course, it would be intolerable. All the great outward realities, marriage, motherhood and war, were things she wished she could flee from. Memories of the white summer midnights of her girlhood in Estonia, filled with the scent of pines and flowers, thronged in her mind, the sea-bathing, the beach fires at Midsummer's Eve, the laughing license allowed boy and girl that night by otherwise strict Lutheran parents. Instead of that an almost unknown man would arrive in the small unattractive flat with his kit and gear, and with proprietary rights in all he surveyed, animate and inanimate—and she would be wholly dependent, without a job and with a child, on him and his wishes. She had met him in the clothes of a herring-gutter. Now she would have to receive him in the drab garments of wartime austerity—without, as she thought, memory or prospect of daintiness, or of ever having been together in a pretty room or in the sun. And what they had missed she did not then see would ever be recovered or compensated for. When he came, two strangers would find themselves shut off together in repellent intimacy.

Coming up from Gib in the long moonlit night, Lowry was also the prey of warring emotions. He felt no doubt that he was going to what was his heart's desire. It was a conviction such as he had not found in other men of his age either before or during the war. From things friends said to him of their own marriages, he got the feeling that "nice girls" were far too good for most of them. Young men went into marriage before they were shed of any of the habits of dormitory or barracks life. Their "experience of life" was largely gained from the promiscuities of young bachelordom. Their concepts of mutuality were atrocious. Charity, a desire to learn, to understand, to adjust were foreign to most of them. He doubted that most of them thought their wives more than wrestling companions. And in his own case there was no question that his driving desire to be with Rosalie was physical. True, in their brief time together in London she had not seemed to find it distasteful, but even the most shadowy allusion to it had been absent from the dutiful letters she had written him. And precious as their small son was to her, she did not write of him as though he were their flesh and blood. It was Madonna and Child, not the Holy Family. But, he said to himself, all this was to be expected. How was he to begin with her, how be natural, how make it clear he still expected to win her. Yet he was sensible enough to see that to revert to the austerity of their Norwegian night would be more ridiculous than chivalrous. Still better be ridiculous than arrogant or possessive about what he did not really possess.

Actually my trouble, he said to himself, is that damn piece of metaphysics I read in the hospital at Naples. Convalescent but not yet ambulatory he had read all the tattered paperback trash that came down from bed to bed each day. One late afternoon an older officer in the next bed said to him, "Here's one of the Great Books. You went to college. You ought to be able to read a Great Book," and he handed him the *Confessions* of Saint Augustine, written when Rome was about to fall to its first alien conqueror.

It was too heavy to read, but opening it at random Lowry read a sentence which in his weakened state he supposed was intended particularly for him. He read it enough times for it to stick in his memory:

But as not only pain may be inflicted but lust gratified on the body of another, whenever anything of this latter kind takes place, shame invades even a thoroughly pure spirit—shame, lest that act which could not be suffered without some sensual pleasure should be believed to have been committed also with some consent of the will.

Now in the Stygian darkness of the plane he reached for his thermos of hot cocoa and poured some in the cup. The plane was cold and the cocoa not even lukewarm. As he tasted it he highly resolved that his meeting with his wife would be such that shame would not invade her.

Determined to be second not even to Saint Augustine, he rang the bell of her flat late the next afternoon. The plane had landed early in the morning in southwest England but the train had not left until noon, coming up through a dismal landscape. He could not hear her coming and the sudden opening of the door startled him. They stared at each other a few seconds. She wore a blouse and slacks and her thick glorious hair was page-boy length.

"Oh, darling," she said. "It *is* all right. I was so frightened it wouldn't be." She kissed him with her lips opened. He pushed his bedding roll through the door with his foot, shed his kit bag and coat, closed the door with an elbow and resumed kissing her.

"There was no trouble from the moment we saw each other," she said afterwards. "I can't imagine what I was so afraid of."

She led him to the crib in the bedroom and he looked down in awe at the sleeper. "I am very inexperienced about people like this," he said, staring at their son.

"I know, so was I, but you get quite accustomed to them. He's very companionable," she said. "How do you think you will like him?"

"I'm not a monster. I like him already," he said, touching the tiny fingers.

"He grows on you. His mother isn't much good to him. She hasn't any more milk. For a peasant that's a disgrace. I feel very ashamed. Dear, I feel terribly keyed up. Can we have a drink and talk a moment?"

"Can I get it?" he asked.

"No, I will. Sit down, it's a very ugly room but it's all lit up now. Stephen, do you think we'll get along all right? Do you want to know I haven't had any 'pity' from anybody?"

"I–"

"Don't say. It doesn't matter, or not now anyhow. I have whiskey for you, but there's only tap water."

As she got the bottle and glasses, he opened his kit bag and took out a small package.

"It isn't much," he said. "I got it in Algiers from a French officer when I first went out. It had come two thousand miles across Africa, and a Roman officer might have brought it from Carthage to his bride in Rome."

In the package was a necklace of ivory and gold, antique, barbaric and beautiful. She gave a little gasp of pleasure, put it around her neck, kissed him and handed him his glass.

"To have a husband come home isn't as frightening as I thought."

"Have you been very frightened about it?"

"Sometimes, yes, particularly yesterday and this morning. Before, that, when I was worried about whether you were safe I had a special train of thought I took comfort in. I'd make myself forget there was war and I'd say, 'Well, now he's washing his hands, or putting on his coat, now he's writing a letter–' "

"Oh I know. I did the same sort of thing, visualizing you brushing your hair, or dressing or getting off a bus, unlocking the door, doing your breakfast dishes, eating with your pretty manners."

"Sometimes I would see you with someone else and be unhappy," she said. "Still, I thought, he can't ask her to marry him. He has me, poor dreamer. Do you realize, if the war is over next year we could still have fifty years together? How could you stand me fifty years?"

"One way would be to make love most of them."

She smiled merrily at him. "Would you like to begin?"

"Oh could we? I wasn't sure."

"Of course. I had no idea I would like you so much. 'You know what?' as you Americans say with your awful usage?"

"No, what?"

"*Ma armaston sind,* I love you. But why do I love a stupid fellow I hardly know who doesn't know enough to say he likes my hair this long, and who, after I give him a child doesn't say my figure is perfect–doesn't compliment me for learning so much hard English usage for him, doesn't think I'm very smart not to spoil my skin with those austerity soaps. There's only enough oil for the baby. A stupid fellow who thinks 'Oh well, it is so I married a peasant, they're not accustomed to anything. I'll just give her another baby and keep her quiet.' You may, you know. I have decided on three as soon as possible."

Now, breathless beside him, ecstasy ebbing divinely away as silently as light, she whispered sleepily, "My dearest, each time it's more glorious. Is it for you?"

"Yes."

"What are you thinking?"

He kissed her passionately again. "I was thinking two things—how much I love you and how soon we can get some breakfast."

"You're such a blessing," she murmured, "because so was I. Peasants always think of food."

5

ON MONDAY MORNING, A LITTLE AFTER TEN, Lowry appeared at Rutledge's office with his financial statement and received a most cordial welcome. Rutledge had already talked to Peale about his bills and, as he had first guessed, found they were a complete oversight. With his anxieties relieved, he had his usual sanguine feeling that the New Year would be a record breaker, and he was pleased to see that Lowry was properly dressed for an office.

His wife had brought him to enthusiastic agreement about the Lowrys and had said Lowry must join the Company if only to satisfy her curiosity as to how and when Rosalie and he had met and been married.

"I don't think we need any palaver," Rutledge said to him. "I take it you're satisfied, and I am. I propose you settle down with us tomorrow and I have asked your principal associates to lunch with us at the club. That's agreeable, is it?"

"Very much so," Lowry replied. "I would like to say how much I appreciate your confidence and to assure you I shall give everything I have to justify it."

"Fine, splendid. Just don't overwork."

"Here is the statement of my affairs you asked for," Lowry said, handing him the sheet of paper.

Rutledge unfolded it and leaned back to read it, shifting his chair slightly after a glance over his shoulder at the light. He read with the slow care of a man to whom reading was not a pleasure. Lowry was not fully prepared for the look of almost appalled amazement that came over Rutledge's face. He was obviously keeping a careful check on himself.

The brief statement showed total assets of some $8000. There were no liabilities, but that a man past forty should have accumulated so little, or have had nothing of his own to start with, profoundly shocked him.

"This is the whole thing?" he asked in a thin voice without looking at Lowry.

"I am afraid it is."

Rutledge gave a little cluck of dismay.

"Do you or Mrs. Lowry have any income from outside sources, your families or trust funds?"

"None."

If they stayed on at the Pierre, Rutledge figured quickly to himself, three-eighths of their assets would be gone in less than a month. He put the paper on his desk and rubbed the bridge of his nose.

"Naturally," Lowry said, "if your requirements are higher, I wouldn't expect you to be bound by anything you've said."

"We have no 'requirements,' as you put it. I suppose we have to consider you've not been in a profit-making organization. I suppose there are a good many reasons for this—inadequate government pay, growing family—"

He stopped in the middle of his sentence. Another case of a man they had taken on several years ago flashed through his mind. Only after he had been with them a month had he revealed the complicated domestic situation which required the company to be on notice as to the payment of monthly alimony to a previous wife and his three children by her.

Rutledge coughed in some embarrassment. He must ask the facts, disliked doing so and felt worried at what they might be. This came of going outside the organization for a man. There were things that you didn't know unless you had some detective agency find them out. He looked so distressed that Lowry felt sorry for him.

"What's the trouble?" he asked. "Feel free to ask any questions you like."

Rutledge cleared his throat. "Your wife and children are your only dependents?"

"Yes, though I've had to help my sister occasionally. Her husband's a chemistry professor in a small college and they've had a rather hard time."

"I see. But your present marriage—that is to say—you have no other family?"

Lowry laughed. "Oh Lord, no. No other family, no other marriage, no breach-of-promise suits pending."

"Well, I didn't mean that, of course," Rutledge replied, his relief tempered by the levity. "Your mother's provided for? I apologize for this seeming to pry, but I take it to be my duty to know just what my juniors are up against."

"My mother has her own money from my father's estate. She has a farm in Ohio which shows a profit."

"From what?"

"Beef cattle, mainly."

"What did you get for your father's company when he died?"

"Only about one hundred and fifty thousand. I was at the war at the time and my brother handled it. I don't imply I should have done better."

"You could hardly have done worse. A hundred and fifty for Lowry Equipment? He must have been out of his mind. The net quick must have been that much."

"It was—"

"Let me see, do I know your brother?"

"Dahlgren."

"Dahlgren, not Dolly Lowry?"

"I'm afraid so."

Rutledge gave a great sigh. "I just never connected the two. I was with two other men in Guy Eliot's office at the Founders when your brother came in and announced that Guy Eliot was a Fascist and wanted to do business with Hitler. Then he went to the *Times* and *Tribune* and tried to get them to publish a letter about him."

"I know," Lowry said. "He's a rather difficult fellow."

"He's been divorced twice, hasn't he?" Rutledge said as though to imply his anxiety had not been wholly groundless.

"Yes. As I said about my finances, if this changes the picture, you're not bound in any way."

Rutledge was not sure whether this independence pleased or displeased him. "Where is your brother now?" he asked.

"He has a small job in Stonington, Connecticut."

"It's not a question of my being bound. The question is, are you the best man for the job? I'm prepared to believe you are, but I'd like some assurance I now have the full story," Rutledge replied.

"I haven't concealed anything. You asked for a financial statement. You have it. I didn't suppose the price of a factory sold in nineteen-forty-four concerned you and I assumed you knew Dahlgren was my brother, and I don't regard the fact that he is as a disgrace."

"Now, now," Rutledge protested, "I'm not criticizing you. I have a very heavy responsibility and if I seem irritable I apologize." He wished, however, he could ask directly about Mrs. Lowry's record. Suppose she were a Communist. Still, the State Department must have been satisfied on that point.

"You may be wondering about my wife. Her whole family were killed or exiled by the Soviets in nineteen-forty except for one brother, her only known living relative."

"Who is he?"

"Armas Lainvee. He's the senior partner of the very rich French banking firm of Delacroix and Company."

"Oh, is that so? Fine. We know them well," Rutledge said, enormously relieved and affable.

"However, you'd better know that my mother was the actress Joan Denney, and that she started her career in the Follies," Lowry told him curtly, getting to his feet.

"My dear boy," Rutledge said beaming, "that beautiful lady

is your mother? My God, how I remember her. Well, well, if I had to go through all this to find that out, it's worth it. Now let's wash out all this other nonsense and get to work. Go for your physical this afternoon—it's just routine—meet me here at nine-thirty in the morning and we'll all lunch privately at the club. Let me see, I don't think I've forgotten anything you need to know, unless, oh yes, one last thing. I told you we're essentially a small business without frills. It's our habit here to answer our own phones with our name, 'Rutledge,' 'Lowry' and not make people go through a song and dance with a secretary. Like to have you do it that way, if you don't mind."

"Certainly not," Lowry said.

Going down the carpeted hall, he asked a passing clerk where Mr. Peale's office was. He found Peale in and told him all was settled, including how to answer the telephone.

"Well I knew it would be," Peale said, "unless you told Rutledge what you told me when you were tight the other night. Do you remember?"

"Certainly I remember. I don't expect to talk to Rutledge as I might to you. I was only expressing to you and the girls my objection to devoting the next twenty years to business. I hope to make enough in ten to do something more valuable or more interesting in the next ten after them."

"You'll find it doesn't work that way," Peale replied. "You can't get a good salary and salt most of it away. You have to live and entertain in a certain way. Besides you'll like the things money can buy—and anyhow you can't make money as a half-time hobby. It takes all you've got."

"I know that. I'm not going to play at it. Quite the contrary. But at the same time I'm not going to be like the fellow we heard about in school who 'was born a man but died a grocer.' "

"What's that mean?"

"You ought to know. It made a great impression on you at sixteen," Lowry said.

"What does Rosalie think about all this?"

"Well, you know she's just a beautiful peasant girl."

"Has she ever heard a word of her family?"

"Only her brother, whom you've met."

"Terrible thing," Peale said. "Is she still affected by it?"

"She seldom speaks of it, but I know that even now she still hopes to hear."

"Was her sister as beautiful as she is?"

"I really don't know. I should think from looking at her and Armas it ran in the family."

"You know I somehow can't picture Rosalie except as she was the other night, gay and laughing yet wonderfully understanding and sympathetic. Was that true about her and the fisherman's clothes?"

"Oh yes."

"I hope you appreciate her," Peale said curtly. "I didn't make a bad impression on her, I hope. I did get a little tight."

"You both made more than an impression," Lowry said, and feeling it was time Evelyn's name was mentioned added, "She felt she had always known Evelyn." He felt he ought to say more about Evelyn and that perhaps she had not wholly approved of all the gaiety.

She had soberly said to the sleepy Peale on the way home, "I hope all this drinking and nonsense isn't to be characteristic of seeing the Lowrys. I must say I couldn't picture her in the Resistance. She seemed to have so little."

"My God, she's beautiful. Don't you think so?"

"She evidently does and rather flaunts it, I thought."

"You mean the dance?"

"The dance and other things."

"But the dance was your doing," he said, and fell asleep in the corner of the car.

Luncheon the next day was in most ways what Lowry had grown accustomed to in Europe. There were a dozen well-dressed, well-informed active men friendly and easy to talk to. The table in the private dining room was set with European care, except for the absence of wine glasses. The menu, however, was wholesome rather than imaginative, the club steward evidently feeling that a baked Idaho potato with sliced steak was a rarity and a culinary triumph. But there was giant white asparagus flown from a hothouse in France. The cocktail tray had had as many glasses of tomato juice as martinis and with their lunch two of the men ordered milk.

The atmosphere was almost fraternal in welcoming their new brother and it was hard to realize these cordial, agreeable men were all, except Rutledge and Johnson, in one way or another his rivals. Yet under their ease Lowry got a feeling of marked self-consciousness about three of them—Peale, Hewitt and Evans—as though each had long ago decided on the impression it was most advisable for him to make and conformed strictly to it. Under the good spirits Lowry felt a lack of spontaneity, almost a sense of personal strain or the excess of a desire to please. But he decided this was nonsense or a reflection of his own feelings of the moment.

Charles Curtis, the treasurer, was in contrast to the others perhaps because of his seniority. He was about the age of Rutledge, rather scholarly-looking, cordial but reserved in manner. In appearance Calvin Hewitt was the most striking, with the fine figure of a college oarsman who with the years has put on a moderate amount of weight. His crisp, closely cut hair had begun to go gray. He had been the handsomest man in his class in college and in most gatherings still was. His face was unlined and in repose had something spiritual about it, blotted out by the breezy manner of a good fellow, and a fund of bawdy stories told in a chuckling undertone to everyone but Rutledge and Johnson. His juniors roared as he told them.

Leslie Evans struck Lowry as rather colorless. He was particularly interested in meeting Thomas Johnson, the president, who Rutledge had said would succeed him at his retirement. He was thick-set, of medium height, about fifty-five. His very dark blue suit was the best in the room and there was an unmistakable air of great ability, alertness and affability about him. He listened more attentively than Rutledge and spoke less, but he gave the impression that he would always know what to do and that it would be the right thing for all concerned. And from every outward thing about him it was hard to believe he had started life as a steel puddler.

The talk turned to where Lowry was going to live and all the considerations that went into it. He explained that he had until summer, when the children arrived, to decide on a permanent place, and would look for a furnished apartment in town until then. The pros and cons of Westchester and Connecticut were outlined—both delightful in theory but hot in summer, all right if the family went to Maine or Vermont, icy in winter, all right again if you were in town January-February. The North Shore, hot in summer yes and now practically uninhabitable west of Cold Spring, but with a fine school at Lattingtown. The South Shore, climatically wonderful, ten degrees cooler in summer, warmer in winter but now gone forever to developments and split-levels. New Jersey? Uninhabitable this side of Bernardsville, very fine there and thereafter. Lowry said he would like to do some small-boat sailing, which they told him still meant Seawahnaka at Oyster Bay. Sailing had come within range of more and more people, with the result that you were likely to find yourself involved with "all sorts" anywhere else around New York.

There was manifest cordiality about getting him and his wife for dinner—what's a good time for my wife to reach yours or can we fix a time now? It was all as nice as could be, of course, and though he was not looking for "good talk," "the art of conversation," "developments in the world of art," "the latest books and plays and music"—but it all sounded about as stirring as a commuter's train schedule.

Yet, when the coffee had been poured and Rutledge made a little speech, it was stirring. What major industry had set out to do, it had done better than anyone else from distribution to pure research. When any Point Four Program could accomplish what Aramco, for example, had in Saudi Arabia for the welfare of the people there, he, Rutledge, would turn C.I.C. over to the Socialists. Competition and incentive were the basic reasons for it. Aramco knew, just as C.I.C. knew, that if they didn't do it, Texas or Shell or another competitor would. And for doing it they received the magnificent incentive of about five cents for every dollar of sales. What gave him the greatest satisfaction was the very meagerness of that incentive. A return like that left no room for doubts as to how the rewards were distributed. But profit wasn't the only thing they were in business for. He had had another great satisfaction in the last few days. In his talks with Stephen Lowry, who was joining them today, he had been able to say with complete truth that every man at the table—and the whole organization—would receive him, help him, and *accept help and advice from him*, as though he had long been one of them. Well, he could see from Charley Curtis's face that it was time to go back and count the money, and he suggested they do so.

Lowry spent the afternoon reading a mass of reports and in several talks with members of the staff, familiarizing himself with credit and collection policies in the "buying" countries and labor and government-control problems in the producing ones. Like the classic revolutionary who on coming to power first calls for his own police dossier, he was fascinated by reports of activities of F.O.A. and the Point Four Program, with which he was familiar, and the detailed and usually well grounded reports on their personnel high and low, whom he knew. He had not realized how attentive American business was to the quality of government personnel abroad.

One report had this to say of his own visit to Turkey:

I went to a cocktail party at the Embassy to meet Mr. Stephen Lowry here on a special investigation for F.A.O. I had heard there was an internal row about his coming as a consequence of his somewhat ruthless correction of abuses by Americans and others, which you probably read about in Time *Magazine. However, he made an excellent impression on everyone, Turkish and American, and put America on the map culturally by asking to be taken over the route of the*

Ten Thousand to the Sea. The Minister of Education took him in his own car. On the trip Lowry "happened" to discuss some farm-school problems with the Minister, who, having heard Lowry call out Thalassa, thalassa *at the right moment on the road yielded on some restrictions he had insisted upon, the project was confirmed and we will build the schools and dig the ditches (photostat of our contract attached). Lowry told me it was all luck and the idea was on the spur of the moment. I talked to his wife, a foreigner, very attractive, and she said he knew how to go a long way around to get his own way. Too bad there aren't more like him.*

A little after four Rosalie made her first telephone call to him at the office. He had sent her to a renting agent and she had been apartment hunting all day. She had found one they could sublet furnished, four rooms and bath, high up, in Gramercy Park. Could he meet her there? She wanted to move that night before the Pierre bankrupted them. This was only $225 a month. She went on to say that it was very attractively furnished, not like a hotel. The people had gone to Florida for five months. "I'm sure they are nice people, and they evidently can read and write—you like that—they have a desk and books, comfortable old chairs. Very pretty china and lamps and things like that and I'm exhausted besides." Could he come now?

"Oh I think so. In about twenty minutes. No waiting to sign or telephone Washington, thank God. These profit-making organizations have an easy, quiet life."

"Dear, there are twin beds. Isn't it a shame? But they're next to each other. It's called Hollywood."

"The apartment house?"

"No, the way the beds are. Don't be long."

He stopped to tell Jim Peale he was leaving and why, and to his surprise Peale looked a little dismayed.

"Gramercy Park?" Peale said. "I don't think that's any place for you to live. Why the rush?"

"We want to get settled and economize. Nothing disreputable about Gramercy, is there?"

"Well no, not disreputable but I never knew anybody who lived there. Children play in it and the Players Club's down there, but I think you're rushing it. Call them up and say you've changed your mind and I'll get a hold of a fellow at Douglas Elliman's."

"Can't wait. Rosalie's there now."

To his surprise Peale went to the elevator with him, saying, "Really, Steve, this sort of thing is more important than you seem to realize. How big is it?"

"Four and bath."

"But listen, four rooms! You can't live in four rooms. How are you going to have people to dinner?"

"Just have four, one in each room. So long."

6

THE NEXT NIGHT THE MEN OF C.I.C. WERE ALL eagerly awaited by their wives, for, whatever their positions, it was Wednesday. The back of the workweek was broken, and the last of the leftovers from Sunday dinner gone. From top to bottom of the office force there would be less grumbling, whether about a dinner party, at home or abroad, or taking the wife to a neighborhood movie; the supply of baby-sitters was better from midweek on; weekend plans, even if only to go see a "married sister," could be suggested, and pleas to be accompanied to the stores "open Thursday until 9 P.M." made, with less chance of mortal groans from husbands. The money market was also easier even if it was another week till pay day.

Of course the eager waiting was not in every case a happy one. While the devoted Mrs. Thomas Johnson waited eagerly to learn whether her husband had kept his promise to go for a cardiogram "by Wednesday anyhow, I promise you, dear," Wednesday was the night that stretched Paula Hewitt's nerves to the limit. Either the hearty Hewitt was all fun and husbandly cheer or, sometime during the evening or even after he was in bed, beginning doubtfully and faraway, he would say, "Oh I almost forgot to tell you. So-and-so's probably going to be in town Friday and wants me to have dinner. I'll have to do it, I haven't seen him in years . . ." He had an inexhaustible list of these mysterious characters, "important to the Company" or someone "I've got to be decent to for old time's sake. Poor old John's had a tough time." They always came to New York without their wives and "I'm not going to have him boring you." What it meant was that Hewitt's current girl could see him Friday. It was always to be "an early dinner, I'll certainly get the ten-three." Thursday night when anticipation was rising in him he might say, "I think I'll drive in tomorrow. Those late trains are so ghastly." In that case his wife knew that toward midnight Friday he would call up and say, "Look, I've been a bad boy and drunk a great more than I should and I really don't want to risk driving out. Do you mind if I . . ." Whereupon she took two Seconals so that she would not keep seeing them playing together.

Once she had called him back at the hotel he vaguely mentioned and the night operator had said yes, Mr. Hewitt was registered but had asked not to be called until eight. "Mr. John Doe of Wichita? No Mr. Doe from Wichita is registered." On Saturday and Sunday afterwards, guilt written large on his face, he was practically uxorious for an hour and a half.

At times the intervals between such Fridays were so long that she thought they were done with, and when on a Wednesday the careful overtures began again she first half believed them and then felt too humiliated and spiritless to question them. More recently she had made it a practice to have two martinis very dry, before Hewitt's arrival both Wednesday and Thursday, so that she only half heard the casually elaborate details.

It was quite different on Wednesdays at the Titcombs'. The Missus got dinner in a pretty little silk number protected by a big apron and they had "a nice glass of sherry wine" together before dinner—Wednesday and Saturday only. Titcomb changed to slacks, strollers, sport shirt and purple velveteen jacket—all very nice—and an evening of cultured comfort over WQXR followed. Looking at his wife, Titcomb would think to himself, "I just wish Mr. Rutledge or Mr. Johnson or Mr. Hewitt or some of the other big boys could have a home life like mine. I've seen a lot in my time and though I'm getting old hope to see more, but I never have and never will see anything as pretty as my wife's face and ways. Everything in the world a man could want in this little apartment. And to think how it came about. A thousand chances to one, more than that more like ten thousand that I worked late that night and walked up Lexington and decided to stop in for a cup of coffee. And there she was, the new night cashier. First time coffee ever kept me awake. Well, you could call it luck, I've always had luck, but I don't know, to me it was just God's hand and I'm not a churchgoer."

Whatever the sad or happy excitement of these people on this Wednesday it was less than that of the wives of Lowry and Peale, who had lunched together at the Colony and who could hardly wait to tell their husbands of their impressions.

"Jim, I am not exaggerating," Evelyn Peale told him, "she's proposing to do her own cooking, except on special occasions, and to make their beds. I'm not sure but I shouldn't be surprised if they were going to do the dinner dishes together."

"This may be only temporary."

"Temporary—what will Edward Rutledge think if he hears it?"

"Well, you don't need to tell him. I can speak privately to Stephen."

"It won't do any good. It's some crazy philosophy of theirs. Of course I can understand that after a government job for years, they have to think about the children's education, but aren't there insurance policies for that sort of thing?"

"Sure."

"Do you realize that they expect to 'save up' for things. That sapphire of hers and that clip they saved for. They 'saved up' to go to the Pyrenees and buy a car. They seem to have no plan for life."

"Well, it may be a queer one but it's certainly a plan. It might even be better than spending all we do."

"Are you suggesting I'm extravagant? If you are, I shall be glad to do the housework."

"For God's sake, don't be touchy. I'm not complaining."

"It sounded that way. Another thing is the way she talks about them in the most adolescent fashion. Of course I like her and I intend to do all I can for her, as I told her—at which she coolly informed me that unless they were working on what she calls their principal errors—they go to libraries and make notes about them—all they like to do after dinner winter evenings is to go to bed and read. I realized on New Year's Eve that she's inclined to be very sexy."

"Is that so bad in a wife?"

"I don't know what you're implying. I think for someone who's been married twelve years it's a little distasteful to emphasize the physical side of marriage."

"Does she? How did she put it? I'd like to hear her exact words."

"I'm sure you would and you had better ask her for them."

"Oh come on, tell me," he said, "any man would be curious to hear. Don't be so serious."

"If I am serious it's because I don't look forward to seeing too much of them. Stephen's all right. He's an American and he went to Yale, but I do hope you understand I can't just become 'best friends' with a foreign woman I don't feel easy about simply because her husband is your oldest friend. I've asked them to dine with us Saturday. The Johnsons are coming, and the Guy Eliots. I had thought we'd have some bridge. But she doesn't play bridge."

"We could play post office," Peale said. "It seems to me you've worked yourself up about nothing."

"Thank you. By the way Gristede's would like a check. I hadn't one to send them. And what about the school bill? I'm on a committee there next week, and I shouldn't like to feel uneasy."

"I said I would pay both bills this week and I will tomorrow."

"Well you better get dressed. The Dunhams are taking us to the theater."

"Any mail?"

"Other than bills there's a letter for you, from Venezuela, it looks like. It's on your bureau."

Left alone, Evelyn, staring sulkily in the fireplace, felt a sense of general irritation with the world and of uneasiness about herself. Life was not easy on $50,000 a year, before taxes, at the standard she felt herself expected to maintain. Some of the wives of Peale's colleagues, as well as other women she knew felt the strain. Cars, a summer cottage, education, servants, entertainment took so much, and you were expected, so at least Jim had taught her to believe, to display a little more each year. And if some little thing went wrong—such as the breaking off of a merger negotiation after Jim was long of the stock or that misbegotten investment in chlorophyll as a cure-all—well it put you badly in the hole. Margin requirements were outrageous. Years ago fortunes, like the one her father had lost, had been made on a five-point rise with a ten per cent margin. There was some stability. But now everything cost so much, so that you thought so much about that you could no longer be yourself.

She was not herself, she realized, in love and affection with Jim, or at least not the self she once had been. A sense of thin ice under them affected all their relations, leaving her with no sense of emotional support. She was sustained in part by a bond of martyr-camaraderie with her friends and other wives like her. Even when they had wads of money, most of them wore themselves out with "activities" and some with isms. Those still climbing felt the same stresses she did—so that they bought a fine boat, like the Peales' new one, on long installments, not for the pleasure it would give them but because it had something to do with business success. Those installments often meant that the allowance for the house, for clothes, for themselves had to come in installments also—and sometimes even be skipped. "When the boat's paid for we can really set something aside." And waiting that far-off event Jim, worried and distracted, increased his life insurance, to the greater unsettlement of their life.

Yet the feeling that she and most women she knew were in the same boat had been a great comfort. One heard all the time of husbands, involved and badly overextended, to whom the great break of promotion or larger participation came and debts were paid and life made easy—and the wife's new clothes were thereafter by Dior or Balenciaga—"My dear, Hattie hasn't dressed me in years."

In the absence of all this it was the sense of contentment about

Rosalie which annoyed her. Cows, not women, were supposed to be contented. When Rosalie had told her they liked best to go to bed and read on winter nights, she had asked somewhat coldly what about the summer.

"Oh the summer nights are rapturous. We lie on the grass and look at the stars."

For all her irritation, she wished she could go to Jim and say, "Let's go to bed and read tonight. We've seen that damn play. I couldn't tell Narcissa so."

The children's nurse came in to say they were ready to be tucked in and she went to the nursery to her maternal duty. She felt a gulf even between herself and them. Rosalie had said that most of what she knew of English and American literature she had learned from reading aloud to the children. The Peale children could read, and besides they had their own television.

"Bang, bang, you're dead," her son said to her as she bent over him. She felt a sudden terror as though she were going to die or lose everything and that the agent of it would be Rosalie Lowry.

She hurried to the bedroom, where Jim was making a bow of his black tie.

"I feel ill," she gasped. "I'm going to be sick. Something dreadful is going to happen to us from that Lowry woman. I know it in my bones. Please take care of me." She sank back on her bed in tears.

"What in the world's the matter?" her husband said irritably.

"Can't you be tender and understanding once?"

"Why do you imply it would be the first time? I shouldn't have said I was an unfeeling or irresponsible husband or father."

"Oh don't talk that way. Be human."

"I'm human. I am also carrying a heavy responsibility. Have I ever denied you anything? I may have demurred at having that last interior decorator in, but I agreed, didn't I, as I always do?"

"Please don't be so noble, I can't stand it. I should think you'd try to comfort me and—"

The telephone between the beds rang and she reached over her head to answer it.

"For you," she said, handing it to him.

"Yes," he said, "this is Mr. Peale. Who? Oh yes, Mr. Bland. No, I didn't. Well, yes, I think so. Can I call you the first thing in the morning. Oh, yes, before the opening, certainly. Right, thank you." He then said to his wife, "That was Bland at Channing and Company. That rise in margin requirements made a bad break. There was quite a shake-out. They want some more margin tomorrow." He sighed through clenched teeth. "It's your turn to be human and understanding and comforting."

She got up and went in the bathroom to repair her make-up. "Isn't it always?" she asked over her shoulder. Her alien alarms were over and she was quite herself again.

Lowry, having comfortably come down in an East Side local to Twenty-Third Street strode along the cold sidewalks to Gramercy Park in excellent spirits. His second business day had gone well. He had lunched alone with Thomas Johnson, liking him even more than at first sight. Johnson said he had been at a symposium at the Harvard School of Business Administration over the holidays and there had been a discussion of why men "kept at it" so often after the financial rewards had ceased to matter. The general feeling had been men liked the power they exercised. He said in his case he liked his job, he liked his associates, and he had a very happy time in his office. He thought most men with any sense did. He never found it interfered with a happy home life or outside interests, and all this talk about having to conform made him laugh. True, you couldn't run a business with a bunch of eccentrics around you, but no one had ever tried to tell him what he had to believe in or whom he was to vote for. He was not a millionaire but he had made a certain amount of money and never had to resort to "tanker deals" with some Greeks on the side to do so. He said that prison reform and the rehabilitation of offenders was his greatest outside interest. He had got into it, he was frank to say, because when he was young an older brother of his had served a long prison term.

"When he finally came out we were all hopeless about what he could do. I went up to meet him and while I was waiting I happened to fall into conversation with the Jewish chaplain of the prison. I told him why I was there and how despondent I was. His careworn face lit up and he said to me, I remember his exact words, 'After half a lifetime in this work, I tell you most people, including offenders like your brother, have an insatiable appetite, when properly aroused, for the good life and self-betterment. And never forget it.' I never have. We have no children and I've been able, thanks to my wife's feeling about it, to start a foundation, a small one as such things go, for this work of rehabilitation. We live rather simply, relatively, because of the commitments we've made."

Lowry wanted to ask how the brother had come out, but it seemed too delicate to ask.

"Let's go into the other room and have some coffee, though I am not supposed to have it," Johnson said. "Would you be interested in what became of my brother?"

"Very much so. I wanted to ask."

"He's the minister of a large church in Kansas City and has served for many years on the State Parole Board. His oldest boy is a Rhodes Scholar."

Over the coffee Johnson said that he hoped Lowry would not let himself be rushed about anything, particularly a foreign-inspection trip, and "if Edward gets impulsive about it, have a word with me. The main thing is to get the feel of the whole business. However, I shouldn't hesitate if I were you to take charge right off and make the decisions."

"I did that with Halleck this morning on that cable from Turkey, where I happened to know the local situation."

"Oh I am glad you did. Halleck wasn't sure about bothering you and I sent him in. I was interested to know that Jim Peale and you were such old friends. I happen to know another old friend of yours and your wife very intimately."

"Oh, who?"

"Alec Channing, the man with the kindest heart and the most intolerable exterior—intolerant may be the word—in New York. It's extraordinary what excellent intelligence officers stockbrokers make. I told Alec it's because their minds have lain fallow for years while the rest of us wore ourselves out. Though actually I have never been able to understand how a specialist executes an order on the Floor."

Lowry laughed. "Neither have I."

"Tell me, where are you living? At the Pierre?"

"Oh no, we were only there for a space over the holidays. We've taken a small apartment in Gramercy Park until summer."

"Well I think that's very sensible. I'm glad to hear it."

The warm lobby of the apartment was pleasant after the twenty-degree cold outside and the elevator rose with old-fashioned dignity through the not-unpleasant odors of cooking.

As he unlocked his door, Rosalie's head poked out of the kitchen. "Modest drinks in living room in two minutes. Darling, it's ages since morning. *Sa Puha Jumal*, you're cold. The first time you heard those words was when I first saw you in uniform. I have much to tell you. Oh these were in that other trunk." And she opened her apron coat on Spanish dancer's pantaloons flared at the ankles and a white Spanish blouse.

"How was your lunch?"

"I have shocked Evelyn Peale and it may ruin your friendship. but *dépêche-toi*. Oh, the fireplace burns beautifully and the concierge told us where to buy cannel coal on Third Avenue. And darling, you should have seen me marketing on Third Avenue. Great bags of food very cheap—how good I don't know. You wheel the bags around like babies and a man on the street was giving out handbills about 64,000 bargains and no questions asked for two days. It was like bazaars in the Middle East. I don't know what to do with all the paper that things come in. But none of the shopkeepers smile at you as they do at home—I mean in Europe."

When he came into the living room in the clothes, plus strollers, in which he had first interviewed Rutledge, Rosalie was on the sofa before the fire, mixing highballs.

"All go well with you?" she asked.

"Oh very. Also much to tell," and he sank on the sofa beside her. They kissed fondly and she sank back against his arm, his hand over her breast.

"This is not," she said, "what the James Peales do when he comes home."

"Poor fellow. What do they do?"

"They dress for dinner with important people. Darling, are you sure you still know Jim? Because the picture you've given me of him isn't Evelyn's. You did think at times in Europe that his letters were getting a little pompous."

"Well, he does seem to think and do the correct thing with a lot of determination. What about Evelyn, though?"

"Well, first, she's unhappy."

"Did she tell you?"

"Oh no, but she never spoke a happy word or had a happy thought the whole time. She took it for granted to start with that I felt the same way. I think everything I said shocked her. You know how we bought this blouse and pantaloons while we were walking the Route de Ria to find Pablo. Casal's house and how we lay by the Route that night watching the stars. Things like that or the pictures you took of me in the wild flowers in Rhodes looking across at Asia Minor—well she is either shocked or thinks we're not *type sérieuse*. She seemed to imply that if a man and woman were happy together they were traitors to some higher loyalty. Her life is made up of the most unimportant outward things—money, position, social obligations. I said that we ran into the last because of your jobs in Europe. And I almost said 'Isn't it divine to forget them and go to bed together' but I knew it would be too shocking. I'm sure they don't like to. I also said we worked on Principal Errors and believe she thought it was *our* principal errors. I didn't tell her. I was afraid it would be too much. You don't mind?"

"No, I was going to tell Jim but he has been so stuffy."

"What's Calvin Hewitt like?"

"Oh I don't know. Nice enough fellow."

"And they're not particularly happy, Evelyn said. I met Mrs.

Hewitt, who was lunching at the Colony. There's much rivalry between Jim and Hewitt as to who will succeed Mr. Johnson when Mr. Johnson succeeds Mr. Rutledge. The Peales' life is based on his succeeding. Did you know that?"

"He hasn't spoken of it. I should think he'd win easily over Hewitt. But I don't imagine it's imminent."

"I used to think the idea of a man *running* for President of the United States must be the funniest sight. But everybody's running here. Darling, don't run, just stay still with me. Oh, and I wrote long letters to each of the children. They're open on the desk, so put a postscript on each one."

He sat down at the desk where the three letters, of several pages each, were waiting.

"My, you've had a busy day," he said, reaching for a pen.

"When I left Evelyn and Mrs. Hewitt, I made another call. I wondered what they would have said if they knew."

"Where'd you go?"

"The Estonian Relief Committee on East Thirty-Fourth Street."

He put down his pen and went over to her.

"Nothing?" he asked gently.

She shook her head, her eyes full of tears. "Nothing, except brave people, a little restaurant and an Estonian newspaper and a bulletin board with questions like mine tacked on it. I wrote one out too and someone had to help me with words I'd forgotten, 'Wanted by their sister and daughter, Rosalie Lainvee Lowry. . . .' "

7

LOWRY DID NOT FIND HIS JOB TO BE A HARD ONE that winter. The heavy responsibilities carried power with them and its exercise was stimulating rather than wearing. The overseas calls from Buenos Aires, London or Madrid asked practical questions: Can you get a mechanical engineer off to us tomorrow? —We need another battery of I.B.M. machines to keep up with labor payrolls at the alkali plant— If we bid on the irrigation project can we count on equipment being here in May instead of July? They were not like the Washington calls of the past asking for "a fuller end-use justification" or saying that the discovery that so-and-so's household goods had gone to Beirut instead of Bombay had become a matter of Congressional Committee interest and what explanation could be made?

If he had any doubt as to the rightness of any decision, there was a group of experienced, friendly men to consult with. He was always aware of the strong understructure of the corporation supporting him. The fact that profit over the long pull was in effect the sole objective greatly simplified decisions. There were no opposition politicians, no minorities, no special interests to contend with as there had been in Europe. His respect for American industry increased. No one wanted his strongest competitor ruined. Strong and fierce as was the drive to increase sales and profits, the announced purpose was only "to get our fair share of the business." What constituted our or your fair share was the subject of certain differences of opinion.

Outwardly his colleagues Curtis, Hewitt and Evans had a certain corporate uniformity of optimism, team spirit and strict attention to business. Curtis, personally the most attractive, was the least forceful and seemed the least ambitious. Evans, dependable and highly skilled, was a little overshadowed both by Peale and Hewitt.

The latter had the gift of "talking business" in equally absorbed fashion with Mr. Rutledge, an officer of a subsidiary or a small customer whom he might overhear arguing with a salesman that a spare-parts delivery was not properly scaled. He would introduce himself at once and take the man off to his private office. There he would ask him as a great favor to tell him how far the man felt C.I.C. was safe in selling ahead. It would quickly develop that the customer and he were "thinking along identical lines" and that both of them felt confident of the outlook as long as proper caution was exercised. By the time he was through the man let himself be docilely led past the salesman's desk to a hearty handshake at the elevator and Hewitt would go back to his office with a word of advice to the salesman. "Never get cluttered up with small claims. Get 'em settled."

As he said to Lowry, "I've never let myself get so busy as to lose the following I had among the little fellows when I was starting." And he had a very nice way about it. He was never too busy to see some old dealer along Lafayette Street, who liked to tell of his family and staff. "I can go into C.I.C. to this day and Mr. Calvin Hewitt will write out my order for me, just the way he used to do. Kept a vice-president of one of the banks waiting while he did it. He's a great kidder. Always makes me sign the order."

It may be added that the bank vice-president was as much impressed as the customer with this evidence that the vast C.I.C. was just what it claimed to be, "essentially a small business in the best sense of the term."

One of his most amiable qualities was the pretense that he was a glutton for a wide variety of foods. Along with conventional wild ducks, quail, salmon and venison from sportsmen friends, special delicacies came in due season from Jewish, Italian, Greek, Scandinavian, New England and Pennsylvania Dutch minorities, for which he had led the donors to believe he hungered or thirsted. His appreciation made a great many people happy and contributed to his reputation of being a very sweet guy.

Lowry got an early respect for Hewitt's knowledge of the business, his devotion to it and his real ability. It surprised him to find certain less amiable qualities present as well, one a form of tale-bearing, where as a friendly mentor, he would say, "I happened to see Rex Thurston the other day and he told me you were old friends. Of course I've known Rex all my life. There's just one thing I think I ought to mention. I *do* think from something he said that he may feel you're expecting a good deal of your friends. It was about that situation in Rhodesia where you asked him to write you . . ."

"What the hell is this?" Lowry said in annoyance. "I met him in the subway and he told me . . ."

"Now, for God's sake, don't go back to Rex about it. He likes you, make no mistake about that; do anything for you . . ."

"Look, it's not a question of his doing anything for me. I . . ."

"Steve, I only told you this as a friend. If I've said the wrong thing, forget it. I am always glad if people tell me . . ."

Another pattern, equally annoying, had to do with something he had "been given to understand" would not be announced for some months to come but when it did would very likely cause a major row. He was not at liberty to say what it was and actually all he could say was wait and see. However, he was making his own plans. To the timid or unwary this was likely to suggest salary cuts, but even those less easily alarmed feared he might have got on to some plan, say, "to move the executive offices out of New York," that dreaded "re-deployment" the Pentagon had taught Big Business. It happened in one form or another all too frequently, and homes, schools and clubs in which families and children were just beginning to be happy had to be abandoned.

As to Peale, Lowry found himself more and more puzzled. He was certainly no longer fun to be with. Consecrated and critical at once as his manner was, Lowry felt a sense of insecurity about him which nothing in his position seemed to warrant. Peale would break off a lecture to him on what Lowry should do, to ask, "Steve, you would say, wouldn't you, that Rutledge has an unusual respect for what I think and the way I do things?"

"Yes, why?" Lowry would answer.

"I sometimes wish it wasn't so marked. I think it gets under Calvin's skin."

Lowry did not believe for a moment that Peale had said what he meant, but he was equally at a loss as to what he did mean. There was something distastefully boyish about it. But in another way there was something insecure about Hewitt also.

He realized that the insecurity did not have to do with the loss of their jobs. It came, he felt, from the complexities of high corporation employment. In his grandfather's time even a businessman "built an estate" by "saving money" and investing it wisely at expanding returns. Investing wisely was a relatively simple thing—there were even prime mortgages paying ten per cent. Such a man's grandson, with perhaps ten times his income, had constantly to think how best to secure his future, after taxes, in a maze of management pools, pension rights or company insurance plans. "Savings" were obsolete. They were what were found in envelopes in the rooms of dead derelicts in Skid Row or what old ladies drew out of the bank to give to confidence men. A man had a savings bank account of a few hundred or thousand just as he might have some early Americana around his house.

But while the distracting worries and rivalries involved in getting ahead bothered and even bored him, Lowry realized that most men seemed to thrive on them. As he more or less unconsciously studied them, he was aware they were also studying him. Rutledge and Thomas Johnson appeared well pleased with him. In effect they let him understand that they found him sound, agreeable and effective. He was in some doubt that his peers agreed with them particularly in his attitude toward "a business lunch" of eight or ten men representing, say, three parties at interest.

Europeans, both industrialists and officials, for all their lack of know-how, did not lunch in masses for business reasons. They frequently ate too much and drank too much, in a quiet way, but if it was really business, the table was only set for three or four at the most.

In New York, however, for such an occasion at least three representatives of Party Number One arrived in the club lounge about a quarter past twelve carrying briefcases. While waiting for the others they opened the briefcases, brought out typed tissues of plans or reports and had "a quick final run-through" of them before the others came. The second delegation arrived. There was a wait for Delegation Number Three from out of town, who inevitably arrived with their overcoats on and had to be escorted to the checkroom, leaving their fat briefcases to the sense of honor of the first arrivals.

The entire group now divided into the washed and unwashed and the former waited for the latter. If Ed and Frank and Wilson did not know Tom and Jerry they were reminded they had met at Atlantic City or White Sulphur the spring before.

Like the most sinister of Red agents, they handed each other "copies of the plan" as the difficult business of bourbon on the rocks, bourbon with branch water, scotch old-fashioneds, scotch and soda no ice and two Gibsons was settled. Lowry always had a perverse desire to order a Jack Rose to break the solid manly front.

Another American custom which Lowry found difficult adjusting himself to was The Dinner for a Cause. Like the Eighteenth Amendment, each was noble in motive and the support and attendance from great corporations was an evidence of the "growing social consciousness" of Big Business.

It was possible to fill tables in the ballroom of a great hotel with a thousand people at a hundred dollars a plate to "honor" a man of good will or celebrate "brotherhood." Dress was "optional," and into the room—gleaming with cathedral-candles on the tables and a profusion of flowers—came the dinner-jacketed corporation officials and the deadheads in business suits combed out of the ranks to swell the crowd. They had scarcely seated themselves when the Committee Chairman on the dais told them, "You would not be here tonight unless you believed in" the cause or the Honor Guest. "That's what you think," a wit would say in a loud whisper. "I'm here because my boss sent me."

The Chairman then announced that they would rise while the Invocation was pronounced and would remain standing to sing the National Anthem. Practically all present heard grace before meat only on such occasions. Lowry always felt somewhat embarrassed by the public tributes to God and Country, though he was a devout believer in both.

When the frequently magnificent dinner had been served and cleared away with incredible efficiency, the Committee Chairman, assuring them of the brevity of what he had to say, introduced the toastmaster in a long speech and, as at political conventions, saved his name for the last three words, uttering it in clarion tones. As it was printed on the left page of the menu it came as a surprise only to a few.

Usually the toastmaster was a hearty muscular Christian who occupied a prominent pulpit, had a TV show and wrote best-sellers. The Chairman usually alluded humorously to his income with some such quip as, "I can deny that my friend and yours is negotiating to buy the U.S. Steel Corporation. He is not. He's after Montgomery Ward."

There were several good things about the toastmaster. You could always hear and understand his loud ringing tones. His rapid-fire jokes seemed to Lowry better than any of the professional radio or TV comedians. Of course it may simply have been that he had better writers. Good as he was, Lowry did not wholly subscribe to the tribute paid him by the man on his left. "Isn't he a sweetheart?" his neighbor asked.

As he introduced speaker after speaker, Lowry slightly had the feeling there had been a breakdown in staff work somewhere.

He got the impression the speakers thought they were addressing another audience. They did not, in the parliamentary phrase, "speak to the point of order"—whether the Cause or the Honor Guest.

Brotherhood, if that was the Cause, was, they implied, now well established, except among the colored races of Asia and Africa, and it would be extended there, after we had used the hydrogen bomb (the A-bomb was as obsolete as race or religious prejudice) on Red China, with the result that our new colored brothers would be able to buy everything that American factories could produce.

Everyone knew that Management and Labor were now in full partnership—where men without regard to race, creed or color were accepted. This had come about because Management had (apparently voluntarily) raised wages, shortened the work-week, and provided insurance benefits. Nonetheless, there were demagogues who were trying to set class against class.

In the whole great gathering Lowry was one of a minority of two who seemed to feel the speeches were less than gospel. The other was a traditional happy drunk in dinner jacket with a carnation as red as his beaming face. "Wherezat old fight? Where's ole Charlie Schwab?" he arose to demand at intervals and then, like Belshazzar the King, drank wine before the thousand.

Perhaps what most troubled Lowry was the complacent confidence in the speeches and the tabletalk around him that the world was faced with no problems which were not well on the way to solution—or to which business or the banks would not shortly reveal the solutions.

Of course all the dinners he attended were not for a Cause or an Honor Guest. There were the "briefings" which Rutledge or Johnson several times arranged for him to go to in one of the white-stone residences with heavy grille-work doors in the East Sixties or Seventies, where fifteen or twenty hand-picked business leaders dined well, with little to drink and, when the servants had withdrawn, listened to a grave, enormously well informed expert from Washington as he told them the all but final secrets of the National Security Council. There was nothing phony, nothing at which to laugh in such meetings. Those present were taken farther behind the scenes of world tensions and into the plans of the American government than Lowry had ever been in any embassy in Europe. And the secrets they were told were never leaked.

Yet with the best of them Lowry had the feeling that he and his fellow diners were only being told, like Bourbon kings, how the status quo could be maintained and nothing of the profound changes or emotions stirring the Jacquerie in Africa from the Cape to Cairo or all southeast Asia.

He did not claim for a moment to know more or have better judgment than the men around him who listened, with occasional requests for more detail, but without variance of opinion. He alone was uncertain both that what they were hearing was the whole hypothesis and what the conclusion should be; while the rest had the singular certainty about it all that housewives or filling-station attendants did when they were stopped by a tabloid's Inquiring Photographer.

Not all the extracurriculum activity was at such a level. At small dinners which the Rutledges, the Johnsons and Colonel Channing gave for them, they met an impressive number of lawyers, bankers, industrialists, who in culture and experience of men and affairs were frequently second to no group in the world. Nor by any means were all of C.I.C.'s competitors and customers the stereotypes of latter-day Babbitts or Collingwoods. Repeatedly Lowry had the feeling, "There is a man with whom I'd like to be on terms of close friendship. Our tastes, our outlook, our view of the Good Life are the same." But there was no time for forming such ties. Such men were not looking to expand, but rather reduce the number of people they knew, not from snobbery but to save some time for themselves. People you wanted to know wanted to be left alone. Experience taught them that any relaxation of their reserve would leave them the victims of undesired and inappropriate invitations. "Come on-a my house" was the plea of the lower four-fifths of the world; my house or "a gallery my wife and I found on Third Avenue with an amazing collection of Hindu art," or "a darling little French place we like to go to. It's off the beaten track and they have no printed menu at all, not even a blackboard. Henri, who runs it, is of course the original Henri," or "We've gotten to know an interesting group of artists and writers I'd like to have you know. Not Village stuff. They're real. I don't suppose there's been such conversation as you hear there since certain voices were quieted in Athens." He tried to think where he had read that last bit.

It was at dinner at the Evanses' that Lowry was most embarrassed by one of these people. He was talking to one of the wives, a dear little enthusiast, and in an unwary moment admitted that Rosalie and he could read and often did.

"Oh this is wonderful. I was sure the moment I met you both that you were that way. You can always tell. Now how would you like to come out twice a month to our Reading Club? We have a buffet meal and a guided discussion. It all started in revolt against such things as the Book-of-the-Month that tell you what you must read. We are archaeologists, in a sense. We're going back to dig up the old books. Right now it's wonderful old Bulwer-Lytton. Of course you know him."

"Um," Lowry said politely.

"I have had a rather daring dream for our next project. You must be as sick as we are of current historical novels. I want us to tackle Harrison Ainsworth. Now do say you'll come, or shall I ask your wife? We closed last year with rather an unusual thing that I don't think has been done before. We divided the founders of The American Academy of Arts and Letters among us—writers, as you recall, like Hamilton W. Mabie, Robert Underwood Johnson, Henry Van Dyke, John Burroughs, F. Hopkinson Smith—those wonderful Colonel Carter books—everyone worked very hard, all of us, on our Discussion Papers and decided to send them to the Academy, which we did. Their secretary, who by the way composed 'Good Night, Poor

Harvard,' aren't you a Yale man? wrote us a very nice letter and we have no doubt our papers are now part of their archives. Do say you'll join."

Lowry said the trouble was that a business trip abroad was hanging over him.

"Well, just come for *Kenelm Chillingly*, which winds up Bulwer-Lytton and we can talk about permanent participation when you get back. And another thing. One of our best friends is a publisher and we'd just love to put your wife in touch with him about writing a book. She must have had wonderful experiences in the Resistance and with the Russians. People are interested in just that sort of thing today. We'll talk more about it."

Rosalie said, when he told her, that it seemed to her most of the women were in one of three groups: the earnest PTA, civic-minded or higher-things class; the resigned but discontented under-analysis group; and the dominated-over, badgered-in-bridge-postmortems, sweet, docile, golf-widow lot, whose husbands were the dullest of all. The only spark about them was their irritability.

"And the husbands?" he asked.

"They have rather shaken my views on peasants versus aristocrats," she replied. "I must admit the simplest, most attractive ones are those who seemed to have inherited money and all of whom knew each other as children and at school and college, and their parents before them. There seems to be as much intermarriage among them as there is in Europe—they're all cousins or in-laws or brothers and sisters. But you know, Stephen, the men have one thing very much in common, whether they're those we met tonight or at the Boys' Club Benefit at the Plaza last week."

"Oh, what?"

"Well, they seem to feel that all foreign women are simply smoldering with passion, without moral sense, and never faithful to their husbands. At the Plaza I was dancing with that icy-looking Van Leyden man. The orchestra was terribly noisy but I was talking about our trying to find a house. He brightened up and, I thought, was being helpful, and I said, 'And if you do know of one you'll call me.' He said he certainly would and then gathered me to him and whispered, 'There's always my apartment. You're marvelous.' "

With all this and the outlook for increasing income and power, Lowry did not feel that the operations of C.I.C. were all he ever wanted to be concerned about. He had been very fortunate in being asked to join them. Their sort of goods and services was essential to the modern world. Their top men were capable of running a country. But to imply for a moment that working for them was anything but a means to an end, which in his case it was, would have been disastrous.

Late one afternoon Peale called to ask him to play squash, and as they strode along Fifty-Third Street to the Hounds Club in good spirits, exchanging the banter of earlier days, some of the old close comradeship seemed to come back.

Both played well in different styles. Peale, holding the mid-court with his still terrific volleying, and Lowry, out of practice, relying on round-the-court angle shots, lost three straight games.

After a shower and rubdown they went to the bar for a drink. On the way to a corner table Peale stopped to speak to several members, introducing Lowry to them.

It was in such contrast to his usual aloofness that Lowry said to him, "You've gotten awful pal-ly."

"I think you'll find it does no harm to let people feel you're interested in them. What will you have?"

"A clear and cold martini."

Peale ordered and then took a handful of peanuts.

"Tell me," he said casually, "you see a good deal of Evans and Hewitt, have they indicated at all who they think will move in back of Tom when Edward steps down?"

"Never been mentioned," Lowry said. "Why?"

"Well you've been there long enough to see the whole picture. Do you think I'm fooling myself in thinking it is likely to be me? Now for God's sake, don't mention this even to Rosalie."

"I'm not likely to, but whether it'll happen I have no idea. Needless to say, if you want it I hope you get it."

"Want it? Of course I want it. I've gone over and over it and I can't see who has a better claim. Hewitt's slightly my senior but they'll never take him. Leslie Evans, well, you know. As a matter of fact, Steve, I sometimes get the feeling it might lie between us."

"Oh nonsense."

"No. I mean it and I base it on what I've heard Tom Johnson say about you. Certainly if it does go that way, no one will welcome it more than I and that's the main reason I may seem to tell you things you ought to watch as much as I do."

"Jim, my boy," Lowry said, "I think there is something you ought to watch, and that's not pressing so. You press at the office and you pressed just now in the court. If I weren't out of practice you'd have been hopelessly trimmed."

"If it is me, I should think you'd follow," Peale went on. "It would be a wonderful thing if after all these years we ended one, two at–"

"But that's ridiculous. Your number two will be somebody ten years younger than I am."

"Just a minute, I want to speak to Henry Dennison. You know him, don't you?"

"Yes," Lowry said. "Go ahead," and he waved at Dennison.

Peale got up and as quickly sat down again. "I didn't see Alec Channing with him. I can't stand that fellow."

Channing passed with a curt nod to Peale and patted Lowry on the head. "Tell Rosalie I want to take you both out for a nice fish dinner," he said without pausing.

"What's that about?" Peale asked.

"An old joke."

"I didn't suppose Channing joked except at crucifixions or something like that," Peale said, motioning to the waiter to bring them another drink. "Getting back to what I was saying about your watching things–I don't mean that this is one–but Evvy told me you told some woman, I forget who, you were going to retire and write a book. You weren't serious, of course?"

"No, but don't look as though I told her I was going to rob the company," Lowry replied. "Did you ever meet Garrett Maynard?"

"Who? I don't believe so."

"Garrett Maynard. He was a partner in Rantoul and Company before the war and he died of wounds in Naples—great loss. I met him in the hospital and he knew he wouldn't live. He told me his greatest regret was that he wouldn't be able to write the book he had planned and he urged me to get someone to do it. Finally he asked me to—and the last letter he wrote was to have his trustee turn over the material he had to me. It's something far beyond my abilities but it is the thing at some point I'd like to try."

"What's it about?"

"'The Principal Errors of Judgment of Rulers and Peoples Since the Reformation.'"

"My God, how'd you happen to tell Paula Hewitt, I think it was, about it? And Evelyn heard about it too."

"Paula used to know Maynard and happened to ask me if I'd ever met him. She'd even heard about the book."

Peale shook his head. "It's just that it gets back to what I said to you the first day, Stephen—you can't make business a halftime thing."

"No, Mr. Peale," Lowry said with a grin.

"It's not a joke," Peale replied.

When Lowry telephoned Rosalie that he would be a little late getting home because of playing squash with Peale, he sounded so pleased about it that she felt glad for him. It had been apparent in their frequent meetings with the Peales that he was disappointed at the gulf which time and distance had made between them. He had been so happy and exuberant about all the reunion was going to mean that, finding they were far from their old intimacy, he was apparently a little self-conscious about speaking of it. At first she had feared that perhaps she was in the way. But with her alone Peale talked much more freely than with Lowry. With him, there was something slightly superior, something critical if not censorious of Stephen's general outlook, which annoyed her. At the same time it struck her that Peale was envious of the full, eventful, happy life they had had in Europe, a shade jealous even of the ease with which Lowry had gained Rutledge's and Johnson's confidence. And there was another aspect which troubled her and of which she had not spoken to Stephen, but which she felt she must.

He came in glowing with health and exercise and told her with usual good cheer of how badly he had lost at squash, and of how Peale's volleying was as terrific as it had been twenty years ago.

"We had a really swell time," he said, "until over a drink Jim began on his corporation prospects—why they should bother him, God only knows—and my business shortcomings. Incidentally I told him about Principal Errors, to his great distress. He *is* so changed. What does he talk to you about? I notice he does a great deal."

"Yes he does, more than Evelyn likes, I think, and more than I do sometimes. He does seem to have a feeling of guilt or inferiority about his war record. I know that he wishes now he'd done the sort of things you did. That may be why he preaches to you about business."

"I never could understand why he stayed in Washington."

"To start with, he was very amusing about your escapades and your girls (I'm afraid you were naughtier than you've ever admitted to me); he has taught me all I know about the Junior League and the Colony Club; but recently he talks almost wildly at times about the Company and do you think he'll succeed Mr. Johnson. But with it all there's a very sweet side to his nature. He has great appeal at times, like a brilliant, troubled adolescent."

"He's always been brilliant but he's also been normal and I get the feeling he isn't quite normal. It could be overwork, or he could, I suppose, have something physical the matter. He brought up this question of succeeding Johnson just now and asked me not to speak of it to you. And you say he has."

"Oh constantly. Stephen, there is something else I'd like to speak of that is very trying. I didn't mean to tell you of it because, well, it's difficult to express. But maybe you can tell me how to handle it."

"Oh. What is it?"

"He apparently craves to talk about sex."

"I do myself," he said with a smile.

She smiled back. "I know, but this is quite different. It's even different from the men who when they find out I am Estonian—which they've never heard of—think it means my days are one long assignation. It isn't so much talking about it as half asking or leading up to the most intimate sort of details or questions—"

"Do you answer?"

"Of course not. Sometimes he justifies it because we know each other so well, or we're both 'grown-up,' or he'd like to compare our views, and the most unpleasant time is when he says 'Evelyn isn't interested,' and I understand him."

"You're not about to tell me he's in love with you, are you? Of course I should think any man would be, but leave that aside."

"Well no, but I must say I think he could easily be, and he has restless hands. I'll be glad when summer comes and we don't have to see so much of them."

"I'll be damned," Lowry said, "and I thought I was one of the least jealous of men. I take it you don't meet him for little lunches and so on."

"I don't but he has telephoned to ask me, and the other day he sent a note by messenger."

"What did it say?"

"Darling, you will be glad to know I couldn't read his writing and I just sent it back."

He laughed. "What a relief. A woman can always read the writing of any man she's in love with, even if it's in Chinese. I should say he needed 'psychiatric help' as they call it."

"I hope this isn't going to bother you at the office."

"Not as far as you're concerned, no. As far as he is, yes. Tell me this, they spend an awful lot of money. Is he worried about that?"

"I don't know. He likes to talk about how much they spend. There's one thing more, and then let's talk about something else."

"All right."

"This is your fault, my dear man. Do you remember how annoyed I was at the Pierre that you left the picture of me sunning for the Rutledges to see?"

"Yes, I was sorry, but I didn't know they were coming."

"And you remember the to-do Jim made about it later?"

"Yes, at the moment, with the champagne, I almost showed him the one in Rhodes for old time's sake."

"Well, I can't find the picture since they were here the other night and I'm sure he took it with him."

"My God, it was on my bureau and he *was* in there alone." Then he added slowly, "He did take it."

"How do you know?"

"Because the summer we were out of college we went to a big coming-out party and the hostess had on some marvelous perfume. The tennis court had been covered for dancing. Everyone of course was out there. Jim said he must have the perfume and he went back to the empty house, found the hostess's bedroom and put the bottle in his pocket. At the time it seemed amusing. Later I didn't think so well of it because some maid was accused. I remember the bulge in the pocket of his white dinner jacket and I swear it came back to me the other night when he came out of the room. I must have noticed the bulge of the picture."

8

THERE WAS NOTHING ABOUT PEALE'S BEHAVIOR or demeanor the rest of the week to suggest he was in need of any kind of help. His only reference to the previous day was in good-natured superiority about his squash. Lowry noticed that on Thursday and Friday he was in long conference alone with Rutledge. All together it seemed ridiculous to suppose he could have taken the picture from the Lowrys' bedroom.

As he was leaving Friday he said to Lowry that he was off Monday night for about three weeks in Ohio ending, he hoped, with a week's holiday at White Sulphur with Evelyn.

"You'll hear the details at the officers' meeting Monday. I'll be in and around Larus most of the time and I'd like very much to see your mother, if you think she'd like to see me. She's near there, isn't she?"

"Right there, really. She'd love it."

"Well, send her a word of warning, will you, and say I'll ring her up? How do I get her?"

"The telephone is Larus 124 R. Look, try to see Sally too, will you, and let me know how they're off for money? Be discreet though."

"Oh sure. Where is she?"

Lowry gave him his sister's telephone and asked what was up.

"Diversification," Peale said. "You'll hear. Look, why don't you and Rosalie drive Evelyn down to White Sulphur?"

"Well, I'd like to but I don't think I should be away just yet."

The brief exchange was so easy and natural, so in keeping with their long friendship that Lowry felt more and more uncertain about the neurotic pilfering. After all, if an attempt to get a beautiful woman to talk about sex were a crime, the jails would be jammed with otherwise law-abiding men. And the fact that Peale was going to White Sulphur probably indicated that he realized he had been overworking. His occasional apathy might be sheer fatigue and he himself be aware of it.

"Well, as you like, but no one would object," Peale said. "By the way, before I go I'm proposing you for the Hounds and you've probably guessed by now that you met several governors the other night, by my being so pal-ly as you call it."

Lowry felt more ashamed. "Actually I didn't realize it, I'm—"

"Oh that's all right. Who are you getting as a second?"

"I suppose Alec Channing, if that's all right with you."

Peale looked a little surprised.

"Is it?" Lowry asked.

"Sure, he's very influential."

At the officers' meeting Monday morning Rutledge was in the chair, Johnson on his right and Peale for the first time on his left. Leslie Evans, sitting next to Lowry, whispered, "I wonder if we're seeing history made. I'd never have believed it."

"That doesn't mean anything," Hewitt said shaking his head. "I knew about it. Stephen, don't run off after the meeting. There's something I want to ask you."

Rutledge disposed briefly of several items and then started some single sheets of figures clockwise around the table. After watching their progress halfway, he put on his glasses and studied his copy. Peale leaned over, pointed to one line with a pencil, said something in an undertone and Rutledge said, "Yes, yes, I remember. You have here," he continued to the rest, "the balance sheet of Larus Earth-Moving and will note not only their strong cash position but their earnings over twenty years, if you didn't already know about them. The family still holds three-quarters of the stock and has had little to do with the company for some years. They're at last all ready to pull out and the management can either put out some preferred stock or it can come to somebody like us. Thanks to the young man on my left they have chosen the path of wisdom and I'll let him tell you about it. Jim?"

"I first talked to Edward about this six months ago and at that time we wondered—"

"I wondered, you never did," Rutledge said with a smile.

"Well, it was felt, then," Peale said smiling, "that diversification could go too far. We finally disposed of that."

"He practically told me I was obsolete," Rutledge said complacently.

"The book value of their stock compared to ours," Peale went on, "makes a three-for-one trade a simple and attractive one. There's a forecast of the effect on our earnings at the bottom of the page."

"Our directors approve but leave the decision in your hands," Rutledge added.

There was a moment or so of silent reading by them all and Evans asked, "What portion of their unfilled orders are government?"

"Under twenty per cent."

"How much abroad?" Lowry asked.

"About the same, well spread over a dozen countries."

"I know Burnham quite well," Hewitt said, "and like him very much. Had dinner with him on his last trip. He's certainly an individualist."

"Well he likes to talk that way," Peale said.

"He bid on some equipment when I was in Paris and the French trade unions raised some question about him and his labor relations," Lowry said. "Hasn't he had a good deal of trouble, or made it for himself?"

"Well, he's opposed to an annual wage, if that's what you mean," Peale replied.

"I thought they had a bad strike."

"No, no. A year or so ago he shut down to do some conversion and his labor didn't like it. Some people said he was pushing automation too fast. To my mind, it was all on the credit side."

"He has a union contract, I take it," Johnson asked.

"Oh no, he's always refused to deal with the union."

"Then I don't like it at all," Johnson continued. "In my view we have no better asset than our labor record. If he doesn't want to deal with them, he can take his business elsewhere as far as I'm concerned."

"I didn't understand Lowry to be making an issue of it—" Peale started to say.

"No, but I am, and it will do no harm to put a few obstacles in Burnham's way—"

"My God, there've been enough obstacles," Peale said.

Rutledge came to his assistance. "I thought, Tom, we could decide on this today. I don't like to delay it, so let's decide, but let Jim tell them his associates have raised that question and want to be sure our general policies will be his."

"You mean just say that and have him agree and then sign up?" Peale asked.

"I don't mean that. I think this is a good time to ask our friend Cramer to have a talk with him," Johnson said.

"I don't want to exaggerate what I heard in Paris—" Lowry said.

"We all understand that," Johnson replied curtly.

"I rather like the idea of having Cramer in," Rutledge said. "How does it strike you, Jim?"

"Well I don't see the necessity but if that's what's wanted, I accept it. I only hope it—"

"Look," Johnson said, "Burnham's a good manufacturer. If he were a good executive he wouldn't have been under the thumbs of that family so long. He doesn't know how to deal with a union official. He ought to be grateful for what Cramer can tell him."

"Of course we don't want to get him mad, after going this far and see him high-tail it off to Duraco or somebody, Tom," Rutledge said.

"Has he shown any signs of doing that?" Johnson asked.

"No, but it doesn't mean he won't," Peale replied.

"And if he does, I don't suppose we'll go broke. I understand from you that when you first saw him, he had no idea where to go, never had had any experience of the sort."

Peale nodded.

"How did you get on to it originally?" Evans asked him.

"From a mutual friend. Like the F.B.I., we have to protect our informants."

"There's no finder's fee involved, I take it?" Curtis asked.

"No. How's it to be left?" he asked. "Cramer tutors him? I get him to promise to be kind and thoughtful with his labor or the French may be mad, then do we go ahead?"

"Personally I want to know first that a union contract has been signed," Johnson said.

"Now what will you settle for, Tom?" Rutledge asked in an attempt to be jocular. "My thought is Jim goes out there and says OK and then he says something like this: 'Now I'd just like to review the question of labor relations and make sure we are thinking along the same lines. We want you to talk to D. P. Cramer.' He does so. The union contract comes along in due time. Now why isn't that enough for us all? After all, Burnham won't own Larus. We will. Doesn't that satisfy your point, Tom?"

"Oh I suppose so," Johnson answered. He felt a prickling flush over his body and his forehead was wet with perspiration.

"Well let's not say yes as though we were agreeing to a funeral. This whole thing's been admirably handled by Jim from the start and I don't want him to feel we're not appreciative. All agreed?"

More or less everyone nodded as Hewitt whispered to Lowry, "I still wonder where Jim got the tip. Oh, this is what I wanted to ask you, what are you doing Friday night?"

"Nothing that I know of."

"Well do you mind," Hewitt asked, "letting me say at home that we're having dinner together? I'll do the same for you some time."

At that instant, slightly troubled at having brought up the matter of the Larus labor record and touched off such a change in the negotiations, Lowry did not catch the import of the question.

"I don't know that I can have dinner," he said.

"No, no, it's just that I want to see someone and I'd rather not tell Paula. I'd just like to have her think we're out with some customer. You don't mind, do you?"

"Well, I suppose not," Lowry said coldly, "but I don't like to involve Rosalie, I mean, if they see each other."

"It'll never come up. Just be a pal this once, will you? I mean, if I say the two of us are out together, that'll end it. I just want to avoid any chance of your calling me that night. You never know what might come up."

"OK," Lowry said, "it's up to you. I'll not tell Rosalie, though."

"Don't want you to. Thanks a lot."

They separated and Lowry followed Peale into his office. Peale's manner was one of tried but polite patience.

"You know," he said, "I don't of course know what's customary in present-day government meetings, but if I may advise you in a meeting here, don't go off half-cocked with ideas. I thought six months' hard, taxing negotiations—incidentally to our great advantage—were out the window. You must know by this time that Tom Johnson is supersensitive about labor. It all stems from that brother who served a jail term."

"I'm sorry," Lowry said, "but I still don't see—"

"Well you saw what it started. Stephen, you must have guessed how I got on to this. You do, don't you?"

"No, I don't."

"You don't realize that Dolly's first wife was a Larus granddaughter?"

"Now that you mention it, yes. I never met her, as they were married and divorced while I was in the Army."

"She told Dolly. Dolly told me. I'll say this for him. All his ex's keep him in mind. Incidentally, I haven't told anyone here it was he."

"I see. In that case I want to be absolutely sure of one thing.

That there is no finder's fee going to be paid Dolly in any form?"

"I said no at the meeting, didn't I?"

"Jim, I don't want to quibble and I don't want to sound righteous, but Dolly has no moral scruples about anything and I can't imagine his doing this for nothing. True, you said no, but you didn't say in any form."

"No is no, isn't it?"

"Not always. You know whether it is or not."

"A finder's fee is a perfectly legitimate thing."

"If Rutledge, Johnson and everybody else knows about it. And if Dolly were in that business. However, do you give me your word he's getting nothing in any way, shape or form out of this?"

"My God, what are you so hot about? Tom Johnson was actually sweating."

"I don't like it, and otherwise I intend to tell Rutledge."

"Well, you'll put me in a nice position, I must say. What's more, the inference that I don't know what's right and what's wrong—"

"Look, Jim, the whole thing is settled if you give me your word."

"Now listen, the corporation is not paying a fee to Dolly. I certainly am not. Burnham's not, so do we need all this 'under oath' business? Rutledge knows Dolly. I didn't tell him about him because I thought it would prejudice the deal. That's all there is to it. It's all I know about. If you'll stop and think, you'll see you've done me and your brother an injustice."

It was all said plausibly and with evident candor. But it left Lowry still uneasy, because he did not feel it was the whole truth.

He said nothing about it to Rosalie that night for several reasons, the principal one being that he did not want to seem to be making a case against Peale every time he spoke of him. The brief interlude with him before the meeting had been so easy and natural that it made him realize all the more how much he missed the confident intimacy of the past and what fun it would be to get back to it. While even now he thought too much had been made of his raising the labor question, he asked himself whether he had not raised it, as men so often did, only for the sake of having something to say. A private word to Peale would have sufficed.

Altogether he was inclined to give Peale more than the benefit of any doubts. So at least he felt until, alone in the bedroom, his eye became aware of the space where the picture of Rosalie had stood. He felt a cold anger all over him, and going to the door called to her, "No sign of your picture?"

She got up from the sofa in the living room and came down the small hall.

"I've looked everywhere for it. I am so furious about it, and it makes me feel so indecent I almost called him to demand it. And I'm not sure I shan't ask Evelyn to let me look for it," she said. "Did you give any sign about it?"

"No. He's going out to Ohio tomorrow and meeting Evelyn in White Sulphur at the end of the month. I may go through their apartment while they're gone."

"I suppose I let you take the picture because it was fun, in all that sun and air, and this is our punishment. I suppose people are always expected to be respectable. I'm most furious because well, I don't know how to say it, but I feel self-conscious even toward you now. And I don't feel happy. The more successful you are, the more separated we'll become. How far's Grosse Pointe from Detroit?"

"Oh twenty minutes or so by car. Why?"

"I read in the paper today about this enormously important industrialist who has 'an estate' in Grosse Pointe and a nine-room suite at his office, where business keeps him three nights a week. Think of it. Can you imagine that in London or Paris? If we took that house in Connecticut, you'd be twenty hours a week, almost a day, going back and forth. I don't know what's to become of us. We have to get a place for the children—"

"Well, dear," he said gently, "everybody's up against this. It's modern life. We can't go live in a chalet in a valley like the song Mother sang in the Follies."

"I could, very happily. I'm still a peasant. But I don't feel like cooking your dinner tonight. Don't change your clothes. You'll have to take me out to some horrible restaurant."

"All right, but try to be cheerful about it."

"Oh you and your cheerfulness," she said impatiently. "Dearest, you're always *riant*, I'm not *riante*." Then she laughed. "Well, I feel better, but Stephen, really, I cannot see what anybody we've met gets out of this life. Mrs. Johnson is absolutely sweet. Their great apartment is utterly homelike, but she's worried to death about his health and all his responsibilities. Evelyn's worried to death that Jim won't get more and more responsibilities. I suspect Paula Hewitt is worried because there are other women. By the way, who is Titcomb? You've never spoken of him."

"Titcomb? Why do you ask about him?"

"Paula knows them and says they're divinely happy."

"Paula knows them? You must be mistaken. He's an old fellow who's head of the mailroom and general factotum around the office."

"Well, you must get to know him better, because he's happy. Get my coat, so we can exercise 'a choice of' on the dinner."

They took a cab to the pleasantly expensive Chateaubriand on East Fifty-Fourth Street, where, over their cocktails, the headwaiter recommended early shad roe and new asparagus. Rosalie gave him a look of mock horror and Lowry said gravely their religion prevented their having roe. The captain looked distressed at his blunder and suggested duckling.

Rosalie said she loved people to have private jokes. "I'm sure Jim and Evelyn haven't any now, or the Hewitts either. I can't understand why so many people marry the wrong person for them."

"The trouble is they stop and think it over too long."

"You mean that the way to a happy marriage is just to see a pretty herring-gutter and marry her?"

"I found it satisfactory."

"Do you realize that in a very few years we're supposed to start diverting the energy of our primitive drives into behavior that is socially and ethically on a higher plane?"

"Where did you read that?"

"I looked up sublimation in the dictionary. Someone told me the —" she whispered the name of the famous couple as the people on the banquette next to them tried to hear what they were saying,"—have done so completely. I suppose Principal Errors of Rulers and Peoples will begin it."

"Oh no," he said. "Give me a kiss. It will make the evening for those out-of-towners next to you."

She kissed him quickly and they heard the woman say in a loud whisper, "I knew they weren't married, Harry."

"Besides," Lowry went on, "the Sidney Webbs at the height of their intellectual production took a break every two hours for a romp."

"The trouble with a marriage like the Hewitts'—"

"You *have* got them on your mind, haven't you?"

"Yes. I like her very much and I feel very sorry for her. If a husband is dull—no ideas, no knowledge, no fun—that's bad enough, but women put up with it. But with someone like them love, or whatever he feels for her, has no tenderness."

"Does she tell you all this?"

"She has told me some. She's the sort of person who would give her life for someone she loved—without complaint, rich or poor, sick or well. What does he have in the office to do so well?"

"Well, he's shrewd, affable, breezy."

"I don't think there's any place but business where that would be enough to succeed."

"Darling, you're mistaken," Lowry said. "There are people just like him in politics, on university faculties, in the ministry, for that matter. He hasn't any doubts about things. I often wish I hadn't."

"What a bore you'd be. I'd still take care of you but I wouldn't love you."

"Pardon me," the woman beside Rosalie said, "but could you folks recommend a good show? We're from South Bend, Indiana, my husband's head of one of the plants. I'm originally from the South. We're staying at the Plaza, we couldn't get on the park side and they gave us a sitting room to make up. This is my husband, Mr. Dilsey. I'm Mrs. Dilsey. How would you like to join us at the show, as our guests? We'd love it. Harry, give your card to Mr.–Mr.–"

"Lowry," Rosalie said.

"Pardon me, but are you two married?"

"Oh yes," Rosalie said. "Three children."

"Really I'd have sworn, I told Harry, you weren't married. You acted so cute together."

"Like to have you go along to a night club later. You pick it," Harry said cordially.

"Well I'm afraid we can't tonight," Lowry said, "though we'd love to."

"Sure you can't now? Do you good."

"No really. What sort of a play did you want to see?"

"Well, we don't like a musical. We really get all we want on TV. We like something with emotion, something you can think about afterwards."

"There's a play about a Russian grand duchess."

"Oh I read about it. And if you say it's good, we'll go. Harry, go call the Plaza."

"It may be difficult to get tickets this late."

"Not for Harry at the Plaza."

Harry paid his check, tipped all and sundry and shook hands with the Lowrys. His wife made them promise to "come in for a drink some afternoon this week. I was so interested in all you were saying to each other." She went on talking until Harry motioned to her from the telephone booth.

"Well?" Lowry said to Rosalie when she was gone.

"Dear," she replied, "what a delight all that outspoken friendly sincerity is and I'm so glad it was us and not Jim and Evelyn next to them. I'm sure the Dilseys are very tender with each other."

They both studied the desserts on the menu for a moment and Rosalie, looking up at the headwaiter, noticed a woman about her age across the room, leaning forward, hand half raised to signal them when they saw her. She was slim and dark, and the smiling seriousness of her face was unusually attractive even across the room. She was with three people, all in evening dress. Rosalie half smiled in return and the woman pointed with her forefinger at Lowry.

"We're being picked up again," Rosalie said to him. "Look up, a lovely woman wants to wave to you. I wish I were dressed."

Lowry looked up. "Oh my God," he said, half rising.

As he did, the woman slipped out between the tables and came over to them.

"Stephen," she said, "I had to speak to you. What a delightful surprise."

"This is wonderful," he said, glancing at her ringless hand. "Rosalie, this is Lorna Hume."

Rosalie put out her hand and smiled, never having heard of Lorna before but feeling certain she should say, "Oh, of course, Stephen has spoken of you so often." Her own feathers stirred if they did not rise, but she herself felt the strong appeal in the attractive face and slim figure. She also had the feeling that Lorna had avoided looking directly at her, as they shook hands, and like Lowry she noticed the ringless hand she had raised to the low neckline of her dress as she reached across the table.

"We're about to have coffee. Can't you sit down?" she asked Lorna.

Lorna glanced inquiringly back at her table, motioned that she was staying with them and a waiter brought a chair, which Lowry took, seating her on the banquette beside Rosalie.

Listening to their rapid-fire news of what each was doing—Lorna was with one of the magazines—their quick recall of things past, Rosalie had a disturbing feeling both of their intimacy and their self-consciousness before her. She saw Lorna break a sugar lump into her coffee and Lowry hold the bowl for her to take a second, then wait with a cigarette while she found a holder in her bag.

"Have you the children's pictures with you?" Lorna asked her. Oh come, Rosalie thought to herself, you don't want to see their pictures. You want me to feel all right about this, but you wish

I would go powder my nose. And so does Stephen so that you could quickly get things straight between you—or on what I am to be told. When could all this have been and do stop looking at him that way, as though you could scarcely breathe. And it isn't necessary to keep your hand across your pretty bosom. She wondered if Lorna had been there to see Stephen kiss her.

Lorna glanced from the children's pictures Stephen had taken from his wallet for her and handed them back with appropriate comment.

"Show her the one of your wife in Rhodes," Rosalie wanted to say, though her feelings of petty hurt and jealousy annoyed her. Lowry scribbled their address and telephone number on a slip of paper and she gave them hers. He said he would remember it.

"He has an elephant's memory for everything," Rosalie said sweetly. While to a degree they made her feel an outsider, she felt a certain wifely pity for Lorna. And her appeal, even when her warm arm occasionally touched hers, was understandable. And she had Rosalie's own way of listening to Stephen, all eager interest.

"I must go back," she said looking at her table, "but Stephen, tell me first where and how is 'Principal Errors of Judgment?' "

"Oh still some years off," he said.

"Not abandoned or anything like that?" she asked.

"Oh no, very much not."

"Every once in a while I've copied a note for you from something I've read."

"You must let him have them," Rosalie said.

"Tell me what," he asked eagerly.

She shook her head. "Some other time or I'll just send them."

"Do," Rosalie said. "Our fourth box is only half full." I didn't have to say our, she thought to herself. It's Stephen's, it isn't ours, maybe it's even theirs.

Stephen and she got up and as she passed them Rosalie thought, Poor lamb, she wants so much to have him kiss her again. Lorna gave her an icy hand in goodbye and called her Mrs. Lowry.

The others at her table rose and she went out with them without looking back.

Lowry sat down beside her a little glumly.

"What are you thinking?" he asked guiltily in a moment.

"Well, many things of course, dear. One is what a lovely name Lorna Lowry would have been."

"Oh I don't know, sounds like a Stephen Collins Foster title. I am sorry I never happened to mention Lorna. We were friends in the thirties."

"Darling, everything is all right, but do be careful what you tell me. You don't have to tell me anything, but I happen to know Garrett Maynard didn't tell you about Principal Errors in the thirties. I think we'd better go."

"Will you have a brandy?"

"Do you need one?"

"I wish you wouldn't feel there's some mystery about this."

"Dear, I don't think there's any mystery."

"What do you mean?"

"Do you really want to ask me all these questions? You've met someone you used to know. She's terrifically attractive and I'm glad you met again. That's all there is to it."

"But I can see you don't feel that way about it."

"You really want to go on about it in this restaurant? Do the lights and the people make it easier?"

"Well, I would like to get it settled," he said with male absurdity.

"It's settled but you won't leave it at that. Do pay the bill. I'll meet you at the door."

She went to the powder room sure that all the women in the restaurant could see that she was a jealous wife, making a scene. And she was angry with Stephen because he had managed somehow to make her feel an alien and angrier at letting herself feel so—after all the years when, though she was an alien, he had made wherever they were home and refuge. "I wouldn't mind," she kept saying to rationalize it, "if he didn't act so like a guilty boy about it."

She looked at her face in the powder room mirror, trying to erase the frown between her brows, but finding herself imitating Lorna's enraptured gaze at Stephen, lips parted as though for his kiss, and then her hand raised to her neckline. But you've been looking at a small comedy, the remembrance of things past—not a tragedy. Why not smile? Why should you be upset? Suppose Lorna loves him. How do you suppose she feels after this brief meeting to leave him with you? You have him, and if he behaved like a flustered teen-ager, when had you supposed men ever wholly grew up? If he were in the habit of deceiving you he would have shown some skill at it. But as she opened the door she nonetheless thought to herself, But when and how did she know about Principal Errors?

Stephen was waiting all smiles and the captain said, "Goodnight, Mr. Lowry. Goodnight, madam," and bowed them out. She took his arm as they waited for a cab.

"I wonder," he said after they got in, "if the Dilseys got their tickets."

"I had forgotten about them," she replied, with unintended tactlessness, at which Stephen sat tongue-tied all the way to Gramercy Park and she realized with a sigh it all had to be gone over.

The silence continued up in the elevator and while he put their things away. Then he followed her dutifully into the unlighted living room, where, knowing it was the wrong thing to do, she stood by the tall windows looking vaguely at the lights of lower Manhattan.

He came over to her, his voice flat and unnatural, saying, "Dear, is everything changed, or what is the matter?"

"Nothing's changed, I suppose, it's just that I don't think—of course I don't know—that I've ever seen you with a former lover before and it's a little disconcerting. I'm very sorry. I don't want to make it hard for you. I don't blame you—but you might have told me about Principal Errors. Please don't be chivalrous and deny you were lovers though."

"Is it just Principal Errors?"

"I don't know what 'just' means. It's a great deal to find I've deceived myself about that. But please understand I don't blame either of you. She's quite lovely. But I wish I hadn't had to see her, because I see her in bed with you now and I keep hearing both of you saying the things we say to each other. Give me a cigarette," she ended impatiently. The fact was that she had not seen them in bed together nor heard what they said—and had been on the verge of kindly laughter about it all—until Stephen, of all people, must choose that moment for sober silence or guilty questions.

"How did you know?" he asked in somber tones.

"My dear man, no modesty is so obsessive as that which a woman displays with a man to whom she was once all immodesty. The dress wasn't so low she had to cover her very nice-looking breasts. I wonder she didn't put on gloves."

"It was before the war," he said.

"And how often after, since you want to talk about it?"

"I saw her in 'forty-eight when I was back."

"Had you arranged to?"

"No, it happened almost like tonight—but she went with me to Maynard's brother's for the notes."

"And so to bed, I suppose? Stephen, I don't know whether I can ever forgive you for making me question you."

"There was nothing," he said.

"Wouldn't she? You must have wanted to. I would if I were a man. Now you've found her, can't she help you with the book? Did you see her in 'fifty-one?"

"Yes."

"Did you correspond in the meantime?"

"No," he said impatiently. "Do stop staring out the window. It isn't the end of the world. I don't care whether—"

"Don't say you don't care whether you ever see her again as though someone who loves you doesn't matter."

"That's the most unreasonable and provoking remark I ever heard," he said, and started to draw her away from the window. "Can't we finish with this?"

"I can't. I'm very sorry. I'm sorriest because for the first time I can't tell you what I really feel."

"Try."

"No, please go to bed and leave me alone."

She looked over her shoulder in dismay as he stalked out of the room like a martyr. She knelt on the windowseat, trying to get at the heart of what was the matter. She had of course been deceived, but in no very grievous way. The thing is, she thought, I have never been sexually jealous before and I had no idea what it would be like. And it's a loathsome state. I want to be told everything and I don't. I'm resentful and still disgustingly curious, and worst of all I have this perverse desire to be had now, this minute. And I feel no tenderness about it and no laughter. If I had any sense I'd go in and say something sweet and silly and then all would be over. There was a foolish pet name she kept for times when he was troubled or depressed. If she could only go in and say it to him now. But had Lorna had some similar tender folly? And who else? But neither of those possibilities really mattered. It only mattered that she could not go in and absurdly say "You're my dear manager" and be sure it would comfort and bring him close again.

He was in the shower when she came in the bathroom in the morning and saw with alarm that there had been a major change in him. His shaving brush was unrinsed, his razor undried and the cap was not on the toothpaste. Hastily brushing her teeth, she put her head around the corner of the curtain.

"Good morning, darling," she said, trying to look *riante* through the spray of the shower.

"Good morning, angel," he said.

"How is my dear, dear manager?"

"Hungry," he said stepping out and kissing her. "Golly, I never left such a mess before."

"I'll dry them," she said. "Stephen, do you realize marriage is a great institution?"

"Oh very great."

"The greatest thing about it is that its pleasures become

habitual. Isn't that profound?"

"I think so. I'm not quite sure."

"For instance," she said, pulling her nightgown over her head and taking his place in the shower.

9

ON FRIDAY OF PEALE'S SECOND WEEK AT LARUS, with all going well there, Thomas Johnson asked Lowry to go up to lunch with him. He said he had two things on his mind. He had wanted to be sure that Lowry was thoroughly comfortable about the business and his associates before being asked to go on a trip. He thought, as did Rutledge and the rest of them, that Lowry's progress or acclimatization had been so rapid and gratifying that, if it suited him, they would like him to make a quick inspection trip to Paris, Madrid, down to West Africa, back through Brazil and Venezuela, say five or six weeks all together. The other thing was that Peale, who didn't know the plan yet, was very anxious to have Lowry join him at Larus and see the setup for himself. Larus had some agents and distributors abroad whom they were not quite happy about and Peale felt that both economies and efficiencies would result from C.I.C.'s own subsidiaries taking over. So, in short, could he go to Ohio and then make the longer trip?

"I imagine the question of your house and the children's coming over will concern you first. Have you found anything you like?" Johnson asked.

Lowry smiled. "The trouble is we've set ourselves a hard problem. We like the waters around Long Island and the space back in Connecticut. And what we like in Long Island is awfully expensive."

"Yes, I realize that. Of course special arrangements can be made–"

"Mr. Rutledge very kindly spoke of that but–"

"You mustn't feel it's anything out of the ordinary. We expect our people to have a decent roof over their heads."

"I'd like to go to Larus very much to see the plant, and my mother lives on a farm near there and hasn't seen my wife since our arrival. She's anxious to have Rosalie and the children for the summer, and if I'm abroad it may be a good solution–that is leaving the decision on our permanent home until I get back."

"The office can stir around while you're gone about a house, and Mrs. Lowry could always fly back from Ohio and have a look. So if it does suit you, will you please make arrangements accordingly?"

"Yes, with pleasure," he said though it was not unalloyed pleasure. He hated missing the children's first reactions to their native land, disliked the feeling of impermanency about a home and increasingly felt that a long life would be insufficient in which to see enough of Rosalie.

Johnson went on to say that Peale's handling of the Larus business was greatly to his credit. Lowry's mother had written Stephen what a delight it was to find Jim the same attractive person he had been in school and college and how good it made her feel that Stephen and he were together again. Peale had written enthusiastically of Mrs. Lowry's management of the property and pleasantly as to her retaining her looks.

Rosalie heard the news of the trip with mixed feelings–of pleasure at seeing the land Stephen came from and his mother but of anxiety for other reasons.

"I suppose we'll see a great deal of Jim, and that does make me a little uneasy, but we'd better forget about the picture and the rest of it and start all over. I feel a little as though I were running out on my English class–"

"It will be only a few days."

"And I wish I could go abroad with you. If your mother's willing to have me and the children for the summer, she'd probably greatly prefer having them to herself. But I realize I must stay or the dear lambs will think we don't love them."

"I hate missing the summer with them, too," Lowry said.

"I know. It's precious having them and it's precious being alone. Oh I'll be so glad when we get all settled where we're going to be."

Lowry had not seen his mother since her visit to them in Paris two years previously and he had never seen the farm she had bought and managed alone after his father's death. The usual thinness of a woman's sixth decade was in her case a slim elegance in tweeds and it was incredible that the woman who met the train was old enough to be his mother or earthy enough to live by animal husbandry. She greeted Rosalie and him, spoke to porters and the driver of her farm truck about their bags in the voice whose enunciation and timbre had, before he was born, been so famous in the theater. He could still hear that high, clear voice calling from the kitchen at their lake at camp in his boyhood, "Stephen, desire your father to burn the garbage while I look at the moon." It made him grin with delight to hear her and to see by her gestures and "business" that all the world, including an Ohio station platform at seven-fifteen on a blowy April morning, with the smell of spring in the air, was still a stage to her.

She linked her arm in Rosalie's and led the way to her small car. "Now," she said, "Stephen you're to be delivered to the Country Club for breakfast with Jim and his manufacturers. Rosalie, can you wait to breakfast at the farm? We'll be there by eight and we can talk until noon. Stephen, I'll pick you and Jim up at the plant. You'll want him to dine, won't you?"

"Yes," he replied.

"We had orange juice on the train," Rosalie said, "and I can wait hours. It's divine being here. I really loathe New York."

As they drove out of the tree-lined streets of the town past the lush farmlands and their well-painted houses with the low wooded hills rolling away northward under an enormous sky, the air smelling of earth and heaven, it was easy to feel this was the Promised Land. Red birds, which only bird-watchers with binoculars saw in New York, were flitting and calling from tree to tree. There was no sign there of what coal-stripping had done to Ohio, or manufacturing to all its *belles rivières*. It looked as it must have to young Washington or the French coming to the confluence of the Alleghany and Monongahela, and it filled Lowry with a great love of the land.

There was a sense of space and vigor about it. The most perfect English inn would have been out of place along such a road. He wished they could pull up beside a long white country hotel with a veranda and chairs, and at the desk a bound register, big as a church Bible, on a swivel so you could pull it around and read the guest names. And then go into breakfast where fried steak, liver and bacon or fresh fish were higher up on the menu than ham and eggs; hot cakes and syrup were a side dish, oatmeal for the ailing and coffee was boiled with eggshells and tea was strong enough to float a silver dollar. It was not nostalgia—he was too young really to have known such things—but it was race-memory. And it flooded over him when he had kissed the two beautiful women in the car goodbye and entered the Country Club.

Jim and two men, their chairs drawn together, were talking business, handing decks of typed tissues back and forth, fishing in briefcases for more copies. They turned to hail him cordially, and he saw that the third was D. P. Cramer.

"Hi, Steve," Jim said, "this is Les Burnham of Larus and I think you've met Mr. Cramer. Well I guess we're all ready for breakfast."

Cramer said, "Yes, indeed," beamed from behind his glasses and shook hands cordially.

Burnham was a big fellow with a narrow head, long chin, long nose and a high forehead from which the hair had receded to a wavy thatch. He wore big steel-rimmed spectacles, had a big voice and a big, almost perpetual smile. He looked what he was, a civic-minded good citizen with no doubts about what was right and wrong, and sure that right would prevail throughout the world if American business were given a chance. To no one could the funds of widows and orphans, or the fate of a man on trial, be more safely entrusted. He believed in God, Country, Yale—Class of 1918—Ohio and the Republican Party. His grandfather had believed in the same things, plus the G.A.R.

Burnham got up and with a hand in the middle of Lowry's back guided them toward the dining room, where they were met by a very pretty hostess who, greeting them each by name, led them to a table. As they sat down, and a white waitress poured water and gave them butter, a colored boy wearing a page uniform in club colors drew four small cups of black coffee and placed them at their right hand. Another colored boy in white jacket and apron appeared with an oven of hot biscuits, toast and rolls, to which they all helped themselves. No one else was in the dining room.

The business of the small coffee both puzzled and pained Lowry. He supposed that it was some nicety brought back from New Orleans by a woman on the House Committee. A pick-me-up brought to master's bedside by a Negro body servant. He saw the page's eyes fixed on them as they ordered scrambled eggs and bacon, and pushing the demitasses aside he began to talk. He was fond of coffee and expected to have two cups in due course, but he neither wanted nor needed this eye opener. The page came sadly over to the table with his pathetic little salver to remove the cups. Lowry wondered if anyone ever drank one. On the boy's face there was a look of futility that touched Lowry's heart. As the boy reached for his cup, Lowry said, "Oh wait, I must have that," gulped it down, thanked the boy and handed him the cup. "Just what I needed," he said.

The boy grinned. "You like another, sir, nice hot one?"

"Well, thank you, not just yet. Did you make it?"

Cramer paused fractionally in what he was saying to take it all in.

It appeared from the talk that Burnham had been called to

Washington on matters unconnected with the take-over of Larus and that details were not yet finally settled. Mergers were an area of business in which Lowry was not expert and he listened respectfully to the others. Two things particularly impressed him—one, that the desire to buy was animated very slightly by Larus's condition that day but rather by what they felt it would be tomorrow. The other was the absence of pressure, trading, "chiseling" on both sides—or of any effort to figure relative book-values down to the last penny. Larus would be part of C.I.C. and its acquisition should be at a price which would leave its sellers, its management and buyers all happy. Thereafter the boundless future of American business would take care of things.

Burnham said, however, that before they got to what Mr. Lowry's organization was going to do for them abroad, he and his associates did want to be clear on the stock-option plans for them.

"As I told you," Peale replied, "the option price is twenty-five dollars."

"Twenty-four dollars, fourteen cents," Cramer interjected.

"It closed night before last at twenty-seven and three-fourths," Peale said with a smile.

"Yes, I know. What concerns us aren't the prices. It's the number of shares we can reasonably expect, having in mind there's been no such plan at Larus and the family had all the stock."

"I don't think you have anything to worry about," Peale replied. "No one's ever accused them of not being generous."

It was certainly true, Lowry thought. In his own case his paper profits on the options issued him were already considerable. Years before, when he had worked for the Founders Trust Company, the directors were thought of at his level as a group of fault-finding rich men who were likely to have people fired for a small mistake. Like God, they saw all he did and usually disapproved. He was there on tolerance. In government service The Department in Washington and The Congress were in a similar capacity, poised to break the careless or the negligent.

Now he found that directors were really a group of philanthropists living in abject fear that "key men" even like him would be lured away by higher rewards elsewhere, constantly trying to boost "officer morale," and protecting them against "small but vocal stockholder minorities" who objected to "option plans." Any man lucky enough to be a "key" in that inner circle had only himself to blame if the years did not bring him reasonable riches, happiness, a full life and something to leave to his widow and children. As to the male children, corporations were very rapidly providing jobs in the succession for the best of them as old "family businesses" had done. A key man did not have to worry about the future of a regular son. He would come along and there would be money for those who wanted to enter the ministry or paint or write or ranch. So assured were the rewards that it was hard to understand why anyone chose another means of livelihood. Why should anyone be a teacher, like his brother-in-law, Robert Breese?

The lesson of 1929 had been learned and everything was taken care of, provided Labor would go on laboring. On that D. P. Cramer had begun to speak. He said first that in every plant he ever ran the door of the president's office was never closed. It was a symbol and more valuable as that than as a fact. Burnham said noisily they had some bad actors at Larus and always had had.

"You have to remember that they've got memories of many years of Pinkerton informers in the plant, right through the La Follette investigation," Cramer replied in his quiet undertone.

"I'd like you or anybody else to tell me how you run a plant without having someone to tell you what the men are talking about and what schemes for grievances they're up to."

"Well, in the first place, friend Burnham, you sign a union contract, and that's what I'm here to talk about," Cramer said.

"The thing is this, Les," Peale said. "Our people all feel it's essential that there be a satisfactory labor contract *before* the company belongs to us."

"At how many dollars and cents an hour?"

"As high, or a little higher than what's paid anyplace else," Cramer told him.

"And I suppose retroactive to the Year One?" Burnham asked.

"Well, certainly retroactive. Mr. Lowry told us at the start of a very valuable contract the Foreign Aid people had to cancel because the French labor unions were bitter about your non-union politics."

"Now we have to please the Frogs too, do we? I thought Mr. Lowry was here to tell me how we're going to increase our export business." In Burnham's ordinary words, he was plainly hot under the collar and Lowry felt considerable sympathy for him, taken suddenly to task about something Peale had evidently not raised before. And he was surprised at the abruptness with which Cramer had tactlessly injected the French issue. Peale looked at him critically as though to say, "Well, you did raise it and started all this."

"I mentioned the French matter casually during a very general background discussion," he said.

Cramer interrupted. "I'm sorry, Mr. Lowry—if you'll think back it was not 'a general background discussion' but a meeting of senior officers to whom the Board had referred the Larus plan with power."

"In any event, Mr. Burnham," Lowry said good-humoredly, "you do not have to placate the French. We all feel a labor contract is essential, but that's a matter for you and Jim and Mr. Cramer to thrash out. The main reason I'm here is that I'm going abroad very shortly and I want to learn as much about your machines and your sales as I can, and then see if our people can't do better."

"You're my man," Burnham said with his big smile. "I'm just a dirt mover and a damn good mechanic. I think trade unions are a curse to the country. Let us get to the office, look over our records and get out to the demonstration lot and my labor-relations man can settle with our friends here any way they like and I'll sign it. Now what's your itinerary?"

"When was this decided?" Peale asked.

"Yesterday. It's comparatively short, six weeks, Paris, Madrid, West Africa, Brazil, Venezuela."

"You'll never make that in six weeks and accomplish anything," Peale said. "I think either you ought to take more time or come back from Brazil and start over."

"I understand you're admirably qualified in Europe and the Middle East, but do you know your South America?" Cramer asked.

"I've never been there but I think I'll get along," Lowry said.

"The political situation in Venezuela last year was so unsettled that I wasn't at all sure how wise we were being about developing there. Bribery, subsidy, placation of the opposition is terrific in all Latin America. As an example, I had an appointment with a member of the Cabinet in Mexico and our agent took two pesos from me for the Minister's Secretary."

"Come on, let's go," Burnham said. "You're not going to Mexico anyhow and I want to show you our machines. You want any more coffee, Mr. Cramer?"

"I never take but one cup."

As they pushed back their chairs, Lowry said to Burnham, "Our Venezuelan agent writes me of a railroad bridge planned to start this year. If you're in the picture, I think C.I.C. is in a position to bid on the whole thing and it's of a magnitude of six million dollars."

"Now you're talking my language," Burnham said with a slap on the back.

"I don't want to throw cold water on it," Peale said, "but I don't think it's got any reality." And as they went out to the car he said aside to Lowry, "Go easy on these plans."

At the plant Burnham got Mather, his labor-relations man, in his office, settled Cramer at his own desk with Peale beside him and said to Mather, "Now forget everything I've ever said and do what Mr. Peale and Mr. Cramer tell you to do. I'll see you all at lunch." He told Lowry, "You may need a sweater on the lot. Strong wind."

"No, I'm a cold-climate graduate."

On the lot Burnham was at his best, operating everything from great excavators to post-hole diggers himself, sprinting alongside another in action, demonstrating the wonder adaptability of the machines by having his twelve-year-old boy couple and uncouple attachments and implements with incredible speed and facility. It was a wonderful morning of sun and air, health and vigor, and by the end of it Lowry at least felt there was nothing C.I.C. needed as much as Larus.

At one o'clock, when they returned to the offices, they found the others had had sandwiches and coffee brought in, with a glass of milk for Cramer, who said they "preferred to work straight through." Burnham asked a few questions and took Lowry off to the cafeteria.

"I guess it's all to the good," he said. "Even Bob Taft used to tell me I'd better come to it. I'll get Deacon, our sales manager, to join us."

They all ate quickly and repaired to Deacon's office and spent the rest of the afternoon reviewing contracts, sales records and order books. About four they went back to Burnham's office, where the other three were winding up their talk and typists were bringing in and taking away the results of their discussion.

"I think we're done," Cramer said. "I have accepted, with some reluctance, Mr. Mather's view that it is best to wait the next call from the Union. He assures me it can be expected within a few days—"

"I told him that Lampson—that's our troublemaker, Mr. Lowry—probably already knew all we've said. It's going to be nice having him as the Union representative," Mather said somewhat bitterly.

Cramer looked at him. "You have no doubt of the wisdom of our decision, have you?"

"No, no, Mr. Cramer."

"Well then, I wouldn't say or think that sort of thing, if I were you," Cramer told him.

It was hard to know what Peale was thinking. He looked very tired, and his manner was formal and taciturn.

"Well," Burnham said, "give me fifteen minutes with my mail and we'll go back to the club and bend the elbow a little."

Cramer declined at once, saying that his car was waiting to

take him to Galion, and Lowry said his mother was calling for Peale and him.

"Oh I'd forgotten Mrs. Lowry was your mother. Wonderful woman," Burnham said. "Well, then, we'll see you and Jim in the morning?"

They said yes and Burnham made a nice little speech to Cramer and then said to Lowry, "Oh, I forgot. My kid wanted to ask you to send him some foreign stamps, if your secretary has time."

"I certainly will and when my boy gets here from Europe I'll get him to write David about 'traders.' "

Mrs. Lowry and Rosalie were waiting in the car, and Lowry presented Cramer to them.

"Both of you in the back," Mrs. Lowry said to Lowry and Peale after Cramer left.

"Did it go well?" Rosalie asked.

"How did it, Jim?" Lowry asked.

"All right," he said. "I'll have to come out to dinner later, Mrs. Lowry. If you can drop me at the club, I've got some things to do and I must talk to New York."

"Talk to them from my house," she said.

"Thanks, but I have a lot of paper to spread out for the talk."

"Do you want me to wait with you?" Lowry asked.

"No, not at all."

"Dinner's at the unholy hour of six, as my cook and her husband have their programs to listen to. Can you manage that?" Mrs. Lowry asked.

He was either so exhausted or disturbed about something that Lowry asked him in an undertone if anything *had* gone wrong. He shook his head and got out at the Country Club looking almost ill.

"I'll come back for you," Lowry said to him in some concern.

"No. I've got one of those Driv-Ur-Self's."

"Jim, you're not ill, are you?" Rosalie said.

"Oh no," he replied, but Lowry, looking at him, also got out and walked up the steps with him.

"There must be something wrong, Jim. Don't feel you have to put on an act with us."

"Why do you say 'put on an act'?"

"I just mean if you're feeling sick, say so."

"I'm perfectly all right, I tell you."

Lowry had never seen the farm before, so it was not coming home in the true sense, but going into it gave him all the emotions of home coming, of stability and of family. The house, built in 1840, had high-ceilinged rooms, high, broad-silled windows and a railed porch in front. To the left of the "front door" was Mrs. Lowry's farm-office with a business desk and typewriter, filing cabinets, shelves of catalogues, County Agent and Agricultural College reports on animal foods, fertilizers and seeds, photographs of blooded cattle and of the mighty Yamoyden Butter Prince Paul III, the pride of the farm. The rest of the downstairs was a lovely country house—to the right a long sitting room, with an L-turn at the end to the open library and next to the office a dining room facing west on a flagged terrace. The beauty and amenity obviously cost a great deal more than Lowry had expected his mother could afford, but he admired the independence with which she had done it and the self-reliance that had led her to live so well though alone. Loneliness was something she had never mentioned in her letters and he wondered what her thoughts must be in the long winter evenings or the long dusks of summer. He had not been aware—perhaps because he was too young when he left home—what the inner relations between his parents had been, except that they liked and seemed happy with each other. His mother had never expressed to him any regret at leaving the stage. Yet it was hard to see how so attractive a woman could be happy without men.

The three of them were in the living room at five-thirty, with cocktail ingredients and ice, awaiting Peale's arrival, when the telephone rang and Mrs. Lowry went to her office to answer.

"I'm sure it's Jim, saying he can't come," Rosalie said. "What in the world has happened?"

From Mrs. Lowry's side of the conversation it was clear in a moment that she was right, and Lowry hurried to his mother.

"Let me speak to him," he said to her.

"But this is such a disappointment, my dear," she was saying. "The Larus operator's a friend of mine. She'll get you here. We can really hold dinner as late as you like. Here's Stephen."

"I'm sorry," Peale said to him, "but I simply can't come."

"Well, Jim, if it's about today I'll come to the club."

"It isn't necessary. I'll tell you, I'll give you a ring later."

"Well all right, but I wish it didn't have to be so mysterious."

"It's not, it's just as I told you, business is a whole-time job." The note of curt hostility in his voice was so marked and uncalled for that Lowry in some annoyance said to suit himself, hung up and walked back to make cocktails.

"He can be difficult," he said as he stirred them, still wondering if he was being derelict in not going to the club.

The menu was the farm's own premium steak, its new potatoes, its watercress fresh from the brook and its asparagus cut the hour before. There was a rough but excellent Chianti that Mrs. Lowry said was made by an Italian family who had a vineyard down the road. It was all delicious, but each of them ate halfheartedly, puzzling over Peale.

When they finished their coffee in the living room and Mrs. Lowry took away the cups, saying she must have a word with her farmer, the cook's husband, Rosalie said, "Darling, you don't suppose I spoiled this in some way?"

"No, of course not, but I have the feeling I ought to go in and find out—"

"Then, why don't you?"

"Well, he plainly doesn't want me around and I dislike barging in on him."

"I think I'll go up to bed and leave you to talk to your mother. She's been darling to me."

"The Stephen Lowrys never knew why they were unpopular," he said to his mother when she came back. "I should have thought Sally and her husband would have made a point of being here."

"My dear, I explained it to Rosalie, who understood perfectly—Sally and he are devoted to each other, but Robert's life is not an easy one."

"I know they have a hard time financially."

"My dear, it is the fact that that very dear little man, each day of his life, has you held up as the final repository of wisdom, knowledge and valor, and, at his slightest shortcoming, is warned by Dolly's horrible example. I don't read psychology but I think your dear sister suffers from brother-images. Still, as Dolly said, 'The fellow may be nuts, but after all she's nuts about him.' Incidentally do you know what styrene—propylene—co-polymers are?"

"No."

"It means nothing to you?"

"Nothing."

"I am so happy for Robert. He was sure you wouldn't and has written a paper on them which I understand has set Dow Chemical, is it, by the ears. Maybe money, money, money."

"Well, good for him. And speaking of money, are you all right, as they say?"

"Why do you ask, dear?"

"Well, the house is so lovely and its things so beautiful."

"My dear, I take better care of money than almost anyone you know. Rosalie and I had a long talk about it today. We're both thrifty peasants and I can live this way because I do an enormous amount of work myself. So don't worry. You're such a blessing," she said. "I don't know where I got you, when I think of all the worry Sally and Dolly have been in their ways. From the time you were a little boy, you were always so responsible—"

"Now, Mother—"

"Don't 'now Mother' me. I was going to add that what would really put your poor, dear brother-in-law on his feet would be to have you do something absolutely irresponsible and have it get in the papers, you know, something not disgraceful but very, very human."

"Well I'll certainly think it over," he said, laughing, and

changed the subject to Peale and the changes in him. His mother said that until that afternoon he had seemed to her as delightful as ever.

"I remember when I used to go to New Haven and you'd both come to breakfast at the Taft with me. How long ago it seems."

She sat a moment in reverie and looked up to see Rosalie in robe and nightdress in the doorway.

"Can I come in?"

"Oh I should say. It'll be much more interesting with you here."

"Stephen, I know it's none of my business, but I have the strongest feeling you ought to go in and see what's the matter with Jim."

He got to his feet. "Actually, so do I," he said. "I'll call him first, I think."

He was at the telephone and the club operator had just told him that Mr. Peale had left with Mr. Burnham about half an hour before, when they heard a car stop in the driveway and the farm dog bark, then a ring of the bell.

Mrs. Lowry went to the door and they heard her say, "Why Jim, how wonderful. We were just talking about you."

Rosalie, conscious of her attire, started to go as Mrs. Lowry brought him in. To Lowry he looked much more himself than he had since breakfast. His manner was more composed and easy and he said he was sorry at missing dinner and being difficult and glanced only casually at Rosalie's negligee.

"I'll tell you what happened, Steve. I talked to Tom Johnson and I got him to agree to Les's and my signing the final papers—which we've done—subject to an oral understanding on an immediate labor contract. I'm getting the train at eleven for New York, where I've got to be tomorrow, and you and Les can wind up without me."

"Would you like a drink, Jim?" Mrs. Lowry asked.

"I don't think so, thanks. I must go straight back, but I did want to say goodbye."

If this is all it is, why the first evasiveness? Lowry wondered.

Surely it was not simply to emphasize his own subordinate position.

Peale said he felt a great relief at getting it all settled and apparently that was all there was to it. Then he continued plausibly, "You see, I wasn't sure how much Cramer has rubbed Les the wrong way and I thought it advisable to get him out of the picture as quickly as possible. And I think Les was very much pleased and took it as a vote of confidence."

"I agree with you," Lowry said. "Does Cramer know?"

"He will in the morning."

"What about White Sulphur?"

"I'm not sure and now I must beat it. Goodnight, Mrs. Lowry, and many thanks."

She kissed him and he turned to Rosalie, making herself inconspicuous in the corner of the sofa. She very quickly put out a hand and wished him luck. Lowry walked out to the car with him and there was no further reference to business. When he came back, Rosalie had gone upstairs and Mrs. Lowry was switching off the lamps. She raised her eyebrows to her son. He shrugged and kissed her goodnight.

Rosalie was in bed in a jewel of a room, bright with pretty lamps and mirrors, a bowl of flowers, and French-blue draperies drawn. He took off his coat and slowly undid his tie. "I suppose that, while it's all true, it isn't the whole story. I never felt more in the dark in my life," he said.

10

LARUS CONTRACTS WITH FOREIGN REPRESENTAtives were cancelable on thirty days' notice, and Burnham sent out such notices the next day after further talk with Lowry. Though there was no urgency and they would like to have stayed at least another day at the farm, Lowry felt they had better take the train that night.

At the office Lowry found that Peale had gone to Washington and that the results of the trip had pleased everyone.

"Tell me," Rutledge asked. "Jim didn't seem to mind Cramer's sitting in too much, did he?"

"No, though actually I didn't see a great deal of Cramer."

"He's an effective fellow. Doesn't like New Yorkers, but as the great Victor Moore once said, he doesn't want to kill us either. I don't think he liked Jim's sudden decision to sign Burnham that night, but we all felt it was very good judgment. Always well to have a little give and take. We're going to try to get Jim away for a holiday. He seemed awfully edgy, but the negotiations have been trying. He's done a wonderful job and he tells me you were a tower of strength."

"Well, hardly that, but Burnham and I got along well."

"Good, there'll be lots more when you get back. Nothing like team play."

* * *

During the early April days before Lowry's departure neither he nor Rosalie, for all their sanguine natures, could quite shake off the persistent feeling of uneasiness. They put it out of their minds, and they rationalized it—and they laughed at it. But it still persisted as the forsythia and the tulip trees blossomed in Gramercy Park, and horse-drawn wagons sold hyacinths in the streets and new candy-stick awnings appeared over little restaurants in the East Thirties and grocers had mint for juleps or the Pascal lamb.

They saw the Peales as often as before, and except for a sense of strain between those two, and a business he made of a kiss of greeting, it seemed to Rosalie that Jim's attitude toward her was more normal and toward Stephen less critical—though still, Stephen told her, without the intimacy of the past.

To this he had begun to reconcile himself, aware that except in the field of actual management Peale was very much ahead of him in corporate vision and experience.

"I not only can't create mergers in my own mind, I don't really understand the workings of them at times," he told Rosalie.

"You didn't go to the Harvard Law School, but I can't imagine anyone choosing Jim to run things instead of you," she replied.

"Well, I don't want to be just dependable," he said.

"It's an awfully comforting thing to many people that you are, from Rutledge down to your mother and me."

"Maybe, but Rutledge talks a great deal of Jim's vision. I worry at times about Principal Errors. I suppose there's something a little ridiculous in someone of my limited education undertaking it. And in ten years, if I have the money, I may have lost the will or the cutting edge. Rich men have seldom written good books."

"Dear, you won't lose the will or the cutting edge. You're a very persevering man. Anyone who could devote three years, wasn't it, to getting me to agree to Arethusa—"

Mention of the connubial secret of Arethusa made him smile. "I was unshakable, wasn't I?"

"Yes, and I have seen you *more* unshakable about affairs of state."

"I am ashamed of being concerned that Rutledge might hear about Principal Errors. Jim considers it madness."

"Why should Rutledge or anyone else care what you do away from the office?"

"You see he would take the stand that anyone has just so much energy and that any spent on Principal Errors would come out of what I should give the corporation. And that if I intend to leave the corporation in ten years he's entitled to know it now."

"But, dear, suppose in ten years they want you to be president of Standard Oil, or whatever, does he have to know that now?"

"No, but that isn't analogous. The creed is, a man is entitled to get as much for himself as he fairly can but he's not entitled to use business as a means to another end. If I should retire in ten years and the book come out two years later, they will all say, 'Oh now we understand why Lowry couldn't or didn't do this or that'—and I'm not sure whether I care about their saying it or not."

She shook her head perplexedly. "I don't understand it. Didn't you say that Rutledge gives an enormous amount of time to the Metropolitan Opera? And that half of Alec Channing's time went to the Yale Alumni Fund? Do they feel guilty about it?"

"Of course not, those are public duties. Arts and Letters are a different matter. If Rutledge knew who Isaiah Berlin is, for example, he'd say, 'Turn it over to him. I'm not adverse to some substantial financial aid, but don't you get mixed up in it.' "

"And he's such a dear old man. Well, if necessary the book can come out as the joint effort of Lorna and Rosalie, disciples of Mr. Lowry. It will be an immediate best-seller, book-club choice. I don't know just how they'll make a movie of it, and our sister savants Rebecca West and Simone de Beauvoir will review it, so you have nothing to worry about. I wish so I could go on this trip with you," she said. "I never worried before about you. I think it was much easier for women when their lords locked their chastity belts on and said, 'Now you look out for the flocks and herds and don't let anyone fly my falcons, and make barrels of mead and salt beef and fish and weave nice tapestries and I'll be back in three years.' At least they didn't have to wait around every morning for the mail. You really will write me every day?"

"Yes," he said, "but now since you won't have to weave tapestries or brew mead, you can work classifying our notes. While I'm in Paris, if I can, I want to find someone to look into why and how the Germans managed to avoid the Renaissance so completely. I doubt that that language of theirs has had any new words added since Caesar crossed the Rhine."

"You'd better also have more work done on the wherefores of the Revocation of the Edict of Nantes. Oh Stephen, I do wish we were rich and you could do nothing else. We'd be together all the time."

When Lowry let himself into the apartment rather early a few afternoons later he heard a rumble of voices from the living room. He looked in to see Rosalie in the midst of an English lesson with four of her Estonians, waved and went to bathe and change.

The lesson ended and her pupils departed as he finished dressing. Rosalie came in and to his amazement dropped in a chair, bursting into tears.

"Why, darling, what in the world?" he asked, his arm around her shoulder.

"Oh, Stephen, one of them was sure she had met Inge and Mother in Rotterdam last year and then it turned out not to be true."

"She was sure it wasn't true?"

"Yes, the name was different and I had misunderstood some Estonian word. They were two cousins—older women. Oh it's happened so often."

"I know, darling," he said.

"I think I'll lie down awhile. Get me an aspirin, please."

Half an hour later she joined him in the living room in a round-necked cotton dress and sandals. "I'm all right," she said. "Sorry to have been a baby. Tell me, what are the men saying—" a phrase in their private idiom.

"Well, they're not saying much. The Larus union contract

came through and everybody's very pleased with Cramer and Jim, though neither, I suspect, is pleased at dividing the credit with the other. Jim has had to go to Washington again, and may not be back before I leave. I had the benefit of some fatherly advice, however. Incidentally, he's looking perfectly ghastly."

"He told me the other night he had lost ten pounds."

"I don't understand it. When we got back Rutledge was going to send him off for a rest and now he tells me Jim refuses to go."

"Perhaps I could have found out. He called and begged me to have lunch with him today. He sounded so unhappy that I think I would have if he hadn't suddenly said something about how I looked when he came in at your mother's."

"Where'd he call you from?"

"I don't know where. It was a booth. He had to put in more money."

"God, that's furtive."

"Speaking of lunching or dinner, dear, when did you have dinner with Calvin Hewitt? Paula told me all about it with great pleasure. Not that I mind, because, as I told you, I think he often has dinner with bad little girls. But for the life of me I couldn't remember when it was."

"Did you tell her that?"

"No, I didn't want her to think you hadn't come home and raved about what a great fellow he was. He says you're a wonderful talker, impress everybody and have a great future and the very big shot you were with thought so too. I told her that all the European potentates felt that way about you and I could never understand how you put up with dull me. But when was all this?"

"I'm ashamed to say it never was."

"It must have been. I even heard what you had for dinner."

"Dear, Hewitt asked me some time ago to let him tell Paula we were having dinner together—"

"So he could be out with some woman?"

"I suppose so."

"Why didn't you tell me?"

"I warned him that I wouldn't tell you and have you involved."

"Very noble, I must say. You thought nothing of letting Paula be deceived–I suppose he would 'help you out' next time."

"Certainly not, but I didn't weigh all the ethical considerations. It's the sort of thing that happens–"

"I realize that but I didn't think you'd do it. Several times in Europe you refused, or at least you told me you refused."

"That's true. I could refuse then for official reasons or even vague security ones."

"So you really have no principles of your own about such things?"

"I do have, yes. It's difficult to expound them in an office. I regret it, but it doesn't seem to me absolutely heinous."

"That's a word I've never heard. What does it mean?"

"Infamous. It's surely possible even you might have done it for a woman friend."

"If you think that, you really don't know as much about people as I thought you did. I would only do it for a friend who was deeply and really in love with someone and whose husband I considered deserved it. Do you consider Paula deserves it? Aren't you supposed to be a friend of hers?"

"Must we go on? I regret doing it but I must say it's a commonplace that is hard to avoid in an office with someone whom you are otherwise working with in a normal way."

"You mean all men do this?"

"No I don't, but certainly many do and more have done it on occasions."

"May I know whether you do it with me, or am I supposed to take it for granted and not ask?"

"I have never done it with you and never will."

"That's really too noble for words. You never did it before? In Europe?"

"No. Can't we drop it, please?"

"But in New York, in business, you readily do it for someone you don't really like and to someone who has never shown you anything but kindness and hospitality. Is that the effect of this Big Business? Suppose Evans or Curtis hear from Hewitt, 'Oh get Lowry, he's glad to be an alibi,' will you agree?"

"It's not likely to happen."

"But you don't say you won't do it."

"I won't do it. May we stop quarreling?"

"I'm not quarreling. I am dismayed that you see this as a casual white lie. Stephen, do you know that for the first time since I saw you I'm disappointed in you? I'm even afraid I feel sorry for myself. If Paula had told me that you had done this, I'd have sworn she was mistaken. Nothing would have convinced me. I realize you think I'm magnifying it out of all proportion. But I was as eager all day to be with you tonight as though we had been separated for months. I took it for granted we were somehow so miraculously still in love that—"

"Aren't we?"

"But, you see, feeling that way I also took it for granted that we were both loyal to, well, love itself—this is a terrible thing to say to you, but protecting Hewitt in this is not greatly different from helping him find a girl, is it?"

"That is a rather terrible thing to say. I don't think I deserve it."

"I don't suppose you do, but it's rather a terrible thing you've done to me too."

"Is it irreparable?" he asked coldly.

"Please don't take that tone."

"Well, is it irreparable? Or do there have to be weeks or months of expiation because I couldn't make a speech on Sexual Ethics at the end of an officers' meeting?"

"You don't need to be so injured. You could be understanding as you usually are—"

"It's difficult, I suppose, because I am ashamed of it."

She was silent a moment and then said, "Well stop being. I've made an awful time about it but I really understand how it happened, and I'm sorry I made you feel badly. Only let's not, well, you know—let the business ruin our lives. I was just thinking of something funny. Suppose this had made a real rift between us and I told Armas why—can you imagine the lecture that European would give his beautiful sister? And come to think of it, poor Paula had a little happiness out of it."

11

MANY UNEVENTFUL TRANSATLANTIC FLIGHTS had not sufficed to give Lowry any confidence that the triumph of aerodynamics in which he and sixty to eighty other people were contained would not fall out of the skies and burst into flames in "the worst accident in aviation history."

The widely advertised comfort, not to say luxury, of the flight, hot and cold running water, self-adjusting seats, individual reading lights, free drinks and complimentary meals, all made it worse. It was always too hot or too cold and the complimentary meals tasted like the leftovers of a flight from Atlanta, Georgia, to Chattanooga. He envied the men who could talk business for sixteen hours with time out for refreshing naps, the others who actually "overslept" or who finished their paper books just as the aircraft touched down. The young mother of an infant in arms confided to him that "if I had shipped him air freight he'd have got more attention," and while it had a modicum of exaggeration, it was not far from his own view of a first-class flight to Europe. He had never been able to read comfortably on a plane, so that he sat with the impassivity of a Mongolian idiot, brooding on whether at the crash he would behave as he would want to, and on the insufficiency of what he would have left to Rosalie and the children. Somber visions of her, a widow, trying to educate three young children on the proceeds of his life insurance haunted him.

If by some miracle he got safely off this plane he would devote his life to the one goal of providing for them.

As alternately the heat or cold and lack of ventilation grew worse, his thoughts became gloomier so that it was only by an effort of will that he could concentrate on the things he had to be thankful for. They were of course numerous—health, an excellent job, a happy home-to-be, children and a beloved and beautiful wife who loved him and of whose fidelity he was sure. Suppose in this human sardine tin he had to worry as to whose bed Rosalie were in that moment! He smiled as the steward gave him his dinner tray and applied himself to its rare delicacies with what relish he could.

His brother-in-law Armas Lainvee was waiting at Orly with his car, as handsome as Rosalie was beautiful, with a striking resemblance to her. They greeted each other affectionately and Armas handed him a cable.

"Your office sent it around," he said.

Lowry tore it open, hoping it was from Rosalie. It was dated from Caracas, Venezuela, and read:

GRATEFUL IF YOU WOULD AGREE TO MY COMING TO PARIS AT MY OWN EXPENSE WHILE YOU ARE THERE FOR PRIVATE REASONS CAN ARRIVE IN THREE DAYS DARAN

"I might as well reply now," Lowry said. "Our Venezuelan agent wants to meet me here."

They stopped for him to cable his agreement and a message to Rosalie and went out to the car. It was only fair, Lowry had always felt, that there should be something to mar the beauty of Paris, and certainly the drive from Orly into the city was about as ugly as any in the world. All that was worst in modern urbanism was before your eyes. Then the car crossed the Seine into the incredible city, discharged Lainvee at his office in the Boulevard Haussmann, moved toward the Bois and out to the Lainvee house back of the trees in the quiet Avenue Henri-

Martin. There was nothing on Fifth or Park Avenues or in the East Sixties like these houses with their cool, high-ceilinged rooms, french windows open to the smell of trees and gardens, all utterly quiet and peaceful. Often as he had come to Paris, long as he had lived there, Lowry was still always struck by the ineffable amenity in which the rich French lived.

By the time he had bathed and shaved, his clothes had been pressed, his linen put away, his shoes polished. He moved with a sense of well-being and a profound respect for the living standards of the wealthy.

He found Piccard, the head of the Paris office, a fussy man who seemed a little over his head in his job. His opening complaints, discouragements and doubts were twice interrupted by a clerk timorously entering to give him what looked like a payment voucher. Piccard apologized to Lowry and went to the outer office. Lowry watched him as he selected a key from a ring in a side trouser pocket and unlocked a wooden cabinet from which he took a cashbox, counted out some paper money and gave it to the clerk.

"Constant interruptions," he said with a sigh on returning.

"Do you pay everything personally?" Lowry asked.

"You may count on that at all times, Mr. Lowry," Piccard assured him. "Here we have security."

In the conversations the rest of the day, Lowry could not see that they had very much else if indeed that, since the wooden cabinet could have been opened with a strong pocket knife. Everything about the office except the wage scale confirmed Rutledge's views on European commercial inefficiency and Lowry considered with apprehension how long it would take to make all the necessary changes. At least as long as his whole trip. Perhaps Jim Peale had been right about the haste.

Back at the Lainvee house he got a call through to the children in Switzerland and the sound of their excited, happy voices brought tears to his eyes.

The night before his arrival Daran cabled from New York, giving his flight number and arrival time. Lowry felt there was good will to be earned by meeting him at Orly and ordered a limousine to take him out alone. As he alighted the chauffeur of another Cadillac came over and shook hands with his driver and Lowry left them to a discussion of the outlook for the tourist season. The New York plane was already in and Lowry asked an attendant to inform Mr. Daran in the *douane* that he was waiting.

He had smoked one cigarette when from behind a high truck-load of baggage propelled by two porters a man appeared whom he recognized, from a picture in the New York office, as Daran.

A more suavely theatrical figure he had never seen. He was of medium height, slim and graceful. He wore a good sport jacket and slacks and what looked like a Charvet tie hand painted with girl angels from the ceiling of the Sistine Chapel. Sleek black hair was parted in the middle and his shaggy black brows were in contrast to his neat mustache. He carried a walking stick which Lowry felt sure was a sword-cane. With him was a young woman.

He greeted Lowry in precise English. Lowry later learned he spoke all Indo-European languages with equal fluency. Turning to the young woman at his heels, he said casually, "Mr. Lowry, I have the honor to present you to the Señorita Beatriz Maria Inclan y Cespedes, natural daughter of the late Benemérito Jefe, Juan Vicente Inclan, and my mistress. I feel it best to be completely frank with you."

"Thank you, I am honored," Lowry said and kissed the offered hand of the Señorita. Her figure, her dark melting eyes, her sensual mouth were in the Carmen tradition but her clothes were both expensive and well chosen, her voice low-pitched and agreeable, her English excellent and her response suitable and without affectation. The flaw in her looks, however, was considerable. Her nose was that of a battered prize fighter.

Daran continued, "You will doubtless have wondered about her nose. I myself find it piquant. To her it is distressing. Many of the late Jefe's eighty natural children have inherited his nose, as Franz Josef's did the Hapsburg lip. In a sense both are the marks of the blood royal. But we live in democratic times. Now let us be off. We have reservations waiting at the Ritz, a rather noisy address, still what hotel in Paris is really quiet?"

Beatriz interrupted the speech to say how very kind it was of Mr. Lowry to come to meet them.

"You will think me quite rude not to have said that before," Daran said. "I am really very touched. The fact is I think I did not thank you for coming because I felt self-conscious, even worried, as to how you were going to regard my bringing Beatriz. Does it offend you? I assure you the Company's interests in Venezuela will not suffer."

"Of that I am sure. Mr. Peale has given us very fine reports about you—"

"Has he indeed?"

"Oh yes and as for—"

"I was never sure he quite trusted me."

"You may be sure, and I am delighted you have been able to bring the Señorita. Did you see any of our people in New York?"

"No, we went from Pan Am to Air France at Idlewild in a matter of moments."

Lowry's chauffeur and his friend were still in conference but as they saw the travelers both came forward.

"I have a car waiting," Lowry said.

"I had arranged for one also," Daran said.

"Mr. Daran?" the other driver asked him.

This is a very thorough and competent fellow, Lowry thought to himself, and anxious to learn more about him and the Señorita Inclan he agreed to drive into the city with them and dismissed his own car.

"I must explain," Daran said, "that the main reason for our voyage is that Beatriz enters the hospital here in the morning."

"Yes, I am so sorry, Mr. Lowry," she said, "that I could not have first met you after I had been operated. I mean operated upon. I always forget and George says, 'My stupid one, my machines are operated. You will be operated upon. Please speak correctly.' "

Glancing down at her, Lowry thought what a desecration it would be for a surgeon's knife to enter that perfect body.

"I hope you will be here afterwards to see," she said.

"I'm sorry to hear this. I hope it isn't too serious."

"No. Would you like to know what they're going to do to me?"

"If you'd like to tell me," he said.

"We have only been lovers a short while and not really before George won the National Lottery and took me to Mexico on holiday. I pleased him so much that he was very sweet and wanted to give me a large diamond or a sable coat. I refused."

"Oh?"

"I said I would very much rather have plastic surgery on my nose. It is so ugly and spoils my face. The cost of coat and the operation was what George calls 'even Stephen.' Do you know what that means?"

"Yes."

"So it is to be done and I may be beautiful. Who knows, he may want me to marry him, though I don't think it likely. He is such a good man. Mr. Lowry, is your wife beautiful?"

"Very."

"How long have you been married?"

"Oh, twelve years."

"And you are not tired of each other, you know, as lovers?"

"I think not."

"I worry about that because in Venezuela so many women cannot hold their husbands as lovers because they let themselves remain stupid and become fat. I read many American magazines on these two subjects. Is your wife American?"

"No, but very Americanized in many ways now."

"That is interesting. George is European, you know. I'm not sure he knows where he was born."

"I have told you where I was born. Now this is what I suggest," Daran said, as the Ritz bagagistes unloaded the luggage, and Beatriz, arm linked in his, looked from the shop window to the top of the Column. "I would ask you to wait now but we must have our bath and confirm our arrival to the hospital. Beatriz enters in the morning. Will you not come back to dine with us at eight?"

"Please do, Mr. Lowry," Beatriz said.

"No, no," he replied. "You will naturally have more fun alone tonight, your first night in Paris. You must forget about me. Actually I am booked to dine with our Paris manager."

"Well then, if you agree, I shall come to the office to see you as soon as the result of the operation is known in the morning. You must not think I have forgotten our business. I have a dispatch case of reports for you."

"Good," Lowry replied, "but let everything wait until you are at ease about the Señorita. And now the best of luck to you both. I am sure all will go well and that the Señorita will be even lovelier, though it is hard to imagine."

"I am sure I shall be free by lunchtime. Could we take it together?"

"By all means," Lowry said, smiled, shook their hands and got in the car.

He was amused by how much he felt drawn to them both. Their special appeal arose not so much from their fantastic plans and situation as from the casual gravity with which they announced them and the matter-of-fact but apparently ardent attachment between them. Daran gave the impression of being one of those few men able to manage the rational and irrational sides of his life as a unit.

He heard from but did not see Daran until the second day following. The plastic surgery was reported as almost certainly successful and the Señorita as happy and eager.

Daran appeared at the office all business. He was enthusiastic about the acquisition of Larus, whose previous agents were a poor lot. Before leaving Caracus he had reached out for orders which would be finalized on his return. The Minister of Roads and Communications was a close friend. Daran believed that his special contribution to the success of Larus would be his spare-parts control and perpetual inventory. The layout he showed Lowry would have been acceptable on the River Rouge itself. As to the regular lines, he did not feel he was getting the deliveries he should. He had made the point strongly to Mr. Peale. When he had heard of Lowry's appointment he had been very happy, feeling that at last there would be some one person in New York to fight his battles and insure prompt deliveries of all he could sell. Here was a forecast—it was beautifully tabulated and coherent—of what he was going to dispose of. He would like to know if such programs and his semimonthly reports were ever really read by anyone in authority. Usually it did not seem so. Modifications which he proposed and which could be readily made were never commented upon. He realized the enormous domestic market to be served first and that Venezuela was relatively small. But if Mr. Lowry would look at this selling-cost analysis he believed it would convince him that he was distributing goods at lower costs than at home. One of the first uses to which he put the proceeds of his National Lottery winnings was to secure reports from two New York management consultants on competitive costs. They were to his credit. He gave an equally favorable report on collections and credit losses. He had a great deal to say about the proposed bridge and his hopes for the contract.

Lowry listened attentively to it all. "There is no reason," he asked, "to suppose the bridge proposed lacks reality?"

"Oh most certainly not."

"Mr. Peale seemed to have doubts of it."

"You mean just in general, I suppose?"

"No, specifically, as I recall, based on what he had heard when he was there."

"Oh I think you are mistaken, if you will forgive me, Mr. Lowry. Mr. Peale could have heard nothing of it when he was there. I myself had not until just after New Year's, when I wrote you."

"Then I must have misunderstood him. Looking ahead, do you want to make Venezuela your permanent home?"

"Certainly not," Daran replied, "if only for the reason that I should not want seventy-nine half brothers and sisters-in-law hanging around my house. I must tell you that after leaving you at the Ritz the day before yesterday, while we were having our bath, I told Beatriz I desired to marry her, irrespective of the outcome of the operation. Please do not think I was overcome by the intimacy of the moment. It was due largely to your acceptance of her and her easy behavior with you. For that I am very grateful."

"I congratulate you," Lowry said. Daran, he thought, arrives by processes of thought at the sort of decisions I reach by impulse.

"Have you something in mind as to a change?" Daran asked.

"Not immediately, but I shall think about it," Lowry replied. He had thought a good deal about it as Daran had produced his reports, while still trying to recall Peale's exact words about the bridge.

"Will you be my guest at dinner tonight? I shall naturally be a little lonely and Beatriz has suggested I dine and go watch '*les* girls' with their clothes off in a night club. It seems a good suggestion. She does not fear rivalry but would herself be ashamed to see a spectacle. That of course arises from having lived remote from centers of civilization."

"I propose you dine with my brother-in-law, Armas Lainvee, and me at Laurent's—"

"With pleasure and you will be my guests at the spectacle?"

"Well, we'll see."

"I shall need to make early reservations."

"All right then. We'll go," Lowry said. He wanted his brother-in-law's opinion of Daran, whose choice of a "spectacle," whose conduct there and comments on it would all be evidence.

That night, as they drove to Laurent's, Lowry told his brother-in-law what was in his mind about Daran. They found him awaiting them, looking very well in a dark suit and tie with a white shirt, viewing his surroundings with evident satisfaction.

"I think Mr. Peale mentioned this restaurant to me," he said as they waited for their martinis. "I believe he said Proust used to come here with the Prince Bibesco. Mr. Peale has a great interest in Proust. To me he is only a name."

Lowry said he had brought Peale there several years ago. "Its greatest attraction is that you lunch or dine in the midst of forest trees in the very heart of Paris. New York of course has no place fit to dine outdoors in."

"Mr. Peale is a man of great culture," Daran said, tasting his cocktail. "Wouldn't you agree?"

Not wishing to let down an absent friend, Lowry agreed, and they ordered their dinner and wine.

"It amuses me, Stephen," Lainvee said, "that, having lived so much in France, you're still unaware they have other wines beside champagne. You're sure you want champagne, Mr. Daran? My brother-in-law, unlike Mr. Peale, is not 'a man of great culture.' "

"Oh I like it very much," Daran assured him.

As they ate their long, delicious meal Lainvee, with considerable skill, kept Daran talking about himself. He was born in 1923 in Europe—he did not specify the country. He had been captured by the Russians in June, 1940, while fighting, as a boy of sixteen, in the Lithuanian army.

"My sister, Mrs. Lowry, and I were with our family in Tallinn that month—"

Daran put down his knife and fork. "You are Estonian?" he asked.

"Yes, of course. Why?"

Daran hesitated an instant and said, "I suppose I thought your name was French." There was a slight change in his manner and he ate his artichoke in meditative silence.

"So far as we know only my sister and I survived that dreadful month," Lainvee went on. "Nothing has ever been heard of my father or mother or other sister, though I have never given up hope. Through the correspondents of Delacroix and Company, constant inquiries are being made. Of course there are millions like us in Europe."

"I know," Daran said gently. "I among them."

"I went to Bonn last week to talk to some returned prisoners of war. One never knows."

"I meant to tell you that Rosalie went at once to the Estonian Relief in New York," Lowry said to his brother-in-law, "and for a brief moment one day she thought she had word."

"You escaped with Madame Lowry, Monsieur Lainvee?"

"No, I was with our forces at the frontier when I was taken. She escaped alone from Tallinn to Sweden and ultimately to

Norway sometime in July, 'forty."

"She was in the Norwegian Resistance when I met her there on a mission," Lowry said.

"I see," Daran said.

"We were united here in Paris as a result of my chancing to meet Lowry at a large cocktail party given by the Marshall Plan people for French bankers."

"I shall always include your family in inquiries I make about mine," Daran said.

"Thank you. I shall do the same for you if you will give me the details while you're here," Lainvee replied, "but let us talk of less unhappy things."

"Just to be clear in my inquiries, it was from the Russsians, not the Nazis that Madame Lowry escaped—you spoke of talking to German prisoners of war?"

"Oh from the Russians, yes," Lowry said, "a year before the Nazi invasion."

Daran nodded. They had finished with the fingerbowls, after the artichokes, before he spoke again.

"In nineteen-forty-six I worked my way on a ship to Venezuela and since then things have gone well for me. I may say I worked hard to make them."

"What sort of a passport do you have?" Lainvee asked.

"Oh I am now a Venezuelan national, not possessed, however, of much love of country."

"You say you are alone in the world?" Lainvee asked again.

"Well yes, except for my mistress, of whom Mr. Lowry has without doubt told you. Tell me—the French couple at the table there—would you know their relation to each other? You may look. They are very engrossed. Obviously she is married. But to whom? To him? One cannot be sure. The relations of men and women fascinate me. Those two are very chatty and happy in each other's company. They have good appetites, so they cannot be unhappy, and they whisper and laugh a great deal. They have the air of wealthy people."

Lainvee glanced at them. "I know him, he's a bachelor, she married. They have been lovers for several years."

"What explanation does she have to give her husband as to dining here with her lover?"

"He may be away. He may be dining with his mistress. Most likely she merely says, 'Charles, I am dining with Raoul tonight. I shall be a little late.' "

"And all is understood?"

"Yes."

"Civilization is so pleasant and cozy. All quite impossible in Caracas. The husband would lock her in her room." He glanced at the menu again, smiled at Lowry and said, "Soufflé au Grand Marnier, please. One lives but once. Pardon my curiosity, but in whose bed will that couple end their evening?"

Lainvee looked at them with a banker's appraising eye. "I should say they had been in his bed before they came. Their contentment and hunger for food are apparent."

"I should like to ask another question," Daran said. "You see, I live far from the centers of culture. I sometimes feel that I put too much emphasis on the carnal charms of women. I suppose there comes a time when one wants something else besides them. Now what is the quality, other than physical, which is most desirable in a woman?" He turned directly to Lowry. "I wish to impress it upon Beatriz."

Lainvee laughed good-naturedly. "Each man to his taste, of course. There are the major qualities—sympathy, understanding, inspiration—but I should say it was some everyday things that mattered most. For example, I always know what time it is without looking. It would irritate me very much to have a woman unaware of the passage of time, believing it four o'clock when it is six."

"Even though she had lost track of time in her passion for you?" Daran asked. "That seems strange."

"Each man to his taste, as I said," Lainvee replied.

"You're not joking?"

"Oh no."

"Mr. Lowry, do you mind giving me your opinion?"

"Well, like Armas, I think it is everyday things. A *riante* nature, tidiness and order—"

"Strange things to want in a woman," Daran said, scribbling on the back of an envelope, "but I have noted them. Tidiness and order is what I would think one wanted in a chauffeur or a cook—or a sailor. *Riante?* A lovely word but in someone always *riante* I should miss the splendors of sadness. Still, I shall tell Beatriz."

Lowry laughed. "Armas and I are not being definitive, you understand?"

"No, but what you tell me is significant. You are married men. I confess Beatriz never picks up her clothes and sometimes it does annoy me. And she often weeps. You may be quite right, you know." He looked at the envelope a moment. "No allowance," he asked, "for national differences—the proud, jealous Latin, the cold Anglaise, the temperamental Jewess? No, you are right not to do so. If in love, they are the same."

Daran's reservation was the only empty table in the crowded night club when they arrived. They edged their way to it, just managed to get their chairs around it and Daran ordered the required champagne. The girls, naked except for an ornate *cache-sexe*, were astonishingly young and lovely and Lowry and his brother-in-law stared at them with no less interest than Daran, or than the other men and women of the audience.

Daran, sitting between them, drank some champagne. "What I like best about a spectacle of this sort is the philosophical questions it raises in my mind. Have the women in the audience come because they do not trust their husbands and lovers without them? Not entirely, I think. They are too curious to see. Why should they be curious about other women? Is it not that in all cultured people there is a desire for more sexuality?"

"If only by proxy?" Lowry asked.

"Oh yes, any way. And let us observe the girls. They are young. They are fresh. It is impossible to have such faces and bodies and spend one's time in drink or dissipation. These girls did not go to bed drunk this morning. They had eight hours of healthy sleep. I would wish I were as free of sexual jealousy as their husbands or boy friends must be. I could not permit Beatriz to do this. And if she were here with us, it would make her unhappy that I so much enjoy looking at them."

"Didn't she suggest your coming?" Lainvee asked.

"Oh yes, but in a tender, generous moment without thinking," Daran replied. "You have nothing as interesting as this in New York, have you, Mr. Lowry?"

"Well there are night club shows but as far as I know—I haven't explored—nothing like this."

"That sketch we are watching—very wicked no doubt, but I don't find it offensive, do you?"

"No, very amusing."

"And so true to life. We must have all had such an experience."

Even in Gramercy Park, Lowry thought with a nostalgic sigh.

"Mr. Peale would not approve. He is a man of fine culture."

"Oh come," Lowry said. "Peale enjoyed himself very much with me in just such a place in Paris."

"He gave me the impression of great strictness in Caracas, though he did talk one night in the Café India about the relations of men and women. Do you know, I never mentioned Beatriz to him. I felt he would not trust my business judgment, if he knew. With you, of course, I had no alternative."

"I don't believe he would have felt it was any of his business," Lowry said.

"Oh, I think he would have. He told me a story—it interests me that with the infinite variety of women's breasts, those of the whole ensemble are uniform."

"That was his story?"

"No, no, an observation of mine. The story I forget."

Lowry saw his brother-in-law turn to look at Daran. It was obvious he had not forgotten the story but had quickly veered off it. He wondered what it was. Daran's picture of Peale's "culture" and respectability he could understand. They were both ingredients of the present Peale.

As they came out of the night club to Lainvee's car, the doorman asked Daran the time-honored question as to whether they would now like to see a "special show." Lowry was curious to hear the answer. Daran handed the man 200 francs without a word, said to Lainvee he would get in last, since he was getting out first at the Ritz—or would they like to go to another club?

They both yawned and said tomorrow had already arrived. Daran sank back in the car. "Very distasteful always to hear a pimp speak. Strange to think that hundreds of people in this area are now professionally performing varieties of the love-act under other people's eyes. I would not deny being curious but I should be too embarrassed to watch, a form of *hipocresía* on may part, without doubt."

As the car rolled down the hill of Montmartre, his companions were so quiet that Lowry thought they had dozed off, but as the car stopped at the Ritz, Daran bounded out, leaned in to shake hands with Lainvee and said, "Mr. Lowry, may I have a word with you, please?"

Lowry got out. Daran seemed suddenly nervous and ill at ease, as though he were going to be sick or, in the afterglow of the evening, he were going to ask for something, like the reimbursement of his passage to Paris.

"Mr. Lowry, there is a very serious matter I must talk to you about in the morning. I shall be back from the hospital by a quarter before twelve. I should not like to discuss it at the office. Would you be good enough to come here to our sitting room?"

"Yes," Lowry said slowly. "What is it about?"

"That is what I shall have to ask you."

"I see," Lowry replied. "Do we have to be mysterious at two in the morning?"

"I am sorry. I must take it in phases. The first phase was bringing myself to mention it at all. I have been working on that all evening."

"Very well, then. I'll be here just before noon. Thank you very much for the amusing evening."

Daran in turn thanked him and called another goodnight to Lainvee.

"What did you think of him?" Lowry asked his brother-in-law in the car.

"I don't know. I was puzzled. His sex interests did not give me much chance to judge of his business qualities. What did he want with you just now?"

"He had something to tell me tomorrow which he says is very important. I have no idea what it is. He's an interesting and likable little fellow, but as to my idea that he might be given the Paris office—"

"Well, I shouldn't judge from this evening. I think there's a good deal to him, and of one thing I think you can be certain. He is not a *chicaneur*."

12

THE CONCIERGE AT THE RITZ SAID THAT MR. Daran had left word that Mr. Lowry was to wait in his sitting room if he himself were delayed, and a page took Lowry to the room. Daran arrived with profuse apologies a little after twelve, saying that, while the bandages had not been removed from Beatriz, the surgeon was very confident. He suggested a drink, which Lowry declined.

"I am so happy," Daran said, "about the operation that I would like to take it as an omen that what I have now to discuss will be resolved as fortunately. Even now I feel considerable hesitancy in mentioning it." There was no question that he was more than hesitant. His manner was uncertain, his face troubled and he moved nervously around the room.

"Have no hesitancy," Lowry said. "We're friends. Say or ask whatever you like."

"Thank you. You are kind, but I have a great dislike of being a fool. Still, best to have it over with." He seated himself and studied his manicured nails and then his polished shoes. "Mr. Lowry, is it proper for me to know what the Morval Project is? If not, then I have no more to say."

"I can't answer that," Lowry replied, "because I never heard of it."

"Does an amount, a special draft or check that is to say, of fifty thousand dollars suggest anything?"

"No, but this is all very vague. Whose draft? Where?"

"The Company in Caracas."

"Originated by whom?"

There was almost a moment's silence, then Daran said, "Mr. Peale on his visit last autumn."

"What you say means nothing to me, but it's quite possible that I know it under another name or that it's some completed transaction I've never heard of. Suppose you tell me why all this comes up."

"Mr. Lowry, I am not trying to make a bargain with you, but if it turns out that my concern, actually my worry about it, is all nonsense, will you say no more about it? I do not want you to think me an alarmist, an informer—a busybody, shall we say?"

"I shan't. Go ahead."

Daran shifted an ash tray, some matches and a package of cigarettes on the table beside him. "You are doubtless aware," he said, "that in Venezuela the Company has made some confidential political contributions and several times set aside sums for some form of social welfare—a clinic at the hospital, substantial prizes for farm improvement, that sort of thing. This may be such a matter which Mr. Peale did not feel I needed to be informed of. When it occurred, I asked no questions. But because of the ledger I felt it proper to write Mr. Peale on three occasions after he left, asking for his instructions. Here are my letters." He opened his dispatch case, selected a folder and handed it to Lowry.

Lowry read and returned them. "What did Mr. Peale write you?"

"He has never replied."

"I see. Tell me exactly how it began. What was done, what was said?"

Daran glanced at his watch. "At exactly this time one day, Mr. Peale came back to the office, after a meeting alone with the Minister of Roads and Communications, and asked me to draw a check in favor of Morval Project for fifty thousand. At the same moment he began to dictate a report on his meeting to my secretary and when I came back with the check and the voucher for his approval, he took the check, initialed the voucher without breaking his dictation. I waited for a pause and asked whether there should be any memorandum with the voucher for the auditors to see. He shook his head, and went on with his report. I still hesitated and he looked at me with a smile and put his finger to his lips. I nodded and left the room."

"What did he say about it later?"

"He never mentioned it."

"Did you?"

"Mr. Lowry, I was in a difficult position. I did not want to be told it was none of my business and I felt that was just what I would be told. I felt convinced that there were good reasons for special silence about it, all the more because of the very friendly personal relations between us. After work Mr. Peale and I were always together."

"It occurs to me at once that 'Morval Project' may be code for the bridge and that with all due regard Mr. Peale was told of it in confidence by the Minister before you were—and that the voucher has something to do with it. What, I don't know."

"That, of course, occurred to me as soon as I heard, but I have reason to be sure there is no connection. Here is the original voucher and check," Daran said, taking them out of his briefcase.

Lowry examined the check. It was endorsed in Peale's hand "Morval Project," and then with his name, and been deposited in Maduro's Bank on the day of its date.

"And?" Lowry asked handing back the papers.

"When I received your cable that I might come to Paris, I prepared a memorandum of matters to take up with you. Morval Project was one. As soon as I got your cable I hurried to Maduro's Bank to buy my traveler's checks. Monty Maduro and I are good friends, and while I waited for the checks I decided to ask him about the Morval account. Of course I gave no hint of any concern about it on my part, simply asking in an offhand manner. His answer has troubled me deeply, though I am sure New

York's reply to you will show me to be a great worrier about nothing."

"What did he say?"

"'Oh that I remember,' he said. 'It was an in-and-out transaction. We made a telegraphic transfer to an account of Mr. Peale's in New York that day.'"

"What had Mr. Peale told him?"

"Nothing at all. He was very affable, talked about conditions and asked Monty to handle this personal matter for him. Well I have unburdened myself. I feel better."

"Anything else?"

"No, I've made enough trouble now."

Lowry got up. "As you say, I am sure we shall have an answer from New York clearing it all up in the morning. I do think Mr. Peale is to be criticized for leaving you so much in the dark. I'm sorry you have had this worry."

"You're entirely frank with me in not saying I have done the wrong thing?"

"Entirely," Lowry said, shook hands with him and left, himself deeply troubled but yet confident the explanation would be satisfactory. I must be careful, he thought, not to stir up a fuss about nothing. Just how to put the inquiry to New York was bothersome itself. He decided on a personal cable to Peale.

DARAN INQUIRING ABOUT MORVAL PROJECT TRANSACTION STOP AS I AM IN DARK MYSELF WOULD APPRECIATE YOUR PUTTING AT LEAST ME IN THE PICTURE

He asked for a reply to Lainvee's house. It came promptly that afternoon, reading FORGET MORVAL ALL IN ORDER.

In the interval before the cable came he had begun to feel grave anxiety about the transaction. Either there was a quick satisfactory explanation to him, if not to Daran, or it appeared that $50,000 had been embezzled. The latter was absurd on every ground, yet the first was equally hard to credit. The alleged telegraphic transfer was, however, only supported by hearsay evidence. Might Daran have misunderstood it?

Troubled and anxious as Lowry was while he waited for the reply, his feelings on reading its smug brevity were of anger as well as anxiety. And it left him in a ridiculous position vis-à-vis Daran. He wrote a reply to go to Peale's apartment beginning "Cannot accept your reply," controlled his feelings and started again:

IN VIEW OF TELEGRAPHIC TRANSFER TO YOU WHEREOF DARAN NOW AWARE YOU MUST SEE MATTER CANNOT BE DISMISSED AS YOU HAVE STOP I DON'T MIND TELLING HIM TO FORGET IT IF I AM TOLD WHAT IT IS STOP NATURALLY DO NOT SUGGEST ANYTHING IMPROPER ABOUT IT BUT IT DEMANDS FULL CLARIFICATION AND I WON'T LEAVE IT OTHERWISE STOP SURE THIS IN BEST INTERESTS OF ALL STOP HOWEVER IF RUTLEDGE OR JOHNSON CABLES ME PERSONALLY TO DISREGARD WILL AGREE ADVISING DARAN THEREOF REGARDS

There was no reply by the second morning following. If, as seemed inevitable, the silence implied a fraud, Lowry felt it impossible to break the whole matter to Rutledge or Johnson by cable. His dilemma and his fears were profound, and after waiting until eleven o'clock he went to Lainvee's office to put the matter before him. Lainvee listened with raised eyebrows.

"Plainly you must clear it up," he said.

"I agree, but there's always the possibility that Jim is out of town or hasn't gotten my second cable. I owe it to him not to be precipitate."

"He owed it to you to answer originally but I realize how you feel. Could you cable the company, possibly in these words, 'Advise me of any developments in Morval situation Caracas'? If it is a company matter they will say so. If not, you haven't put Peale on the spot. You could of course telephone him, but I shouldn't think it could be handled by telephone."

"It could of course, if there's nothing to it."

"Would it perhaps be wise to go over what Maduro said to Daran again, with Daran that is?" Lainvee asked.

"No, not without knowing more myself. I would appear to suspect him and Peale both."

"Have you any reason to believe Peale would embezzle money?"

"Put that way, no," Lowry replied. "But in view of minor things, in a way equally disturbing, I feel considerably alarmed."

"Such as what things?"

"Well, he has an attachment to Rosalie which is distasteful to both of us. Some of the things he has said and done suggest he's either ill or under an unusual strain. Yet his standing with the senior officers is very high," Lowry said, and then added, "I think I will cable the office as you suggest. I must tell Daran something by tomorrow at the latest."

"And if it turns out to be a very ugly thing, what will you tell him?" Lainvee asked.

"I can only hope it won't come to that. Hell, there must be an explanation. There's one grim comfort, if it is embezzlement, the only dollar-free country he visited was Venezuela."

"True," Lainvee said, "but an embezzler is never at a loss for methods to fit his needs."

But when the Company's answer to his cable came about five o'clock it read, QUESTION NOT CLEAR WHAT OR WHO IS MORVAL. He replied to them, MUST RETURN BRIEFLY TO NEW YORK LEAVING TOMORROW NIGHT, and cabled Peale at his apartment and Rosalie to the same effect. Though there seemed no alternative, he was still half sure he was making a fool of himself about nothing and that facing Rutledge, Johnson and Peale they would say, "Oh Morval, of course, the word was garbled in transmission. We had not idea what you were getting at. Morval is the confidential project the directors decided on . . ."

He telephoned Daran, asking him to wait at the Ritz the next morning for him and went there at ten.

"I have been in touch with New York about Morval and as it is difficult to give the whole story by cable I've decided to go back for a day or so, since there are several other matters here that need decision. I'll probably be back before you're ready to go."

He could see that Daran knew this was not the full story but Daran replied, "I am afraid I've put you to a lot of trouble about something that is not *gran cosa.* You do understand I felt I must speak of it?"

"Of course, you have done exactly the proper thing. Beatriz progresses?"

"Oh yes, very well indeed. She will be eager to have you see her on your return." He hesitated. "I hope I shall not have lost Mr. Peale's good will by my interference. You realize how much I admire a man of his culture." He said it as though Lowry and he were errant materialists. "I was at the Château of Versailles yesterday. I had never seen it before and wished to be able to show it to Beatriz without a guide. I saw something which pleased me very much. The gardeners and workmen still wear the sort of blue smocks they did when the Queen was there. But one of them rolled out of the gates of the Great Trianon driving a tractor of ours. Monsieur Piccard has done well."

"I'm afraid it got there under the Marshall Plan," Lowry told him.

"If you can, Mr. Lowry, you will let me know, please, as soon as possible whatever I should know about Morval and, if I may say so, I believe Monty Maduro should be informed."

"I shall do both," Lowry said. They shook hands and Daran walked to the elevator with him. There was a brief pause before Lowry touched the bell, as though both felt something more should be said. Then Daran made a wry face and went back to his room.

A hired car was waiting and Lowry told the chauffeur to take him to the Sorbonne. He had looked forward to the day, after perhaps a first week of strict business, when he could visit the young woman working for a doctorate in political science who had done special research for the Mutual Aid mission when he was part of it, and turn over to her some of his questions regarding Principal Errors. Now it required an effort of will to interview her.

A warning blight from the Morval Project had spread over all his own private plans and projects. Ominous as this situation was, tragic as it would be to become the instrument of a friend's downfall, the extent of the blight still amazed him. Something had happened to him. The whole hitherto dominantly optimistic and resourceful side of his nature was deeply affected, and actually before there were any but circumstantial reasons to justify it.

If Principal Errors had real importance or value, as he was sure it did, it would still have them, whatever Peale had done or whatever happened to him. But a devilish inner voice he had never heard before kept saying, "You see, one must never put anything before or even beside the benefit of the C.I.C."

Other doubts assailed him. He had known how to ask for and use other men's opinions on official matters. He had never had to seek advice on a personal matter. But here was a situation where he was not at all sure of what was the fair, the kind the right and the necessary thing to do, and for the first time on any major issue he was uncertain as to what Rosalie's views would be.

In a slough of indecision, which disgusted him with himself, he told the chauffeur not to go to the Sorbonne but to take him back to the Company's office, where for the rest of the day he listened to Piccard's complaints and frustrations.

13

EARLY IN THE MORNING OF THE FIRST TUESDAY in May, Rosalie answered the telephone to find Colonel Channing calling.

"About a house," he said. "I happened to see one for sale over the weekend you may like. I made some inquiries yesterday and the reports are good. However it's thirty-five years old."

"Oh where is it?" she asked breathlessly.

"Well, it's in Ridingtown, Long Island. Now of course the place isn't what it was. It's overcrowded and no longer distinguished socially. But it has lots of nice people Steve would know and even a few fourth-generation families are left. It has climate and salt-water sailing and I don't quite see how, in an incorporated village like it, this house could become less desirable, certainly not in the next twenty-five years, but of course we never know."

"How much? What type?"

"Asking price, forty—French farmhouse. The thing is, can I drive you out to see it this afternoon?"

"Oh would you? What about a school?"

"A very good private school close by. I must warn you that with lilacs, apple blossoms and dogwood all out any place this week in May looks better than it is. And this hasn't 'a view.' "

"Never mind—how much land?"

"Not much, two acres."

Channing approached the house by the roundabout sand road "around the water." Its gate was on a lane off the main roads, and as Channing turned the car into its gravel drive, there was no doubt in Rosalie's mind that this was where she wanted to live. The whitewashed brick wall on three sides, the high hedge along the lane gave a wonderful seclusion. In the near distance she could hear the rhythm of two hammers falling, that most homey of country summer sounds. And as for "a view," miles of sunlit tidal waters were visible from the second floor windows. There were enough maples and birches in one corner for windfall logs for the winter and the apple and dogwood trees were in full blossom. The air smelled of sea and lilacs and cedars, the last, with their burgeoning branches, looking like Victorian ladies—and Rosalie wondered why people ever smoked so much they could not smell the springtime or the sea.

Trees and walls and hedge were far enough off for the sun to light each of the rooms at some hour of the day and now westering it came through the french windows of the long sitting room facing it, even lighting the empty bookshelves of the study adjoining. Rosalie looked around, mentally placed lamps and furniture, bought curtains and carpets, rolled a piano from one corner to another, asking Channing how many bedrooms and baths as she did so. And when she had scampered upstairs to see them she called down with peasant thrift, "Will they take thirty-five, three thousand in cash?" Channing thought they might.

So after a stop at the agent's she was driven back to New York in high spirits to cable Stephen, only to find the cable announcing his return. He gave no reason and she thought merely what a lucky break. She was making lists at her desk in the apartment when the doorbell rang, and answering it she found Peale waiting. Bubbling over with excitement, she started to tell him at once of the house, feeling so happy that momentarily she did not resist a kiss or pay attention to his arm around her. Then she quickly put it aside and took him in the living room.

"Aren't you delighted for us?" she asked. "And best of all, Stephen's coming back."

She motioned him to a chair. His outward appearance was faultless as always, but his handsome face had a haggard intensity, which disturbed her and made her feel she must be wary of what he was going to say or do. She remained standing, leaning against a table, and then broke off her ecstatic description of the house to say, "Jim, is something the matter? You seem all queer." She wanted to ask him to leave and was embarrassed to see a slight stain of lipstick near his mouth. He leaned forward, elbows on his knees, looking down at his clasped hands between them. She felt like saying, "Not the approach pathetic, please, not today."

"No, nothing's the matter," he said very quietly. "There are several things I have to tell you. I wish you would make it easier by sitting down here. I wanted you to have dinner with me, then I thought possibly you'd fix something for us here, so we could be alone."

"But my dear man, I have no desire to be alone with you, and I have a thousand things to do about the house and Stephen's arrival."

"Do you know why he's coming back?"

"No, not really. I mean, no, not at all."

He got up, and still very quietly, said, "You know I'm desperately in love with you—"

"Now you must really go. I can't listen to such things. Come now, off with you," she said as though she were sending a child away.

"What is your feeling for me?"

"Stephen thinks you're his closest friend, and so I am a friend of yours, but I shan't be if you go on."

"I think Stephen is coming back because of me."

"Oh you can't have told him such nonsense."

"I have told no one, not even Evvy, who has left me for good. I couldn't live with her, wanting you as I do."

"But this is monstrous," she said. "I won't listen to it."

"I think you must listen to it," he said. "Stephen cabled me he is coming back about a business matter that I bungled. It could have been set right, if he hadn't made this headlong decision to return. He must have realized that. Therefore, I'm afraid it's something else. I'm afraid he must have been told something that I said about you. I want to beg you to forgive me. I hope you'll have some pity. I think if you could understand how I felt when I saw you after dinner at Mrs. Lowry's, the love, the desire, the horrible jealousy I felt. It was cruel to let me see you that way."

"You really mustn't say any more. You must go."

"But you've listened to me all these weeks. You have let me speak of intimate things to you—"

"Tell me exactly what Stephen may have heard about me. How could you have told anything he didn't know?"

"Wrong as I have been, let me kiss you again—please, please."

"Don't come near me. Tell me this thing you've said."

He regained control of himself and spoke again in a matter-of-fact tone. "I was with a man who seemed to have devoted his life to the pursuit of women. It was after dinner in a café. We had had a great deal to drink. He had story after story of his experiences, I realized how little I knew of such things. I think I wanted to impress him. He told me about being at the opera in Berlin shortly after the Occupation. It was *The Tales of Hoffmann.* A Russian general, a shaven-headed Mongol, came in with a beautiful German girl dripping with sables and jewels. It was during the gondola scene. On the gondolas were lovely naked girls. The music and the beauty, beside the Russian beast and the naked girls on the stage, were overpowering. I thought of how I had somehow missed such things. He said it was at once beautiful and macabre beyond belief, because in the opera house the stench of the unfound bodies from the bombing was still noticeable."

"Oh how horrible. Stop it."

"Yes, but the fact that he had seen it made me envious and I had reason to want him to think me as experienced as he. He dwelt on the Russian and the courtesan with him and I told him

I knew of a similar thing. I said there was an Estonian girl of whom I knew who had married an American officer, letting him believe she had been violated by the Russians in Tallinn, whereas actually she had been the acquiescent mistress of their general."

He said it all as though it were nothing. He had spoken of something which the years and Stephen's love had let her seal away, yet which lay silent at the base of her feeling of insecurity in America. Even in her cold horror, she felt the deep warmth of gratitude to Stephen that he had never asked and gradually dispelled all need to speak or even think of it.

"I mentioned no names," Peale was saying. "It was simply that you were the only woman I knew–I hadn't met you yet–who had been under the Russians."

She said a silent prayer to let her forgive him for Stephen's sake. Then the thought flashed through her mind, how could he know what had happened to her in Tallinn? Stephen could never, for all their closeness, have mentioned even the fringe of it.

"You made this up. But why, why did you think any such thing happened to me?"

"Your brother Armas said one night in Paris that you had suffered greatly before you escaped."

"I suffered. I had lost my whole family, everything."

"I knew there was more when Stephen first sent a picture of you and when I saw the portrait in Paris."

"Why will he have had to hear this?" she asked exhaustedly.

"I told it to Daran in Caracas last fall one night in the Café India. Daran likes to talk of women. He is certain to have told it over a drink, as I did, because he said he would always be asking himself and other people which the husband would have preferred."

"How could you have done this dreadful thing?"

"I don't know. I don't know why I have done many things."

"Why have you come to me? What did you expect I would do?"

"I came because I needed and want you and because you have

been in peril and I never have. I know in my soul it's this story I've told and nothing else that brings Stephen back—and perhaps I hoped that this was Fate's way of bringing us together."

She turned to look at him. Sick as he must be, there was really so little change in his face since she first saw it New Year's Eve, no sign in it of the monstrous thoughts which went on behind its mask. If anything, his outward appeal was greater, most of his arrogance gone, a look even of heartbreak about him.

"I stole that picture of you in the sun. It never leaves me," he said.

I must get it back, she thought. That is the first step.

"I knew that," she said quietly, "so does Stephen. You must give it back to me now as your first atonement."

Slowly he reached in his breast pocket for his wallet and took it out.

"Put it on the table," she said, fearing to take it lest she touch him. She rubbed her lips, trying to sort out the confusion in her mind, overwhelmed with pity for Stephen. True or false, the effect of this story would last forever and it would be she who had somehow broken this long brotherhood. And was it not even possible that some time, however much he appeared to have disregarded it, even he with his self-control, might not say to her, "I can stand it no longer. Even though Peale could not know, *was* there any truth in the story? I must know exactly what did happen. Everything!"

Or suppose that by good fortune Daran had not told the story and that Stephen was returning wholly on account of business and that it was put right. What reason could she give him why she could not see Peale again? And how could they be together in C.I.C. and not meet constantly? Or what effect would it have on Stephen's career if his colleagues knew there had been some break between him and his closest friend?

"What *is* this business trouble which you think is not bringing him back. May it not be that?" she asked.

"I did something rather impulsive and unwise in Caracas, something I shouldn't have done but it's impossible to suppose Stephen would return because of it and bring it into the light, with God knows what consequences to me before I can put it right. I know him too well. We're too close for him to do that to me."

"He might say he knew you too well to believe you have done whatever you have or that you could have talked to Daran as you have. What you have done is either to lie or steal, isn't it?"

He winced as she said it and a look of such utter despair came over his face that even then she almost pitied him.

The telephone rang and she picked it up automatically. Peale could hear Thomas Johnson's voice on the wire.

"Mrs. Lowry, I'm downstairs, having just had a call from Alec Channing about the house, and I wanted to see what we can do to help before Stephen gets here. May I come up for a moment?"

"Of course," she said. "Jim Peale's here also."

"Tom Johnson?" Peale asked in a matter-of-fact tone and got to his feet as though nothing had happened. "I'll let him in." She watched in amazement as he stopped to glance in a mirror and rub his cheek with a handkerchief. Then hearing their voices, friendly and easy, at the door, she had the feeling that she must have misunderstood all that had happened, or that it hadn't happened at all. She looked in a mirror, almost startled that there was no visible change even in her. She turned the picture face-down and in what felt like someone else's voice said as they came in, "Wouldn't you like a drink? A Tom Collins?"

"Well yes," Johnson replied.

"I'll get it," Peale said, and went out to the kitchen.

"Alec said you were really pleased about the house and I thought our Legal Department could handle the title search and all that stuff, and if you like we'll have our Service Department round up painters and electricians or anything else you want. Stephen left you a power of attorney?"

"Oh yes. Well, if you can do those other things, it will be wonderful."

"Edward wanted me to say he'd send over his gardener to meet you there whenever it's convenient. He'd like doing it so don't hesitate to say yes."

Peale came in with the frosty glasses and they all cheerily drank to the new home.

"You're all too good to us. How can we repay this sort of thing?" she asked.

"Friends are supposed to help friends," Peale said, lighting a cigarette. From everything else he said and did, and his easy manner toward her and Johnson, one would have supposed he was what he was believed to be—affluent, successful, untroubled about business or domesticity, at peace with himself and those around him.

"You haven't heard why Stephen's coming back, have you?" Johnson asked. "I hope he hasn't picked up some bug."

"No I haven't heard," Rosalie replied, "but he thrives in any climate on any diet, particularly Paris."

"Probably got homesick," Peale said.

"And who can blame him?" Johnson said with a smile at Rosalie. "Jim, you have no idea what this Morval Project he cabled about is, have you?"

"Not the slightest."

"When do the children arrive?"

"On the *Queen*, Wednesday of week after next."

"Alec says you gave him a check to bind the bargain until 'when, as and if' the title's clear and I'll have them push the search and get in touch with you."

"How soon do I have to let the warehouse people know about our books and furniture?"

"I'll see about that," Peale said.

Johnson finished his drink, declined another and said he must be off.

"So must I," Peale told him.

"If my wife were out of town," Johnson said with a laugh, "I'd take the lady to dinner. What's the matter with you young men?"

"I've already been turned down," Peale replied. "Sure you won't change your mind?"

"Quite sure. I have too much to think about."

Johnson put his hand on Peale's shoulder. "Tough luck. Good-bye. Now call one of us whenever you want. Delicious drink. Just what I needed. James, my boy, I'll give you a lift uptown."

As she drew her hand back from Johnson's she had the feeling that she must tell them both to wait, implore Peale to tell this pleasant older comrade he had done something that he wanted to put right, that if she could only do that, Johnson, hearing it, would say, "Well, this isn't so very bad. I think we can fix it up. I'm glad you told me," and somehow all would be fixed. She looked at Peale, almost willing him to speak, feeling like saying, "I'll go in the other room while you tell Mr. Johnson."

But as Johnson turned to go, Peale picked up the picture she had left face-down by the telephone, put it in his side pocket and followed Johnson to the door.

14

WHENEVER STEPHEN LOWRY HAD BEEN HOMEward-bound to Rosalie, the "duty" of meeting him had been one of the happiest things in the world. His journeys truly ended in lovers' meetings annd there was always a sense of new and expanding horizons in their lives. It was all delightful—the care to look pretty for him, the special blouse or dress, the fresh gloves, the hairdresser's work the day before, the momentary shyness, the first little wave of greeting and the consuming intimacy even in the crowd.

Now for his return from Paris, New York put on one of its show days, the temperature in the sixties, the humidity down to the level of a barometer's reading and visibility unlimited. The Army oculist in London had said of her vision, "With your eyes you see infinity," and so it seemed to her, watching the skies from the platform at Idlewild.

On the plane Lowry was the prey of bitter depression. It was an article of his faith to scorn advice if he were going to do something, however generous or quixotic *for* someone. But here he had to do something *to* someone and he would have welcomed the advice of anyone who could show him a way to avoid it. All the way west, he ransacked his mind to find some explanation of the transfer that was not a guilty one, or some way he could avoid being the agent of his friend's ruin. It was selfish, doubtless, to consider himself, but his ugly business, like a spreading blot on clean paper, would stain all the happiness of his life. A hostile occupying power would be in possession of Rosalie's and his life together, for how long he did not know.

So also Rosalie felt as she caught a glimpse of him through the customs window at Idlewild.

He came out at last, still trying to decide whether to tell her then and there and "spoil it all" or in the motor, or in their apartment suddenly say, "There is something I have to tell you."

She ran to throw her arms around him and kiss him, and tired travelers smiled a little at the pleasant sight. He seemed to her half aloof and distrait even when he kissed her. God, please let it not be about me, she prayed.

"You're alone?" was the first thing he asked.

"Yes."

They walked arm in arm to the car the Company had sent her out in and as he looked back for his porter, she said, "Darling, I know there's some trouble about Jim and something he's done. Don't let it spoil your coming home to me."

"How do you know?"

"He came to the apartment. He was very upset. He didn't say what it was except it was something in Caracas that could be put right. Is that what it is?"

"Well, it's in Caracas. I hope it can be put right."

"It's nothing affecting you and me directly?"

"Of course not," he said, kissing her again.

Oh, she thought, now the skies can fall and I will shoulder them.

"But if it's what it looks like, it will be ghastly for all of us and ruin for Jim. I can't believe it. Dear, it looks as though he had embezzled fifty thousand dollars from the Company."

"Oh," she gasped, "I had no idea. Why while he was there, Mr. Johnson came and no one would have known anything was the matter."

"Let us hope I'm wrong. It's always possible. If I am not, I have the horrible duty of accusing and ruining him. It's almost more than I can stand to think of—"

"What will you do first?"

"Oh see him at once and give him every chance."

His baggage was stowed in the trunk and they got into the car, Lowry pressing the release of the window which shut them off from the chauffeur.

"Our new house isn't far from here. I wanted you to see it on the way in for a minute. I suppose now that's spoiled too. It's a precious place. What do you think?"

He shook his head bitterly. "I don't think I can. This is really so ghastly."

"It's all right. I understand. Tell me how the children sounded."

They tried to talk of the children, and Armas and their old haunts in Paris he had seen, and the new house, but it was an effort, the end of which led constantly back to Peale.

In the apartment they kissed for a moment, standing in the bedroom and then he sat down to dial Peale's number.

"Sandwich? Some coffee? A drink?" she whispered.

"First two after I have a shower and a change of clothes," he said, and then, "Jim, I've just arrived. I'd like to come to see you, if it's—" He stopped short of the word agreeable and fumbled for another.

"Come ahead."

"I'll be there in about half an hour."

"I'll still be here in an hour," Peale answered.

When Lowry was ready to go, Rosalie kissed him and said, "Darling, I know how terrible this may be for you. All my heart goes with you. I feel so close to you. It's a nearer nearness even than danger was, leaving Norway or even than if we had made love just now."

He held her to him a moment. "It worries me," he said, "that someone from the Company may call you. I don't want anyone to know I've gone directly there until I'm sure there's no solution of it. Can you stand not answering the phone if it rings? I know it's always nerve-wracking."

"Yes, I won't answer."

Peale was alone in his silent apartment when he reached there about two o'clock. He came to the door, tall and straight, gray flannel trousers well pressed, a fresh white shirt unbuttoned at the collar, street shoes polished. His thin, serious face had its spiritual look, and a lock of dark hair, usually smoothly brushed, fell across his forehead.

"I almost forgot and said I was glad to see you," Peale said.

"I am glad to see you," Lowry replied with a pat on the shoulder. They walked into the living room full of beautiful things, with the painting of Evelyn and the children looking down from over the fireplace. The flowers on piano and table had begun to lose their petals.

"Do you want a drink? There's still some unpaid-for liquor in the apartment. I've let the servants go."

"Of course not," Lowry said, drawing a long breath. "Look, can you tell me straight off that there's nothing wrong in this Morval thing and that I've made a great fool of myself? You must know how desperately I hope so and how terribly I feel about it."

"If you feel so terribly, couldn't you have given me some chance to fix it? Did you have to cable, did you have to rush back here?"

"Then it is true?"

"It's true that I took the money. Are you going to Rutledge about it?"

"Jim, what alternative have I? It's not only my duty—it hurts even to use such a word with you—but if I don't, it can only make things worse in the long run."

"But there's only this one little thing. There's nothing else, except straight-out debts."

Lowry got up and walked over to the window, unable to look at Peale.

"How much are you in the hole all together?"

"I don't know—with this and debts—I just don't know; over a hundred thousand dollars. Nothing I couldn't pay back in a few years by strict economy. I'd get rid of everything. Evelyn's gone her own way already."

"She knows about it?"

"No, there were other reasons. How did Daran happen to bring it up? Did you ask him to come to Paris?"

"Before he knew I'd be there he made plans to bring a friend to Paris for an operation. He cabled me asking if I minded. The third or fourth time I saw him he asked me to find out from you what he was to tell the auditors when they arrived. He said he had written you several times."

"So you were suspicious?"

"He showed me the voucher and the draft. Maduro told him just as he was leaving about the transfer to you. I asked you for an explanation."

"Couldn't it have waited your return?"

Lowry managed to control his impatience and weariness. "I don't want to hurt you," he said quietly, "but you must realize I was sure the whole thing would be cleared up in a brief cable to me."

"So now Daran knows. What does he say?"

"He doesn't know. He's a very remarkable little fellow about not prying."

"So everyone's behaving splendidly but me?"

Lowry looked down at his shoes. "You know I'd give almost anything to help you, and I have no desire to humiliate you. No one I know will, but it will be hard to help you if you feel this way. Men have recovered from far worse than this. You can be one of them."

"What are you going to do next?"

"Jim, unless you have a reasonable alternative, I must tell Rutledge."

"I knew this would happen," Peale said almost in a tone of grievance, "when it was sprung on me at Larus that you were going to Venezuela. I telephoned two men I knew in New York that night and tried to raise the money. I was sure I could. It would have meant nothing to them. One was away and the other insisted on details of why I needed it. I did everything I could. I went to Washington to see Granville. He refused."

"Why didn't you tell me then?" Lowry asked. "Instead of—but never mind. I don't want you to feel worse."

"No, but what would you have done if I had?" Peale asked quickly.

"I can't say definitely except that I would have done everything in my power to help you raise the money and put it back—"

"And said nothing to Rutledge or Johnson?"

"Under certain conditions, no."

"You mean like a promise from me not to do it again?"

"I don't know what the conditions would have been," Lowry answered impatiently, wondering why he had got himself in the witness chair. "I only know that I would have done all I could."

"To prevent my ruin?"

"Yes, yes."

"Then, Stephen, what is the difference in doing it today? Fifty thousand dollars is no huge sum. Rutledge would have paid an outsider that and more for Larus any time. Why do you feel—"

"Jim, surely it's clear that now it's gone too far. You must see that."

"When the men I appealed to before you left turned me down, I was surprised, I was hurt, yes, but I told Rosalie I couldn't believe you were coming back to do this to me. I can't quite believe it now," Peale said.

Lowry could see that his surprise and the tears in his eyes were real. "I hope you have some idea how I feel," he said.

"But what's to become of me, what am I to do? You'll send me to prison, I suppose, dear God, for fifty thousand dollars. I'd better end it out a window at the Yale Club."

In spite of his provoking pretense that he was somehow the injured one, and under the theatrical threat of suicide, Lowry realized how truly frightened and lonely he must feel. He had hoped to find something better with which to make a start in helping him. He told him he was confident prosecution or prison would be avoided by his going at once to Rutledge. Peale's answer was an incoherent outburst about the hundreds of thousands of dollars he had made for C.I.C. and the respect Rutledge had for him. Finally Lowry asked him if he preferred to go to Rutledge alone.

Peale, head in his hands, said, "Oh no. Please go, please do your best for me."

"Of course I will, and Rutledge is no avenger. But this will shatter him as it has me. I think we'd better not try to say any more now. It is a fact, though, that there's nothing else like this? If there is, it's best to tell me."

"No, there isn't, there really isn't."

"Well, try not to feel too badly. We'll all do what we can." He reached out to put a hand on Peale's arm and as he did he could feel him tighten his big muscles so they felt tough and hard as whipcord. Strange how men's vanities lasted. "You have cash to get along, I take it."

Peale nodded. Trying silently to detain him, rubbing the hall rug back and forth with his heel, head down, watching it, he said at last, "I am sorry to have involved you."

"You never know," Lowry replied, "where comfort will come from. I'd like to repeat what a man said to me once during the war about someone in a far worse situation than yours. I don't know whether it's true and I don't know whether I believe it. But I think I do and I think it's true. He looked at the man and he said, 'You know he doesn't realize it, but God's still got a plan for him.'"

15

LOWRY CAME DOWN IN THE ELEVATOR, THROUGH the lobby and out to Park Avenue past a parade of flunkeyism which would have enraged Thomas Carlyle. He felt like telling them to save it for Peale's last exit. The doorman, in his court vestments, whistled a taxi to the curb and Lowry got in, giving the driver his address. He received it with a half groan and a contemptuous wag of the head. Lowry wondered why he disapproved.

As they drove down Park and on into Fourth Avenue, it suddenly occurred to Lowry that the only American money he had left was a ten-dollar bill. When they stopped for the light at Twenty-Third Street he apologetically so informed the misanthrope in the driver's seat and asked if he had change. There was no reply and at Twentieth Street he repeated the question. The man looked back at him with withering contempt.

"Mac," he said, "I've got change. Today even children carry change for ten dollars."

Lowry laughed. As nearly as he could remember it was the first time since he had been at the night club in Paris. Then he thought of what lay before him, and what had already happened to him made him wonder when he would laugh again. Everything would be affected. In a few moments he would be alone with Rosalie and be unable to be himself, with half his mind absorbed by his grim call on Rutledge. Was there still any way that could be postponed for Peale's benefit? Even if he could personally replace the money that night, he was still in honor bound—that incredible, intangible duty—to reveal what had been done.

The two hours he had been gone had been bad ones for Rosalie. The telephone had rung several times and once, nerves on edge, she had almost answered it. She felt a terrible anxiety that, whether Daran had told the story or not, Peale, breaking down in full confession, might have told it and there have been a fight between him and Stephen.

The skies had lowered under rainclouds and there was a sense of tender pathos in the evening light, with the blossoms of the tulip trees falling in the Park, an hour for lovers alone together. She heard Stephen's key in the door and hurried to meet him.

"It's as I feared," he said. "He gave no reasons. I asked for none. Now I have to tell Rutledge." He sank down on the sofa, sitting a long time in silence, his hand over hers. "He says he tried to raise the money as soon as he heard in Larus that I was going to Venezuela. If he had told me then I might have been able to do something. I don't see how I could have foreseen anything like this, but it doesn't make it any easier."

"Darling, I don't think anyone could have done anything for a very long time. Come and rest awhile."

"I'd like to call Rutledge—"

"Call him later."

"I don't want him or Johnson to call me first. It could be very difficult."

"I'll answer and say you're asleep. Nothing is more natural after your trip."

"Will you rest beside me?"

"Of course."

He was unable to rest, his mind constantly coming back to the question of whether there was anything he could still do. She lay watching him as he paced the room, thinking how he had never before been unable to find peace with her.

The telephone bell burst out and she answered quickly.

"I'll speak, whoever it is," he said.

She listened an instant and then handed it to him.

"Stephen," Peale said, "I can't stand it. What did Rutledge say?"

"I haven't called him yet, Jim. When I do I'll only tell him I want to see him. I can't talk about it by telephone."

"Won't you be able to put it to him just as something that's happened, that isn't indication of a whole disaster? It's just one thing."

Rosalie could hear each word.

"I'll put it the best I can, but you must realize that it will be a terrible blow to him."

"Does Rosalie know?"

Lowry sighed. "Yes," he said.

"Would you and she let me come down there?"

"Oh no," she whispered to Stephen.

"I really think I'll lose my mind here alone."

"Jim, I'm not heartless, but it won't help to come here. You must try to face it by yourself." He hesitated and then said, "I'll come back, if it'll help, for a few minutes after dinner."

"Oh Stephen do you have to?" Rosalie said, half in tears.

"Please do," Peale said and hung up.

"I'll start supper," she said, getting up. "There's some vichyssoise and some chops and some asparagus vinaigrette. Would you like a drink?"

"Oh, I guess so, yes," he said wearily.

When she brought it in the living room to him he was calling Rutledge's house in Long Island and his voice had regained its timbre and he spoke with his special, distinct clarity.

"Well Stephen, welcome home," Rutledge was saying. "The new house too much to wait for, or what brings you back? Haven't picked up a bug I hope."

"No, something came up which I felt demanded consultation and I reluctantly came back. Would it be possible for me to see you at your house in the morning?"

"Of course it would. Come to lunch, bring your wife and we'll drive over to see the new estate and take my head gardener along. Stay the night if you can and we can drive in Monday morning. I'll have the car pick you up at what, about quarter to eleven?"

"I think I'd better come out alone by train."

"Nonsense, I'll send the car. But is anything the matter with Rosalie?"

"Oh no but, well, I should like to talk to you alone and I must come back."

"This sounds damn mysterious. Is something wrong?"

"I know it does and I'm sorry to sound that way, but—"

"Well at least give me an inkling of what it's all about. Piccard turned out to be a Commie?"

"Oh no."

There was a silence at Rutledge's end and then he said, "I know you wouldn't go through this unless you felt it necessary, so come along, and if I don't sleep tonight it's your fault."

"I would have waited until morning to call you, but I felt I had to be sure you'd be free."

"I'll be free, but I still can't understand why Rosalie can't lunch with us. However, you're the boss."

"This is so frightful," Lowry said to Rosalie. "I feel like the lowest type of informer and I hate springing surprises on people. What in God's name is to become of Jim?"

"Darling you must try to think how much worse it could be for him if someone hostile to him had found it out."

"But when I think of all these years—"

"I know, but you must try not to think of them. What distresses me most is that it will be so long before you can be happy again."

"I don't feel as though I could ever be. The rest of my life this will hang over me, unless somehow I can get him on his feet again."

"He must get himself on his feet. Remember what the chaplain said to Mr. Johnson about his brother."

As soon as he finished supper, he left for Peale's apartment and when two hours later he came back, looking worn out, Rosalie was in bed trying to read. He shook his head sadly. "In a way, the worst of it is he has yet to say anything which makes you think he realizes what's he's done, or for that matter that makes you sorry for him now. I feel sorry for the man he was."

"Did he tell you any more about anything?"

"No."

The butler took Lowry's hat and led him through the sweet-smelling country house, dim and cool under its awnings, to where Rutledge was waiting in the warm sun on the flowery terrace from which shallow steps went down to the "wild garden." Beyond it Lowry could see some young children playing around their nurse, their shrill little voices the only sound breaking the Sabbath peace. It seeemed almost impossible that he could break his grim news amidst such peace and beauty.

Rutledge put down the news section of the Sunday *Times*, moved a paperweight across it and came forward with his hand out.

"Well, you look fine. What's all this about?" he asked, pulling a wicker chair forward. "Hope you like that chair. I can't stand these damn modern things that fall over with you in them. Will you have some coffee or anything at all?"

Lowry declined. He still had no idea how or where to begin, whether to "prepare" Rutledge or tell him the worst forthwith. He felt in double-duty bound—to make it as easy as possible for Rutledge and to put it to Peale's least disadvantage.

"This is extremely difficult for me," he said slowly.

"Now look here, if you've hashed something up and we're in a jam about it or it's cost us a lot, never mind. Such things happen. Just let me have the facts and we'll deal with them sensibly. No one's going to take advantage of someone's honest mistake."

"I wish it were that," Lowry said. "I must ask you to be prepared for something far more painful. I judge it's best to tell you straight out. It was my misfortune to discover in Paris that Jim has embezzled something like fifty thousand dollars of

Company funds. I've been over it with him and it is a fact. I have come to you only after satisfying myself there is no way we can put it right."

"Jim? Jim Peale?"

"Yes."

"You're absolutely sure?"

"Yes."

"Good God. Who knows this?"

"You and I and Daran. I hope I've done the right thing in coming to you."

"You've done exactly right. What a horrible experience for you. What does he say?"

"I spent yesterday afternoon and some of the evening with him. Beyond confirming it and assuring me no one else was involved, he said nothing that really helped."

"Evelyn doesn't know?"

"He says not."

"My God, what's his explanation?"

"He hasn't any really. Pressure was all he said. Expected to pay it back."

"Part of the guilt's mine. I knew, though he denied it, that he was spending too much money. Is there more to it? I mean, a woman?"

"No."

"He had five hundred dollars in unpaid bills on his year-end statement. That must be a drop in the bucket."

"He spoke of that. I should have said he asked me to see you alone. I suggested that he come out and tell you."

"What did he say about the five hundred dollars?"

"It was pretty involved. He felt, so he said, that was as far as he could safely go. He was in such an emotional state, naturally, that I didn't press him."

"He's not going to add suicide to our troubles, is he?"

"I don't think so. He mentioned it and for what it's worth promised to do nothing desperate. I was his friend and I told him I'd continue to be. I emphasized that he must pull himself together if anyone was to help him."

Rutledge rubbed his face with his hand.

"There's always more to some piece of madness like this than the mere fact of stealing money. I've had such things before, never so close at hand."

Lowry wondered what Rutledge would say if he knew about Peale and Rosalie.

Rutledge was pacing up and down. This is the man, he thought to himself, looking at Lowry's grave face, whose evident love of "fun" I was once worried about.

"Is he bonded? I don't think so," Rutledge said.

"No, he's not, fortunately."

"Go back now, if you will, and tell me how you came on it," he said.

Lowry gave him the long details of his talk with Daran.

"You didn't tell your brother-in-law?" Rutledge asked him.

"Yes I did. I asked his advice."

"Well you've been living with it. What are we to do?"

"It's hard to say. In Jim's present state he wants everybody told—directors, stockholders, the whole organization and the newspapers. It's the only atonement he can think of—"

Rutledge interrupted him. "It just doesn't seem possible he can have done this and gone on his usual way with all of us and now he wants to unload it on us."

"It seems to me what Jim wants or says he does is an indication of what we ought not to do. In other words, the knowledge of it should be limited to as few people as possible—yourself, Tom and Charley Curtis."

"You don't mean with Jim staying on?"

"Oh no, he'll have to resign of course."

"Well, we can't take a fifty-thousand-dollar loss and not tell people what it's for."

"I'm not suggesting that. I can put up some, say ten per cent of it in cash. I'll put up some more if you'll loan it to me or assist me to borrow it. You may feel you want part. I don't offer to do this in any excess of generosity."

"But what's going to become of him? What's he going to live on? Have you any idea of how much he owes?"

"He says about a hundred thousand, but I don't think he knows. The trouble is he hasn't anything."

Rutledge sank into his chair. "All of it comes back to *me*. I've made myself responsible for the men we have. I thought I was doing everything humanly possible to prevent the slightest temptation to such a thing as this. I never gave half as much attention to our profits as I have to our personnel. Think of it! New Year's Eve at the Pierre, there we all were together like a family—you had absolutely no inkling of anything wrong? He said nothing to you at all? I remember his greeting to Rosalie—"

"I had none at all. The only change I've seen since then is that he has been less fun to be with."

"Rosalie like him?"

The question startled Lowry. He wanted to say how Rosalie felt had no bearing on the case. He realized he had inadvertently not included her in those who knew of the embezzlement. He did not want to tell Rutledge that Peale already had seen her and at the same time he saw "a solution," if there was one, as depending largely on everyone's telling the full truth. But for Rutledge to know of Peale's behavior toward Rosalie would destroy any chance Peale had. And besides it was impossible to reveal it.

"Yes, she liked him," he said briefly.

"Has he given any indication of what he thinks we'll do about this?"

"I told you he would like the worst to happen."

"Yes, no doubt he would today. He'll get over that of course. I wonder if even you realize how he's managed to erase most of my own pleasant dreams," Rutledge said with a bitter shake of his head. "Do you know whether Tom's in town?"

"No, I don't. Do you want me to see him or call him for you?"

"No, you've had enough. This mustn't spoil Rosalie's pleasure in the new house. I shouldn't tell her if I were you. No need for her to know."

"When you asked who knew it I didn't mean to leave her out. She knows it. Peale hinted there was something wrong just before Tom came to the apartment when she found the house."

"Why did he have to tell her?" Rutledge demanded angrily. "To have her intercede with you? My God, Tom told me about his being there and that Jim was all helpfulness. Do you mean to say Rosalie already knew it when Tom talked to her?"

"Only that there was something."

"But you say Evelyn doesn't know? Why should he tell Rosalie and not his own wife?"

"I suppose that to confess first to Evelyn was more than he could bear. And he told me she was away."

"And he had to tell a woman first because she would be kinder to him than a man."

"I tried to be kind to him."

Rutledge sat a moment staring out where his grandchildren were playing. "I'll go in and call Tom and if he's in town I'll drive in with you. Will you be at home this afternoon if I need you?"

"Certainly. I did tell Jim—"

"That you'd let him know how I took it?"

Lowry nodded.

"It's a marvel how quickly men want someone else to take the consequences of their mistakes. Tell him I listened but you can't tell him what I'm going to do because I don't know."

They drove back to the city in silence on the almost empty westbound lane on the Parkway in the face of the enormous outbound traffic.

Late in the warm afternoon, while Stephen and Rosalie were napping together, Thomas Johnson telephoned. He spoke in his usual calm voice and said that after a long talk with him and Charles Curtis, Rutledge had gone back to Locust Valley. Both Rutledge and he felt, on the strength of what Lowry had said, there was no useful purpose in their seeing Peale, though if he made an issue of it he would do so. Rutledge would not unless for reasons of which he did not know.

"If you feel too badly, Stephen, about having discovered this, why don't. From what Charley tells me, it would have been discovered in a matter of weeks anyhow. Now if you can, try to get Jim's resignation tonight and bring it with you in the morning–simplest possible form, just 'I hereby resign,' etc., will do. Well, that's it, I guess."

"What about the money?"

"Curtis already has a check for it."

"I told Edward I'd–"

"No, no, forget it, nothing to do with you. We're sorry you've had to have all this. Very sorry."

"Uh–is Edward all right, as they call it?"

"No, I'm afraid he's not. He's badly broken up. We won't be in until after lunch, that is to say after a special directors' meeting downtown. Oh, one last thing–we feel it essential that Evelyn be told at once and if Jim won't we want to ask you to tell her."

"Oh Lord," Lowry said.

"I know. Try to get him to. We understand she's at her aunt's in Southampton. Get a car to drive you down in the morning."

"All right. That all?"

"No, one thing more. Daran should also be told at once. Is he likely to inform all Latin America?"

"Oh no. There's little doubt he already suspects the truth and having it confirmed will make him feel very badly. He had a great deal of regard for Jim. I'm sure no one will ever hear about it from him."

"Edward says you talked to your brother-in-law about it."

"Yes."

"Is it asking too much for you to telephone him requesting that he tell Daran? We don't want to shift the responsibility but–"

"I'll be glad to telephone him. He met Daran at dinner with me."

Johnson gave a sigh of relief. "It would be the greatest help. Please make clear how much we appreciate it. That *is* all for the moment then. Goodnight."

"I could hear most of it," Rosalie said, stretching. "You poor lamb–"

"Well I'd better go to Jim now. I hate to leave you here."

"You can drop me at Paula's and call me there when you're through and we'll have dinner somewhere. Don't look quite so sad, darling, they're not going to do anything to him. That's what he's most afraid of. When will you call Armas?"

"In the morning."

"Can I speak too?"

"Of course."

16

PEALE'S ATTITUDE THROUGHOUT LOWRY'S WHOLE visit that night was that of a man condemned and sacrificed by those he had thought were his friends. He had apparently not expected his verdict would come so swiftly and he signed the resignation almost as though it were his pardon of them. The fact that no other action against him was intended seemed to make no impression, nor did he seem grateful that the money had been replaced. If anything, he seemed to resent being spared an interview of confession.

Lowry said to him, "They have done it this way because they thought it would be easiest for you. I myself have asked as few questions as possible for the same reason, but if you want to talk about it or why it happened, please do so."

"It isn't that so much," he replied. "It's the terrible way that almost without a word, men I thought believed in me have simply cut me off, just taken scissors and done it. Not only cut me off from C.I.C. but apparently right out of their lives. You yourself last night, you wouldn't let me come to your apartment. I'm untouchable. Compare Tom Johnson's treatment of me with this Foundation of his. I'm like a man on a desert island, put there and left by his shipmates. I don't know what I'm expected to do. Am I expected to eat, to shave and bathe in the morning, go out, do what? Am I to speak to people? Am I to call people up and say I'm an embezzler? What are the rules? What does a man in my case do?"

"I don't think there are any rules. It sounds trite, but time, each day, will help, I think."

"Time's a great healer, is it? It's more likely a great destroyer."

Lowry paused a moment. "There's the practical matter of how your affairs stand. If it'll help, we can go over it together now and make some sort of a statement to talk to a lawyer about."

"I couldn't do it now."

"Evelyn has to be told. Are you willing to see her?"

"No, definitely not. I'll not see her."

"Then I'll have to. Is there anything you want me to say?"

"No, just tell her that the bad she so easily saw in me is now apparent to all. Tell her her judgment is confirmed by Edward Rutledge."

"Please don't think I'm preaching or that it's easy for me, but you must rid yourself of this bitterness. If you feel you've been victimized, you must forgive. Rutledge and Johnson haven't victimized you. They're brokenhearted about it. You must know that I am."

"But it's not going to affect your career or that book or your life with Rosalie. Those will all go happily on. I'll be someone you used to know."

Peale talked on in the same fashion for another hour. Consciously at intervals, so it seemed, referring to suicide as the only solution. Lowry finally left, saying that he would see him as soon as he was back from Southampton and extracting a vague promise to "do nothing extreme" before then.

Hoping the exercise would clear his mind, he walked back to Gramercy Park, saying to himself that people who talked about suicide didn't commit it, but fearful of being called during the night to hear of a plunge from a window or of gas turned on in an oven.

"I don't think the worst will happen," Rosalie said when he told her.

"People say that, but it does happen. I don't know what to do. I can't help saying to myself that he is behaving badly about it, that I'd try to be a little more stoical, but, my God, I don't know what I'd do if I were in his place. I say to myself that I'd never get in such a mess, but who knows even now how he got into it, little by little—"

"I think he'll be all right in the long run."

"You mean remake himself."

"No, he'll just float back to the top somehow, because even now he obviously doesn't blame himself, has no sense of guilt to weigh him down."

"I wish I thought so," Stephen said.

He telephoned Evelyn early Monday morning to make an appointment. She said she would see him though it was useless to think he could persuade her to return. He reached Southampton at eleven o'clock, driving a hired car, and asked her to guide him to where they could talk in seclusion. There he told her at once what had happened.

She lit a cigarette and said unemotionally she was not surprised. She had expected something from the letters coming to the house from Venezuela. Since she felt no attachment of any sort for him, she felt no obligation to stand by him in any way. Her aunt was only too glad to have her and the children with her. Peale could do what he liked with the contents of the apartment. There was literally nothing in it she ever wanted to see again.

"I hope this isn't too disillusioning for you," she said. "I suppose you expected a fine gesture, 'for richer, for poorer' and so on. The only person I'm sorry for in all this is you, Stephen. It was sweet of you to drive all this distance to tell me. Oh, I'll give you whatever jewelry he's given me that I have here and he can sell it—there's some in the safe deposit also. I'm afraid I've rather shocked you."

"Well it's not for me to judge," Lowry said, "though I suppose—" He paused. Relief though it was to have it taken so calmly, he was shocked, perhaps a little horrified.

"I know what you're thinking," Evelyn said, "but of course you don't realize that I've disliked him for a long time."

"I suppose that's one way of putting it," he said. "I'd like to ask why, because I can't abandon him and I need to know as much as possible to help him."

"My reasons won't help you. I disliked him for deceiving me, for making a fool of me about the money we were spending."

"But you weren't deceived until just now and you say you've disliked him for a long time."

"Yes for his intolerable superiority, because he thought I was stupid, for the withering tone in his voice with me, for his constant correcting me, interrupting me, moving things from where I put them, boasting of his physical fidelity to me, acting starved sexually."

"There was no other side to it?"

"I suppose there was. To start with I was very much in love with him. I did things to please him I didn't want to do." She gave a grim little laugh. "I was very innocent then. I think he was. We were high-minded about how far we went before we were married. Do you mind if I don't talk about it any more?"

Lowry thought for a moment. "You'll want to get a divorce sometime, I assume, and meanwhile there are bound to be questions about some household details. Is there any lawyer who can act for you?"

"Yes, I suppose my aunt's lawyers would be willing. I'll speak to them. Stephen, I don't like to worry you like this—please don't be angry—but there's nothing between Rosalie and him is there? He's been mad about her since New Year's Eve."

"Well not on her part certainly," Lowry said. "What do you think he should do—or what I should try to do for him?"

"I shouldn't try to do too much. A dear old man, gentle and kindly, came to see my aunt last week. She told me that he was a monster until he was past forty. Jim is still pubescent, I think that's the word."

Recounting the interview to Rosalie that night, Lowry asked her if she felt the same sense of shock about it that he had.

"I don't think I do. I understand her feelings," she told him. "Living as man and wife without love must be emotionally the most destructive thing in the world."

A week later at nine in the morning, Peale walked into his new club, found a bench, and settled himself to read the want ads in the *Times*. He had resigned from the Hounds, the University, the Yale, a yacht club, a lunch club and a shooting club in Georgia to join the one that required no proposer or second—Bryant Park, with its floating, changing membership of white-collar unemployed. Its central location, its ready access to the room on the second floor of the Library where Poor's *Manual of Corporations*, Holmes's *Green Book* and the *Directory of Directors* could be consulted made it most convenient. On Forty-Second Street was a hole in the wall where the worst sandwiches and coffee in the city were served. Partaking of them was a form of penance that solaced the guilty soul.

He had a room in a cheap apartment on West End Avenue which held everything he had kept—his clothes. He had a new "special account" with a number in a branch of a bank that was not a member of the Clearing House.

What surprised him most was how quickly things could stop—mail, invitations, telephone calls. He had been at the active center of a great corporation. Yet when he had called Charley Curtis to offer to come in to explain or complete unfinished work, to meet him privately with details, Curtis had said, "Oh we needn't bother you with that, Jim, we'll pick it up all right. Anything we can do for you?"

This was while he was still at his Park Avenue apartment and he had hesitatingly asked whether Harold Titcomb could be sent there to help him see to the disposal of its contents. Curtis had said certainly, adding, "Harold of course doesn't know what's happened and there's no need to tell him."

Officially only the senior officers did know. The rest of the organization had heard that "Mr. Peale had left the Company to enter another field, but is not yet ready to announce his plans." Titcomb, however, knew pretty well what had happened. He was distressed about it—"We've never had anything like this of course," he said to his wife—but his real anxiety was that Mr. Rutledge had not been at the office since Mr. Lowry's return and he was afraid "he was taking it pretty hard."

At Peale's however, he was efficient, matter of fact and tactful, dealing with the men who came to bid on rugs and furniture, overseeing packing and shipping—going himself with some of Peale's clothes (anonymously buying some of the "sports outfit" himself) to a secondhand dealer "who was recommended to me."

To see himself stripped of possession was agreeable to Peale. Lowry went with him to an attorney on the more complex business of deciding whom and what he could pay on his debts. Aside from the embezzlement, and after crediting some chattels that could be returned—including some jewelry Evelyn had left in the apartment—his debts and bills were over $50,000. The attorney and Lowry advised him to keep $1000 to live on until he had a job. The attorney drafted the letter he was to send certain creditors in the hope of avoiding legal action and consequent public bankruptcy. Of it all he said little to Lowry except that he now felt no bitterness toward him.

"Had you not discovered it, I see now I should have gone on to worse things. 'Murder leads to lying,' Oscar Wilde said. I didn't tell many lies. The thing I don't understand, Steve, is that nothing ever turned out right. I never had any luck. Other men have speculated—well, what's the use of talking about it. What do you think I should do?"

"For the moment, get any job you can that's respectable."

"I don't suppose there's anyone I can go to and ask for one."

"I don't like to say this, but I think it's inadvisable. A good job is bound to raise questions—"

"I know. I did see Bill Le Grand of Chevelux. I've spent a small fortune cultivating him and the first thing he asked was, 'Jim, there's nothing funny about your leaving C.I.C., is there?' "

"If you can get a small job and give this time to blow over, something will come up where you can come back. It's hard, but I think it's what you have to do."

"What do you think I ought to do about people I know asking me to dinner or that sort of thing? A few might. I suppose that'll take care of itself after I move and they don't know where I am."

"I don't want to give advice, Jim, as though I were some pundit. I think it's the sort of thing that, however well meant, would be very trying. I realize the loneliness you'll feel, but to see people socially—oh, well I can't say it, but don't do it. Don't let people feel sorry for you that way."

"I never thought you believed in hair shirts."

"I don't. I believe in fun. It wouldn't be fun."

In spite of a drugstore breakfast in contrast to the frosty fresh orange juice, the eggs poached in milk, bright with paprika, with a dash of tabasco, the broiled bacon, the trimmed, hot toast and delicious coffee of the past, Peale settled on a bench in Bryant Park, feeling wonderfully free of care. He had lost or thrown away a number of things on none of which, at the moment, he put great value.

The realization on awakening that morning that he was no longer in love with Rosalie—was not tormented, as for months he had been, about what she was doing alone with Lowry, or when he himself could see her or how he could win her accord—was an almost priceless relief. The fires of desire and curiosity were wetted down. A woman member of the Bryant Park Club was scanning the want ads on a bench across from him and the morning breeze blew her skirt now and then above her knees. He saw it idly but did not have to go on gaping. He realized suddenly that he had no further interest in the picture of Rosalie in the sun still in his pocket, and getting up with the determination of a man setting out for the Pole he crossed the Park and went down Forty-Second Street to the Times Square post office, where without looking at the picture he mailed it to Rosalie. It gave him an illusion of strength of mind and will, and he felt that in now desiring Rosalie no more than he did Evelyn—which was to say not at all—he had conquered something.

The more he considered it the more it seemed to him that much of the aberration which had led to the embezzlement could be traced to his unmanageable desires for Rosalie. He remembered being with Lowry in Paris in 1950 when she was in Switzerland and another picture of her, very *spirituelle*, Lowry had shown him. He remembered exactly what had happened the next afternoon when he had been at a conference. The economists and diplomats around him had been busy with their doodles. And he had fallen into a daydream about her, beset by curiosity as to whether she were faithful to Lowry. And then of what it would be like to be the lover of such a woman. He had wished he could have an affair, if not with her, with one of the tall, beautiful women of the high world he was meeting—women of such aloof and distinguished beauty it was inconceivable to think of them in bed with anyone, yet women said to have the great men of Western Europe as their lovers. At a dinner that night he had tried to direct the talk with the women either side of him toward sex and seduction. One would not listen and the other, listening attentively, finally said to him, "You see, what you say is *ni drôle ni douce* and it must be one or the other."

He felt out of it as he did with the men, who, it seemed to him, sensed he had not been closer to the war than Washington and let drift into their talk what he felt were deliberate allusions to it, the more barbed because they were so innocent—"Oh no, that day I well remember I was in Blois" . . . "At that time De Marsac was still with Le Clerc."

Well, now at least all such things were off his mind.

When half an hour later he walked into the crowded anteroom of one of "the better placement services; we handle only men of executive caliber," he doubted whether soldiers like Lowry or the former Resistance leaders he had met in France had faced an ordeal requiring more courage. He had looked on the lobby directory for the floor number and gone to the waiting elevator. The operator looked at him and said, "Stairs right there."

"To what?" Peale asked.

"Placement Service. One flight up."

How the man knew where he was going he had no idea, but it was like a blow in the face. He turned, pushed open the door and climbed the stairs. There were said to be almost no unemployed in the country but the anteroom was jammed with men filling out forms, waiting on the edge of their chairs for their names to be called, getting up with a confident, jaunty air when it was, turning away sorrowfully when it was only the message "Nothing today. Mr. Peterson suggests you call around in about a week. Oh yes, your name's right at the top of the tickler."

At lunch at the Hounds Club there would not be as many polished shoes as there were in that room. Nowhere, except in a similar anteroom, would there be so many men trying to be what they were not—confident, calm and unworried. Practically all carried briefcases. There was of necessity in so packed a room a No Smoking sign. Men drifted to the corridor for a cigarette, trying to stay within earshot of the receptionist's voice. Her manner was cordial and agreeable and she laughed at each one's pleasantry. The older men, forty-plus, were naturally the most pathetically pretentious of all. The younger ones talked with each other, exchanged tips, rated other agencies—but the older sat tight to their seats looking through address books or suddenly making sure again the six copies of their "résumés" were in their briefcases. Well, Peale thought, they must get jobs for some people, or they couldn't pay the rent.

He went up to the receptionist.

"What kind of a position are you looking for?" she asked.

"Executive, I guess."

"What was your last salary?"

He hesitated and then told her the truth. She was accustomed to hyperbole and handed him the forms with a pleasant smile. He walked slowly over to the wall desks and realized he had never carried a fountain pen. The agency supplied none, and after a moment he asked a man who had completed his form if he could use his. The man hesitated, obviously afraid he would never see it again, and then said yes but he'd have to have it back as soon as his name was called. So Peale began to write the story of his life. Reading it back, he did not see how he could hand it in. Why should a man with such a record need a job? The only references he gave were the officers of C.I.C.

He returned the pen and walked over to the receptionist, who glanced through the form without comment and told him to be seated. Twenty minutes later, like the lowliest of the waiting men, he had grabbed a discarded tabloid of the day and was reading it. It was an hour before Mr. Peterson could see him.

"Your last salary was five thousand," Peterson asked, looking up from the application.

"Fifty."

"You'd better find me a job," Peterson said. "You have a remarkable record. I wouldn't think you'd need us. What happened, a freeze-out?"

"Something of the sort."

"And your former competitors don't want you?"

"I prefer not to go to them."

"Frankly we don't have jobs at that level going begging around here, though of course clients do come to us in special cases. I placed a man last week at twenty-five thousand. Don't know just what to say about you, though. I'll look around, what's your minimum?"

"Five, I suppose."

Peterson chewed his lip a moment. "No real sales experience—Oh and you don't have a car. Well, give me a call, say, Thursday. Meantime if anything comes up, I can reach you, let's see. Oh yes, your telephone's here. OK."

"You will do your best?" Peale asked him.

"That's what we're here for."

Peale went back to his club in the park. More men, many evidently life members, had come in. Some checker games and two of chess were in progress. The backgammon-dominoes tradition of the Hounds was not observed. There were no facilities for letter writing, their discarded newspapers and magazines were less interesting than those at the Hounds but otherwise it was much the same—except for some excellent recorded music played from the Library during the noon hour. He knew men at the Hounds who lived in Connecticut because of the New York State income tax but who were in their chairs in the bar daily by 10.45 and stayed there until the 5.10 train. The new club had similar habitués. He could think of nowhere else to go, no one to telephone to, no one to lunch with, no one to write to, no one even to talk to and he wondered whether he would sit there idly until the autumn chill drove him and the rest into the main reading room to doze over the *Mirror* or *News* concealed in a volume of the encyclopedia.

Thursday morning he went directly to the Placement Service without telephoning and to his surprise the receptionist, after checking, said Mr. Peterson wanted to see him in about twenty minutes. Looking around the room, he felt he had already moved up to some seniority.

Peterson got up and put out his hand.

"Now we've got something which I don't know whether you'll want or not, but I take it you don't want to be hanging around. Am I right?"

"Absolutely."

"OK. Excello Extrusion, it's a plastic outfit, manufacturing, factory in the Bronx, want a high-class credit man. They do a nice business, owners built it up from a shoestring and ride around in Cadillacs. They make a point of wanting class. What do you say?"

"How much?"

"Start you off at seventy-five, a week that is."

"At least the taxes on that aren't too much."

"I think you'll like these people if you'll take 'em as you find them. They're smart, a little on the rough-diamond side. Want to try it?"

"By all means. Any idea how to get there?" He started to say he had never been in the Bronx.

"Subway. Here's your card. Hope you land it."

The head of Excello Extrusion was P. J. Cronkhite, who had the business in the palm of his hand. He told Peale they worked long hours in this shop and they wanted a go-ahead two-fisted credit man with vision who wasn't primarily interested in his biweekly salary check but in his future and the company's future, a man who could turn a customer down for credit and still make him want to do business with Excello and nobody else.

Candidly, did Peale consider himself that man?

Peale said he did.

"No objection to working nights?"

"No."

"I want somebody with class. This organization's got class. You look as though you had. Am I right? Peterson down there told me you had."

"Well, I think that's for you or him to say."

"Fine; like a fellow to be frank. Now if you like you can take off your coat and go to work now. Check your credits on your orders coming in, get your holdings out of the way and get me a report on everything overdue thirty days. Like to see the whole thing in the morning. Have your collection letters on 'em ready too."

"Whom do I dictate to?"

"Oh you don't write your own letters?"

"No."

"Sorry to hear that. Well, you can use my girl some of the time."

The rest of the day Peale learned a good deal about "little business."

Speeches in the *Congressional Record*, if nothing else, always left no doubt that small business was one of America's chief glories. Large business was "soulless," "monopolistic," "geared to profit-making." Its managers were outrageously enriched by their own votes of high salaries and bonuses to each other, although this practice could be condoned where the managers "came up the hard way."

"Small businessmen," in contrast, were kindly, often the victims of monopolistic competition and although in need of federal protection against loss from big business, were large taxpayers and the backbone of free enterprise. How without profits they managed to pay such large taxes was not clear.

If all this was true, Peale found that Cronkhite and his associates must be of some commercial third sex. They had neither the brains nor resources to make a budget or plan operations. They did have a twenty-four-hour devotion to the business and a multitude of customers whom they alternately cursed, cheated, crawled to, "entertained," joked with and insulted. Seller and buyers, however, seemed quite happy about it.

As Cronkhite had said, he had the business in the palm of his hand. Stamps could not be bought until a frightened clerk told him what the last had been used for. Suppliers' bills were paid late with full discount taken and endlessly argued about. Wages were paid by check after the banks had closed for the weekend. The office lacked the most essential statistics, but the "girls' rest-period time-book" was scrupulously accurate.

With his training and experience, Peale did not find his work difficult, except for the condition of the files and the fact that he was expected to do his own filing. By the normal closing time there was a good deal of order around his desk and Cronkhite, with his partner, Ruthven Halperin, stopped "to look things over" on their way out.

"You'll be out of here by nine. I like the way you go at this, Peale. Ruthven, Peale came in to take potluck with us and as I remarked to you just now I think he's very sincere and I've got plans for him. You agree with me, Ruthven?"

"Absolutely."

"I'd like you in early, Peale. Want to talk to you about distributing the mail. You strike me as a doer and I want to see you go ahead fast. Want to get everything systematized."

Peale put in fourteen hours each on Friday and Saturday and spent most of Sunday alone at the office. Order had indeed replaced chaos. Monday morning he arrived in time to open the mail and have it on the desks of the people it concerned by nine o'clock. He was rather pleased with how quickly he had grasped the business.

He was busy at his own desk when Cronkhite came in at nine-thirty and a few moments later Peale heard a roar from his office. Its door opened and Cronkhite bellowed across the room, "Peale, C.U."—the usual summon to the Presence.

He went in to find Cronkhite in a rage.

"What the hell do you mean by distributing the mail before I saw it?"

"Look, Mr. Cronkhite, you told me you wanted people at work at nine. You said yourself the mail was late getting to them. Anything you need to see as president is on your desk. You shouldn't waste your time on every detail. Where your men are in doubt they should come to you. I read every letter carefully. The way I've done it is the right way."

"Well," Cronkhite said, "I don't want to bawl you out for an honest mistake, but you see we're one big family here. If we don't, my top associates and I, see all the mail one of us may get the idea we're holding out on him and by the way, never, but never, give Halperin a bank letter unless I say so. I want to think this over. I'll talk to you later."

Peale went back to his desk. The air apparently had cleared but he was aware that the staff, sensing that he had been called down, were going in one by one to see Cronkhite with letters, orders and invoices. Shortly afterwards Cronkhite went out and did not return until after three. A moment later Peale's phone rang and the office operator said, "Peale, P.J. C.U.

He went in again.

Cronkhite began, "Do you know that submission of a fraudulent balance sheet by mail is a federal offense, whereas if it's handed in it isn't?"

"Certainly."

"Wanted to be sure, that's all. How do you like it here?"

"Very much."

"Like to stay?"

"Yes sir. I hope you're satisfied."

"Your work's all right," Cronkhite said, "routine stuff, of course, all laid on the line for you." He paused. "You're not very frank, are you, Peale?"

"I think so."

"I don't. Why did you leave your last job? What was this 'management disagreement' you put on your application? I want to warn you now I know more than you think I do, so be careful. What's the matter, are you afraid to answer?"

In the near panic he felt, Peale realized several things: that only by a miracle had Peterson and Cronkhite not pressed the question before; and that Cronkhite had a right to a full answer. Yet even in the few days at Excello he had begun to feel some security.

He must not lose this job. If he did, he was done for good. He was ready to do anything—to lie his way out, to beg for a chance, anything—to hold it. If a man like Cronkhite could fire him he could never hold up his head.

"You know what I think," Cronkhite said, "I think you had sticky fingers. You were a pretty big shot, you went to Yale, I know the type, honest little business like this not good enough for you in your Brooks Brothers clothes."

They're not Brooks, they're Pooles Peale wanted to say. Otherwise his mind was a blank. He could find nothing to say. Cronkhite gave the impression of having waited all his life for the malevolent satisfaction of seeing another man brought utterly down before him. Peale had read of otherwise respectable men arrested in vice raids. He felt like one of them. He wished he could be defiant and tell this bully to think what he liked and stalk out, but he was too frightened.

"Got you on the raw, eh?" Cronkhite asked. "Well now suppose I told you I had a plan for you?" God and Cronkhite, Peale thought. "You'd be relieved, wouldn't you?"

"Yes."

"Well, we'll see. We'll see what my partner thinks," Cronkhite said, lifting the telephone. "Halperin, see me," he told the operator.

Halperin came in with his sickly air. Cronkhite, ordinarily contemptuous of him, placed his chair and spoke almost deferentially to him.

He drummed on the desk with his fingernails. "Ruthven," he began, looking at the ceiling, "you and I have been partners together for a good many years, ever since we came out of Poppe Paper Box, scarcely more than kids, to set up our own show. We had dreams then. They haven't all worked out. The best ones have. Maybe we're not going to be the richest men in the cemetery but we can sleep at night on God's green earth meanwhile. We've never had any secrets from each other. I've known your problems. You've known mine. That's the way it's going to go right on being."

He paused to frown at Peale, who was standing. "Ruthven, Peale has taken some money. He's admitted it."

"From us?" Halperin asked, as though he wondered where he could have been.

"Before he came with us, from his old crowd. Now, Ruthven, don't get excited, don't say what I know you feel like saying, what I felt like. Now he had trouble getting this job and of course if he loses it, under these circumstances, he's going to have one hell of a time getting another. You and I believe in the same God, different parts of the same Bible and we've got to think of a fellow human. We can't, at least I hope you'll agree with me, turn him out like a dog. I see a way out of this. I see a way that you're going to say is a damn fool way, maybe so, but instead of letting Peale go, I'm not only going to give him a chance, I'm going to show him we've got confidence in him. Do you agree with me so far, Ruthven?"

"Perfectly all right."

"How about you, Peale?"

Peale took a long breath and expressed his appreciation.

"This is what I'm going to do. Peale got this job without telling us the whole story. We're paying him at the rate of thirty-nine hundred a year, that's on a week-to-week basis of course. You understand that, Peale?"

"I do."

"Now you remember the qualification we set. I think you'll agree that they haven't been measured up to by you. But I'm not going to take advantage of that—you can stay right on as Credit Man at thirty-six hundred, that is to say three hundred dollars a month, and I'll overlook what you didn't tell me. OK?

"That isn't all. I told you I was going to show you more confidence and I am. Miss Blake, who has been our cashier and head bookkeeper, is leaving us, Peale; you'll step right into her shoes. We won't replace her. We'll throw the whole thing together, cash, books of account, credit, that's the way it should be, and I figure you'll have plenty of time to handle the whole thing. May take a little night work, may mean a short lunch hour some days, but you can do it. You're young still, you're strong as a horse and you're going to know you've got our confidence. Now Ruthven, will you go along with me in this, the way you always have?"

"Perfectly all right," Halperin said.

"There it is in a shell of nuts, Peale. It's strictly up to you, but remember this. I'll be living in our checkbook and our cashbox and don't you forget it for one little minute. That's all."

17

THAT AFTERNOON THE SENIOR OFFICERS OF C.I.C., each of whom had been privately apprised of the reasons for the Peale resignation, were requested to meet with Thomas Johnson in the Board Room at four.

Since his return Lowry had been impressed by the decency and good manners of their not questioning him. Each had let him know they sympathized with his reluctant part in it. There had been no "long-suspected I could have told you so's," and even Hewitt, with unexpected delicacy, had left a handwritten note for him, reading:

Dear Steve:

It occurs to me Jim will have to have funds to go along on and I just want to say that I'll join you, and any others, with my share. Let me know. Probably best if you could act as banker.

He remembered the emotions with which he had said to himself, to Rosalie and to Rutledge that Peale was his friend and he would stand by him. Was he doing so, he wondered. He had not felt, nor had any of those who knew, that there in Peale but for the grace of God went they themselves. Yet what Peale had done had not been conceived in cruelty nor brought material suffering to anyone. It was not heinous, not a sin against the Holy Ghost. It was quite possible that all of them, from Rutledge down, had sometime in their private lives done a more shameful thing, forgiving themselves or been forgiven without any outward effect on their lives. But Peale had broken trusts which bound them all to one another and common sense required that they no longer trust him. They had shown all the charity that reason permitted. He must remake himself.

Yet as Lowry thought of all the happy, golden times of their youth, of the confidences between them, the half-formed hopes and plans they had shared with each other, it was difficult to leave him alone in the sorrow, humiliation and perhaps even terror he must feel.

Johnson came in after they were assembled and went to stand at the head of the table. He did not look well and his manner was more formal than usual.

"I felt it best," he said still standing, "to get you together for an announcement that will distress you all. I shall want your advice on the best way to tell the organization.

"As a result of what has happened, Edward, against my protest and those of the other directors, has resigned as chairman and from the Board. Nothing we said could alter his decision. He took the position that he had assumed sole responsibility for the selection of our higher personnel and that if, in some way, he had not been derelict the tragic action of Jim Peale would not have occurred." Johnson paused, looked down a moment and then continued, "I suppose I would have been less than human if I had not looked forward to the time when I would succeed him. But I assure you I thought of it as something in the future.

"Coming now as it has, you will realize there is no pleasure in it. Two men for whom I felt respect and friendship have, as it were, gone down to make room for me. I am not at all sure I retain either the buoyancy, the optimism or the qualities of leadership necessary. I shall need far more help from each of you than Edward did.

"All that I say is very hard to put into words. I think what I most want to say is this. It would be easy to install closer supervision, tighter controls—even, if I may say this, for us to permit suspicion or doubts about each other to take root. Nothing of the sort must occur in any part of the organization.

"So much for that. How and what shall we tell the staff?" Johnson asked, sitting down.

"I am sure I speak for us all," Curtis began by right of seniority, "in pledging our support to you and in sharing with you the feelings you naturally have as to how it has come about." There was a murmur of assent from around the table. " 'Least said, soonest mended.' I suggest we multigraph a brief announcement and have it on everyone's desk when they come in in the morning. Let it go to plants and branch offices by regular mail. I'll have Harold Titcomb in, after we've drafted it, and ask him to stay and handle it personally."

Johnson nodded. "One of you go over it with Charley, will you? I think I'll go now."

They all got up and shook hands with their new chairman.

"Tom," Curtis said, "I think you ought to tell Harold. It will be an awful blow to him. He was idolatrous about Edward."

"I know. I don't think I can tell him. One of you do it, or, better yet, get him in here and let him sit down with you," Johnson said and then paused, leaning against the table, rubbing his forehead. "A decision used to be a simple thing and now the smallest one has to be considered. Titcomb has been here longer than any of us. I have the feeling that he's entitled to hear the whole story, if he's to be trusted with the announcement. I'd prefer that, I think."

"I guess we'd better tell him," Curtis said when Johnson had left. "What do you think, Steve?"

"I think so," Lowry said and Hewitt, with the others, agreed. When Titcomb came in, Curtis pulled out a chair for him and Evans offered him a cigarette.

He listened gravely, without a word, to what they told him about Peale. His jaws tightened at the end and he gave a sad little shake of his head. Then they told him about Mr. Rutledge and what they wanted him to do. His emotion, as his eyes filled with tears and his voice trembled, eased the tension they all felt.

"This is a terrible blow to me," he said, wiping his glasses.

"It is to us all, but we realize you two have been associated longest. Tell us how you think we'd better phrase it in the announcement," Curtis said.

"Well, as simply as possible. I wouldn't say 'we regret to announce.' It'd be too much like a death notice and it wouldn't be fair to Mr. Johnson. Mr. Rutledge wouldn't like it either. We'll have to pretend things'll be the same, but they won't again, never, never."

"Try a form of words, Steve," Curtis said.

Lowry wrote it out in pencil and showed it to Titcomb, who took off his glasses to read it, nodded and handed it to Curtis to read aloud. No changes were proposed and they each went back to their desks without further word, but in a few moments Hewitt came to Lowry's office.

"I don't need to point out to you," he began, "that Tom said nothing about the presidency or the fact that there are only three of us left. What thought have you given to it?"

"None, I should say."

"Well, of course you've had a good deal on your mind, as we all have, but I've been doing some rather tall thinking. I can't tell you anything now but something has happened that puts me in a position to take advantage of this and I wanted you to know, Steve, I'm also thinking of you. I think the world, as we all do, of Les Evans, but Leslie's best friend wouldn't claim he was any world-beater. That's about all I can say now. Tell me, by the way, does Rosalie know all about Jim?"

"Well yes, she does."

"I haven't told Paula anything except that he's out. Of course she's curious, pestering me with questions, but I think the fewer people who know, the better. Don't you agree?"

"Certainly as a general practice, yes," Lowry replied, in the dark as to where this was all leading.

"Charley hasn't said anything about how much of his stock Edward's holding on to, has he?"

"No."

"Well, we'll see what we shall see," Hewitt said and went out with an air of breezy mystery.

Profoundly affected as he still was by Peale's downfall and now by Rutledge's resignation, Hewitt's reference to taking advantage of it further depressed Lowry. He realized that in his personal life he must shake off his depression, if only for the sake of Rosalie and the home-coming children and although he was not in a mood to conspire or to battle for their places, with Hewitt as an ally. But it had been grimly borne in on him since his return that he could not leave his office troubles on his desk at five o'clock and take them up again in the morning.

He found Rosalie at the apartment hot and voluble, after a day in Ridingtown with painters and carpenters. Paula Hewitt had driven out with her.

"Darling, she pestered me all day with questions about Jim, where he is, what he's doing and above all what it was he did. Calvin's told her nothing."

"So he told me today, in evident disapproval of your knowing."

"Of course, they're not at all close as we are. Did he tell you about Paula?"

"No, what?"

"Did you ever hear of a Miss Samantha Suydam?"

"Oh yes, she died the other day at ninety-six. She had one of those 'original Standard Oil fortunes.' "

"Brace yourself. Practically all of it goes to Paula. She was her great-aunt."

"My God, she's enormously rich then, enormously. And now she's going to buy a great block of C.I.C. stock for Calvin. I'll be damned. Really, it's too much."

"What?"

"That fellow in Rutledge's place."

"Oh no," she said. "I'm very sure she has no such plan. There have been too many Friday night dinners. Oh no, you can be sure what she'll do, because it will be the exact opposite of what I'd do in her place. Master Calvin will have to watch his step. She isn't sorry for herself any longer."

"I wouldn't think so, with all that money."

"Speaking of money, of which we're spending an awful lot, I realize, could we have an economical dinner at Hamburg Heaven?"

"Yes. How's the house?"

"Divine, the Rutledge garden crew arrived in a truck and dug and planted and rolled the whole day. And the painters are almost through. Oh there's a letter from Dolly for you."

"Oh, sit down a moment," Lowry said.

"What's the matter?"

"Mr. Rutledge has resigned." Then he told her what had happened that afternoon. "I feel very badly. We all did." He told her more about Titcomb.

"Oh I do too. Not because he's retiring, but that Jim should be the cause of it," she said, and went over to sit on the arm of his chair. "Won't it be almost the same with Mr. Johnson? It could be so much worse if it were a stranger."

"Of course it could be. I suppose in a few days it will seem just the same." How quickly, he thought to himself, we all crave the comfortable assurance of familiar ways and people and surroundings and to avoid "new adjustments" or "getting accustomed" to new things. How poignant the words "a stranger in a strange land." How lost and lonely Jim Peale and all the uprooted of the world must feel.

"Who will succed Mr. Johnson?"

"Nothing was said about that. The offices might be combined I should think for a while, but this Suydam money may change it all. How like Rutledge it was to have his gardeners over there today, when he must have wished he'd never seen me."

"I'm sure he didn't wish that. Do you want a drink while I bathe?"

"No thanks. Hurry though, I want a shower myself. I'll get Dolly's letter."

He took off his coat and tie and sat down in the bedroom to read it. As he took it out of its envelope, a check fell on the floor. The letter read:

Dear Stephen:

I was in New Haven last night on some Class Business and ran into Stu Winthrop in Mory's. He is not, you will recall, a happy drinker and why the Founders Trust stands for it I have never understood. I attribute it to the boyish shock of now silver hair he has retained. In any event he told me, and I regret to say some others, about Jim.

Although, as you have often so fraternally reminded me, I am a man without conscience, I am not without my own type of pride. Your acquisition of Larus, after I put Jim on to it, resulted in my receiving $5000 from a lady who had briefly shared my bed. I had intended dissipating it in Europe. However, here is my check for it in Jim's favor. See that he gets it, and do not write me a brotherly letter.

Yours,

D

Lowry sighed and put the check and letter on the bureau. "A decision," Johnson had said that afternoon, "used to be a simple thing and now the smallest one has to be considered." He supposed it was legally Dolly's money to do with as he liked.

Rosalie came out of the bedroom. "Read the letter," he told her. When he came out to dress she said, "It's of course quixotic of Dolly, but won't it be a help?"

"I suppose," Lowry said grimly, "it will be a help, though what Jim Peale should do with it, God knows. I was sure at Larus something like this was in the wind and he gave me his word, or so I thought, that it wasn't. I felt it essential that my brother not get anything out of it, unless everyone concerned knew it. What a mess."

The days of that midweek passed without special incident at C.I.C. The staff responded to the announcement they had found on their desks Tuesday morning with round robins, to Mr. Rutledge of good wishes for a long, happy life in his well-earned retirement and to Johnson of a pledge of the same efforts and loyalty they had shown in the past to "your predecessor." A plan to levy tribute for a silver tray with their names on it for Mr. Rutledge was quashed by Curtis. There were questions in the washrooms as to how "this ties up with Peale's leaving" and some gloomy prophecies that "we haven't seen the end of the changes, you just wait and see."

Without saying why, Lowry telephoned Peale to ask when he could see him, suggesting they dine alone at the Plaza. Peale said he would be "working nights" until Friday and they fixed on it.

Johnson himself was not in the office Wednesday or Thursday, and without Rutledge or him the operations of the great corporation went on, the staff giving the illusion of needing no higher management—as an orchestra does playing a symphony without apparent regard to the conductor.

Late on Thursday afternoon Curtis went in person to the offices of Lowry and the other seniors. "I have some rather bad news," he said to Lowry, "and I don't want to tell you and the others here. Can you be at my apartment at five-thirty? Don't leave the office together. I don't want to start any talk."

The Curtis apartment was on Fifth Avenue facing the Park and Lowry, leaving just after five, walked slowly north to it, wondering what it could all be about. He could not avoid the fear that they had found Peale's fraud was not limited to the Venezuela matter.

As he crossed Fifty-Seventh Street, Hewitt caught up with him. "What the hell do you suppose this is all about?" he asked. "I swear Charley was so ominous I've been searching my own record. Have you?"

"Well, I'm ashamed to admit I have been saying to myself it can't be about me," Lowry said.

"I don't know whether you saw the will of Paula's great-aunt in the *Times*. At least I've got something to fall back on. I don't know why the hell I should think of that, but Charley did give me the creeps."

At the Plaza they crossed to the east side of Fifth, looking up at "the surf-leap of granite coming down from the North." The next twenty blocks still held for Lowry the mystery and magic of a foreign city—outwardly impregnable wealth and stability dwelt there. The white stone of the buildings was bathed in gold and the sky was blue and high. The rush and democracy of the city had stopped. Motors drew up silently at the canopied entrances and doormen obsequiously bowed their occupants in. Outside some of the private houses elderly caretakers, coatless in clean shirts, hair slicked down, contemplated the end of the day.

Curtis was waiting for them in his study, standing with his back to the fireplace, where a great copper pitcher was ablaze with colored peonies. Evans and Hardwick were already there. There was a small bar with bottles and glasses in the corner of the room. Curtis made no gesture of invitation toward it, but closed the door after Lowry and Hewitt.

"You'll feel I brought you quite a ways for what can be told in a few words. But I didn't see what else to do. About two o'clock this morning Tom had a heart attack. They're the most dangerous kind, I'm told, if they come when you're in bed. He's at P.H. They *think* he'll make it, but it's the end of his working days. Months of convalescence at the best. An invalid life if he does make it. It's really only a hope that he will. Well, that's all I can say."

Something between a whistle and a groan came from the listeners.

"I might say," Curtis continued, "it really has nothing to do with Jim's affair. It was of long standing—though I don't suppose that helped. I don't know how you fellows feel. I feel damn near like an orphan."

Lowry thought of his first talk with Rutledge, the ten-twenty-year plan, the fixed succession. All that had seemed so permanent had to do with mortal men.

"It's really that bad?" Evans asked. "I mean, can they be sure this soon, these new drugs and all?"

"They're sure," Curtis replied.

"I don't want to seem heartless," Hewitt said, "it hits me very hard, but what's it going to mean? What will the directors do? It ought to be you to move up. We'd all be in back of you."

Curtis shook his head. "I suppose, I hope at least, it will be one of us. It won't be me. I'm too old. I'm well, I know as well as you do I haven't the range."

"How's Mrs. Johnson?" Lowry asked.

"Brave but pretty broken up, a little bitter that he's been allowed to do so much," Curtis said, sighing between his teeth. "I hate to think of what people will say, three of us in a matter of weeks. They're going to wonder what sort of show we've been running."

"Please have a drink if you feel like it," he added. "I don't."

No one moved.

Hewitt walked over to the window and looked out at the Park, hands in his pockets. "If the directors are smart," he said, "they'll see the best answer to what people may say, will be to fill Tom's place at once from the organization."

"They will see that, won't they?" Evans asked Curtis.

"I don't know. For so many years Edward not only dominated the Board but Tom and he represented us. I can't say, I don't think any of us can, that we *know* the directors. We're acquainted with them, yes, and that's about all."

"Let me ask how they took the news about Jim," Hewitt said.

"Well, Edward shut them up, really, took the whole onus of it. They were pretty horrified, naturally."

"It's funny, but do you know," Hewitt said, "Jim had only to wait for this? Do you see him at all, Steve?"

"I am seeing him tomorrow night," Lowry said, "first time in ten days or so."

"What's he doing?"

"He's credit manager of a small plant in the Bronx."

"They had an investigating agency call Tom about him the other day," Curtis said. "Wanted to know why he left of course."

"What did Tom tell 'em?" Hewitt asked.

"He didn't say. Well, I think we've said all we can. We'll just have to carry on. Sure you won't have a drink?"

"Thanks no," they all said.

On the sidewalk, however, Hewitt said he needed one. "We ought to talk this over together and make some plans. How about it?"

Evans agreed. Hardwick hesitated and looked at his watch. "Steve?" Hewitt asked.

"I don't think I will, thanks. It needs more thought."

"You taking a cab home?"

"Yes, can I drop you?"

"You might, at the University corner."

They called a cab, Hardwick saying he'd catch the East side subway to Grand Central. In the cab Hewitt said, "The thing is this, Steve, it should be one of us. If we can agree among ourselves on the setup and put it up in determined fashion, the Board will snap at it. You can be sure that holding the organization together will be their prime thought. I'm fortunately in a position to be of help to us all, as I want to be. Come on in and have a drink. Let's explore it."

Lowry again declined, his main reason being that he was not ready to be a triumvirate with Hewitt and Evans. It was foolish to suppose he himself had a chance for the succession and unlikely that they would support him if he did—and he did not feel that either of them was a choice he would support.

"Perhaps just as well he didn't come in," Hewitt said when their drinks were served. "I don't think he could contribute anything and he's got a mark against him now. Incidentally you've probably heard about the Suydam money—"

"I have indeed. It's staggering. I'm very happy for you," Evans said.

"Thanks. Of course it has its advantages. I didn't want to refer to it even indirectly with Charley just now, because I certainly am not going to be arbitrary in using it. But Les, I want to ask you something. Tell me if I'm wrong. I find a certain coldness, an air of superiority about Steve I don't wholly like. Does it strike you that, after all, his treatment of Jim was a pretty coldblooded business? I haven't heard that he made any effort to save him. He certainly didn't come to me. Did he to you?"

"No, no, he didn't," Evans said.

"Straight to Rutledge. Now mind you, Les, I'm not saying that was wrong. I'm not saying Steve hasn't got a conscience. But, I don't know, maybe it's all this foreign service; but take today, wouldn't come in, didn't want to talk to you and me. You know these lone wolves who don't like to be on the team can make a lot of trouble. Of course I may be doing him a big injustice. I sometimes get the feeling his heart's not in his job."

"Why do you say that?" Evans asked.

"He wants to write a book. He told Paula. Well, Les, I wanted you to know how my mind was running and I wanted you to know that if it comes to heavily increasing my holdings, I'm thinking of you. I'm only sorry that Steve feels he doesn't want to be with us, but maybe it's all for the best. Sometimes takes a long time to know a man."

Rosalie heard the news about Johnson with sorrow. "His poor wife," she said, "she's been so afraid something would happen. It's all turning out so differently from what we expected. Everything was going to be smooth and happy—and it hasn't been. And it all comes from outside. It's almost as though we were being shown that people can't live as we planned to—our own lives, with love and happiness."

"I know," Lowry said, "and there's also the question of ambition—I wouldn't welcome Hewitt or Evans as a superior. And Hewitt at least is getting set to start a scramble for the top. I'd be no good at that—"

"But they'd never put him over you. There's nothing to him."

"Oh there's a great deal to him. It's what he's most interested in. He hasn't got you or Principal Errors. He can't be expected to feel as I do about Jim."

"You're seeing Jim Friday night?"

He nodded.

"You won't let anything interfere with the weekend at the house or meeting the children? Because you mustn't."

At six-thirty Friday night Peale met Lowry at the Plaza. He appeared very tired and depressed but his clothes looked well as always and his shoes were polished. They had a table by the window. He declined a cocktail and a cigarette and asked for some scotch and water.

"Laundry's so damn expensive," he said. "I've given up smoking."

"How are things going?" Lowry asked. "You look better."

He smiled grimly. "I set myself to take whatever happened. I am trying to. I don't know that I can keep it up," and he outlined the blackmail Cronkhite had extorted as the price of the job. "The work is nothing. As a matter of fact, I'm invaluable to them but the humiliation is relentless. I sometimes think I'm being provoked to have a fistfight with Cronkhite. But I don't know where I could get another job. I suppose I could go away somewhere but if I'm a stranger there might be more questions. I must say I hope every night the mail will have something."

Lowry started to tell him about Johnson but stopped, feeling it was unnecessarily cruel. Every ordinary topic would seem a cruel reminder to Peale of his apartness: domestic happiness, personal plans, business situations, views of men or events or books—above all, references to the happy past were like the classic mention of hope in the house of a man who had been hanged. Worst of all was the fact that Lowry felt a pharisaism in himself that he was unable, in spite of his lighthearted nature, to clear the air and make it possible for Peale to be his old self.

"What do you do with your evenings?" he asked.

"Work, most of them, or walk or look at the river from Riverside Drive. Only one person I knew has tried to see me. Are you in your new house?"

"We expect to be this weekend," Lowry replied, thinking how wounding everything he said must be.

Peale studied the menu, declined anything for a first course and ordered some fish.

"Sure you won't have anything else?" Lowry asked.

"The fish seems to be the most inexpensive. I mustn't indulge myself after a diet of spaghetti and meat sauce."

Lowry had the feeling that he should deprecate or even protest the renunciation and the martyrdom as excessive, even morbid, but he said nothing, not knowing what he would do in such circumstances and aware that the weak and frightened invent strange patterns for their comfort.

He ordered strawberries and cream for them both without consulting Peale and then over their coffee he handed Peale the envelope with Dolly's letter and check. His face flushed as he read it. "Before you say anything," Lowry told him, "I want to say that disirregardless, as someone has well put it, of anything else, I see no reason why you should not accept it. Dolly's a grown man and a free agent."

"But he doesn't owe it to me."

"He has not been conspicuous in his life for generosity or kindness. Let him indulge in it for once."

"But I wouldn't know what to do with it. Give it to Rutledge, turn it over to the lawyer to prorate. After what I've been through I don't want to be accused of preferring creditors."

"Well you haven't gone through bankruptcy, so I don't think that arises. What would you like to do with it?"

Peale stared out the window at the horse-drawn victorias waiting across the street. "I will have a cigarette, if I may," he said, took it and lit it without turning his head.

"If it doesn't go for tax arrears, have I committed a felony?"

"I don't think so. I can find out."

"You sound as though you had some idea, what is it?" Peale asked.

"No, I haven't. I'd like to see you use it in a way that would give you the greatest sense of relief."

"Stephen, I implied to you, I guess I told you, that you had the whole story. I held something back."

"We all do that, don't feel too badly. Don't tell me now if you don't want to."

"I kept it back because—"

"Listen, you kept it back because you couldn't stand any more at the time. Now time has passed, you've recovered a good deal and you can face it."

"Do you actually think I've recovered any?"

"Of course I do. You really do look better."

"It isn't much of a recovery to accept money from Dolly. Could we walk over to the Park and find a bench? I'm more at ease on park benches."

Lowry paid the check and they crossed the street and walked until they found an empty place.

"This is much harder to tell than it would have been that first Sunday. I'm ashamed of it now. Well, here it is briefly. In talks with Daran he brought up the bull market. He said that besides the Lottery he was doing well but he'd like a hedge in the U.S. I let him understand I was doing well in the market. He asked me to take five-thousand and invest it for him and let him know in a year how he stood. If it was lost, that was life. At the time I intended to invest it, or I think I did. Maybe I always intended to keep it. I'm not sure but what, actually, I suggested his doing it. I paid somebody with it. Can I send Dolly's money to Daran?"

And that wonderful little man never mentioned it, Lowry thought to himself.

Peale was still talking. "I know it's no solution to anything but, Stephen, if I could just get one thing checked off."

"Go ahead," Lowry said, "check it off."

"He made no mention of it to you?"

"None."

Peale sat in silence for a moment. Then he suddenly asked for another cigarette and Lowry wondered what was still to come. Peale took the cigarette and then handed it back.

"Big gesture," he said.

"You wanted to say something?"

"No, that's all. Thanks for dinner. I'll walk home through the Park. They sometimes knock you on the head in the lonely paths. Goodnight."

Lowry gave him a pat on the shoulder and said goodnight.

18

AFTER THE WEEKEND OF HIS RETURN, THE RELAtions between Rosalie and Stephen had been so normal that her anxiety and distress over Peale's story had considerably abated. And it was impossible for her to feel rancor toward someone brought down to the dust as he now was. Of course the new house and the children's imminent arrival helped. The thought of really settling somewhere for a long time, of having neighbors as friends—a new experience for them (in Europe their "friends" had been made largely from officialdom; thus far in New York from companydom)—was a great comfort. No one connected with the company or its customers lived in Ridingtown, though Stephen had found both men and women he had known and liked in school or college.

She came back to Gramercy Park pleasantly tired and excited after Friday in the new house. She had engaged two maids and Stephen had ordered a new car and a secondhand station wagon from the Ridingtown dealer. By Tuesday, the eve of the children's arrival, Stephen and she would dine from their own china, with their own silver and sleep in their own broad bed, like prosperous peasants attached to the land.

Stephen had gone directly from the office to meet Peale. Hearing his key in the door when he returned from dinner, she hurried as always to greet him and poured out half her happiness as he kissed her.

Then she asked, "What about Dolly's check? Would he take it?"

"I'll tell you all about it in a moment, first though—" and he asked about utilities being turned on, moving-van arrivals and final alterations at the house. Satisfied, he said, "He took the check. He's an extraordinary fellow. Even now I don't know whether he told me the whole story."

"About what?"

"Well, it seems that he told Daran—what's the matter?"

"Nothing. Someone walked over my grave, I suppose."

"No, really, what's the matter?"

"Stephen, nothing. Go on."

"He told Daran about his profitable market operations and Daran gave him five thousand dollars to speculate with for his account. Jim just used the money to pay someone else. He's going to use Dolly's check to pay Daran."

"What else did he say?"

"In a way that was all, except about these people he works for, but it did seem to me, just as we were separating, he wanted to say something else and couldn't. I didn't press him. I do think he's really trying for rehabilitation—big word."

"So you think next time there'll be more?"

"I rather think so."

"So do I," she said slowly, "and I know what it will be. I dreaded your hearing it. I wanted to spare you—and now I am going to tell you."

"Why darling, what is all this?"

"I'm going to tell you for the same reason he will—because you're stronger than we are and will know what to do. It's not about anything that's happened between him and me. Is that a relief?"

"Yes, though I didn't suppose it was."

"I know I'm a weakling to unburden it on you."

"Oh nonsense, what's a healthy husband for? Just tell it."

"It's about Tallinn that June."

"Oh."

"Jim told me that he had told Daran—this is so horrible—that he knew an Estonian girl, married to an important American, who had let her husband understand the opposite of what was true. That actually she had been the acquiescent mistress of the Russian commander. He told me two days before you came home. I was in terror that Daran had told it. I really never suffered as I did that first weekend you were back, because I thought Daran had told it and that you might believe it, you were so aloof."

"Oh, you poor angel," he said, putting his arms around her.

"It's better that you know, isn't it? Now if Jim wants to confess, you won't have to listen. I was afraid if he told you you might have a fight. Dreadful things were in my mind. I was afraid you might kill him. You will forgive him and forget it, won't you? Please do."

"I'm thinking of that wonderful little man, Daran. I can remember the moment at dinner with Armas when he must have decided not to tell it when he was asking questions about men and women," he said slowly. What a mercy he had not told it and that Peale, in some agony of remorse, had not. "You're all right?" he asked her gently.

"Yes, if you are, I am."

"Then let's forgot it. It was faraway and long ago. I am not one who can brood."

"My dearest, I hope I am with you, I suppose I will be, on the Day of Judgment."

"Why particularly, though it would be awfully cosmic without you?"

"To hear you politely advise the Omnipotent not to take it too seriously."

They were at breakfast the next morning when Mrs. Johnson telephoned to ask if he could come to see her at ten. She received him looking haggard and drawn but in noble command of herself. The terrible hush of tragedy filled the beautiful rooms of the apartment.

"Tom wishes that he might see you," she said. "There is so much he wants to tell you, and a great favor he has to ask you. I am to ask it for him. I hope you can grant it."

"Of course, whatever it is," Lowry said.

"You will understand that the Foundation's future worries him terribly. He isn't worried about the Company. There are all of you to look out for it, but the Foundation needed more time, more money, more surety of which way it should go. What I am to ask you is, will you take the post of treasurer at once and become one of the trustees. I'll still be one for a little while. The others are Henry Dennison, whom you know, and Benoni Bailey, professor of sociology at Yale. Tom had all but persuaded Walter Caithness, with all his money, to come on. He's sure that you'll be able to."

"This is a very great honor," Lowry said. "I'm quite overcome, but there must be many better suited."

She gave him a wintry smile. "But you will say yes? It's so essential—Henry Dennison is in his mid-sixties, Walter and Professor Bailey are sixty. We need you. May I tell Tom it's settled?"

"I only hesitate because I know so little about it. You're sure it wouldn't be better for you both to look around a little more?"

"We're quite sure. You must, however, realize that it will eat into your leisure."

"There's also the question of my being out of the country at times," Lowry said, thinking also of Principal Errors and the lien they had on his leisure.

"We've thought of that. It won't matter. There's a paid staff of three who are very competent."

"Well," he said, "I'll do it and I'll do my best."

"Oh, thank you so much. I'm going at once to the Medical Center to see Tom."

"It's Saturday, but do you suppose I could go down to the Foundation office and go through some files, so I can be thinking about it over the weekend?"

"Yes. Here, call Mr. Draper, the administrator. He lives just across the street from the office and he can meet you there." She smiled again. "Tom told me to put him on notice you might want to see him today."

Lowry telephoned to him and to Rosalie, telling her that he could not go to Ridingtown until after lunch.

"I'd better go out right away," she said. "You can phone me which train you'll take out and I'll meet you. Is it something bad?"

"Oh no," he said. "I'll tell you later."

She was waiting on the almost empty platform for the 3.37 and as he walked toward her, she made in miniature the gesture of putting out her arms to him.

"Oh darling," she said. "I feel so wonderfully American and suburban and housewifely. It's divine. And to pay for part of it I'm going in to my English class one whole day a week. Paula will be away and I can use their apartment. Your classmate, Kenneth Hopkins, or his wife rather, called to ask us to cocktails—Beach and Country Club governors and school trustees to be there—and the whole Classified Directory wants our business. What about the business that kept you in town?"

He told her in detail. "I can't tell yet how much time it's going to take. I did keep thinking about Principal Errors, but I couldn't say no, of course. Their confidence in me was very touching and I realize that I haven't been very conspicuous about 'public service.'"

"But you have."

"No, not in the sense of doing something for nothing for people I never heard of."

Cocktails at the Hopkinses' were pleasant and the drive home about a quarter of eight was past settings of peace and amenity —pleasant houses set in well-kept shrubbery, with green lawns that cost small fortunes to maintain in the dry sandy soil, cars passing with handsome men and women in evening clothes on their way to dinner parties. While it was all a simulacrum of country gentry, there was an atmosphere of neighborliness and common interests.

"I had a lovely time," Rosalie said to Lowry, repeating what she had told her hostess. "Everyone was agreeable, but there is so much planning and organization about it all."

"There has to be to keep a place like this at all country when it's so near New York."

"I know, but sometimes I did feel as though I were in a dog-show with all the governors and trustees judging my points—and their wives asking us to 'show' at dinner. I suppose it's to be expected, but really the curiosity of people because I'm Estonian is amazing, though one woman put me at my ease by saying they used to have a splendid Estonian man and wife 'who did absolutely everything around the house, including the laundry.' But dear, even the women there this afternoon who knew Paris as well as we do were dying to know what really happens inside the doors of French *maisons*. I thought they meant *maisons tolérées* and said they'd all been closed since the war. Much confusion."

They were alone all Sunday unpacking and settling, hanging pictures, putting books away, moving furniture, one of the happiest days of their lives, feeling it was to have whatever permanence mortal man and woman and their children could achieve. Nothing marred it, no sorrows of their own or others.

"I love you in shorts and shirt, you look so *b e e g* and strong and brown," Rosalie said admiringly as Stephen, outdoing himself, broke up barrels and packing cases with his hands or carried them like a Sudanese bearer to the cellar for later firewood.

"I'm not in bad shape," he agreed modestly, "and as I have often said, you always look very well in slacks. But I've never understood why women like to get into them so much."

"Really, you amaze me after all the years of watching me dress. Don't you realize they involve two less garments? No garter belt, no slip. Stephen, I have a big money-making idea," she said, straightening up from a packing case of European pictures of places and people. "We don't want to keep all of these pictures. Why can't we make up nice selections and sell them to the less fortunate, who don't enjoy our extensive connections with European potentates? There's two of Charlie de Gaulle autographed, five of you with the Prefect of Lyons—won't one do? Three views of you with the whole Turkish government looking at Atatürk's statue. I don't suppose this one of Nous, Roi d'Egypte will bring much. Here's you outside a housing development at Padova. I can't seem to find Lollobrigida in the crowd, but we could say she's there. Who's this with you in Morocco, Allah Akbar in person?"

"Let me see. That is Bou Aziz. All his sheep had the mange. Keep that one. He was a very nice fellow. Wanted to come to America."

"Why is Franco smiling so in this one? Had someone just shot a nesting ortolan at three paces?"

"As it happens not, he was admiring the famous General Motor two and a half ton, six by six. It was just before I told him I drove one for the Loyalists."

"Oh here's the big money, the Balenciaga opening, reading from left to right, the Duchesse de Saint-Simon, Elsa Maxwell, Mrs. Stephen Lowry and other reigning beauties and notables, including that maharani you were after."

"I never was after any maharani."

"Well, it may have been me then."

"Please."

"Dear, I meant that you were after. Do we want this set of Mommsen? It's not our period. We could send it to the Alsop brothers."

"They have a set. I need it for reference."

"Then my little bookworm shall have it and his mummy will cut the pages for him, as soon as he gets her a drink and gives her a big kiss. I'm having such fun."

By Monday morning the office knew of the grave illness of Mr. Johnson and, though they did not yet know he would never return, speculation as to his successor was in the air.

Lowry, sure that he would not be chosen, thought it equally unlikely that any of his immediate colleagues would be. It was only reasonable to think the directors' selection would be a good one and that he could work effectively under whoever it was. He talked to Curtis about the resumption of his trip.

"Well I think you'd better not start off again, until we're more settled. Part of Jim's work will fall on you—and anyhow you ought to be here to make your own mark with the new president."

"Still no idea who it will be?"

"Not the slightest. Are you chafing to be off?"

"Far from it. Our children arrive Wednesday and I'd like to spend the summer in our new house."

"No reason why you shouldn't," Curtis said.

At nine Wednesday morning, the Lowry children, all in dark blue jerseys, the boys in gray shorts and Lainvee, the daughter, in a gray pleated skirt, were first down the gangway of the *Queen*, tumbling into their parents' arms; they had "almost seen" an iceberg; they had been on the bridge and steered; they had been polite; where and how was Smoky? Half the ship's company came to say goodbye and they had to visit most of the alphabet to say goodbye to their other friends.

"Dear, at least they're not sullen," Rosalie, slightly teary, said to their beaming father.

In the all but deep-country quiet of Ridingtown at night—with the children happy and healthy, wild with delight over new friends and scenes, advanced swimming lessons, tennis lessons, sailing lessons, vain at the awe they created at beach and country club jabbering French or Italian at each other; dinner on the terrace with them as waiters and waitress; lying on the grass with Rosalie looking at the starry heavens as they had on the road near Casal's house—the various fates of Rutledge and Johnson and Peale seemed far off and at times half forgotten. The sense of home-at-last was all pervasive and with it the feeling that all the peace and happiness would last forever and that neither they nor the children would ever grow older.

Lost like young lovers in each other, neither of them had heard the telephone ringing, when their eldest son's voice called from the terrace, "Dad, it's for you. It's Colonel Channing. I've had a nice talk with him. Goodnight Mum, goodnight Dad. I'm pretty sleepy now. It's ten o'clock. Oh boy!"

They hurried in together and Rosalie ran upstairs to see that all was well.

"Stephen," Colonel Channing said, "I have been out to dinner and found a note here to call my brother. I thought you'd want to hear right away what he had to say. I hope I'm not disturbing you."

"No, no, we were star-gazing."

"There was a special directors' meeting of your people late this afternoon. D. P. Cramer was chosen to succeed Tom. My brother says they were all taken aback afterwards at the speed with which they voted. It shows what one determined man can do. William Adams Delano, of all people, got the idea and rammed it down their throats. What do you think of it?"

"Well I hardly know," Lowry said, himself amazed. "He's all right, he's—it doesn't seem possible though. I should have thought he was—"

"Oh I know, to me he's a good accountant and beyond that a nobody. My brother thinks that Cramer proposed himself to Delano and that all the moral platitudes Delano gave out were supplied by Cramer."

"Had this been in the air?"

"I don't think so. How do you stand with him, Cramer that is?"

"Well I think all right, though I've only met him twice."

"As soon as they voted, Delano brought him in and he made quite an impression on them—very high moral tone."

"When does he start?"

"Monday morning. That's why I called you."

"Do the others know? Hewitt and Evans, I mean."

"They'll probably hear. Charley Curtis of course knows."

"Was Rutledge at the meeting?"

"Oh no. Well, you've got the weekend to get adjusted."

"Yes, many thanks. Goodnight."

19

MONDAY MORNING HAROLD TITCOMB ARRIVED AT the office at eight o'clock as usual. The early shift of his mailroom was already at work. As he entered, his assistant looked up, and then came quickly toward him, making motions to say nothing and do nothing.

"What's up?" Titcomb asked, as Lever took him by the arm and drew him to the door.

"I got here at seven-thirty. I heard voices in old man Rutledge's room and I looked in. Two guys and a dame I never seen are in there yak-yaking, furniture all changed. Go ahead, 'make the connection.' "

"Who did they say they were?" Titcomb asked.

"I didn't stay. I beat it back here. Ten minutes ago the young one was here asking me if I was Titcomb. I told him no. He says where are you. I say on the way in. He's got your name on a paper and he counts how many boys we got sorting and he goes back. I swear to God he leaves me like dumb-foundered."

Titcomb was like dumb-foundered himself, though he did not admit it to Lever.

"Just go ahead with the work. I'll find out," he said and walked, very quietly, to the open door of Mr. Rutledge's former office. What he saw, without being seen, appalled him. He felt sure the senior officers like Hewitt and Lowry and Evans would be as shocked as he was. They couldn't have known of this or they would have warned him. So that in loyalty he ought to warn them. He knew the night-wire desks as well as he knew his own street address, hurried to the most remote one and dialed Hewitt's number. A maid said he had been in the country for the weekend and would go straight to the office from there. Mrs. Lowry said Mr. Lowry had already left for his train.

"He's making his usual eight-thirty-six, Mrs. Lowry?" he asked.

"No, he got the eight-one. He ought to be in the office a little before nine. Is anything the matter?"

"Oh no, nothing. Just wanted to speak to him," Titcomb said assuringly and went back to the mailroom. Lever came over to the door and Titcomb said, "I recognize the older one. He's that D. P. Cramer—been in here a lot. I imagine he's just using the office for a few days, or it may be an audit. I'm going down for coffee, be up around nine."

"I never known you to take coffee at this hour," Lever said.

Titcomb tried to smile and make a joke, but he could think of none. He could only remember a phrase he had read in a book, "An era had ended," and he didn't want to believe it was true.

Elevator traffic was still light and the starter was positive none of the C.I.C. officers had gone up while car Number Seven with Titcomb was coming down.

For half an hour he did sentry duty by the elevators and at 8.50 to his infinite relief, Lowry turned the corner and saw him.

Titcomb drew him quickly aside. "I've been watching for you. The place has been torn apart. That Mr. Cramer who used to come in—you remember New Year's Eve—he's in Mr. Rutledge's office with a secretary and somebody else. All his furniture was moved in over the weekend, the starter told me, the three of them were there all Saturday, Sunday. My God, Mr. Lowry, what's happened? They could at least have told me. Mr. Rutledge or Mr. Johnson wouldn't do such a thing without letting me know. I've been one of the first to know of any move for over forty-five years. They always consulted me. I didn't want you or Mr. Hewitt to walk in on it like I did."

"That's awfully nice of you, Harold–"

"You didn't know, did you?" Titcomb asked in a shaken voice.

"I got a phone call quite late Friday night that Mr. Cramer had been elected president and would be in today but I had no idea of this weekend move. We'd better go up."

"Maybe I was wrong in getting so upset about this," Titcomb said in the elevator. "Lever did say the other fellow with Mr. Cramer was out asking for me around eight. Maybe I should have gone in right off."

"Oh well," Lowry said cheerily, "it doesn't make any difference. Mr. Cramer is a very nice man, you'll like him."

"I don't know. I just don't feel that way about it. Of course, I've always had Mr. Rutledge or Mr. Johnson to go to and I guess I relied on them too much."

"Well, they relied on you–we all do. Mr. Cramer will too."

The staff had begun to reach their desks and to start the day's work. It seemed to Lowry as he passed them that they were all consciously trying not to look toward Rutledge's door. He paused there and Cramer, looking up, called, "Oh, glad to see you, Mr. Lowry. Come right in, both doors will always be open to the whole organization. You–you do know what's happened?" Cramer glanced at his wrist watch as he said it.

"Oh yes, I wish you all sorts of luck and–"

"This is my secretary and girl-Friday, Jane Wilkins," Cramer said. A severe-looking woman of fifty said good morning. "You had a quick trip abroad, didn't you? I'll want to hear about it later. Oh–John, come in. Mr. Lowry, this is my son John, who's coming to act as my personal assistant. Just back from his two years in Korea. Graduate of the Wharton School. John just check again on whether that old fellow in the mailroom's in while I talk to Mr. Lowry."

"Right, Dad," young Cramer said, giving his hand to Lowry and taking it away in one movement.

"Titcomb's in, he came up with me. He's always in at eight, and was this morning. I had asked him to do something for me."

"Leave it, John. That explains it satisfactorily."

"Right, Dad."

My God, Lowry thought, is this "Right, Dad" going to be standard procedure?

The elder Cramer, smiling benignly, said he had only had in mind catching any slackness that the interregnum might have let creep in. "You can be sure I'm here to learn from you all. Till yet I know very little of the whole picture." *Till yet,* Lowry wondered. "Any fear on the part of anyone in the organization that I'm here to interfere or make changes should be very and most definitely nipped in the bud. And I hope you'll spread that around. Now don't let me keep you."

"There was one thing you wanted to ask Mr. Lowry, Dad," John Cramer said.

"And that was?" Cramer asked indulgently.

"You wanted to know how long the Venezuelan manager would be in Paris on personal business."

"Yes, you're right. Can you tell me, Mr. Lowry?"

"I should say he would return in a few days, probably this week," Lowry said. "Originally I had thought I'd be back in Paris in a few days."

"I see, and then this ugly business detained you?"

"Well yes."

"You can give me the details later, but perhaps, John, you'll make a note to remind Mr. Lowry to have Mr. Doran return via New York."

"I'll do so," Lowry said.

The father waved his son away with paternal pride. "Fine boy, isn't he, Mr. Lowry? He's got the sort of qualities I lack. He's Phi Beta Kappa, by the way, the honor society. I don't know how many Phi Betes, as they call them, we have in this office."

"There are several, Mr. Curtis and Evans both among them."

"You weren't so fortunate?"

"Yes, I happened to be," Lowry said.

"Oh well, that's splendid. John and you will be working very closely and being so close will make it all the better. Of course there's a great difference between the generation that's been in Korea and yours in that other war. I think in it men used to feel that if you just came out alive, that's all you wanted. Isn't that so?"

"To a large degree, yes."

"You see these younger men are keen about business. Feel absolutely free to call on John and use him whenever you want to. Don't let what he's doing for me interfere. Want to make a note to cable Doran?" He pushed a pad and his own pencil forward.

"I'll remember; his name is Daran, not Doran, by the way."

"Thank you," Cramer said.

Lowry left the office and, passing young Cramer's and Miss Wilkins's desks in the anteroom, was staggered by the amount of papers they had already managed to assemble. Correspondence folders were high on both desks and a drawing board with graph paper on Cramer's as well. An electric typewriter swung from a bracket on the side. As Lowry passed, Cramer did a lightning calculation with a slide rule and entered the result on the graph.

Hewitt, somewhat breathless, eyebrows lifted questioningly, met him outside the door.

"True?" he asked.

"Yep," Lowry said, "Have fun. I forgot to pledge my support. Make a note to do it."

That day and the two following Cramer and his son and his secretary behaved very much like a close-knit family of three who had just moved into a large apartment house occupied by tenants of long standing. They spoke to their neighbors in a friendly way but kept very much to themselves. The feverish industry of young Cramer and Miss Wilkins continued, as files were returned and new ones taken away. Cramer himself occasionally emerged and, as it were, spoke to the people in the next apartment smilingly, but his assistants were in and out with a somber air of detached consecration, as though they were wholly self-contained and had no contact with the outer world. The office staff, largely without guidance except for the article in the financial section of the *New York Times* and a multigraphed pronouncement from D. P. Cramer beginning "Today I assume the heavy responsibilities . . . and bespeak the help and good will of all of you," went ahead with their work, and gave Lowry the impression of Don't-look-now. The headquarters staff arrived early and worked late and the more worried of the office workers began to lengthen their own hours. It was very difficult to break at 4.55, when through Cramer's now always open door they could see the three within just settling back to new self-assignments.

With Curtis, Hewitt, Evans and Lowry, Cramer's attitude was of smiling, almost embarrassed detachment and confidence. He questioned nothing, and showed no desire to interfere or even participate in the day's work.

He was like the congressman who had made the long trip to France in '45 to assure the officers and men of Lowry's outfit, "You boys are doing fine."

"Of course you realize," Hewitt said to Lowry on the morning of the third day, "this won't last. This fellow will be into everything and that son of his will stop being so goddamn deferential. I wish Cramer would stop referring to himself as 'a worker in the vineyard.' "

"I judge he is a man of deep religious conviction. He describes our Export Department as doing business in great waters. He also observed that 'a man is right in his own case, but his brother cometh and judgeth the matter.' I took it Jim was the man and I was the brother."

"Did he mention this god-awful dinner he's giving? Us and our wives?"

"Oh no, not really?"

"Yep, tomorrow night. Command performance. I don't want to rub it in, Steve, but I think all this might have been prevented if you'd felt you could spend a little time to make some plans with me after we left Charley Curtis the other night. However, don't think for a moment I hold it against you or that I'm dropping them."

Later in the morning Cramer came to Lowry's office to tell him about dinner. Mrs. Cramer, he was sorry to say, had "not yet come on from the West," but he wanted to "get the family together" right away. He seemed as cheery about it as a Lord Bountiful. Dinner would be at six-thirty at his hotel. Just Miss Wilkins, his son, and the four of them and their wives—a simple dinner "that won't keep us late."

So indeed it turned out. A line on the bulletin board in the lobby of his hotel read, "Mr. Cramer's dinner, room 1013, 6.30 P.M." They went up to find Miss Wilkins presiding over a tray of tomato juice, which Hewitt supposed at first glance must be Bloody Marys. The son had a fine salver of canapés. It was all very folksy, husbands and wives next to each other on either side of the beaming Cramer. "Large coffee with" the three-course dinner and an abundance of hard-shelled rolls. Jellied tomato soup—"He's nuts on tomatoes," Evans whispered to Lowry across Rosalie—roast beef with baked Idaho potato, broccoli and a fine blueberry pie for all. Fresh hot coffee with it.

"How do you as a Frenchwoman like American cooking, Mrs. Lowry?" Cramer asked.

"Exquisite," Rosalie said. "But I'm not French."

"Be that as it may, I don't think we'd use the word exquisite about cooking. It's wholesome and substantial."

"Oh very."

"For example, there's about eleven ounces of prime steer in each portion of that roast beef. I understand you eat a good many frogs' legs in France and of course they are abundant in this country too. The finest I've ever tasted were in Chattanooga. They were served with a side dish of creamed asparagus. Cole slaw went with it. And you, Mrs. Hewitt, are frogs' legs your favorite also?"

"No," Paula said judiciously with a side leer at Rosalie. "I like ham and eggs with red-eye gravy."

"That must be good," Rosalie said.

"Yes, it's a dish that Arkansas is famous for and *there's* something that *is* practically exquisite, Mrs. Lowry, as you said."

"And substantial."

"Yes, you're right. Another delicacy I'm very fond of is Lake Superior whitefish."

Lowry nudged Rosalie with his knee and shook his head at her with a slight frown. She was not sure what he meant, but made no comment on the whitefish as Cramer asked Mrs. Curtis who her favorite columnist was. He said that his was David Lawrence. He felt there was vision there and Miss Wilkins was always good enough to clip it out and have it on his desk when he came in. He went on to say that he put a high value on members of the family getting together in an informal homelike atmosphere and had made a point of it wherever he was. This was the first of such dinners which would gradually be extended to all the staff heads.

His men guests listened to him mainly in silence, so that Lowry could not help feeling a little sorry for him. He was plainly making an effort to impress them with something, but he was also trying to please. He told his women guests, looking from one to the other, that his one goal was to be helpful. "I'm not a taskmaster in any sense of the word," he said.

At that Curtis unbent a trifle to say how pleasant working with him was.

Cramer looked around the table and told the waiter to give Mr. Lowry more coffee. "I remember that extra first cup you wanted in Larus." Then, startling them all, he said in his low confidential tone, "Tell me, we're all together here, what is your explanation of Mr. Peale's conduct? You all know him better than I. Mr. Lowry, you knew him best, you were very old friends, I'm told."

Nonplussed by the question, Lowry finally shrugged.

Cramer turned to Curtis. "Looking back, friend Curtis, do we now see anything which should warn us in the future?"

"I don't believe anything like that will occur again."

"Isn't a fact that before it happened you would have been just as sure this wouldn't happen?"

Curtis's normally pale face reddened and he lit a cigarette without replying.

"The reason I mention it now," Cramer said, "is because I

have great faith in woman's intuition, and I want to ask you ladies if any of you, and you all saw a good deal of him, had any intuitive warning. Mrs. Lowry, let me ask you?"

As she hesitated, Paula Hewitt said, "Let me say this, Mr. Cramer, none of us had an intuitive warning. Jim Peale is a friend. He was a brilliant, complex individual. He still is. I don't think any of us want to talk about him. Do you mind terribly?"

Lowry felt ashamed that he had not said something of the sort as Cramer replied, "Certainly not, Mrs. Hewitt. I merely sought guidance."

Mrs. Curtis murmured something about the lateness of the hour—it was all of eight-forty—and Cramer pushed back his chair, telling them what a good time they had had. They left in a body, leaving the hosts, so the latter intimated, to settle down to a solid evening of work after a duty well done.

"Nothing less than the 21 after that," Paula said in the crowded elevator. "I need a lot of red-eyed brandy poured down my throat. Calvin and I will go ahead and have jeroboams of it waiting. What a dreadful person."

The Curtises got in the cab with them, and as the other four waited, Evans said to Lowry, "What in hell can the directors be thinking of? They must know this fellow. What's the explanation, Steve?"

"I don't know. I suppose he has ability and that underneath he's sincere. It may even have been well meant."

"Oh stop being cheerful," Rosalie told him. "I can't stand it. That son and that Wilkins woman and worst of all him. When's his wife 'coming on from the West'?"

At the 21 the Hewitts and Curtises were seated with empty chairs between them, to separate the lovebirds, as Paula cheerily announced.

"I'm not taking this lying down," Hewitt said as they settled back. "I'm not referring to his question about Jim, but the fact that a man like that's been put in over us. I'm going to Delano in the morning and demand an explanation. I don't have to take it and I won't."

"That's the sort of direct action my late great-aunt always

believed in. She would have sent for Delano and you can hardly do that, Calvin, can you?"

"I'll damn well see him," he said, glaring at her.

"What are you going to do, Stephen?" Paula asked him.

"I don't think it's any good doing anything until we see Cramer in action. We can't very well go to Delano and say, 'This fellow gives you a damn commonplace meal when he has you to dinner and asks questions in rather poor taste,' which is about all we have specifically to complain of."

"I think you're right," Curtis said. "We'll know more when he stops sending for files."

"In his way," Lowry went on, "he even seems to be trying to make people like him. He may turn out to be quite effective."

"I don't question his being effective," Hewitt said. "It's the spectacle of our ineffectiveness I'm talking about."

"Oh, let's give him a chance," Lowry said.

"He needs a chance like a tiger needs claws," Hewitt replied.

Curtis moodily agreed with Lowry, and his wife, glancing at her wrist, rose, saying, "Heavens it's long past nine o'clock! You must all come and have a nice baked potato with us some night."

"I'm going to have another drink, Paula. Sit down." But Paula also rose and picked up her evening bag. "Well, do you mind if I don't gulp my drink?" Hewitt asked surlily. "I think I'll stop in the Hounds a minute. Delano might just be there and I could bring it up casually."

"No indeed. Do try. He's probably there with his boon companions. Lowry, where's your car? You can drop me," Paula said.

Curtis said he had ordered his car and they would take her, since the Lowrys had to go all the way to Long Island. They left Hewitt to brood briefly on the morrow before having a telephone brought to the table.

"Darling," Rosalie said, when they were alone, "you're always so charitable about people. Do you really think Cramer won't be too much to take?"

"I think he may be, but I didn't want to get into a cabal with Hewitt."

"I know, he's dreadful. Did he mean that about the Hounds?"

"Delano is a senior warden and is about as likely to be in the Hounds at this hour as Cramer is."

"Paula must know that."

"I'm sure she does. Between Cramer and Hewitt I prefer Cramer."

"I know, but it seems such a shame. And to think Mr. Rutledge's views on Europe annoyed me that first night. Do you suppose Jim knows about Cramer?"

"Probably, from the *Times*. I'm afraid he will have felt very badly."

She moved closer to him. "Dear, if it does turn out to be too unpleasant, you mustn't feel that because of me and the children–"

"My dear girl, I am well placed in a fundamental, well-managed industry. One or two difficult personalities are always to be expected. If I can't get along or compete with them, I'm no good anyway and wouldn't be any better in anything else. I have the additional good fortune to have you and not to be Jim Peale or Calvin Hewitt, so, everything is all right."

"You have me all right, but you have a new and expensive house and thousands of dollars in school bills ahead of you–"

"Nonsense, I enjoy them and I intend to enjoy what I'm doing. There's nothing coming–you might give me a kiss."

When the guests had left and the waiters cleared away, Miss Wilkins and John Cramer stood ready for their coming assignment. To their surprise, Cramer said he was tired and that he had a personal letter he must get off. Miss Wilkins sat down at the desk, pencil and dictation book ready.

"No," Cramer said, "thank you, Jane, but I am going to write it myself."

"Anything wrong, Dad?"

"No, everything's fine. We'll breakfast at seven-thirty."

"Some men will just do and do and do," Miss Wilkins said to John in a tone of proud sorrow as they went down the corridor to their rooms.

Cramer seated himself at the desk and squared a sheet of hotel paper before him.

Dear Mildred:

Well, the banquet hall's deserted and I have sent John and Miss Wilkins off to bed. It's been a hard day and I don't know just what to tell you about it, because I'm not sure how I feel about the dinner I just gave my principal officers and their wives.

I went to a good deal of pains in selecting the dinner and in having everything nice. Food-wise it was fine but either all New Yorkers are "stand-offish" or these particular ones aren't very wholehearted. I even got the feeling at times it wasn't appreciated.

Mrs. Curtis and Mrs. Evans seemed like nice women but Lowry's wife is French, I understand. Lowry himself had very little to say. John has heard it said that he's conceited. Hewitt is more of a regular fellow but his wife "snapped my head off" at one point while we were all discussing Peale. Jane has heard that Lowry plans to bring Peale back in the company. Needless to say I'll put the quietus on any such idea.

I freely admit I feel a little bothered and very lonesome for you tonight and wish you were here. Tomorrow I'm putting in new and stiff procedures. It's all a challenge and I know what I'm doing but I had counted on a little more friendliness. You would have thought Lowry would have wanted to give his new president his own account of the Peale business, but not a word. At dinner he shrugged it off when I opened the way for him.

Fortunately I have Mr. Delano's absolute trust and confidence and I know I have yours, and those are all I need.

Your affectionate husband,
D. P. Cramer

He addressed and stamped the envelope and walked out to drop it in the chute. A man and woman got out of the elevator as he did, the man with a key in his hand. Cramer could see, with half an eye, she was not the man's wife. It gave him an unpleasant start to realize something like that could happen in a hotel where he was staying and where Mrs. Cramer had stayed with him, and he went moodily back to turn in for the night.

20

THOUGH HE TOOK THE TRAIN A HALF-HOUR before his usual one, Lowry arrived at the office to find his secretary was also in. Along with the personal mail she gave him, with raised eyebrows, was an office memorandum asking that a carbon of all letters go to the president's assistant. She said Mr. Cramer would like to see him at nine-thirty. There were air mail letters from his brother-in-law and Daran.

Lainvee's said simply that he had seen Daran and given him the facts, and that Daran had accepted them with little comment but obvious sorrow. His manner had added to Lainvee's already favorable impression.

Daran wrote:

Mr. Lainvee has told me the story which, you may be sure, will be held in the strictest confidence by me, even from Beatriz. It has made me profoundly sad that this could happen to a man of such broad culture. I cannot think of him as having done it but rather as it having happened *to him, like being struck by lightning.*

Your cable asking me to return to Venezuela by New York was received and I shall duly inform you when that will be.

The operation has been a wonderful success. I feel if we

return to Venezuela, seventy-nine other Inclans will come to Paris, which will ruin Paris, if anything can.

I hope when I say I am wholly at your orders, you will understand it is only the truth.

He marked the letters for his personal file and looked through the business mail and cables. It had been some days since the principal officers could have been said to give close attention to the Company's affairs, and some weeks since it had had a directing head. Yet the effect of strong organization, the training and experience of the second rank was such that the great business rolled on of its own momentum.

As Lowry went through his outer office to see Cramer, his secretary hung up her telephone and stopped him. "That was Harold Titcomb," she said, "he's been let out. He wants to see you."

"What the hell," he said angrily. "Who did that?"

" 'President's assistant,' " she answered, making a face.

"Tell him I'll see him when I come back."

Since the day Jim Peale's personal things had been packed and removed from his office by Harold Titcomb, the room next to what was now Cramer's had been used by out-of-town visitors for very small meetings. As Lowry passed it he saw that John Cramer and a new secretary, obviously chosen by Miss Wilkins, had been ensconced there. It was a natural arrangement, convenient for the Cramers, and there was of course no reason why they should not have done it. Somehow he found it irritating. But why should he? Was the place to be kept empty as a grim reminder?

He went through the president's open door to find him all smiling affability.

"Well," he said, "I thought we had a very nice family time together last night."

"We did indeed," Lowry replied. "It was very nice of you to have us."

Cramer made a deprecatory gesture. "No more than I should

do. I wanted to talk to you and the others this morning about some organization matters. I shall of course be mainly concerned with the broad policies on reserves and dividends. The directors insist on that," he added with a shy smile after a brief pause. "That will mean I shall have to ration my time very carefully."

"Oh, I agree," Lowry said.

"Till yet I have always made it a point to give my own attention to details. One learns a great deal that way, but," with another gesture evidently intended to illustrate the weight of his responsibilities, "that is no longer possible."

Lowry nodded.

"Therefore I would like everything to come to me through my assistant, where it can be—"

"But—"

Cramer held up his hand with a father's indulgence. "I know what you're going to say, and you needn't say it. My door will still always be open to everyone. I'm sure, though, I'm going to have your wholehearted help in easing my burden. Isn't that right?"

"Naturally. I'm not sure, however, that I understand just what you intend to go to your son."

Cramer smiled. "In the company John is not my son. He is a functional assistant with a separate establishment. But to answer your question, in three words—the Day's Work."

"I'm afraid I'm stupid, but I don't know what that means. Are the officers to have a daily meeting with him?"

"Oh no, they are simply asked to keep him advised and to come to me through him with any problems."

"Well, as to the first, such figures as cumulative sales and shipments, collections and so on by countries with comparison to last month and last year go to you now from our department. So with other departments—financial, subsidiaries, branches. You contemplate something more than this?"

Cramer put the ends of his fingers together and looked over his glasses at Lowry. The time had come to speak firmly. "Let us assume for the moment I do, have you any objection?"

"I don't object to your having any figures or information

you want. I would object, if you don't mind my saying so, to what sounds like a form of direct supervision."

"Friend Lowry, have you ever heard it said that the man who resents supervision can never efficiently exercise it?"

"No. Has it been said?"

"Is that levity?"

"Not in the least. Well, shall we see how it goes as to the Day's Work and if you don't get what you require, we can talk again. There are two other matters I'd like to mention."

"Certainly. I'm here to help."

"No doubt you have heard it said that in management, no one should be given information he can't use. I don't believe you or your assistant can use the information in every letter I write. I imagine my associates will feel the same way. I suggest to you withdrawing this notice about carbons of all letters and that you leave it to your officers' judgment to send you a copy of anything you ought to know about."

"Now why should you resent a simple business request? There's nothing personal in it. I'm not inferring there are secrets in your letters. What possible objection can you have aside from some fancied injury? You surprise me. Aren't you given copies of the letters your subordinates write? If you aren't, then I *am* concerned about the way our foreign business is being run. We'll leave that, however, for a later date."

"I have neither heard nor spoken a word about this 'copies of all letters memo,' but I am sure my associates will object, as strongly as I do, on their own. But aside from all that, I doubt that your office has even considered the weight of papers they would receive or where they'd put it, let alone read it. This is rather a large office. I take it that like all major administrators you want your officers' advice. In this case mine is to withdraw the memo."

"You had two matters, you said. What is the other?"

"Yes, it's personal. I mention it and it may be I am misinformed. I heard as I came in that Harold Titcomb has been dismissed."

"That is very and most definitely the case."

"Well, like you, I'm rather a newcomer in the organization

but I understood very early that Titcomb, the oldest employee here and one of the most efficient, was to stay as long as he wanted to. If he is not leaving by mutual consent, I think it's a mistake and I believe it will be widely resented at all levels. Do you mind telling me what happened?

"Is the mailroom part of the Foreign Department?"

"No, but I'm a friend of the head of the mailroom," Lowry said with a smile.

"Titcomb has been let go because he's over age, inefficient—"

"No, he's not inefficient."

"Will you please not interrupt? He's been dismissed because I'm president of this organization and I hire and fire and I don't want him around any longer and I'll hear no more about it from you or anyone else. I wonder if that is clear?" His voice remained at its utterly unemotional level.

"Clear, yes, but not, I think, the sort of good judgment you're noted for. Is that all?"

"Well not quite, friend Lowry. You spoke just now of my being a newcomer like you. Of course that isn't so. My close, my very close relations with the Company go back many years, but I do appreciate how you feel. Your friend Peale is gone; Mr. Rutledge, who found you, is gone and now Mr. Johnson. You feel strange, not quite at home yet, uncertain, possibly resentful, with your first trip turning out badly. Now don't have any such feeling. We're all sure you're going to do very well."

"I wasn't aware of such feelings at all," Lowry replied.

"Well," Cramer said comfortingly, "sometimes it takes us a long time to know ourselves."

Hewitt was not in yet but Evans was waiting in Lowry's office with the carbon memo.

"What in hell—" he began.

"Mr. Lowry, you should be leaving for the Johnson Foundation meeting. I phoned you'd be a little late," Lowry's secretary said.

"Thanks, I'd forgotten."

"Before you go," Evans said. "I don't see why this damn memo isn't enough for Calvin to see Delano with. And today."

"Look, we can't go to see Delano on a detail like that. It would be absurd."

"Damn interfering, sanctimonious, little piker—"

"And it won't help to call him names."

"Do you mean to say you didn't protest?"

"I advised him to withdraw it. I've got to go."

The rest of the morning with two of his fellow trustees, Henry Dennison and Walter Caithness, whom he had persuaded to come on the Board, was a satisfactory one for Lowry. He was brought somewhat abruptly back to his own problems at the end of it when Caithness asked him how he liked the new boss. Dennison paused to listen to his reply.

"I'm interested too," he said. "Cramer was very effective on rescue work for the bank some years ago. He has an amazing grasp of figures."

"Well," Lowry said, "he has been there only a few days. He's been very nice, had us and our wives into dinner. He—" He was trying furiously to think of something in Cramer's favor. "He goes about things differently from Mr. Rutledge or Tom, of course."

"Was this story about Jim Peale as bad as it sounds?" Caithness asked.

"I don't know what you heard. It's a tragic thing. He was a great friend of mine."

"Forgive me, I didn't mean to pry. What's he doing?"

"He has a small credit job."

"Do you know Delano well?" Caithness asked.

"Hardly at all."

"Would you like me to get him to lunch some day?"

Lowry hesitated. "I'd like it very much," he said, "but I think I'd better not do it at this time."

"I know him very well of course," Caithness said. "He's responsible for Cramer. What I don't like is that he's telling too many people about Jim Peale and he talks about having put a watchdog in Tom Johnson's place. Well, I can see your point.

We'll leave it for the present, but don't hesitate to call me if you change your mind or need any help."

"That's very nice of you."

"I don't know how Henry feels, but I should think Cramer would drive you all crazy and I'll bet he does," Caithness said. "But I admit he's always gotten results."

On his return to the office his secretary said Mr. Evans and Mr. Hewitt would like to see him as soon as possible. He found them both in Hewitt's office, looking angry but dejected.

"We both talked to him separately about this goddamn memo —and got exactly nowhere. Now what are we going to do?" Hewitt asked. "And for God's sake don't be calm or broad-minded about it. I could throw the sanctimonious son of a bitch out the window. If you had come in the club when we left Charley Curtis the other night and we'd gone then, as I wanted to, to see Delano, Cramer wouldn't be here today. Are you going to send those carbons?"

"Well, if we do, a few days should make it clear even to him that it's impractical. If we don't, we're starting a row with him on a detail. Any directors would back him up—a new president's entitled to familiarize himself with operations in whatever way he thinks best."

"So you're just going to take it lying down," Evans said.

"He can always say," Lowry continued, "that it's simply a temporary expedient, and that he was quite amenable to suggestions."

"I won't do it. I don't have to and I won't," Hewitt said and walked out.

"My thought is that if we have to fight, there'll be better grounds than this," Lowry said to Evans.

In his own office, his secretary told him that the president's assistant had been in and asked where he was and on being told wanted to know how long he had been a Johnson trustee and how often meetings were held.

"I thought you ought to know," she said.

He took a long breath. "I suppose I should. But I don't want us to get in the frame of mind where we think there's something important or personal in everything that office says or does—"

"Then I shouldn't have told you?"

"It isn't that. I appreciate your telling me, but don't let yourself get worked up about it. Don't let the staff bring you stories and rumors. Things will settle down in a few days. Now about the carbons—" he sighed again, "send them in for the present."

"Just as you like," she said. He could see that she thought poorly of his attitude and that her feelings had been hurt by what she felt was a rebuke to her loyalty to him. And the probability was that in self-protection he would need to know all the stories and rumors she could tell him. Still, if that was the case, the whole thing was intolerable anyway. What Cramer had said about his feelings was absurd, but it made him wonder about something else. Had not all the sudden changes, the new rivalries, the injection of Cramer's trying personality made it much easier to forget the purgatory Jim was enduring and in which he was finding it easier and easier to justify leaving him alone?

He now, almost above all, wanted C.I.C. to be what Rutledge had said it was on New Year's Eve and in his welcoming speech at the luncheon. And the change seemed ominous. For the first time he felt that C.I.C. had some of the attributes of a Cause and to be something, more than dollars, sales, options, in which all the qualities of his character were involved.

About four-thirty Rosalie telephoned to say her class was just over and when could he leave.

"I'll be on the sidewalk here at ten after five," he said and looked up to see Cramer in his doorway. Involuntarily he hung up in mid-sentence.

"Can I have a moment, friend Lowry?" Cramer asked humbly.

"Certainly."

"Just two things in passing. I've got to go to meet Mr. Delano at your Hounds Club. I've been thinking, after talking to you and friends Evans and Hewitt, that since you all seem to feel so strongly about those carbons possibly I was wrong. I hope I'll always be big enough to admit when I am. In any event, I've rescinded the procedure, but I'd appreciate it if you and the others would make personally sure John gets carbons of anything he should have."

"We certainly will," Lowry said. "And if I seemed balky this morning I'm sorry."

"Not at all, not at all. I wanted to tell you as soon as I decided but you were out. I hadn't realized you were on the Johnson board until John told me. I want to say I'm very glad to hear it. I want to be sure all our men—even where it's small-town community chest or something like that—feel free to use company time or facilities on projects of civil or human betterment. Well, I mustn't keep Mr. Delano waiting." He blinked and beamed on Lowry, backing to the door, where he paused. "Feeling better about things now, friend Lowry? Your phone is ringing." And he left with a smile.

It was Rosalie and Lowry said, "I'm sorry. Cramer came in and I was—what's the matter?"

"Darling, I'm not at Paula's. I'm at the Relief building on Thirty-Fourth Street. Could you come there for me, please?"

"Yes, you're not ill? You sound as though you were crying. I've got to sign some mail."

"Just hurry. I'm all right. I'll wait."

He signed his mail, approved two cables which Halleck, a department manager, brought in and left. The sight and sound of the traffic on Fifth Avenue told him a fast walk to the Lexington Avenue Subway was the quickest route and he strode along in and out of the home-going office workers.

He found Rosalie sitting in their car parked near the Relief building. The fine new car and Rosalie in her pretty clothes were a contrast to the rundown street and the tired-looking, shabby people passing. He went around to the driver's side before he spoke to her, and looking at her, as he got in, he thought he had never seen her look so badly. The health of both of them had always been so abundant that sickness never occurred to them.

"My darling, what is it?"

"I'm sorry to be a baby, but I didn't feel able to drive," she said and burst into tears. "I don't know what to do. I suddenly feel afraid of everything, even of going home. Please take care of me."

"But I will. Is it some definite pain?"

"Oh definite—everything terrible isn't definite. I gave the lesson down here. It wasn't until it was over that one of them spoke of what day it is. Stephen, it's the anniversary of Tallinn and I hadn't even remembered. I'd let myself forget Father and Mother and Inge and I was happy and carefree."

"But dearie, there's been a fourteenth of June every year and you've been right and wise not to dwell on it."

"No, I haven't. These other people, these little people remember it and mourn for it and I have pretended it all happened to someone else. Maybe I was able to put it out of mind before, because we were in Europe and for tens of millions of people there were days like it. But here there are no such days except for refugees like me. When I work with these people here, burdened even with the problems of food and shelter, I feel like some rich horrible emigrée. I haven't the right to the house and our kind of life—"

"What do you think the children and I would do without you as you are?"

"As I am? You don't know how I am. I see now I should have made you listen in Norway or in London, instead of being beguiled into relief and then love with you."

"Darling, this is very foolish. You had forgotten it. I never think of it."

"But don't you see—"

They were entering the brief approach to the Midtown Tunnel, passing the planting of trees, sick and rickety-looking from the dust and fumes of the motor age. The exhaust and the air brakes of the bus ahead of them drowned her voice. "I can't hear you now," he said, and they sat without speaking until they passed the tollgate on the Long Island side.

"Now what is it?" he asked, sure he was right that the past should be left done.

"It was a *crise de nerfs*, I suppose," she said. "I can't begin again. You're very comforting, but sometimes you're a little inhuman."

"What's the package?" he asked.

"A bathing suit like mine for Lainvee. She wants us to be twins."

21

THE FLOOD OF ORDERS, FOREIGN AND DOMESTIC, with which the next week opened was like nothing that had been seen since the outbreak of the Korean War. All the world's dammed-up buying power seemed to be loose. It engulfed the president and the headquarters staff. No one had any time for them. In the rush which continued all week, even Titcomb stayed at his post unnoticed by them.

Few things in everyday life, except a change in the weather, are as tonic as an enormous and profitable buying wave. Dreams of avarice become reality for high and low. Otherwise anxious or miserly men go home to tell their wives "I'll make it, you spend it." A great rainbow of bonuses to come arches the sky. "A few more days of this and we'll have to enlarge the organization. We'll be weeks catching up as it is," Personnel says.

When Wednesday's record-breaking total was in, Curtis sent word to the other three that Cramer was in his office and would they come in for just a minute. Coats off, sleeves rolled up, Hewitt's tie askew, they appeared.

"I'll only keep you a minute," Cramer said. "In the face of this I've wired all our purchasing agents to meet me in Chicago in the morning. I think it's where I can help most—to make sure just how our inventories will stand up to it. With the business we've got, if we get a quarter of what's pending I'm afraid we may be caught with our pants down. It certainly looks like the real thing and I propose staying right in the Chicago office—"

"I think that's wonderful," Lowry said.

"Charley will be on the teletype to me as soon as the mail and cables are cleared tomorrow." Cramer paused and beamed at them all. "Well, sell 'em, cowboy."

"My God, what a relief," Hewitt said to Lowry as they went back to their offices, "and if anybody knows Middle Western suppliers he does. And not a word about 'my son, John.' "

"You see," Lowry said, "wait for the breaks."

"He's not such a bad little fellow," Hewitt told him, as though that was what he had been saying right along.

All the rest of the week orders continued to pour in. "The biggest five-day dollar volume in our history," Curtis said. They were all on the teletype and telephone to Cramer several times a day. His calm, his resourcefulness, his knowledge of components were amazing. He was never flurried, sounded as fresh at five as at nine in the morning, and there was something wonderfully reassuring in his quiet-voiced reiteration, "Take the order. I'll produce it."

The story began to spread throughout the organization that this was the usual "Cramer luck," that whenever he had been put in to man a company a "Cramer market" followed. At the clerical level it quickly became an article of faith, but after a visit from William Adams Delano on Friday afternoon Curtis told Lowry he had also dwelt on it.

"I never heard such nonsense," Curtis said. "Cramer has had his share of failures, plenty of them, but Delano talked as though ten thousand customers heard he was here and decided it was time to buy. He actually tried to tell me that Cramer's presence has gotten people on their toes, broken down our complacency and all the rest of it—with something to the effect that 'when the moral risk is prime. other things take care of themselves.' I had to ask him how in that case he accounted for the fact that the whole industry was flooded with orders and that if anything Stanley Rutkin and his Forty Thieves had probably sold more than we had. You know that sanctimonious air Delano has, well I swear it almost led me to say I didn't think Jim Peale—to whom he referred several times—had done anything so awful after all. I felt like telling him I helped myself to a hundred grand every now and then when I was short."

"That," Lowry said, "is the sort of remark I am supposed to make, not you."

"We've certainly cashed in on Larus," Curtis said. "They've never had such an order book."

Curtis's cynicism was not shared by Hewitt. "I see this all a little differently," he confided to Lowry. "While Cramer's arrival had nothing to do with this buying, it's plain he does have luck and I like to play with lucky men. This is bound to soften him up and he's going to be much more easy to handle. I think I can handle him. For one thing of course, my personal position being what it is now, I can speak with a good deal more independence. And Cramer is the sort of fellow who respects money."

"What's the plan?" Lowry asked.

"I'll tell you this much—you'll be the first to know. Don't say anything to the others. The fact is, Steve, I've got a very high regard for you personally and as a businessman—"

"Much obliged."

"But I'm not always sure you feel the same way about me—"

"Now Calvin, as you say, you're 'a very dear personal friend.' "

"Don't be facetious. I'm serious."

"Oh come, enough of that."

"I suppose you do think I whore around a lot because I asked you that time to say we were having dinner. Well, actually I don't, a great deal, and I'm cutting it out from now on. Paula's a wonderful girl—"

"Look, I've got to leave or I'll miss my train."

They said goodnight and Hewitt went along to Evans's office for another confidential talk.

The buying wave tapered off at the end of the next week, though with sales continuing slightly ahead of the same period the previous year.

On Wednesday Titcomb came to Lowry's office. In all the rush his firing had been largely forgotten.

"Mr. Lowry," he asked, "have you ever heard of a fellow named John Dryden?"

"There was an English poet of that name."

"That's the fellow. You know, two weeks ago when I was let out I went to see Mr. Rutledge. He was the way he always is, but he said there was nothing he could do. He was finished, he said, and would soon be forgotten down here. Sort of brought tears to our eyes thinking of the past and all the New Year's Eve afternoons. But then he said to me, 'Harold, remember this line by John Dryden and let it be your comfort.' He said it and then I got out my pencil and wrote it down because it made me feel pretty good. I'll read it to you. 'But what has been, has been, and I have had my hour.' Well, I have and I'm not going to spoil it rowing with someone like that Cramer after the type of men I've been associated with. I'm leaving now. Do you know what I'm going to do first?"

"No, what?"

"My wife's waiting for me. We're going to take a taxi all the way to Fulton Street, Brooklyn, and we're going to have dinner at Gage and Tollner's, where I used to go years ago. They been there since before I was born. Not a change. Well, they got air-conditioning, everything else the same, wonderful food, expensive but I've got money saved. I've got my pension. It's a wrench to go, I'm not saying it isn't, but it's a great thing to know when you've had your hour, like I have. I just been in on the greatest ten days in our history. I might have missed that but I didn't. I guess I must be twenty-five, thirty years older than you, Mr. Lowry, so let me say this, be sure you know when you've had your hour and don't hang around. You can think of me in about thirty minutes ordering two lobsters for my wife and me. There's one last thing I want to tell you. I said to you the morning that Cramer was first here, 'He's going to tear the place apart'—well he still is, and don't forget it."

Lowry shook his hand. His good sense and good cheer were

touching, but as he went out to say more goodbyes, Lowry felt a little ashamed of his own relief at what had happened and that he would not have to wrangle with Cramer about it.

Cramer was back the next morning. With his return his personal staff returned to life, their desks, piled with folders, looking like miniature waste piles outside a chemical plant. He deprecated the thanks and congratulations with which he was greeted and said that all the credit belonged to them and the men in the field. He was proud of each and every one. There was only one thing to be feared—and he did not fear it—but there was always the chance of people getting complacent and coasting. That must be watched. Till yet he had not seen a sign of it. He wanted to add a word about vacations. He wanted to be sure his key men got away for a complete rest. He was sure they had made their plans and he wanted nothing to interfere with them. He realized, he said with a boyish smile, that he was not a very good one to preach that gospel—Mrs. Cramer had been trying to get him away for years—but he believed it even if he hadn't hit the trail for some ten or twelve years. Either John or he would personally take over any of their desks if anything vital was pending.

No one had supposed their vacations were to be interfered with but something like a shudder went over them—in spite of all his new camaraderie—at the thought of being away while he was there.

"Oh, one last thing," he said. "I'd like those in the clerical staff who've been working overtime to have a day added to their weekend on a staggered basis."

"You were certainly right in opposing our seeing Delano," Hewitt told Lowry as they left Cramer's office. "The fellow is really all right. I'm going to be able to start talking to you about my idea, probably on Monday."

Just after lunch there was a cable from Trinidad confirming the sale of two pressure vessels on which they had bid the previous week. The components had been the subject of several calls to Cramer in Chicago and Lowry went in to tell him that everything had come out all right. Miss Wilkins said Mr. Cramer would not be back but could be reached at Mr. Delano's late in the afternoon.

"Well, if he calls you might tell him the pressure vessels came through."

"He already knows it, Mr. Lowry," she said, returning to her work.

"I don't think he could. The cable just came," Lowry said.

"Under the new procedure," the president's assistant, who had come in, said, "this office gets advance action copies of all cables where more than two hundred and fifty thousand dollars is involved. We had ours at twelve-thirty-five."

"I see," Lowry said, steam from his control valve all but filling the room.

Here, of course, was intolerable interference on which he must fight. It was an issue on which anyone with any common sense would agree with him, but what was it going to avail to get one more procedure rescinded when Cramer's thinking—to dignify the mental process—could originate them to start with. For the moment he himself was too angry to feel disheartened. Hopeless as the whole picture looked, it must arise from lack of experience; it must be something which Cramer himself would rescind when he understood it. Nonetheless he could hear that low-toned, unctuous voice asking, "But friend Lowry, what possible objection can there be? I'm not trying to do your work. I'm simply trying to keep myself informed. Surely I have that privilege."

"Did you know about these advance action copies of our cables going to Cramer's office?" he asked his secretary.

"Yes, the Cable Room is buzzing with it."

"Why didn't you tell me?"

"You didn't want 'stories and rumors' brought to you and you told me not to 'get worked up.' "

"Miss Marshall, you are an intelligent, attractive young woman, but you would try the patience of a saint. I am not a saint."

"I'm really very sorry. I know I should have told you but everything is so changed and there's so much trouble being made and I feel so sorry for you."

"There, there, I'll weather it."

"But what are you going to do about this?"

"I can't do anything until 'that Cramer,' as Titcomb called him, comes in after the holiday."

He was busy most of the afternoon with his department heads on the analytical report of the last two weeks' sales. The bugbear which hangs over all foreign departments had already raised its ugly head. What were they going to have left to sell? The foreign quotas of production had been filled, running over. Yet most markets had indicated that while there would be a lull, demands had not been filled, particularly on forward deliveries—they had sold into February—and especially on spare parts. The outcome of the meeting which went for typing was the sort of thing which Cramer ought to like and in which he could be helpful. It ought to ease the way Tuesday morning.

They all got up, grinned at each other, stretched and picked up their papers.

Halleck, the best of the department heads, a young man of thirty, hung back, motioning to Lowry that he wanted a moment alone.

"Can I say what's on my mind?" he asked.

"Sure."

"I'm wondering whether we oughn't to have had John Cramer sit in on this. It might have been wise."

"I can't see what possible use he would have been."

"He's talked to me several times and he wants to get in on such things and says his father wants him to—the Day's Work, he calls it. Well it's just a suggestion."

Lowry thought a moment and then he said, "Tell me, between us, are you personally worried because I didn't get him in?"

Halleck neatened his papers again. "I'm absolutely loyal to you personally, Mr. Lowry, but yes, I think I am worried. It may sound ridiculous to you but I have the feeling that I'm going to be in a jam because I didn't tell him we were going to have the meeting. I'm pretty damn sure he'll be over to ask me what we were doing in here."

"You wouldn't feel easy about telling him politely to go ask me, would you? I can see you wouldn't."

"It makes it awfully difficult. If you should go to him now and tell him, he'd know I told you and he'd think—oh hell, I don't know. I suppose I'm scared about my job. We've just bought a house and we're expecting a second child in October. You know how it is."

"I do indeed. At the moment I can only make one promise that I'm sure I'll be able to keep—go tell him anything you like, say what you like about me for that matter, and you have my word I'll not hold it against you. I ought to be able to tell you your job and future are safe as long as I'm satisfied with you."

"You know," Halleck said, "I feel a lot better. You might have given me a lot of assurances and I might have relied on them. I'll take my chance with you."

"Thanks. Let's be practical. I ought to know more by eleven Tuesday morning. If I were you, I'd beat it now before the president's assistant catches you."

Lowry passed Cramer's office on the way from the Conference Room to his own. To say anything to young Cramer would certainly appear now to be at Halleck's suggestion. By Tuesday he ought to know whether "trouble" could be made for him or not. So that he strode past the open door, seeing from the corner of his eye that both workers in the vineyard looked up at him and that Cramer pushed back his chair to rise. Halleck was just disappearing toward the elevator.

"What now?" Lowry asked Hewitt, who was pacing up and down his office. "Let's call it a day. I don't want to hear the best plan in the world."

"Read this goddamn piece of insolence," Hewitt said, red with anger.

"Must I?" Lowry said wearily and then he did read it. "Oh, I see."

"I'm going in and knock his teeth in right now. Do you want to come watch?"

The paper from John Cramer to Hewitt read:

The President regards it as important that no officer or member of his family keep any touch with Mr. Peale.
Will you let me know if you have any comment?

"Come on," Lowry said, "I'll leave with you. We don't want a row in here. Come on, quick."

"I haven't seen or spoken to Jim since he left, but if I had who the hell's business is it? I said before and I say now I'm fixed so I don't have to take this sort of thing. I'm going to knock this guy's teeth out as a public service."

In the end Lowry got him into an elevator and down to a bar without meeting Cramer, where they had a drink and wished each other a pleasant Fourth of July.

"I'm afraid," he told Rosalie when he came down after a shower for a drink on the terrace, "I'll have to unburden myself about the office. It's rather a mess. I think it's likely to get worse." He told her about the day. "You see, outside of aggression and apparent malice, it seems to have no real reason. Take the memo to Hewitt. What reason? We didn't each get one. Why is he capriciously picked out?"

"Darling, in this case, there may have been a reason. Not a good one, a cause not a reason perhaps. It has to do with Paula. Calvin knows nothing about it and she doesn't intend that he shall. She tracked Jim down and had him to lunch. Young Cramer saw them."

22

TWO INCIDENTS OVER THE FOURTH OF JULY weekend contributed to Lowry's uncertainty as to the best tactic for Tuesday morning with Cramer. The first was a comic interlude at the Hopkinses', where Rosalie and he were dining.

The hostess, greeting them alone, said, "Kenneth will be down in a moment. Do try to cheer him up. He's been in a state about something at the office. Does everybody have these office troubles, or is it just Kenneth?"

"It's just Kenneth," Lowry said with a grin. "All other offices are little paradises."

"Oh, you too? That's such a relief. I hope yours is nothing trivial!"

They all laughed. "This is just one man," she continued.

"That's what it always is," Lowry said.

"But he's a partner. He's always against everything and the other partners wear themselves out getting him to agree to something. He never agrees. He let's them override him, saying he's just a partner around here and what he thinks doesn't matter. This has been going on for years."

"Ken didn't take a shot at him, did he?"

"No, but I'm afraid he did give him a shove and a chair got upset and Ken says he's going to buy a chicken farm and leave the ratrace to rats, one of the most original plans I've ever heard."

Hopkins, looking clean and handsome in a white dinner jacket, came in as she was talking. "I never shoved him, Marcie. I simply got up in some natural exasperation and I happened to bump into him and his chair fell over. Steve, you can see how it happened. I'd like to leave it at that but the other partners think I ought to tell him it was my fault and I'm damned if I will. All through the war at W.P.B. there was a fellow who was constantly demanding 'overriding priority' and now I have to hear the damn word all day from one of my own partners."

"*Till yet, friend Hopkins*, I thought only I had troubles," Lowry said.

"What's this?"

"That is the patois in which the new president of a certain large corporation speaks," Rosalie said.

"Why you poor guy. Let me fill your glass."

The other was a telephone call from Walter Caithness Sunday morning. "In view of our talk the other day," Caithness said, "I thought you'd be interested in this piece of gossip. I played golf with Bill Delano yesterday and he volunteered the information that our friend, Cramer, spoke in the highest terms of you and considers himself very fortunate to have you there. Delano alleges he was not satisfied with all the officers but was emphatically so with you. I thought you'd like to know. I gather Cramer is considerably impressed with your being with the Foundation. Let me know how things go."

Lowry was human enough to be very pleased, particularly at Caithness's taking the trouble to call him.

At the office Tuesday morning there was an unopened cablegram addressed to Lowry on his desk. It was from Daran announcing his arrival that day, saying he would telephone from the Waldorf as early as possible. Miss Marshall gave him the report from the Friday meeting which the Stenographic Room had produced over the weekend.

Lowry read it through carefully and decided then was as good a time as any to see the president. He went in to him with a cheery good morning. As usual, Cramer's smiling affability and the quiet, considerate tone of his voice were half disarming. Lowry handed him the report and said what it was.

"Oh I am very glad to have it," Cramer said. "I was wondering what you planned about something of the sort." He glanced through it quickly with the seeing-eye of the experienced reader. "I can see there's a good deal in it we'll need to talk about. I hope John was of some help to you in preparing it."

"I don't believe he knows about it yet."

"You didn't ask him to sit in on it?"

"No."

"Well," Cramer said with a new smile, "I don't want to start off this fine Tuesday morning with any discussion, but I think it would have been the nice thing to have asked him. But we won't go into that now. What can *I* do for you?"

"I have a cable that Daran arrives today and I thought you'd like to know."

"Oh that's very good. I wondered if that had been forgotten in all the rush. Of course I'll want several talks with him, particularly on that bridge, which I'm determined we must get. Arrives today," he repeated and wetting his forefinger he flicked through what Lowry guessed were some advance copies of his cables. He felt it was meant to provoke a question about the procedure and said nothing. Cramer repeated the operation and glanced through some other papers on his desk in some evident annoyance. "When did you hear about this?" he asked without looking up.

"I got a personal cable from him."

"Where can I reach him?"

"Oh he'll use the desk in my outer office."

"You don't know where he's staying?"

It was clear that Cramer hoped for and expected either an outburst about lack of confidence or an aggressive assertion of his responsibility.

"At the Waldorf."

Cramer put both hands flat on the desk.

"The Waldorf?" He wagged his head. "Well, I won't say I'm astonished but I am going to ask, friend Lowry, whether you aren't letting your department in for a good deal of expense. I know how easy it is for people to indulge after a buying spree such as we've been through but I think I'd just reconsider the Waldorf. I wouldn't dream of staying there. Of course you may be thinking of all that we owe Doran—"

"Daran."

"Daran, because of Peale, and I've thought of it, and we may want to do something, but that's not the way to do it."

"You see, Mr. Daran has made this trip for private reasons at his own expense. I'm not in a position to tell him what hotel to go to."

"That's a different matter, then. You most certainly and very definitely cannot tell him. Anything else? Anything holding you up or bothering you?"

"Not at the moment," Lowry said and went out confident that he left Cramer more puzzled than he himself was. While this was personally gratifying he knew it was not the way to run a business. Or rather, it was a way if Cramer's objective was to provoke Calvin Hewitt and him into resigning.

The thing seemed to go deeper than petty and capricious interference. Cramer's reported praise of him to Delano might be a shrewd device which would allow him later to say to Delano, "I really thought the world of Lowry. You remember I spoke of it but he's going around with a chip on his shoulder, uncooperative —a sort of passive resistance. Of course he may not be a well man." If Cramer wanted new officers of his own selecting, if he wanted to up his son immediately, this might be his reasoning as the way to achieve it. And the depletion of Lowry's cash for the down payment and other expenses on the house, and the September school bills did not leave him in too strong a position. Rosalie and he were living with careful regard to expense—cash for everything but house and new car—but living as they were expected to, based on assumption of continuity and expansion which might no longer be justified. What made it worse was the feeling that it could all be cured by agreeing with Cramer in everything and telling him what a genius for administration his son had. The fact that he felt he could forecast Cramer's moves made it no easier. If he let the advanced action matter and the Halleck situation go until a more propitious time, Cramer could say, "But why didn't you bring this up at once? 'Silence gives consent' is an old saying. I asked you time and again if there was anything troubling you and you said no." On the other hand if he made an issue of them that morning he could hear Cramer's low-voiced "Now friend Lowry, what possible . . ."

Halleck appeared as he sat down at his desk. It was plain the poor young man had had a bad holiday.

"I'd like to get this off my chest, Mr. Lowry," he said. "I feel badly about it but I don't see what else I could have done. We were going to Jones Beach Saturday around eleven. I was polishing the car and my wife was fixing the lunchbasket when John Cramer and his father drove up. They couldn't have been nicer, thought I had done wonders with the place, came down and saw my workshop and power tools, and it all ended by their coming to the beach with us. We all went in except Mr. Cramer, Senior, and he said he was a good baby-sitter, so he was down with my fellow making a castle in the sand; really he was wonderful."

"That's fine," Lowry said.

"It made a terrible difference to my wife. They both said I had a big future and she'd been sort of scared and worried about what I told her about Friday afternoon and ducking out. Well the long and the short of it is, after we ate, my wife took a nap, and we got to talking and—" Halleck drew a long breath "—I told them about the report and Mr. Cramer said, 'Well you boys will work more closely together next time, I'm sure.' I hate to say the rest. I don't know what you're going to think. I don't know just how it came out but I told John Cramer I didn't tell him at the time because you didn't want me to."

"I suppose at that point Mr. Cramer went up and got six ice cream cones," Lowry said.

"As a matter of fact he did just that. How'd you know?"

"It was inevitable. Well, don't feel badly about it, if you do. It's all right with me. By the way, Daran will be in today or tomorrow. How are the preliminary figures on the bridge coming?"

"We're building up as far as we can without definite specs."

"Cable this morning and ask when they can be expected. Daran will want to know."

When Halleck left, Lowry telephoned Rosalie and told her of Daran's impending arrival.

"Tell me honestly," he said, "do you have any objection to having him and his Beatriz at the Beach Club for dinner?"

"Tell me honestly yourself, dear, do you mean because of what I may think of her, or because of what he may be thinking about me?" It was the first direct reference either had made to Peale's story since she had told it to him and her tone was not her pleasant one.

"It's just," he said lamely, "that I thought I ought to ask. I didn't mean anything sinister."

"I know. I'm sorry. I don't know why I said it that way. Ask them by all means, or I'll telephone her if you like."

"That won't be necessary and anyhow I don't know how they'll be registered."

"You think of everything," she said with a pleasant little laugh. "Don't be mad if I sounded touchy."

It was three o'clock before Daran telephoned that they were settled at the Waldorf and that he was at Lowry's disposition. There had been the usual nonscheduled stop at Gander for a new oil pump.

"Are you both tired out?" Lowry asked.

"Not at all."

"Well, would you like to drive out to our house about five and dine with us at the Beach Club? We can have a swim before dinner."

Daran said he would be very pleased. Might he consult Beatriz? Lowry waited.

"She asks what should she wear," Daran said.

"Any light dress and a light wrap. It may be cool there."

Daran spoke again to Beatriz. "She asks do you mean a cotton afternoon dress?"

"Precisely."

Daran lowered his voice conspiratorially. "It is not to be known at the hotel of course but we are not yet married, owing to legal delays there would have been in France. Will your wife understand?"

"Certainly."

"Then we come with great pleasure. Thank you. You have your own car in town?"

"No, I'll get one."

"No, no, I insist. It can bring us back," Daran said. "Oh, you will find her face now very beautiful."

So indeed Lowry found it when he met them, and he was again impressed by the mixture of ease and piquancy in her manner. He had brought Daran a copy of the analysis of the two weeks' sales, for later reading.

"Your president's assistant, another Mr. Cramer, a son I gathered, telephoned after I spoke to you, asking me to dinner tonight with him and the father. I put him off indefinitely until I knew your plans."

They were both very charming at the house when they met Rosalie. Beatriz said she brought special greetings "from your brother. He was kind enough to have us to dinner at his own house."

"Did you bring a bathing suit?" Rosalie asked.

"We both did. They are in the car."

Daran viewed the Beach Club, bright with its boxes of petunias and geraniums, the pool gleaming in the late sun and the ocean rolling in, with obvious pleasure.

"I very much like luxury," he said.

The women went off together to the dressing room while the men waited.

"As I wrote you, I have said nothing of Mr. Peale to Beatriz, so I should like to ask you now how is he and should I see him? I'm quite uncertain what is desirable."

"Well, he has a job. I see him occasionally and of course he's going through a very hard time."

"He wrote me sending me a check. I really don't need it and had forgotten about it—well, I say forgotten, I'm afraid that is just a pretense, an effort on my part to—well I really don't need it, that is not pretense. It has all made me very sad. Poor fellow."

"We're all very sad, of course, but he must make his own wav back, it seems to me."

"Yes, I suppose so. Oh, there are the ladies."

They came forward in beautiful contrast to each other and Rosalie handed Lowry the key. He paused for a word with her as Daran went ahead.

"You could both make a fortune in part of those suits in a Paris night club," he said.

"Beatriz," Rosalie whispered to him, "would never do it. Such modesty I never saw. I knew you'd want to hear but I got never a glimpse of anything except her back."

Two hooks in the bathhouse were hung with feminine attire, the most intimate uppermost. Daran took off his coat and hung it carefully over some lacy panties, a wisp of a brassière and a garter belt. "So difficult for Beatriz to understand modesty. You must forgive her."

Lowry felt the least he could do was to put his own coat over Rosalie's slightly less chic froufrou. He did it solemnly.

"I fall too easily into pretense," Daran said, bending over to untie his shoes. "It was my own possessiveness and jealousy that led me to say that."

Both guests swam almost as well as the Lowrys, which was to say very well indeed, and before dinner they went up to the balcony bar, looking down on the ocean, in good spirits.

"Goodness is so puzzling," Rosalie said to Stephen as she prepared for bed that night. "There is Daran, living in luxurious sin on the proceeds of a lottery prize, yet I have never felt more goodness or consideration for others in anyone. He had obviously never said a word about Jim to her. She said she had seen but not met 'Mr. Peale' and thought him very handsome, and where was he? I could tell that he was afraid something she said or one of her questions might hurt me. When you went to order dinner and she spoke of all her half brothers and sisters and started to ask about my family, he guided her away from it. He was so worried that that was why, when she asked me where I had learned to swim, I told them about Estonia. I thought it would make it easier for him. You didn't tell me Armas had been to Bonn."

"I know. I thought it would only make you feel worse."

"Being afraid to hope because you may be disappointed is very cowardly, I'm afraid. Beatriz was very sweet when we went to powder our noses. She said she could hardly wait to be married and conceive, that he was so good she wanted to give him a family."

The full specifications for the bridge were in the mail the next morning and Daran, Lowry and Halleck spent an hour on them before Daran went in for his interview with Cramer. Lowry told him he might as well tell Cramer the specifications were in.

When Daran returned he made a face at Lowry and held up his hands in a gesture of bewilderment. "If you don't mind," he said, "we shall talk about it a little later. I am perhaps a little confused. I am to have dinner with him and his son at six-thirty. I suppose I have never had dinner at six-thirty before. The young Cramer has gone to look at the specs with Mr. Halleck. He has taken his slide rule. I shall probably leave for Caracas tomorrow night."

The day passed quietly. Hewitt was back from Philadelphia but kept to himself. In midafternoon Lowry fixed a meeting of Evans and his engineers and calculators, as well as John Cramer, with Daran, who gave them a general fill-in on the bridge.

When he arrived the next morning, Lowry found Daran waiting for him. So was an envelope "From John Cramer for Mr. Lowry," which he put aside.

Daran began, "We return to Caracas tonight. I shall remain

there whatever reasonable time you feel necessary for the Company. But I now resign my position as your manager in Venezuela."

"My God, what's happened?" Lowry asked.

"In all countries businessmen talk a good deal of nonsense and I am accustomed to such palaver. But Mr. Cramer not only talks nonsense and deception but he insults my intelligence by thinking I do not realize it."

"You mustn't resign," Lowry said.

"I have," Daran said with a smile. "You undoubtedly did not intend to make it easier for me to do so, but you have. I am not like Mr. Cramer. I don't want to make a virtue of it. I am going to do something I prefer to do. I wished, as it was, to leave Venezuela. Your brother-in-law has offered me a very fine position in his bank in Paris if I was not happy. I accepted it by telephone this morning. It will be much better for Beatriz to be in a cultural center like Paris, though of course there is nothing like Paris."

"Are you sure my brother-in-law and you didn't settle this before you left?" Lowry asked.

"No, most certainly not, Mr. Lowry. It was wholly conditional and if my intelligence had not been insulted last night, I should not have done it, much as Beatriz insisted."

"What was the nature of the insult?"

"Well, first about Mr. Peale. How perceptive I had been from the start. Many compliments, but I said I was not perceptive. It never occurred to me, to start with, that anything could be wrong. Even in Paris had you told me to forget it, I should have. I told Cramer that. He talked about the satisfaction it must give me to have had this wrongdoing exposed. I said it gave me no satisfaction and it must have almost broken your heart as a friend, because I shed tears when Mr. Lainvee told me and I was only an admirer of Mr. Peale's culture. But of course all that was by the way. He then asked me if I did not think it would be better for me to agree that my rate of commission and my bonus on the last three weeks' business be reduced."

"Not really?"

"Oh yes, really. You understand that if I had been told 'Daran, you never expected to make this much money and we're not going to pay it,' well perhaps I would have thought it over. But to be told I would be better off without it in the long run—which was how he put it—that was too much. And there was much else I did not like. Something called 'Headquarters Reports' to his son, not to you. Many small-minded things from a small-minded man. And then he told me I was to make no effort to see Mr. Peale. I couldn't bother my head to answer." Saying that, Daran smiled and then began to laugh. "The end was very funny. At the time I was greatly disturbed. You see whenever I answered back, both Mr. Cramers were all soap and oil with me—how valuable I was, how they were thinking of me, how anything they could do, how the commission on the bridge would of course not be reduced, and so on, so nothing would do but they must walk back to the Waldorf with me. Well they did, a little before nine. As we came up the stairs from Park Avenue we met Beatriz just coming down to dinner. She looked absolutely charming, though in street clothes, which I told her she should not have worn to the Sert Room at that hour. But she had been to a movie and not taken time to change. I hesitated a moment, remembered being told I was not to see Mr. Peale, which had very much annoyed me. So, rebellious, I just said goodnight to them, excused myself and joined her." He laughed again. "Isn't there an American joke, 'You don't resign, you're fired'? I walked up the steps to the Sert Room with my arm around her waist."

"Wonderful," Lowry said. "Though your resignation is very depressing I know you'll both be very happy in Paris."

"You must understand that if it makes bad difficulties for you, I will hold it up."

"It doesn't, in that sense, but there are a lot of difficulties," Lowry said.

The morning cables had brought word that negotiations for the building to house a proposed assembly plant of road-making and farm machinery near Smyrna had reached the final stage. A question of law under existing treaties had been raised on duty-free passage and Lowry judged it of sufficient interest and importance to talk to Cramer about, and to be used in opening a wider discussion.

He found Cramer largely indifferent to the issue, which plainly he did not fully understand, finally interrupting rather brusquely to say it was after all a mere detail.

"I want to tell you something," Cramer said, "and I can only hope it's news to you. Your Venezuelan friend took dinner with us last night. Of course like all foreigners he's evasive. But from something he let drop John guessed that he had a woman with him at his hotel and we went over with him intending to make certain inquiries after he left us. There was no need to inquire. There she came flagrantly dressed, half exposed, and he hurriedly left us, overcome with embarrassment I could see. Did you know this? You must have. You saw him in Paris. Why was I not told?"

"Told what? I met Mr. Daran and the lady he is to marry in Paris where she had gone for an operation. My wife and I had them at our house night before last. What was I to tell you?"

"Your wife and you had an immoral woman in your own house?" Cramer exclaimed. "I can't believe it." He pondered the question a moment and said, "Have they got separate rooms?"

"I don't know anything about it."

Cramer hesitated. "Irregular as it is, if they have separate, nonadjoining rooms I'd overlook it, I think. Can you check that, or shall I have John do it?"

"I'm afraid the answer is now immaterial. Mr. Daran has just resigned."

"Mr. Lowry, I must ask myself what can possibly be back of the obvious fact that, whether it is intentioned or not, or what the cause may be, you are gradually destroying the organization. Apparently, I say apparently, Peale should have gone. As to Daran, except as he may now turn vindictive and sabotage the bridge, I'm satisfied to have him go. But isn't it significant that both these men were highly thought of by you? I must ask myself whether Mr. Rutledge or Mr. Johnson might not still—but we'll leave that. Let us come back to Daran. You regarded him highly?"

"Yes, I still do."

"Now tell me, when he resigned—a man as you believe of value to your company—what did you do to persuade him to remain?"

"I saw that his decision was taken and there was nothing I could do."

"This is amazing. You mean to say you did absolutely nothing? Felt no impulse of duty toward your company? Is that what I'm to tell Mr. Delano?"

"I should think you'd tell him a man in whose morals you had no confidence had fortunately resigned."

"A man like that will have just one goal—to make trouble for us in Venezuela. I suppose John, possibly with young Halleck, had better go there. I suppose you got no hint of Daran's plans?"

"Yes, I did. He's leaving Venezuela as soon as possible."

"To do what?"

"To join my brother-in-law's firm in Paris."

Cramer was speechless a full half-minute. Then he shook his head and said, "This is the most flagrant—no, I'll say no more now. I don't trust myself to speak."

"Before I go, I'd like to see what this is about," Lowry said, took the envelope from John Cramer from his pocket and opened it. The memorandum inside read:

The President would like to know full circumstances of payment of $5000 to Mr. Dahlgren Lowry in connection with Larus. May I say you will advise him by Friday?

"Why in the world do you do things this way?" Lowry asked.

"In other words, you're saying I'm entitled to the information but you don't like the way I ask for it, is that it? Let's get this clear, friend Lowry. Is it policy or procedure that's chewing you?" Lowry waited so long to reply that Cramer asked, "Or could it be that just maybe your conscience hurts you because I have had to learn from outside sources what you should have told me? Could it be that?"

It was almost impossible to know how to put his objections. Cramer wore a varicolored coat of paternalism and provocation. It had probably been fifty years since anyone had been able effectively to say "A gentleman doesn't do something like this." Yet that was the basic issue—that Cramer was not a gentleman but pretended to be. If he were told how Rutledge or Johnson would have acted in his place, he would say, "Well if I've got to beat around the bush with a lot of sweet talk to get a few facts out of you. . . ." But the worst of it was that he may have been entitled to know as soon as Dahlgren's check was received. Lowry asked himself whether on receiving it he would not have asked Rutledge or Johnson for advice, if either had been there. Because he put no value on Cramer's opinion, had he been entitled not to ask for it? Had he in fact not taken the easiest way and thereby been unfair to Cramer? Even now wasn't the healthy-minded thing to blow up, get mad, have a row, clear the air and be friends again? Or admit he had made a mistake and accept the passing unpleasantness that would follow? Business is business, as some sad, fierce thinker had said.

"Understand, I'm not going to drop the matter," Cramer said.

There was enough of a threat in his tone to stiffen Lowry's resistance, and he said, "Before the Larus deal was final I was assured there was no finder's fee to be paid in any form. I was apparently deceived, but the whole situation has since changed and I cannot see that our interests were in any way involved. What happened has turned out to be a highly complicated personal matter among outsiders. I feel no obligation to say anything about it."

"Have you benefited personally by this?"

"Certainly not, nor has my brother."

"Then why not tell me? Why must there be this constant pulling in different ways between us? It's not my wish or doing."

This man is such a liar, Lowry thought. Unquestionably Beatriz was not "half exposed" last night. Unquestionably he lies to himself about his own motives.

"I'm wondering this, friend Lowry," Cramer continued, "do you need a vacation? You've had a difficult spring getting your family together. You've had this Johnson Foundation business and I know you're having family worries. This must worry you, having taken on a big new house of your own, growing family. You see, things come to me. People realize I've got the interests of all you men at heart. Now would it be wise for you to get away? I'm only thinking of you. We'll forget the Larus matter till a later day."

The man's amazing ability to pick up scraps of intelligence was less disconcerting than his ability to change his color like a chameleon and the trick of shearing off—like a fish in a tank—with concern for his opponent's welfare before a final clash made it almost impossible to explain to anyone else why dealing with him normally was impossible. Yet through all his anger Lowry kept asking himself, "What's in him that others see and I don't?"

Then as though nothing had happened, Cramer's face relaxed into a broad, benign smile and he said, "You know what might be a good idea, for you and me to get a quick bite of lunch and go out to the ball game together. And eat peanuts and drink pop with our coats and ties off. What do you say? It's only eleven o'clock."

Lowry picked up his papers. "Thanks, I've got to be with the lawyers on the Smyrna matter this afternoon and I want to see Daran off."

He telephoned Rosalie about the resignation and asked her to pick him up at Idlewild.

23

THE ELDER CRAMER TOOK HIS SON DOWN TO lunch at the Louis XIV Restaurant. It gratified him to have the corner table where he had once seen John D. Rockefeller, Jr., having a bowl of soup with one of his sons, and he and his son ordered a simple lunch with the careful economy of a multimillionaire.

"I don't suppose, John, there's a man living freer of animosity than I am," Cramer told his son.

"You're right, Dad."

"In all the situations I've been put in to straighten out, at the end I had everyone's good will. I bore good will to everyone. I don't want you to think I have any animosity toward Lowry."

"Oh, I know that, Dad."

"Then why can't I seem to get him to go along? The trouble is, John, the fellow's got a queer streak. That wife of his isn't French at all, she's Estonian. It's as though our nice American girls weren't good enough for him. He's headstrong, he's mulish—"

"I don't think, Dad, you're ever going to be able to get him on the track. You've got the rest of them eating out of your hand."

"Just now I tried to smooth things about by suggesting we go to the ball game. No, wouldn't do it. I phoned Mr. Delano just before lunch about Doran joining Lowry's brother's firm. He was shocked and horrified. Lowry will never know it from me, but I saved his job for him. I don't know that I could do it again."

"Would you want to, Dad? He's a pretty expensive luxury, it strikes me."

Daran, busy about packing and tickets, was unable to lunch with Lowry but said that on the way to Idlewild he would have some advice on the bridge bid ready. He saw no reason why his assistant could not file the finished bid and performance bond but that he would go into the matter thoroughly before leaving Caracas. Lowry, wishing to avoid the Cramers at the club, also went around to the Louis XIV, with Hewitt.

The Cramers saw and waved to them as they went to their table.

"I'd give a lot to know what they're talking about," Hewitt said to him as Cramer said the same thing to his son.

"I had an exasperating talk with him this morning," Lowry said, and told Hewitt about Daran. "I thought Cramer was trying to force me to resign and at the end he asked me to go to a ball game with him. What about that plan of yours and that note to you?"

"Something unexpected came up about my plan and it's held me up. I haven't said anything about the note meantime. May just have to play along for a while," Hewitt said gloomingly. "I sometimes wish Jim were back with us. He could have managed Cramer."

They were studying the desserts on the menu, when the headwaiter came up to say Mr. Lowry was wanted on the telephone. He went to the booth, where Miss Marshall told him Mr. Dennison wanted to speak to him urgently. She gave him the number of Dennison's office.

"I'm just going to lunch with Bill Delano and I want your side of this story about your brother-in-law luring your best Latin American representative away from you."

"My God," Lowry said, "has Cramer told him that? This is really too much."

"Well, what is the story?" Dennison asked in the tone of a

man a little tired of being called on to settle someone else's troubles.

"It's very simple. Cramer provoked Daran into resigning by proposing that his commissions be cut on these recent sales. Told him it would be better for him. My brother-in-law had met Daran in Paris–"

"Through you."

"Yes, through me," Lowry said angrily. "And told him if he wanted a job in his bank any time, he could have it. Daran has taken it. As I said this is really too much, Mr. Dennison."

"That's all you know about it?"

"Certainly it's all I know about it and I don't like the implication."

"Let's not be touchy about little things. I called you to try to help."

"Well, I appreciate that but–"

"I must hang up because I'm late now. I'll talk to you later," Dennison said.

Lowry slammed the telephone back on the cradle and started back to his table. Hewitt, all smiles, had joined the Cramers and all three were pointing to the vacant chair awaiting him. He walked over with what grace he could and pushed young Cramer, who had risen deferentially, back in his chair.

"I settled our check, Steve," Hewitt said. "They're bringing our coffee here."

"I was just saying to friend Hewitt here," Cramer said, "that I want to make a two-three-week swing around the plants and I want him of course to come along. You see no reason why the boys won't get along all right without us, do you?"

"The boys will get along all right," Lowry said, "because the men will look out for them."

At this witticism, Cramer threw back his head and laughed heartily. "Love your sense of humor, friend Lowry," he said. As for Hewitt, a considerable change had come over him. He gave the impression of a man who has made his peace with God.

In the office they parted with hearty we-must-do-it-ofteners,

Hewitt stopping at Lowry's door for a final word.

"I think, Steve, you've been right about this right from the start and I give you credit. We'd have made damn fools of ourselves by going to Delano or anybody else. D.P.'s perfectly reasonable if he's handled right and he couldn't have been more cordial about my going on this trip with him."

"Well, I'm glad. Is D.P. the new form of address?"

Hewitt ignored the question. "I wanted to tell you this. As you know I've said nothing about that memo relative to seeing Jim. I'm glad I slept on it. There's been absolutely no mention of it and it occurs to me that it wasn't intended for me in the first place. Typographical error. I think it was meant for you. Everything points that way. You've had all the contact with Jim. I can bring it up diplomatically on the trip and I'll do so. I think I'm going to be able to get a lot of things squared away for us all."

"Good for you," Lowry said.

"John's going with us, by the way, which is a mighty nice gesture."

"I see," Lowry said. "Toward whom?"

"The executives–shows D.P. has full confidence in them. You know perfectly well how you would have felt if he had been left here."

Though the cat was away for three weeks, neither the mice nor the men in the office engaged in play. The office was an agreeable and stimulating place which men and women could leave at five with a sense of accomplishment and without anxiety for what would "come up in the morning." True, some of the sales which had looked so good two weeks before were canceled as difficulties over letters of credit or exchange or delivery dates arose. But those were things to which all were accustomed, part of the pattern of business. There had been no miscalculations of price or shipping costs, no errors in transmission. No one had to go to his superior to say, "I don't know how it happened. I made the calculation. It was double-checked but there it is, it's my mistake." No branch office had to cable or telephone that they had sold 10 not 100 units or a 100 not 10 and "buyer insists on full delivery. Has discussed with American Consul."

Though it was a little dismaying to Lowry that the mere absence of the two Cramers could make for such contentment and satisfaction in his work, he found himself happier in it than he had been at any time. And the fact that Hewitt was also away made life more agreeable. Evenings and weekends in Ridingtown were perfect, after the all but Arabian heat of the city. At least for the time being Tamargo, Daran's second man, was operating successfully in Caracas, and at the end of the second week after Daran's departure, the engineers and calculators came up with the final price on the bridge. It was put on Lowry's desk for signature and dispatch and Curtis himself brought in the performance bond from the surety company. All that experience and care could do had been done. Each page of the supporting calculations bore the varicolored initials of the calculating experts. The profit, while large, was in line with the risks and time involved. There was a sense of elation and confidence in the office over their entry into bridge building and Evans and Curtis, with most of the principal subordinates, came in smiling to watch him sign.

"We're sure we're right?" he asked, looking around, pen in hand. "Speak now or forever hold your peace."

"Go ahead," Evans said.

Lowry signed. He told Miss Marshall to send the telegram that it was done and what the price was which Mr. Cramer had requested. If they were the successful bidder, as he felt they would be, though the credit would not be his alone, it must inevitably make matters easier with Cramer.

He felt a great relief, mixed with elation, that all he could do had now been done, felt grateful that the final decision on the margin of profit, though approved by Curtis, had been left to him and had not had to be argued out with the Cramers. He wished Daran were still in Caracas to share in it and thought of the not unpleasing self-importance with which Harold Titcomb would have put on his hat and coat and gone out past the fountain and the flowers to the Venezuelan Consul next door to have the papers notarized. And most of all he thought of the pity that Jim Peale, who had really made it possible through Larus, should not even know of it. To call and tell him at his wretched desk in the Bronx would of course be cruel but he felt like doing it and telling him his part was not forgotten and that better days were coming, quoting to him—as they used to do when they found something stirring or beautiful—a phrase he had read of Augustus John's: "Look, O my brothers, do you not see the Rainbows and the Bridges of the Beyond?"

He reached for his telephone to call Excello Extrusion. He would say, "I was thinking about you, Jim, and wanted to know how things were going." Then he hesitated, thinking of the dreadful heat and humidity that had plagued the city for a week and how much a weekend by the sea would mean to Peale. And Tom Johnson's words, "A decision used to be a simple thing. . . ." He could not, whatever his pity, ask Peale to Ridingtown with Rosalie. But he asked Miss Marshall to get Excello.

When she connected him he asked to speak to Mr. Peale. The operator said he was no longer with the company and no, they didn't know where to reach him. He felt a sense of alarm and of responsibility. Whatever Peale had done, he had himself said he would stand by him. He told Miss Marshall he would be back in about an hour, or if he were delayed he would call her. He considered telling Charley Curtis and decided against it, doubtful that that kindhearted man would feel it was his responsibility.

He took a taxi through the wilting humidity to the West End Avenue address and rang the bell of the apartment number where Peale had had a room. A woman answered the ring, with the door on a chain and said Mr. Peale had moved out a week ago.

"Did anything seem to be the matter?" he asked. "I'm a friend of his."

"No, he paid up with me, left money for his laundry."

"He left no forwarding address or anything?"

"No, he was out late for him one night, about eleven-thirty. I had to get up to let him in, as I put the chain up at eleven. He was all right. He got a call at six-thirty the next morning and he was out of here by eight."

"Do you know who it was called?"

"I was that sound asleep I didn't even know whether it was a man or a woman. You're a friend, you're not a cop, are you, because if you are this is a respectable place, no funny business."

"No, no, I'm a friend. He wasn't upset by the call, you wouldn't say?"

"I don't think so but you couldn't tell about him. He was 'cool,' as they say."

Lowry thanked her and left. Other than to call the lawyer whom Peale had seen several months ago, he could think of nothing to do. The lawyer said he had last seen him on May 15 and had had no communication since then. The only encouraging thing was that he obviously had not left Excello with any charges against him; but the Rainbows and Bridges of the Beyond faded a little as he thought how doubtless some morning Cramer would tell him, in his obnoxious undertone, where Peale was and what he was doing.

There was a telegram from Cramer on his desk when he got back.

CONGRATULATIONS AND GOOD LUCK HOPE WE HAVE NOT BEEN AVARICIOUS

He thought about Cramer. In a sense he had failed with Jim. Somehow such brotherhood as he thought existed should have forewarned him of the impending crash and let him prevent it. In a totally different relation he must not fail with Cramer. If, as he thought to himself, he was the better man he must make the qualities which he believed in—tolerance, good will, belief in the best in people, serenity—prevail over Cramer's devious ways and provocative pettiness. To get along with men like Rutledge, Johnson or Caithness was no great credit to him.

That Friday even Ridingtown was under a pall of heat and humidity. The land breeze made the Beach Club if anything more uncomfortable than farther inland, where the famous ten degrees cooler in summer was no longer a fact. The Hopkinses were coming to dinner and before going to meet Stephen's train Rosalie telephoned Marcia to have her husband come in shorts and shirt.

"I'd like to go to the Equator and cool off after that train," Stephen said. "I'll kiss you after I've washed my face. We got the bridge bid off."

"You poor lamb," Rosalie said, "it's been suffocating here, so I can imagine New York. We have a very cool dinner, cold consommé Waldorf, cold chicken and artichokes, and melon and Château d'Yquem."

"Good," he said, "I wish I could have a swim."

"The ocean was horrid, seventy-nine degrees, and the pool seventy-five. I left the shower running at home to have it cold for you."

"You're an angel. You look cool."

"I'm wearing just more than a single garment, and heatproof make-up. Gin and tonic, lots of ice before dinner?"

"Yes, strengthening if not cooling," he said. "Can I wear shorts and what Lainvee used to call her 'short-dress sleeves'?"

"All laid out and I told Marcie."

The Hopkinses arrived and Rosalie, coming out on the porch with the bowl of ice, found the two sunburned men sprawled in long chairs. "You look like two White Hunters. I feel like somebody on safari in an Elspeth Huxley book."

"Women always want to sleep with White Hunters," Lowry said.

"Not on such a hot night. Look at that ghastly sunset."

" 'With a mouth that was red like a lion's it drank the blood of the sun as it slaughtered sank,' " Hopkins said, turning to look at it.

"My, Ruark writes well, or is that Hemingway?" Rosalie asked, handing him a gin and tonic.

"You're right, Francis Thompson Hemingway," Hopkins said. "I'm a great reader."

Marcia held her lighter to the White Hunters' cigarettes. "They do love service, don't they, these big, strong, literary men."

"On high-class safaris," Lowry said, "the memsahibs wear jewels at dinner with their pajamas and mosquito boots. Where are your jewels? Where are your mosquito boots?"

"Is that a wounded water buffalo under those lilac bushes?" Hopkins asked.

"That's Smoky drinking out of the birdbath," Rosalie said.

"Not the birdbath, the waterhole," Stephen said. "Save me the trouble of clapping my hands for another drink, please."

"Yes, Bwana. I wish we were all on safari."

From inside the house there was a sudden thunder of feet and a tumult of voices.

"The bearers have evidently mutinied," Stephen said. At which their three children and two neighbors' burst through the door.

"Dad, can we run six times around the house and will you time us, Dad, please? Here's your watch. Can we, I mean may we? Don't say no, Mum, only six times."

"Will you please speak nicely to Mr. and Mrs. Hopkins?"

Richard, evidently not having seen the Hopkinses, controlled himself. "Oh, how do you do, Mrs. Hopkins? I'm very glad to see you. How have you been feeling?" In the midst of a courtly bow, he handed the watch to his father. "Can we, Dad? Good evening, sir, how have you been feeling?"

"Thank you–not very well. Too old evidently," Hopkins replied.

Lainvee curtsied to Mrs. Hopkins with a polite murmur of greeting, ending in "And no fair, no girls, isn't that so, Dad?"

The others were queueing up for bows. "Just bow," Rosalie said, "don't put out those filthy hands. And you may not run at all in this heat."

"Then can we listen to you drink? Please, so we can play 'come for cocktails,'" Lainvee pleaded.

"Who wants to play that?" Richard asked scornfully. "Dad, won't Mr. Hopkins and you play batting practice with us, please? It's as early as anything. You'd like it, wouldn't you, Mr. Hopkins?"

"Dears," Rosalie said firmly, "it is time for Martin and Christopher to go home. It is time for you to have baths."

"And no wet-towel fights," their father interjected. "Honor bright, now."

"Yes, Dad. Mum, will you be up?"

"Yes, dear."

They trooped happily off with polite goodnights.

"Have you ever thought of giving them vitamins?" Hopkins asked. "Think of wanting to be timed around the house. God be merciful to me, a sinner, but leave us go back to the peace of Africa and another drink."

Darkness brought small abatement to the damp, breathless heat of the day, and a moment's radio news announced, "No relief in sight from heat wave gripping the nation." All four of them were slightly intoxicated from weather and drink.

"Why don't we go for a swim in the channel from our dock?" Marcia asked.

"Our suits are at the beach," Rosalie said.

"There are spare suits in the boathouse," Marcia said. "Come on, you'll sleep better."

"I'm for it," Lowry said. "No crocodiles in the channel, are there?"

"I'd love it," Rosalie said. "I'll get a shower cap." She scurried upstairs and came down with an odd pair of trunks for Stephen and an old suit of her own.

"Why do we need suits?" Hopkins asked. "There's no one around the dock. Don't bother to get your car. I'll bring you back."

"Oh we better take the car, so you can go straight to bed. One more drink, Ken?"

"Well, you've talked me into it."

"Kenneth, don't have another. You've had enough," Marcia said.

"Oh nonsense. White Hunters drink enormously, besides the channel may be damp."

Lowry got up and went for his car as Hopkins made himself a final drink. When he brought his car to the door, Marcia was waiting.

"They're following. You have to take me," she said.

They drove through the winding lanes to her house, with the lights of the Hopkins car glaring in his mirror. As they turned in their driveway they heard and saw Hopkins's rear wheel run over the large white-painted stone at its corner. Rosalie and he were laughing as they got out of the car.

The house was dark except for a hall light downstairs and the garden path to the boathouse dim in the moonless night. A hundred yards way across the hedge they could see lights in the bedrooms of the Eadies' house. The only sound, as Hopkins led the way to the boathouse, was the slap of water against the dock and the rhythmic bumping of a rowboat against it.

"Tide's running out. Look, Lowry, why any suits at all. It's marvelous without them. What do you say, Marcia?"

"I don't mind. Anything to please a White Hunter in the dark. Rosalie, are you game? It *is* divine."

"Oh I know, and it's terribly easy to persuade a Balt not to wear a suit. It *is* dark, Steve."

"No proposing Hawaiian double-oars, Ken, if we girls agree, and everyone keeps their distance, and girls in first. Stephen's hesitating, he's so righteous."

"No, I'm not hesitating. I suppose we are sure no one's around."

"Bwana, the jungle around you is full of Walt Disney's photographers with night cameras. My advice to you is to wear trunks."

Lowry unbuttoned his shirt.

"No, no, girls first. We'll leave our clothes on the dock, Rosalie, by the ladder. You can dive. There's ten feet of water there at low tide."

"Is it all right, darling?" Rosalie half whispered to Stephen.

"I heard that," Hopkins said. "People think I can't hear when I'm drunk, which I am not, very, hear all, see all. There will be nothing to offend the most fastidious lady in the land, Mr. Lowry. Just a nice bathe, as those English call it."

"In with you," Stephen said to Rosalie.

"Keep your distance," Marcia called from the ladder, getting out of her dress.

"You'd think Steve and I were sex maniacs," Ken said.

"Who knows you better?" Marcia called and dove in, with Rosalie after her.

"Oh it is marvelous. I didn't think I'd ever be cool again. What's the little bobbing light out there?"

"Buoy. Don't go near it. Barnacles," Hopkins replied as he dove in and swimming strongly headed for mid-channel.

Stephen followed and swam to where Rosalie was. " 'Like a white lily floating on the peat hags dark waters,' " he said, taking her in his arms.

"Hey, none of that," Marcia called. "Ken, don't go out too far. Isn't it marvelous to feel the water flow all around your arms and legs! I wish Kenneth wouldn't go out so far."

"He used to be a fish," Lowry said, treading water.

"He still is but a rather heavy one and certainly a tired one tonight. Kenneth, don't be antisocial, we're having fun."

"See you soon," he called back, his voice carrying clearly over the water.

"I'm going to have two dives and call it a night. Rosalie?"

"No, a long float and a backstroke sprint and I'll be in."

"Believe it or not, I'm cold and I'm gulping. I'm going in. I'll put towels by the ladder," Marcia said and swam away from them toward the dock.

"Darling," Rosalie said, "not since we were in Rhodes, do you remember?"

"Um," he said. "Every detail."

They saw Marcia go up the ladder and scurry into the boathouse. "Go dive nicely," Rosalie said and turning on her back, started farther out. They were then about twenty-five yards from the dock, Hopkins perhaps a hundred.

In the long submerged seconds of his jackknife dive, Lowry did not hear the sudden, frightened call from Hopkins.

"Oh God, Steve. Come out. I'm all in. I can't make it. Mean it."

As he did come up and shook the water out of his eyes, he heard Rosalie answering. "I'm coming. Try to float. I can tow you in."

"Try, hurry," he heard Hopkins gasp and then Marcia ran

to the edge of the dock calling, "Steve, untie the boat. I'll get the oars."

Rosalie, swimming strongly, also called to bring the boat. He realized in an instant that it was better to get the boat in spite of the risk to Rosalie of Hopkins's panicking and pulling her under. Marcia still naked, panting, ran out dragging the oars.

"It's all right," Stephen said, "Rosalie's a lifesaver."

"Hurry Steve, hurry. Ken, we're coming, darling," Marcia called, sliding down the slippery incline to the boat, holding the oars.

Lowry had the painter loose by then and was over the side fitting the oars in the locks.

"Stay here," he said.

"No, no, I'm coming. I can row."

Over the water he heard Rosalie. "I've got him but hurry, Steve."

"Try to get him on his back."

"I'm trying. I can't."

"Steer," Lowry ordered. "I'll row." The light boat skimmed over the quiet water.

"I can see both heads," Marcia said. "We're coming, we're coming. Oh God, they're in that current, more on your right. They're being swept toward the buoy. Oh God, if they miss it."

"Steer for it ahead of them. We better be against it."

He thought of the deadly embrace of a drowning man around Rosalie and wanted to yell for her to save herself. He looked backward enough to see them forward on his right and made the terrible decision between them and the buoy.

"Crawl past me quick so you can tie up. I'm going over after the next pull."

Marcia slithered past him like a snake as he shipped his oars and slid over the side. The sweep of the current was terrible. After the first kick he made no effort to swim against it but only to keep his position.

"Don't fight," he yelled at Rosalie. "You'll drift here in a second."

"I've tied up," Marcia said.

"Take the oars. Keep broadside to us. It's all right I've got them," he answered as the two floated against him. "Can you make it?" he asked Rosalie.

She was panting hard. "Yes. He's terribly hard to hold. Have you got him?"

"Yes, hang on to the boat till you get your breath." He turned on his back and pulled Hopkins on his back beside him. Rosalie kept beside him, watching the boat, gasping, "You're all right. We're almost there. About ten feet."

"Go ahead," he said, turning his head to see his way. "In over the stern." Then all three of them drifted against the boat and with one hand on the gunwale he held Hopkins and himself. He suddenly realized he was not sure Hopkins was still alive. His mouth was open, the water splashing in and he felt as dead as a wet floursack. It was a marvel that Rosalie could have held even his head. Already he felt as though his own arm holding the boat would be pulled out of its socket.

"Try to get an arm and a leg over the stern," he said to Rosalie. "But don't try to pull yourself up until you've got your breath."

She made one effort and splashed back. Marcia leaned over the stern. "I've got my legs on the seat. When I lean over put your arm under my shoulder. Wait till I get an arm between your legs. Say when you're ready."

The second seemed eternity before Rosalie said "Ready," and he almost lost his own grip as the boat pounded up and down. Then it steadied and he heard her breathing above him and knew she was safe. Marcia's head was over the side and she was begging Kenneth to speak.

"Oh Steve, he's not dead, is he?"

"No, I can feel his heart."

"We can hold his wrists until you get in."

"It won't help. We can't get him in that way. Have you got any flares?"

"No."

"Slap him hard across the face. Harder. Ken, try to help yourself. You're all right."

Hopkins made no answer.

"I'd better try to get us on the buoy. Pull up closer, easy though."

"You'll be cut to pieces."

"I'm all right again," Rosalie said. "If I get in the water can't the two of us lift him enough for Marcie to pull him in? She's very strong."

"I don't think we can get him out of the water. I could tow him in but I think he needs to be on his face—I'll try the buoy. It will only cut my feet. Get us around, stern in. Easy now."

Marcia took the oars and maneuvered them in and Stephen, towing Kenneth, edged along the side. As he did, Rosalie slid into the water beside him and took some of the weight on herself.

"Wait, you can kneel on this bait box," Marcia said. There was just room for it between the supports for the bell and light.

"Rosalie, can you hold the boat? Grab that iron beam. Watch your fingers."

"Oh."

"Marcie, undo the painter and tie it around the seat. Good. All right. Let go, Rosalie. I'll slide out on the bait box face-down. I think we can manage. You and Marcie hold him half a minute. Now I've got him. I'll lift him head first and dump him in."

"Wait," Rosalie said, "I've got a foothold. I'll help lift."

"Oh God, he's like ice," Marcia said.

"All right, heave."

Hopkins's head and shoulder topped the stern an instant, Marcia tugging at his shoulders, and then he slipped back, Rosalie losing her footing.

"It won't do. I've got him," Lowry said panting.

Then across the water they heard the wail of a police-car siren and its searchlight from the boathouse lit up the water halfway to them. They could see two policemen on the dock and some other people, and a police voice called, "Are you in trouble out there?"

"Yes," Marcia called. "A man is drowning."

"We've radioed the Coast Guard. They're coming."

"Get a boat from the next dock and hurry."

"OK, hang on."

Rosalie slithered back into the boat. Stephen saw blood running down her thighs where the barnacles had sliced her. She lay flat facing him, holding one of Hopkins's wrists. Down channel he heard the horn of the Coast Guard patrol boat coming toward them, and saw the police putting off from the dock.

"Get a doctor and blankets," he yelled to the people on the dock.

"OK," they called back.

"You'd better lie down on your stomachs," he said to the girls. "We'll get Ken in the other boat."

Then it pulled up beside him. "It's Mr. Hopkins. Get him in your boat." Even for the two police the lift was a heavy one, and for a moment Stephen felt so exhausted he was not sure he could row ashore.

The officers glanced at the women without comment and one set about artificial respiration immediately.

"We'll row in," Stephen said. "Get him there as quick as possible. He's swallowed a lot of water."

"It's running out of him. Sure you can make it?" they asked. "There's another of our cars now, if you want 'em to come out for you."

"No, it's all right," he said, climbing into the boat with Rosalie and Marcia. He could see the lights of more cars and hear more voices around the dock. "Get your partners to shoo the sightseers away, will you? We've lost our suits."

"Yeah, so I see," the one who was rowing replied.

As the police left, the girls scrambled onto the stern seat, their arms around each other, Marcia sobbing against Rosalie. Stephen thought of the nightmare dream of being naked in a crowd, which would be reality at the dock, and started to row slowly after the other boat.

"Stephen, what will we do?" Rosalie asked.

"We'll manage. I wasn't sure we would. Are you badly cut?"

"No, it just hurts. It's only the front of my legs."

"Do you think Kenneth will live?" Marcia sobbed.

"He'll be all right. You'd both better turn over. We're coming into the lights."

"Call to somebody that there are big towels in the boathouse," Marcia said, "though I don't care who sees me, if Kenneth is all right."

He backed on his oars, twenty-five feet from the dock and swung around to watch the four officers bring Kenneth up the ladder. Then Dr. Hovey's voice called to them that he was there. Only three figures besides the police were on the dock, but he could see a ring of spectators farther back.

"My shorts and shirt are by the ladder," Stephen said. "I'd better swim in and get in them and I'll bring towels to the ladder for you. Can you take the oars, darling?"

"Yes, hurry. I'm awfully cold. I hate to have you go in the water again."

"Nonsense," he said, slipped in and swam to the ladder.

A woman, crouched by it, called, "It's Mary Hovey, Mr. Lowry. Are you all right?"

"Yes, can you hand down my shorts? They're there."

"Yes, and I have towels for the girls."

"Oh good. Come in," he called to them. "Mrs. Hovey's here with towels."

"And brandy," she called. "Ken's coming around."

Chilled as he was, his thin shorts and shirt felt like warm parkas as he got into them, and reached up for the towels.

"Back in," he said to Rosalie. "The rope's at the stern."

She swung the boat around and he caught the painter and wound it around his arm.

"Go ahead, Marcie," Rosalie said, shipping her oars neatly.

He gave her a hand. Mrs. Hovey reached down to help her. Rosalie followed.

"You poor angel," he said, wrapping her up in the big towel. "You were marvelous."

"Darling," she said, " 'when children are bad, they always, always get hurt.' "

Past midnight they reached their house. Dr. Hovey, uncertain as to the extent of shock, had ordered Kenneth to the hospital. Marcia had gone off in the ambulance with him. The police completed their questions and answers in their patrolmen memorandum books. Dr. Hovey, after a glance at Rosalie's ugly, slicing wounds, told them to go to his office for a better look. He had already telephoned the hospital.

Lying under the bright light on his table, with Mrs. Hovey on one side and Stephen the other while the doctor washed off the blood, Rosalie, trying not to wince, said, "Darling, I have been immodest for the last time in my life. Hereafter I'm going to be swathed like a nun."

Dr. Hovey roared with laughter, "That's what they all say. It's no better than a drunkard's repentance. You're all right. Nothing to do. Salt water's done it."

When they turned into their drive, the house, looking strong and secure in the moonlight, was dark except for a table lamp lit in the hall. They went upstairs together to the boys' room. Both were lying in the deep sleep of childhood and Rosalie carefully removed a baseball bat, a fielder's glove and some wearing apparel from each bed. Across the hall a small-girl tea rose was sound asleep amidst complete and tidy order. Shoes were together, robe over chair and clean clothes for the morrow laid out. On the night table a book with a marker in it was beside the lamp. A fingernail buffer was centered carefully on top of it.

With a sigh of maternal love Rosalie kissed her and Lowry and she stole across the hall to their room. The darkness was heavy with French perfume and they lit the lamps on a scene of chaos. One evening dress was on the floor, two others on the bed, four pairs of evening slippers and a selection of lace panties were scattered around the room. The glass-topped dressing table was covered with a snow of bath and face powder and the tops were off all the bottles of perfume. On the table was a sheet of paper on which in lipstick a small hand had written:

Dear Mummy:
I hope you had a good time. I had fun dressing up.
Your Darling LAINVEE
P.S. I washed my face well afterwards

P.P.S. Peter has written to Daddy under your telephone
P.P.S. Smoky was quite sick. It was too many eclairs.
Too bad.

Rosalie handed the note to Lowry. He read it through. "They know they are not supposed to feed the dog," he said pompously.

"Feed the dog!" Rosalie cried. "Look at this room. Look at my dressing table. What horror has Peter written you about?"

The scrawl under the telephone was a brief man-to-man message.

Dear Dad:

A man came and wanted to take a picture of Mum and you. He said he had one he got at Mr. Hopkins's dock but wanted a better one. I guess he will be back.

Smoky didn't make much of a mess. I guess eating grass is bad for him. Hope you had a neat time having your picture taken.

Your loving son,
PETER

Lowry read it aloud.

"Stephen, who could it have been?"

"Maybe no one. Possibly a reporter."

"Oh, how could I have let us get in such a situation! I should have said no. I knew it at the time. Somehow Cramer will find it out–"

24

AT FIRST LIGHT THAT MORNING LOWRY WAS awakened by the wind and rain driving in a full easterly against the bedroom windows. The wet, cold air felt wonderfully tonic as he got up to close them. The wind was battering the trees and he could see the gray channel waters cresting and tumbling in under it. He softly closed the windows, turning to watch the quiet sleeper in his bed, the woman who had swum through those waters. Then he stole out to the children's rooms and closed their windows. How safe the house and those in it now seemed. As softly as possible he slipped back in the warm bed and Rosalie, still asleep, moved closer to him, pillowing her head on his shoulder, so that her hair tickled his chin and nose. The most beautiful and thoughtful of women, he mused with regret, never seem to realize how unendurable that can become. He endured it as long as possible and then moved very slightly away, whereupon Rosalie, moving closer again, announced in clear grieved tones, "Now you've wakened me. Why can't you lie still? You're worse than the children. I want to sleep."

"I can't sleep with your crowning glory tickling me. I'm going to get up. I'll be very quiet. I'll get my own breakfast. I want to work on Principal Errors. It's a wonderful day, as raw and wet as Scotland."

"How *can* you be so vigorous? What time is it?"

"Oh, about five."

"It's ten after five," a small voice from the open doorway said. "Can I get in your bed, Mummy?" Lainvee asked.

"Go back to bed at once," Rosalie said sternly.

"Can't I even watch Daddy shave?"

"Lainvee," Stephen said, "your mother's very tired. Now go back to bed, dear."

"I never get to do anything. I've been down to see Smoky. He's all right today."

When Lowry shaved and bathed and came back in the bedroom, Rosalie was sitting up sleepily examining the cuts on her legs. She sank back on the pillows and pulled up the covers.

"Would you like me to bring you some orange juice and coffee?" he asked, hastily dressing.

"Please not, for four hours. I don't understand you. Are all men as bad as you?"

"In what way?"

"This awful getting up early. I should think the marriage bed would be ideal on a morning like this."

"Well, I'm hungry and I feel very active," he said.

"If I weren't so tired and mangled I'd make you come back just to show you. Close the door after you and turn that telephone off, please." As he bent to kiss her she saw Peter's note on the night table. "Darling, you don't suppose anyone really took a picture of us, do you, or that there'll be anything in the papers?"

"There might be something in. After all, you did save Kenneth's life. But certainly nothing to worry about."

He fixed himself a fine big breakfast, retrieved the morning paper from the rain-swept doorway, glanced quickly through it and settled himself behind the closed door of the library with the notes of Principal Errors. Later he vaguely heard the maids and then the children come down to breakfast.

It seemed to him he had never seen so clearly the direction the book was to take or realized how far organized its material already was. Synopses of several chapters flowed from his pen, themselves full of fresh ideas and points of view. Half superstitiously he said to himself that things came in cycles. All the events of C.I.C. culminating in the bid, and even the near-tragic night before had to have happened to give him this sense of lift and freedom.

The house was still utterly quiet except for the beating rain on the windows and it was almost ten o'clock when the telephone beside him rang.

It was Kenneth Hopkins calling from the hospital, full of apologies, gratitude and questions. He was quite recovered and going home after lunch. He would never forgive himself, etc., etc. Lowry soothed him and returned to work as the phone rang again.

"Oh, Mr. Lowry. This is Bill Eadie. I hope you folks are all right. It was quite by chance we came in when we did and I phoned the police. Have you heard how Kenneth is?"

"He's fine, I just spoke to him. He'll be home after lunch."

"Good. I understand your wife is the real heroine. That current is absolute hell. We wondered if you'd care to come over for a drink before lunch."

"Well, thanks a lot but I think Rosalie is going to have a day in bed—"

"Sure, I understand, well, we'll give you a raincheck, ha, ha, ha, good day for it."

Lowry resumed his studies. There was only a brief lull before the next call, which was answered simultaneously by Richard and Rosalie and himself. A little girl wanted Lainvee to come for lunch. Lainvee took the phone from Richard.

"Oh I can't possibly, Lindsay. I have to talk to Mummy as soon as she wakes up, because she had her picture taken."

"Dear, your mummy is awake," Rosalie said from the extension.

Some minutes later in a white housecoat, looking tired but beautiful, she appeared in the library. "Nice, quiet morning," she said. Lowry shook his head sadly and reached again for the ringing telephone.

"For you," he said handing it to her. "Jane Alden, long distance."

He could hear both ends of the talk that followed.

"Bill Eadie just phoned us, darling. How *are* you?"

"Oh fine."

"We're cursing our luck at not having come to dinner and being up here in Connecticut out of it all. How did you manage that enormous Kenneth?"

"Steve and Marcie and the police did most of it."

"Listen, darling, can anyone hear me?"

"I don't think so."

"I'm dying to know, was it one of the Hopkins's special after-dark swims?"

"What do you mean?"

"Birthday suits?" she whispered. "You can be sure everyone will suppose so, so it's best to laugh and say yes if there are jokes about it. Only you do have to be careful about Mrs. Rossiter at the school. She absolutely refused to have those darling Van Tromp children after Sheila was on such a party there while Vannie was away. Save all the dirt for me, dear, I'll be back Monday after lunch."

For the rest of the morning neighbors continued to call and in the brief intervals, the children alternated in telephoning their familiars about the rescue, Lainvee finally moving its exact point somewhere outside American territorial waters.

"It's like a funeral, dear," Rosalie said, legs stretched out to the fire, "when they say 'she had so many friends.' "

"I've been thinking—" Stephen said.

"In this tumult. You really are wonderful."

"That I wish we could fly to England and spend ten days at Oxford really working."

"Dear, we haven't the money."

The telephone rang again. The caller said he was Joe Casey from one of the news agencies and that his partner, Rudy Ekler, had got a shot of them at the dock but he'd like to come and get another and there were just a few points they wanted to be clear on.

"We got you clear, Mr. Lowry, the vice-president of Continental Industrial Company, that's right, and Mr. Hopkins is a lawyer.

Got his firm all right." He evidently spoke through his teeth and from one corner of his mouth.

"Well I'm not *the* vice-president and my company is Continental Industries Corporation, but we don't want a story in the papers about it."

"Somebody told us your wife who made the rescue is foreign. Do you happen to know where from?"

"Now look, Mr. Casey, we don't want to make a performance because one of our friends swam out a little far and we gave him a hand. That's not news. It would be news if we'd left him."

"Listen, Mr. Lowry, it's news and it's my hard luck it was too late for the morning papers, but when all parties don't have a stitch on, it ought to be good tonight and tomorrow with Ekler's shot. So give us a break and we'll give you one, dignified account of a very very heroic deed. This Hopkins guy weighs two hundred pounds, the cops say. Think of what a heroine your wife is. The TV show Thrill of the Week's going to want her. Where'd you say she's from? I'm just asking you to cooperate a little."

"I appreciate it, Mr. Casey, and I know you have your job to do, but really we haven't anything to say."

"OK, if that's the way you want it," Mr. Casey said and hung up.

"Well," Stephen said to Rosalie. "I don't know whether I was wise or not. I suppose if he's sore he'll make more of it, but I can't imagine their having space for it."

"I heard the 'didn't have a stitch on' part. You certainly have to think ahead in this country. I am so mad at myself. Do you suppose they'll print it?"

"Oh I don't think so really. Would you mind my reading this synopsis to you?"

"No," she said. When he finished she said it was very good and asked, "When will we know about the papers?"

At three o'clock he splashed through the rain on foot to the village for an afternoon paper. The news dealer came up to him and said there was nothing in about them yet but there was a later edition came out on the 5.01 and if he liked a boy would deliver it if there was anything.

"Mighty exciting thing. A thing like that could put Ridingtown right back on the map, Mr. Lowry. Good for business. Hope Mrs. Lowry's all right. Big man, Mr. Hopkins, wonderful how she could manage."

"How'd you hear about it?" Lowry asked him.

"Oh I heard first thing. Mr. Eadie's chauffeur came in, oh about eight o'clock, to get a pack of cigarettes and several people told me. Rudy Ekler married a cousin of my wife."

"How did he happen to get there?"

"Oh, he's got a special short-wave in his car and when Mr. Eadie's call went out to the prowl car, Rudy picked it up and he was at Mr. Eadie's soon as anybody." He straightened some magazines with half-exposed women, as Cramer would have called them, on the covers. "I don't see that that Code and that Czar is helping these much," he said. "People still buy 'em."

Rosalie was asleep again when he got back and he resumed work on Principal Errors. Looking much better, she appeared for tea just as the newsboy brought the later edition. There was brief mention of the heroic rescue, but no picture and no reference to clothing. It did say Mrs. Lowry was a society matron and mother of three, and gave Hopkins's weight.

"You see," Lowry said, putting his arm around her, "conscience doth make cowards of us all. Now can you take a little more active interest in Principal Errors?"

"Yes sir," she said meekly, "but it wouldn't have been very nice, and it made me ill to think about Mr. Cramer. Let's play games with the children tonight. They've been awfully good all day."

When Lowry went down in slippers and bathrobe for the papers Sunday morning, with the rain still falling, he found, along with *Times* and *Herald Tribune*, unordered copies of two tabloids and a local South Shore paper. And there in the last three was the "true-facts" story, with Ekler's shot of Rosalie and Marcie on the dock wrapped scantily in towels. There was a wealth of detail, biographical and otherwise about Diving Godiva, café society's candidate for the Carnegie medal, who had first swum as a girl on her estates behind the Iron Curtain in Estonia before meeting the dashing war hero now a New York executive.

The *Times* and *Herald Tribune*, in their dull way, gave a few prosaic lines to the story. Lowry read the other accounts again, feeling ill himself. The telephone rang.

"Mr. Lowry, this is Schantz, your paperman. I sent you both the tabloids. Will you want me to set aside any more for you to send your friends before they're sold out?"

"No, thanks very much. It won't be necessary," Lowry said. He wished there were some way he could spare Rosalie. He wished, in fact, he knew just what to do. You couldn't buy up a whole issue and you could no longer horsewhip editors. And he supposed if he had read it about someone else he would have been amused. He supposed the Hopkinses would, if anything, feel worse. Hopkins cut a poor figure in the stories and his wife was "reported under sedation" in contrast to the strong, steel-nerved Lowrys.

He tore out the various pages and went upstairs. Rosalie yawned, stretched and turned back the covers for him in one gesture.

"Dear," he said, "here are the stories. Before you read them, remember that everybody won't see them and of those who do most won't care and between laughing or crying over them, it's better to laugh, and—"

"Undressed?"

"Um, yep. However, if in addition to being undressed, you had swum ashore and abandoned Kenneth, the story would be worse."

"It's all very well and very considerate of you to laugh about it, but I should have known enough to say no."

"Dear, but for Ekler's unlucky presence and the fright over Kenneth, it would have been a delightful experience."

"That's just it, Stephen, you're not supposed to do such things, and when you do they get found out."

She got out of bed, quickly donned a robe and went into the bathroom, locking the door behind her. Lowry dressed and went downstairs.

At breakfast even he felt that the children all looked at their parents with accusing questions in their eyes, and that even the maids were drawing their garments aside.

"I feel simply horrible," Rosalie said to him later in the morning. "I am sure the children know, probably from a friend who heard her mummy and daddy discussing it. I'll be ashamed to go to the Beach—outside of the fact that my legs are a sight. I've behaved as though I had no sense of decency or responsibility, or not a care in the world. I resent the attitude people have about European women and I act as though you had found me in the Place Pigalle. I am horrified when I think of what I would have said to the children if they'd done it. 'Mrs. Lowry, *do* tell us about nude mixed bathing in the Baltic. You were always accustomed to it, I suppose. All the men envy Kenneth so.' I can hear the women. And a few months ago, the thought of Jim having that picture of me made me ill."

"Dear," he said patiently, "stop worrying about it so. It's over with."

"You always say to me things are over with, when they're not."

Late in the afternoon a telegram arrived for Mrs. Stephen Lowry. It was from Chicago and said:

HAVE SEEN TIMES ACCOUNT YOUR DARING RESCUE PLEASE ACCEPT SINCEREST CONGRATULATIONS ON THIS NOBLE DEED IN WHICH MRS. CRAMER AND JOHN JOIN ME WE THANK GOD YOU ARE SAFE

D. P. CRAMER

"You see," Lowry said, "that's all it was, 'a noble deed.'"

Shortly afterwards Stephen's mother, having driven into Larus for the *Times*, telephoned in great pride and excitement, and when they had subsided a little she said, "Rosalie, it's such a blessing that Stephen isn't the hero, because it would be a final blow to poor dear Robert. As it is, Sally is, I think, making him miserable because he wasn't smart enough to marry you instead of her. The poor man can do nothing like her brother, not even marry a real lifesaver. You're all right, are you, dear?"

"We are at the moment," Rosalie said, "but I think you ought to know—and let Robert know—that in a fit of madness I, as well as the other three, did not wear anything at all and the tabloids tell all about it."

"Oh, my dear, how divine. Send them to me sure. What a lark! Oh to be young and beautiful."

"I don't feel that way. I'm very ashamed of it, but I thought you ought to know."

"Well," Mrs. Lowry said, "don't take too many austere vows in your remorse."

At eight Monday morning Kenneth Hopkins telephoned in a weak and hollow voice. "Steve, are we speaking?"

"Sure."

"I wouldn't blame you if you weren't, but do you want to drive in? I don't know that I can face the club car. I'm dreadfully sorry and ashamed to have gotten you in the papers."

"I've been thinking about the club car, but I think I'd better face it. Thanks though."

"I'm terribly, terribly sorry about it."

"Well cheer up. It isn't a tragedy. We're all alive."

The club car was an ordeal. There was no direct reference to it but the faces of the fellow travelers were either hidden behind newspapers, around which they occasionally peered as though wanting to be sure this was "the man, who," or they wore fixed smiles of charity and fellowship, as though to say, "You're still a member of an exclusive club car"; a third section kept grinning, if not leering, with the implication that Stephen could give them the juicy details over a drink later.

A presidential aspirant had met the press on TV Sunday night and talked about "human dignity." Lowry thought he had himself not displayed much on Friday night.

Almost the entire office force stopped him with questions or congratulations as he made his way to his office. No tabloid clippings were in evidence, but as he passed the president's open door he saw Miss Wilkins busy with desk scissors on some paper.

His telephone was busy for an hour with congratulations mixed with brilliant jests of friends such as, "What the hell was the matter with you, lose your waterwings?" So far as he could judge, Miss Marshall's inquiries and congratulations gave no indication that she had read or heard of the true-facts story. Yet he felt a little uneasy and wished he had not once so strongly emphasized his wish that she not carry tales.

Rosalie telephoned him toward noon to say, "I realized after you left that the question of where Jim is would come back to you this morning."

"My God, I had forgotten it."

"Well, a letter written to me yesterday came in the mail and I managed to read it because I had an awful feeling it might be, well, nonsense because of the paper. I still have that on my mind, you see, but all he says is: 'Dear Rosalie, I just read in the *Times* of your very brave rescue of Kenneth Hopkins and want to send you my most heartfelt congratulations. I have been very fortunate in being able to leave Excello and have real assurance of getting everything straightened out very shortly.' He doesn't give an address. Are you relieved?"

"Yes, but what can he mean 'get everything straightened out'? Mailed from New York?"

"Yes."

"Well, thanks, darling. Are you all right?"

"Um, managing. The *South Shore Breeze* called up and wanted to take pictures of the house and of me with the children. I couldn't face the Beach yet. I sent the children over and was at loose ends, so I've done quite a bit on Principal Errors. I was amazed, darling, at how much you got done yesterday. You're so smart and so precious. Can I keep you a minute more?"

"I should say."

"Now don't laugh at me because I say this badly. But when I was feeling depressed about the swimming and the tabloid and all—and I had one of those awful female dreads of your only loving me physically—I thought how wonderfully blest I was that we have Principal Errors, and I'm a small part of it even if

I'm only an Estonian peasant. No more now. I love you. Goodbye."

Just before lunch Curtis came in and spoke nicely of the rescue and Stephen, by now feeling that he had been right about few people reading the tabloid story, told Curtis of Cramer's telegram to Rosalie. Curtis seemed unimpressed. "I thought you might care to read this," he said and handed him a letter from Cramer.

While in Lebanon yesterday I took my friend Bresnahan into my confidence as to my serious doubts about the value we were getting from Frank Parry's services as head of the engine unit. I was not at all surprised to have Bresnahan fully agree with me. He believes as I do that if Mr. Rutledge and Mr. Johnson had not had their sympathies worked on by the fact that Parry has a domestic situation and that backward child he would have been out long ago. I think you will agree that one of the best ways of determining a man's value to this company is by asking what a competitor would pay him. Do you know anybody who would want Parry? True, the plant is not badly run, but that's not enough. I am sure you will agree that we don't owe Parry a thing. Bresnahan, as you know, is worth upwards of a million dollars. His quarry, his store and his fertilizer-spreader company in Lebanon are among the smallest of his companies. I think, in fact I have reason to know, all we have to do to get the fertilizer-spreading company for a buck and a dime, as the boys say, is to throw the engine company under his son-in-law, who runs the spreader company. I met the son-in-law, a very well conducted young man, nice young wife and lovely children, and a doer, belongs to everything around here. I enclose the spreader company's balance sheet and earnings since the war and wish you'd let me have your estimate of the effect on our earnings of this change and your idea of what we should pay for it. The son-in-law only draws 8000 and bonus, figured on spreader-units shipped. Parry, you realize, has been upped to ten. I think we might fix young Shattelcutter's salary—his uncle is Senator Shattelcutter of Iowa—at 12, but you may think this too high. Still other economies will more than offset it. John has met Shattelcutter and agrees with me he's a doer. I think this can be handled as a matter of executive action and doesn't need to go to the Board, though I would of course tell Mr. Delano and have no doubts of his agreement. I think all this shows how important it is for us all to get out in the field.

D.P.C.

"We stayed in town yesterday because of the storm," Curtis said, taking it back, "and I found myself reading some Walter Bagehot. I copied this bit. It may interest you."

Lowry took the slip of paper and read:

A large corporation is exactly the place where a vain and shallow person in authority, if he be a man of gravity and method, as such men often are, may do infinite evil in no long time and before he is detected.

"I suppose I've got to do as he asks."

"But Charley," Lowry said, "you can't let him do this. I've only met Parry but we can't let this happen to the poor guy. He's had a terrible life."

"I know we shouldn't," Curtis said. "I suppose I'm tired or old, but I don't have the mental or maybe it's the moral energy to fight. You feel strongly about it. I was sure you would. Why don't you fight the battle? You write Cramer what you think I should."

"I don't think I can do that," Lowry said.

"You see, it really *is* easier to tell people what they ought to do—"

"I meant I didn't see how I could do it effectively. The letter isn't to me. It's not my business. It would only annoy Cramer and probably harm Parry's chances. I should certainly think though that a strong refusal from you would be enough."

"Stephen, I'm sorry for Parry but I don't want a row with Cramer. I've got four years to go before retirement."

"Well, you're not going to spend them agreeing to things like this, are you?"

"It's difficult for you in the prime of life to realize how much you want peace after sixty. If you don't want to write Cramer—and I see no reason why you shouldn't, say I told you about it—then see Delano or Channing. Tell them how strongly you feel."

"But, Charley, you've known Parry all these years. I haven't. I know almost nothing definite about his record."

"I suppose you're right but about two minutes ago you said '*We* can't let this happen to him.' Now it isn't 'we' when it comes to doing something."

"It's so absolutely clear that you are the natural person to do it. You're the senior officer next to Cramer. It's your area. You can say no and make it stick. For the moment just write Cramer you'll discuss it when he gets back, then tell him it's a mistake, and if he persists, tell him you won't stand for it."

"You've been subject to a great many annoyances from him, more than anyone here, I think. Have you ever told him you wouldn't stand for it?"

"No, I haven't."

"You've said each time there'd be better grounds to fight on?"

"Yes."

"Well, Stephen, I'll tell you this. I don't think you want a showdown with Master Cramer any more than I do, and as far as I'm concerned Parry will have to look out for himself. I'll take that Bagehot slip."

25

LOWRY SPENT A TROUBLED NIGHT. BEFORE LEAVing the office he had tried again, and futilely, to persuade Curtis to stand in Parry's defense. Curtis said he was sorry he had shown him the letter. If it was not his own concern it was certainly not Lowry's and he quite agreed any move by Lowry was both uncalled for and certain to make matters worse. There was no reason for Lowry's conscience to trouble him. He knew enough about psychology to say that for a man to intervene on behalf of someone he scarcely knew, and in all the circumstances prevailing, would be absurdly quixotic and unrealistic. Parry had to take his chance, as he himself would or as Lowry would if things went against them. And as matter of fact it was true that, whatever the cause, Parry had not set the world on fire and tended more and more to withdraw from it. There was something in Cramer's feeling they needed a doer.

"All of us let ourselves get sentimentally worked up about Harold Titcomb. And what happened? Harold's fine."

Before breakfast the next morning he went downstairs to put in a call to Hewitt at his hotel in St. Louis to say how he felt about it and ask what he could do. But as he asked for Long Distance the futile absurdity of the call seemed so apparent that he hung up.

He reached his office at his usual hour and was told at once Mr. Hewitt was trying to reach him from Chicago.

"Steve, I didn't want to call you at home last night but I thought you ought to know. Cramer's got all that stuff about you in the tabloids from Miss Wilkins and he's really on a tear. I'm doing my best to quiet him of course, but he's out for blood. You know the high moral line he can take. Well it was something to hear. I can't advise you what to do but I'm frankly worried. You know, 'This naturally ends his usefulness,' 'flagrant disregard of proprieties,' etc., etc., 'It'll look nice in our credit file at the banks.' I don't want to talk any more, in case he comes in. Just watch your step. Have some story ready."

I suppose, Lowry thought to himself as he sat back, this is the feeling Jim must have had when I said he couldn't come down that Sunday evening. I suppose it's the feeling Parry will have. So I'd better get rid of it. What bothered him most, for the moment, was how for the first time he would be able to keep an important secret from Rosalie.

Along in midmorning Paula Hewitt telephoned Rosalie to say, "My dear, how are you after that thrilling rescue? I want to hear all about it but I've actually called about something quite different. You wouldn't want to come in to lunch, would you?"

Rosalie hesitated a moment. "I really don't think I'd better, but why don't you come out? It's lovely and cool."

"I think I will, if you're sure it's convenient. Is two o'clock too late? I'm counting on some help from you." Rosalie detected a tinge of anxiety in her voice which was somehow comforting to her. It was a relief to think someone else needed help.

Paula arrived a little before two in a flowered cotton dress of staggering cost and simplicity. Asked about a drink, she said tomato juice only. There was no sign of anxiety about her. She loved the house, the garden, the weather and the food, and even Smoky, who sneezed heavily and backed away snarling after a sniff of the delicate fragrance about her. Rosalie thought how unworthy of herself it was to wish Paula had been anxious about something. Hearing the "sordid details" of the swim she showed all her pretty teeth and said, "What an absolute riot."

Rosalie stiffly changed the subject and asked in a hollow voice, "You said you were counting on some help from me?"

"Yes, but there's an awfully long preamble to my problem. I hope you'll be patient. I'll wait till we've lunched."

"Do you mind if I have a gin and tonic after all?"

"Certainly not."

Over the coffee Paula said, "Well, to begin, did you hear from Jim?"

"Yes, I did, a nice little note about the rescue."

"I told him to write you. He wasn't sure that he should yet. He told you he'd left those awful people?"

"Yes."

"Evidently he didn't tell you what he was doing."

"No, but he said he had hopes of getting everything straightened out."

"Oh I *am* so glad he said that. It's still hard to convince him."

"Well, what is he going to do?"

"You can't guess?"

"No."

"Want to try Twenty Questions?"

"Please not."

Paula lit a cigarette. "First today," she said, with a smirk. "Although not accurate yet, in every detail," she continued calmly, "I think you'll understand the situation more clearly if I tell you we are living together."

Rosalie choked over her coffee. "As—as, well—"

"Yes, I suppose so, that is to say, we go to bed sometimes. Of course Jim is beset with inhibitions about sex, but you know I'm not of a very amorous nature, so that I can help him. For some reason, which I see no need to dig up by the roots, he has never been able to set his sexual desires in order. He has frequently gotten drunk in an effort to reach a lower level of behavior, without succeeding of course."

"Paula, are you sure you want me to hear this?"

"Sure, it all bears on your helping me. But to go back. I told you about my taking Jim to lunch the first time. He was pathetically pleased at having someone he could talk to, and he talked a great deal. I'm not sure whether he wanted me to be his mother or his big sister or his mistress. What he wanted was someone who didn't care what he'd done or what his shortcomings were—and I told him I didn't. I suppose at the time I was flatttered and certainly very moved at having someone bare his whole life to me. Well, I found myself doing the same. And I concluded that in a very odd way we needed each other. And I'm not such a fool as not to realize that if I didn't have all this money he wouldn't need me so much. But I didn't tell him that. In a long, roundabout way, he asked me to let him spend the night with me, and I agreed."

"But—"

"What he really needed was to get it out of his system. But Evelyn was unable—and who can blame her, certainly not I—to see that there may be urges to erotic license—in part, this is a quotation—having nothing to do with love. Your swimming party is something of the sort. It didn't mean that—"

"Paula, it was not erotic, not in the least."

"Dear, I wouldn't be too sure, but let me go on. Just a minute." She opened her handbag and glanced at a scrap of paper. "Oh yes, as I said I'm not particularly amorous—in fact I'm shy about it—but I had no objection to indulging him or helping him create some unreality—without shock, or surprise or censure. And as soon as it's over, we're very companionable. But you must grasp this. I don't make the mistake of saying Evelyn was all wrong for him and I'm just right. I'm sure now that he and I are both rather shallow people who are at our best when everything's pleasant, and of course as I say, with all this money, you can have an awful lot of pleasantness. Unfortunately at our third meeting, our third, yes, deep remorse, deep shame and self-accusation overcame him and he left me at eleven o'clock never to see me again. I spent a horrible night because I then realized that the one thing I wanted was to get him on his feet and out of those horrible places he was working and living in. I telephoned him at six in the morning and I said I cried all night, which wasn't quite true, and that I needed him, something which I doubt anyone had ever said to him. For which I was grateful.

because if any of his friends had said to him after his resignation that he was needed, for anything, anywhere, by anyone, I wouldn't have gotten him."

"But Paula, dear, I see what you mean, at least I think I do, but how will it all end? After all, there's Calvin and there are all of Jim's debts—and, I don't know, the world at large, I suppose. And besides, can it be good for him to go on that way?"

"It's good for him all right. You'd hardly know him. As for that money thing, I'm giving him the money to pay everybody. We don't know how to do it with Mr. Rutledge and I hope Stephen can think of a device."

"Calvin?"

"I have already devoted half my life to being deceived and made a fool of by him, so that I'm not feeling too responsible. And he has dear Mr. Cramer to comfort him. What a joke that he daren't tell him, just when he writes me they're seeing everything eye to eye. But he can have the apartment. I have another one."

"Isn't it difficult about seeing people?"

"No, we don't see them. That will all straighten out. I can see you're shocked and I understand."

"Please don't think I'm censorious, it isn't that."

"I'd understand if you were. But you must understand this and you must make Stephen understand it. For all the good there still is in Jim, regeneration by atonement, expiation, that sort of thing is beyond him, far beyond him. He would not have been able to hold on at Excello, he would have gradually drifted down. It would have been hopeless. There's no iron, cold iron in his soul. You may not know, but Stephen told him God still has a plan for him. Well, I'm the plan. Now as to your helping us."

A slight shiver ran through Rosalie. We can't have them here, she thought. Birds of a feather—Fifth Amendment exhibitionists; an embezzler with an adulteress under one roof. Liberty Hall! *Fay ce que voudras!*

"You mustn't think I've lost my head or my heart in all this," Paula said.

"Oh no," Rosalie told her.

"I see Jim's faults perhaps more clearly than anyone else. The thing is, though, that he is still malleable. That's a sort of quotation also. I mean it isn't an original word that I knew. Gold is the most malleable metal, that is, it can be hammered into new shapes. There is a basic fine gold in Jim. It's what Stephen saw in him originally. His faults are many but they don't exasperate or bore me. He's not even a congenital liar. In most ways he's very conventional. Of course he can't be trusted with money, but on the other hand he has a great deal of sense about it. He lacks soldierly qualities such as Stephen has, but he has many of the best qualities of the dilettante or idler." She announced it with a happy sigh as though such qualities were the fine, final flowers of Western civilization. "He is still pathetically devoted to Stephen and yearns to regain his good opinion."

No, no, Rosalie said firmly to herself, we cannot have them out here.

"You must have seen how much Jim imitated Stephen and wanted to be like him."

Even wanted his woman, Rosalie thought.

"What he wants most to do now, as soon as I think it's all right, is to write and publish a book, and I think it would be a very good thing for him to do. It may seem unfair for him to be able to do it before Stephen writes that tome of his, but it would do the world for Jim."

"Well, why doesn't he?"

"The trouble is I'm sure he's chosen the wrong thing to begin on. It could come later, though. Have you read Marcel Proust?"

"Um, not all."

"Well, of course I had only heard the name and knew nothing about him—"

"Wait a minute, Jim isn't going to write a book about Proust, is he?"

"So he says, isn't it ridiculous? He's not very good at French. But wait till I tell you. I discovered that this man Proust wrote one book in over twelve volumes and that Jim, like a little boy, took them with him when he went to West End Avenue—only them. He wanted me to read them. Well, it would have taken me through the menopause. So I went up secretly to talk to the Suydam Professor of French at Columbia and got him to give me two hour lectures on Proust. And of course he is very good and very funny—Proust that is. Jim wants to write on 'The Comic Spirit in Proust.' "

"The Comic Spirit is one of Stephen's big ideas."

"I told you, dear, how Jim imitates him."

"It isn't original with Stephen of course."

"No matter. My Frenchman told me," Paula continued with that acquisitive sense of the very rich, "that while the satire and comedy—there's a character funnier than Malaprop, who seats men in order of their impotence—are marvelous, there's a frightful amount of Lesbianism and homosexuality all through it and I don't think Jim is ready for that, not ready for it himself, I don't mean of course; I mean that he isn't out of the morbid state sexually enough himself to be objective, though of course there's no question of anything like that about him. But it would be a situation too precocious for him. Those aren't my own words."

"Paula, have you been going to an analyst?"

"Well, to get advice about Jim, I am talking to the chief psychologist at the Suydam Clinic."

"So what is the alternative?" Rosalie asked.

"That's where you can help us. I propose that I take Jim to Europe for, say, six months and that we put a whole *équipe*—wonderful French word—in Paris and Oxford on Principal Errors under Jim's supervision. Say you'll try to get Stephen to agree."

"Does Jim know about this?"

"To a degree. Don't feel that it wouldn't be all Stephen's book. What we do can be dismissed in a line's acknowledgment, but it would provide Jim with one of the disciplines he needs."

"Stephen would certainly do a great deal for Jim, but I don't think he would like this idea, Paula. I really don't."

"If we get material and give it to him to use, I can't see the harm. I should think it would help him."

As she said it they heard the far-off whistle on the firehouse in the village.

"What's that?" Paula asked.

"Four-thirty."

"I must go. If Stephen agrees, you won't oppose it, will you?"

"But I know he won't agree. He's not changeable."

"You can't say that. Everybody changes. Look at me. Ask Stephen to call me. Here's my new number."

A horrible thought struck Rosalie that Stephen might agree, might say, "Of course it's a compromise, but it would save an enormous amount of time and trouble." She saw him gradually losing all control of it, seeing it slip more and more firmly into other hands.

Then she heard the burst of children's voices and they tore out on the terrace. "Oh Mummy, we played channel rescue all day. All the kids were playing it and Penny Rossiter saved Peter at the deep end of the pool."

Half an hour before, Lorna Hume had telephoned Stephen.

"Stephen, it's Lorna, do you take a train at the Long Island about five?"

"Yes."

"Could I meet you for a few minutes outside the bookstore on that level?"

"Yes, where are you now?"

"I'm at the apartment and I don't want you to come here."

"I wasn't suggesting that, but isn't there—"

"I would rather make it there and it will take only a moment. Quarter of five?"

"All right," he said, and at that time was waiting as the commuting rush streamed past him, wondering, as people do, which direction she would come from. He felt vaguely uneasy that she had something she must say about the tabloid story, then he saw her, cool and trim-looking, at the top of the steps leading to Thirty-Fourth Street. They both waved as she ran lightly down the long stairs, but as they met her smile was so sorrowful that it touched his heart.

"I hope you'll think this was better in the end than writing or telephoning you or having you at the apartment or meeting for a drink. I tried to think it out."

"What is it?"

"You don't know about Principal Errors?"

"Well, I know I'm working on it."

"Stephen, my dear, still my very dear, it has been written by Professor John Bancroft Twombley of Harvard and is about to be published, with the full title, by Dunstable and Company."

"Oh," he said. "How's it possible? Not the same book as mine?"

"Yes, here, this is in the trade paper this week."

She handed him a clipping.

Loud and louder paeans from the editorial offices of Dunstable and Company about the new book on which the Sales Department foresaw a modest two thousand going to libraries. The Volume-of-the-Month for November. All this for a volume of erudite research on which Professor John Bancroft Twombley of Harvard has been engaged for ten years. The book is entitled The Principal Errors of Judgment of Rulers and Peoples Since the Reformation. *There is a strange and tragic story of the source of the book epitomized in its dedication to the memory of Colonel Garrett Maynard, who died of wounds received at Anzio. Professor Twombley, then in the American Intelligence, met Colonel Maynard there, when himself a casualty, and was given by him the idea of the book . . .*

"I feel so terribly at telling you. I don't know what I'd do if we were alone. I still don't know anyone who can take things as you do. I wanted to be unselfish and have you able to go straight to your wife. That's part of why I met you here."

The commuting rush was increasing, men and women discarding cigarettes to find the change for an evening paper, or another pack of cigarettes. Two sweepers with pans and brushes had given up and were also leaning against the bookstore window. The non-red-capped porters were offering their services with their pathetic smiling deference, "Jus' take you to the gates. They won't 'low us to go down."

"It still doesn't seem possible. I never heard of Twombley. Funny that I missed him among all the professors I've written to." He straightened up and patted Lorna's arm. "I suppose the only thing that matters is that he was better equipped than I and it will be a better book. Can I keep the clipping?"

She nodded, said goodbye, my dear, quickly and left him. All the way up on the escalator she held her hand up to him. He turned and went for his train. Monday morning he had not wanted to go in the club car because of the rescue story. Now what did it matter? A great quadrant of his inner life was lost, and hereafter his only familiars would be the bankers and brokers, lawyers and executives of the club car. He had never been any better than they anyhow. Several of them would probably have had the moral courage to go to Parry's assistance.

26

ROSALIE, SEEING STEPHEN DRIVE IN, CALLED FROM her window, "Why darling, how lovely. I'll be down in just a moment bursting with news. Paula's been here."

He walked into the library and sat down, looking at the long table with the boxes of notes with their dividers and markers, the results of so many long, happy hours in many places. He had not told Rosalie of the moral conflict he was going through about Parry, or of Hewitt's call about Cramer and the tabloids, and now he did not want to tell her their book was lost. The synopses he had written Saturday and Sunday were back from the village typist in three sets and Rosalie had put a jug of small golden zinnias as a paperweight on the first copy.

He heard her coming down the stairs and she burst in, gave him a quick kiss and pushed him down on the sofa.

"Paula, Paula Hewitt and Jim are living together! That's why you couldn't find him. She's paid, or is paying, all his debts."

"Keeping him?"

"I know it sounds like that, but it isn't just that. She was here and it was touching, it was comic and yet it wasn't ridiculous or sordid—she's frightfully practical and she seems to understand him, I think. And, believe it or not, she says she needs him, and I think she does."

"My God, I thought he had it in him to make something of himself."

"It will sound strange to you, but I think this way he may," she said, and told him more of what Paula had said.

He nodded finally. "Well, I suppose she's right about him. But what will they *do,* keep going on round-the-world cruises?"

"Oh no, he wants to write a book on Proust."

"But he doesn't know anything about Proust. That's fantastic."

"Paula realizes that. She's even been to see the Suydam Professor of French for a 'briefing' on Proust. But what she wants to start with, and apparently he does, is to go to Paris and for you to let him put a whole *équipe* of researchers on Principal Errors at her expense and turn the results over to you."

"On my book?"

"I told her, of course, you'd never agree—"

He looked down at the rug, leaning forward with his elbows on his knees, his hands clasped between them, sitting as Jim had the afternoon at Gramercy Park, and she felt a sudden fright that he was going to agree. She slipped her arm around his neck, turning his face toward her.

"I said to you about Jim once that I thought I'd be more stoical. I don't know that I am."

"Oh, darling yes, yes you are," she said, kissing him.

"I've already lost the book. Someone else has written it. Please read this," and giving her the clipping he got up to put the boxes back in the lower shelf. She read it quickly and followed him, her eyes full of tears.

"Oh my dearest."

He smiled grimly, looking down in her face.

"It's over with," he said. "I must see whether I can practice what I preach."

"Don't put the notes away, don't say it's over with. There'll be something, something even better." She pressed herself to him.

"I've had an unbroken run of luck from the moment you came into Pastor Larsen's hut. I couldn't expect it to last forever."

"How did you find out about it?"

"Lorna Hume saw the clipping and brought it to me at the station."

"Just now?"

"Yes."

"Perhaps with her you would have finished it in time. Oh darling, why did this have to happen?"

Lowry saw Cramer with his son in train sweep through the office at eleven-thirty the next morning. They moved so rapidly that one felt only power brakes would stop them at their desks. A boy distributing the second mail stepped out of their way just in time. They were set, it was obvious, to plunge into work. He wondered where Calvin Hewitt was.

Within a few minutes Miss Marshall said the president would like to see him at once and he went to his office.

Without his usual greeting Cramer said, "Do you know where we can reach Mrs. Hewitt?"

"No I don't. Is something the matter?"

"I've brought him back from Chicago a sick man. John and I took him to his apartment and got him to bed. His wife wasn't there and the servants didn't seem to know where she is."

"Is he seriously ill?"

"We had to leave before his doctor got there. I am not a physician. When a man vomits all night and looks like death I call him seriously ill."

"Appendicitis?"

"He has no appendix and he had no chest pains. It's not his heart. He's overworked—I don't know what it is. Where in the world could his wife be?"

"He had no idea?"

"If he had, I wouldn't be asking you."

"Well I'm sorry, but I don't know."

Cramer's usually benign face was wrinkled with anger and impatience and, wholly unlike himself, he kept rapping on his desk with his knuckles.

"Did you telegraph him in Chicago?"

"No, why do you ask?"

"He got a telegram from someone, the bell captain told John, that seemed to start this. I thought it might have been from you about this disgraceful incident in the papers. I had already seen it, as had Calvin, and David and Jonathan couldn't have tried to do more on your behalf than he did with me. I never thought I'd live to see the day when an officer in one of my companies would be written up in a scandal sheet. I said to him, 'How can corporate responsibility be entrusted to a man capable of such reckless disregard of the proprieties as this?' My work has been with men whose names don't get in the papers unless it's some fine community effort. Are you still a Johnson trustee?"

"So far as I know."

"We might as well have this out. Miss Wilkins, find out if Mr. Hewitt's doctor has been there yet or if Mrs. Hewitt has been found. Now, sit down. When Calvin showed me the clippings about you—I had not yet received them from Miss Wilkins—I had been deeply moved by the apparent heroism, as my telegram showed—he minimized it all as your good friend. And he told me what I should have guessed, I suppose, that your real interest in life was not your company and your job here, but a book on which you spent half your time. What's the name of this book again?"

"I did not spend half my time or any time except weekends on it. It was called 'Principal Errors of Judgment of Rulers and Peoples Since the Reformation.' "

"Give me an example of these principal errors."

"Well, the belief until a few years ago that the Jews would never fight for Israel and that the desert Arabs would sweep them into the sea in a week."

"In other words you sit in judgment on one religious group, many of whom are our good customers, and you make it unlikely that people like Aramco would buy machinery from us?"

"It's somewhat academic today, as someone else has written the book and is about to publish it."

"This is not a subterfuge because of the papers to keep your name out of it?"

"No. Do you mind coming to the point of all this?"

"There you are, that perpetual chip on the shoulder. That resentment toward me, such as has been so apparent in every way—my getting advance action cables, my seeing Mr. Doran. You seem to feel I'm against you. Not at all, not at all, but I am for the Company."

"So you would like me to resign?"

There was a pause, and when Cramer spoke again it was with his customary tone of unction. "Friend Lowry, those are your words, not mine but, and this is as friendly as it is frank, I wonder whether, no doubt with good intentions, you are one of those men who give 'the kiss of death' to whatever you engage in? Peale, Doran and so on, and, if what you say is so, evidently to your own book. And when the directors put them all together and then read how you and a member of your family and your friends amuse themselves—"

"I'd be careful, if I were you, Mr. Cramer. I'd strike out that last sentence. And make quite sure you never refer to it again."

"Are you threatening me?"

"I suppose so, yes."

Cramer, pinching his face like a barber testing the work of his razor, blinked at him a moment.

"Well, I have work to do," Lowry said briskly and left.

Even now what to do, where to turn and stand, was a problem. In all that had happened so far with Cramer, however provocative —including even his abominable reference to the rescue—the directors, or even friends like Colonel Channing could well say, "Cramer has his objectionable points, he may not be a gentleman, but it still seems to come down to the fact that his personality is so strong that you can't handle him."

He dialed Hewitt's apartment and after saying who he was, Hewitt answered.

"How sick are you?" Lowry asked him.

"I'm not sick except deep inside. I know you know about Paula, Steve. Have you any idea where I can get ahold of her?"

"No."

"I'm going to call the Pinkertons and get her traced."

"I wouldn't call them. I've read they don't take divorce cases."

"This is no divorce, Steve. I want her back, that's all, before Cramer knows about it. I'm going to begin perfectly calmly. I'm going to say, 'It's time you and I went back home, Paula.' If she agrees, as I strongly believe she will, well then that's that. I don't believe for one minute they've gone all the way. Paula isn't much on that, wouldn't be interested, she'd be too modest. It's just that all this money has gone to her head. Get her back in harness and she'll be all right. Funny how your mind works at such a time. I got to thinking last night about when you're married for years, all the little things you do for each other—brought tears to my eyes—there's somebody who knows how you take your coffee. She gets you new razor blades before you run out, knows what you like to eat, runs the house. Why I'd be lost without Paula. We men don't realize what a job running a home is. You know, this is an example, I *never*, but never, saw anyone wash our windows and I never saw them when they needed it. My clothes were always pressed. All I had to do was throw them over a chair. I haven't the foggiest idea who pressed them. It's been years since I knew who did the laundry. All those little things. I suppose you think I'm sentimental."

"Not at all."

"Steve, I want you to know I did everything I could for you with Cramer."

"So I gather."

"If the Pinkertons can find Paula, I'll have to go there and fight it out with Peale. My honor demands that, but I tell you I'm sick of responsibility. I'd just like to see Paula and me get away from responsibility and cut the towing ropes. Did you ever hear of a book called *Walden, or Life in the Woods?*"

"Yes. I've even read it."

"Well, I never pretended to be literary, but Sunday on TV there alone in a hotel room in Chicago I heard a talk on it. The author, this fellow Thorold—"

"Thoreau was his name."

"Whatever his name was, he made a life for himself without responsibility. Do you happen to know whether he was married?"

"I think not."

"Sick as I am, I think if Paula won't come back—though I'm very sure she will—and wanted to settle with me, I don't know what would be fair—maybe ten, better still twenty per cent of the Suydam estate. I think I'd take it and live in Vermont."

"I should think even ten per cent would be a million dollars."

"About, I guess."

"Well Calvin, the possession of a million dollars would only involve you in new responsibilities. People would want to get it away from you."

"I only say this to you, Steve, I've been hurt deep inside and I'm tired of slaving and if Paula persists, then she's got to pay for it. Isn't that the sensible way for me to look at it? I hope you're going to be all right. I'm worried about it, though you've got to learn to be more careful. I suppose on a sickbed you get a perspective. You don't know a trustworthy detective agency, do you?"

"No, I don't. Have you tried the yellow pages?"

"No, I suppose I could do that. I hope you'll keep in touch. It's a time when a man appreciates his friends."

Miss Marshall signaled as soon as Hewitt had hung up, to say that Mr. Devers, one of the engineers, was waiting and wanted to see Lowry at once. He said to send him in.

Devers was a tall man, with the same pointed features, the high receding forehead and steel-rimmed spectacles of Burnham at Larus. Lowry did not recall having said more than hello to him in the eight months, though he had heard Evans speak highly of him, especially in connection with the calculating on the bridge bid. Across the outer breast pocket of his coat was a stockade of pens and pencils with a slide rule. An outsize slide rule with a sheaf of papers was in his hand and his hand was shaking violently.

Instinctively Lowry knew at once what he was going to say. He got up to hear it standing.

"The bridge bid," Devers gasped, "it's out five hundred thousand dollars. There's an error in man hours. Everybody picked it up without catching it. It looked right. It's not my error originally. Have we got time to withdraw?"

"No. How did you happen to recheck this?"

"I got nervous about it."

"Does anyone else know?"

"No sir."

"Mr. Evans out?"

"Yes sir."

"Are those your work sheets?"

"Yes sir."

"Miss Marshall, bring me the work sheets on the bridge bid, please." She brought the folder quickly. "Now show me where it occurred," he said to Devers.

Well, there it was, the original calculation OK'd at the point of error by all, including Evans. Lowry started his own calculation in pencil, Devers breathing down his neck as he followed them with his slide rule. The error was now so palpable that it was as though they had all been hypnotized when they passed it.

"I feel pretty sick, Mr. Lowry."

"There's a lot of sickness around evidently," Lowry replied. "Miss Marshall, see whether Mr. Cramer's gone to lunch, please." She returned to say Mr. Cramer was having a glass of milk at his desk. Lowry picked up the papers and walked to his lonely execution. He said as unaffectedly as possible that he was solely responsible for something that had happened and then he told Cramer what it was. If Cramer listened pitilessly, it was with the professional calm of an auditor. With an auditor's control and competence he followed Lowry's finger through the two sets of work sheets.

"Naturally I'm not a bit surprised," he said, picking up all the papers and handing them back. "Leave these with my assistant, if you will, please. What do you propose now?"

"I've known of this only a few moments longer than you have. I've not had time—"

"Have you telephoned Caracas to see if we could simply not bid?"

"They've already filed and it was effective when we had it notarized at the Consulate here."

"Miss Wilkins, ask John to come here, please."

When he came in, his father said to him, "Mr. Lowry has something to tell you. Be good enough, Mr. Lowry, to go over it all again in the same detail. I may have missed something."

Lowry went through the humbling business. Young Cramer listened aghast, trying hard by glancing at his father to ape his impassivity. It was plain the error had not been covered in his textbooks.

"You see the whole situation, John?"

"Yes, Dad."

"Not a very nice one, though what was to be expected. Have you thought of what you intend to do, or is this 'just one of those things that happen' in your eyes?" he asked Lowry.

"Without minimizing my responsibility, I may say that this line of talk is not conducive to clear thinking."

"Are we expected to feel sorry for you, or for the stockholders who must take the loss? Am I supposed to be pleased that you have no suggestion at all as to what to do? Unlike you, I'm said to be a slow thinker and I see the way out."

"Then may I hear it?"

"I want to talk it over with John. I'd like to have Calvin Hewitt's views, but I suppose that's impossible."

"I have not told Mr. Curtis yet."

"I hardly think that matters. Is it asking too much for you to hold yourself in readiness in your office, or can you tell me where I can reach you?"

"I'll be in my office," Lowry replied.

It was not until after five, with the office rapidly emptying in spite of the president's return, that Cramer appeared in person at Lowry's desk. It had been apparent from the normal behavior of Halleck and the other department managers that nothing was known of the error and Curtis had been downtown the entire afternoon. Evans was reported at the tidewater plant, in New Jersey.

As Lowry went back over every step of the bid's preparation, he could not see where even now he would have done anything differently. Every care and control possible had been used. But all the justification in the world was not going to avail him. "While it was not your responsibility, Mr. Lowry, personally to prepare the figures and aware as we are that Mr. Evans and Mr. Curtis had the same duty and responsibility as you to satisfy themselves no error existed, nonetheless taking this, and various other things into consideration, adding them all up, we feel the best thing all around is to make a settlement with you on the most friendly and favorable basis for you, looking to the discontinuance of your services." That was about what they would say, he supposed. A bitter pill, a bleak prospect.

"I want to say first and right off," Cramer began brightly, "that I very much regret my attitude and what I said in our talk this morning. You were entitled to consideration which I did not show you. I hope you'll accept my apology." He put out his hand and Lowry took it.

"Certainly no apology is necessary but it's very nice of you to say this. I feel very badly about it, to put it mildly. I know what a blow it must be to you."

"Now you mustn't feel too badly, because we're going to find a way out of it. I've got to leave again now. Could you come to my hotel at seven tonight for a further talk?"

"Certainly."

"Tell your good lady it's my fault. Then I'll see you at seven?"

"Good."

In speech and manner Cramer appeared completely sincere and of good will, yet Lowry wondered to himself what had caused the change of heart. Had he seen Delano and not gotten the free hand he expected? It was very puzzling. He wished he had not once told Miss Marshall not to listen to rumors or encourage gossip. He would give a good deal to know where Cramer had been and, as he thought of it, where Curtis was. In his place Cramer would have known. So would Hewitt.

He was glad Rosalie was out when he phoned that he would not be home for dinner, as he was not sure he could have kept the reason to himself.

Miss Marshall looked in to say goodnight.

"Anything wrong?" she asked.

"No, why?"

"Miss Wilkins smiled in the washroom just now, but I know you don't like office gossip."

"That is true," he said.

By six, when he left, the office was almost as empty as it had been the afternoon of New Year's Eve. He went down to the drugstore in the lobby and had a sandwich and a glass of iced coffee, glanced through an evening paper and started uptown on foot to Cramer's hotel. He was still too early and sat down to wait impatiently in the lobby. At two minutes before seven he went up in the elevator and rang the bell at Cramer's door.

Cramer opened it himself, and going in Lowry saw over the back of a chair facing the south windows the crisp hairs of Hewitt's head.

"Hello," he said, "are you feeling better?"

Hewitt looked very worn. Cramer said that friend Hewitt had insisted on getting out of bed to be of whatever help he could, as soon as he had heard of the trouble. "There'll be just the three of us and we're not going to have anything to say about who's to blame. We're going to be constructive, not destructive. Calvin suppose you start us off." Voice and manner were benign.

"Well, Steve, I wouldn't be a bit surprised if when D.P. gives you his plan, you were to tell us you were hours ahead of us and it was rolling."

"*Have* you done anything yet, friend Lowry?" Cramer asked.

"No."

He waved the no aside and said, "That's all right. Go ahead, Calvin."

"I think I've told you, Steve, that I've always made it a point to keep the good will of the little fellows I started with. Never got too big for them. Now in your way you have that same quality."

"You and I had some words about Doran's resignation," Cramer interjected with a smile. "You were right. I was wrong. You kept his good will, helped him get a job."

"I wouldn't say that about the job."

"It amounts to the same thing. You didn't say anything *against* him to your brother-in-law."

"There was nothing to say."

"Steve, there could have been," Hewitt said, "in the case of that Morval check, which Daran signed but did nothing about for six long months—until, I suppose, he got frightened—he was running very close to charges of subornation of fraud."

"No, no, that's absurd," Lowry said.

"Not wholly absurd, friend Lowry, if you read the statute and review some of the decisions which were shown to me this afternoon. But, go ahead, Calvin."

"You take it from there, D.P."

"Thank you, Calvin. Now friend Lowry, the way out of our problem is apparent. You can pick up that telephone right there and put a call through to Paris for your brother-in-law or Doran. I leave that to you, explain what's happened and have Doran go to the Venezuela Ambassador in Paris—let him give the Ambassador the whole story, including this list of benefactions C.I.C. has made to Venezuela. The Ambassador can tell Caracas whatever he pleases, so long as all present bids are thrown out and new bids asked. Just a minute, please, *just* a minute, I quite understand some money will have to pass, but it will be a manageable amount not a disaster. When in Rome, well, you know the old saying. You see how perfectly the whole thing meshes—your brother-in-law's natural desire to help you, let me finish, please, Doran's chance to make up—"

"And the Ambassador?"

Cramer chuckled. "I guess I needn't tell you about Latin American diplomats after your long experience."

Hewitt got up and came over to put his hand on Lowry's shoulder. "Steve, believe me, it's the thing to do and you can do it easily. I'm absolutely satisfied it's right, that's why I'm here. D.P. thought that there ought to be a third person present who was a close friend of yours, so that he would not seem to be exerting any pressure on you."

"Take your time," Cramer said with a glance at his wrist.

"Is there any more to this?" Lowry asked.

"No," Cramer replied. "There are details, but they're going to be left to your own good judgment."

"Well of course I would never do what you propose, so there's no more to say," Lowry said.

"How's that? Wait a minute–"

"Steve, it's your only out. What's a relative for when you're in a jam?"

"Mr. Lainvee wouldn't be a party to it any more than I would, nor would Daran, which, by the way, is his name."

"You seem to be taking a moral tone," Cramer said, "about a business proposal, while a matter of primary morals didn't bother you at all. You insult, if I may be permitted the word, Mr. Hewitt and me by implying we have asked you to do something improper. All we have done is suggest a way for you to get out of your trouble."

"Does Mr. Delano know of this?"

"Naturally he knows," Cramer said, "of your trouble. What we have said here is within these four walls and between the three of us."

"You told him. What did he say to you?"

"I was obliged to call him out of a meeting," Cramer said. "I can only tell you he was aghast."

"Well, I shall see him in the morning," Lowry replied, "and tell him what I propose."

"Suppose you tell *us* now."

"Steve, let me urge you to consider what it would mean to you to have the solution on its way before you see him. I think I can speak for D.P. when I say, with this book of yours now out of the way, as he tells me, we can forget bygones."

"We certainly can," Cramer added. "I have never been ruthless in any situation. If you feel I can put it to Doran better than you, well and good. Or Calvin can, if you prefer that."

"You don't seem to understand, I will not allow it to be put to Daran or my brother-in-law."

"We have been frank with you. Why can't you be frank with

us?" Cramer asked. Lowry looked at him. There was something almost and truly pathetic in his tone. He was not the shifter, the turncoat, the little valiant that Hewitt was. He was one of those men without any ability to see himself as he was and he was in water far over his head. Sure that blame was as clear-cut as an arithmetical error, he wanted to be sure it was all Lowry's before it was all his own.

"There is nothing more I have to say tonight," Lowry told him and went to the door.

Hewitt followed along to the elevator. "You're making a big mistake, Steve. If you don't like Cramer's idea, and maybe you're right—I only got in on it to help out. It isn't my idea—but at least take him into your confidence. He can help you and he can still make an awful lot of trouble for you if you won't let him help."

"We've been waiting since a few days after his arrival for an issue that was worth a showdown. Now we have it. That's all there is to it."

"But you can't be sure, Steve, it won't go against you. I don't see how it can go any other way. Consider that."

"Calvin, how well it has been said for several centuries that death and taxes are all you can be sure of. You'd better go back to your bed."

27

LATE IN THE AFTERNOON ROSALIE DROVE UP TO her door and got out of the car, hot, sticky, exasperated and anti-American. That morning as she had stood in the library trying to think what was the sane and sensible thing to do with all the Principal Errors material, what would make it easiest for Stephen when he came home, the cook had appeared with one bare foot enormously swollen from an insect bite and demanded that she be taken at once to her sister in Brooklyn, where she could "have some care." Dr. Hovey's arrival and assurance that hot epsom-salt soakings would cure it by night, Rosalie's own assurance that she could have a complete rest did not shake her strong death-wish to be with her sister and have her see the foot in full bloom before the end.

The way to the city of boarded-up churches was a difficult one, though vestiges of its once Victorian charm—trees, a street of detached frame houses amidst a long line of brownstones, another like a close in England, the occasional glimpse of block-long "back yards" full of trees and shrubbery—fascinated her. The married sister and her "neighbor upstairs" with their children were waiting on the sidewalk outside their Classon Avenue home in the evident hope that a mad dog had bitten their relative.

"Oh no," Rosalie said, "it wasn't the dog."

"It was that dog, all right," the cook said. "It's his fleas and the ants all over the place—"

All glanced at Rosalie. She said she was very sorry and carried Helga's large bag up the steps. Helga made her way up backwards, lifting herself from step to step.

"Well, will you call me when you're better, Helga?" Rosalie asked. "You must rest until you're entirely well."

"I don't know when that will be, Mrs. Lowry. The pain's already running up my leg, like in the groin. It costs you plenty when you have to have them off," Helga replied as though she had already had a number of pedal amputations.

"Well, we expect to pay for everything," Rosalie said.

"Money doesn't buy a leg," the married sister said. All the children began to cry and the neighbor upstairs made a general comment on the heartlessness of certain people.

An hour and a half later, guided by an Unseen Hand, Rosalie reached Garden City for shopping she had to do for the children. Coming out to drive home, she found herself in the worst of the afternoon heat, the seats of the car hot, the steering wheel almost blistering and the westbound traffic of factory workers homeward bound at its height. The way back was one long detour around "construction ahead," new roads, new sewers, new shopping centers, new developments, and massed bulldozers knocking down trees, past signs proclaiming that she was in the fastest-growing county in the state and nation. Oh to be in a county or country that was not "going ahead fast."

She got out of the car with an armful of bundles. From the garden side of the house she heard the children yelling, and stopped in dismay. In a moment they would come tearing around the house in filthy dungarees, the boys two-gunned, and there would be *bang, bang, bang,* as the law-man dropped the bank robber and his moll. And she remembered the Russians coming into Tallinn and the frightened children, and what had happened that terrible day in Norway when the Nazis caught two little boys playing at killing a soldier of the German Reich.

The whole world seemed a caldron of sorrow and disappointment, violence, ugliness, disorder, greed, embezzlement, stupidity, and near-scandal which she could no longer face. Yet she must face it, wash and tend her children, cook dinner for them and a husband . . . and then tomorrow and tomorrow.

She hurried into the cool, dim house, hoping to bathe and change a very damp and wrinkled linen dress before she faced the children. They ran her to earth by the hall table and she looked at them in amazement as they embraced her. They were all clean and scrubbed, all of them in spotless shirts and shorts.

"Oh Mummy, we're *so* glad to see you," Lainvee said mounting the table to hug her. "The most wonderful thing. We're going to have a club and you will be Head and Daddy will be storyteller and Richard will be treasurer and we meet every Sunday evening and I thought up the most wonderful name for it. The Sprikeling Club, you know like a Sprikeling day. Oh Mummy, say we may and Daddy is storyteller but members, like Peter and me and Richard, can tell stories too, like when we were children and used to say 'didja,' 'member?"

Richard broke in. "And Mummy come out now in the hammock and tell us about when you were a little girl in Estonia. Please Mummy, it's as cold as ice in the hammock."

"Please Mummy, about Uncle Armas teaching you to swim. If you're tired, we can bring you a gin and tonic out there."

"Oh darlings," she said, "I don't need a gin and tonic."

"Why are you crying?" Lainvee asked. "Because you don't know what happened to Grandmother and Grandfather? Would you like to tell a happier story?"

"No," she said, sniffling a little. "Any story you want, but wouldn't you like me to have a bath and change my dress first? I'm so sticky."

"Oh no, you smell best of any mother in whole Ridingtown and Penny Rossiter thinks so too," Lainvee said.

In the hammock she told the often told tale of herself as a child on the Baltic dunes, amidst many corrections and reminders of omissions from them. Smoky came to listen, sitting torridly against her ankles. They all sighed happily when she finished.

"Didja 'member," Richard asked, "when we had the house on the Boulevard des Invalides and how much that bathroom cost and we couldn't afford it and Uncle Armas got mad because Daddy wouldn't let him give it to us and you said he was right but it was going to be awful having dirty children?"

"And now we have all these awful bathrooms everywhere," Peter observed sadly.

Then with cries of "Me, me, me" all three children were off in a flash to answer the ringing telephone. The winner, Richard, called his mother. She came to answer, hoping it was not Stephen to say he would be late.

"Mrs. Lowry, this is Martha Rossiter. I've been trying to get you but you were out."

"Oh I'm sorry, no one told me."

"I should like to see you right away and unfortunately I must be here. Could you come to the school? I can't very well explain over the telephone."

"Why yes," Rosalie said. It could mean, she supposed, but one thing. She was being summoned, politely enough, to testify in her own behalf before Ridingtown's high court of respectability. Anger, shame and embarrassment surged through her. She must go to this arbitrix and promise never to do again what she had no intention of doing, or to make any promise, if only her children were admitted to the school.

"I'll explain but, on the off chance that Lainvee might want to play with Penny, would you come alone?"

Rosalie said she would.

When Stephen reached home about nine she had not returned. The children told him where she had gone and he called the Rossiters' house. The maid said Mrs. Rossiter had gone out to dinner and then the movies, but what movie she did not know. She said she didn't know Mrs. Lowry by sight but yes a lady had been there and left in her car about five-thirty.

"What did your mother wear?" he asked Lainvee.

"That blue linen. She had it on all day."

Yes, the lady had on a blue dress. Yes, she would leave a note for Mrs. Rossiter to call Mr. Lowry, what was the number and how did he spell his name?

He sent the children off to bed, waited while ten minutes took twenty years to pass and called the police, gave a description of Rosalie, and the license number of the car, and asked if any accident had been reported. They checked and said no. He hesitated, thinking of the attempted and successful rapes in cars of which the local papers had been recently so full. "You would know, wouldn't you, if something more serious had happened?"

"We'd only know, Mr. Lowry, if it were reported or a body or abandoned car were found. Nothing so far. We'll have our cars on the lookout."

He remembered the caveat from Jane Alden about the school but whatever Mrs. Rossiter might have said it was impossible to suppose so essentially levelheaded a person as Rosalie could have been overcome by it. So that the anxiety and fear of accident or foul play increased. She had left the house before his message about being late so she would not be at some friend's for supper. Nor even have gone somewhere for a casual cocktail after a trip to Brooklyn and Garden City in the blue dress. And she was not one of those people who stop for a minute and have no idea of the passage of time. In that she was not Armas's sister for nothing. Anxiety became almost certainty that she had been waylaid. Yet a former Resistance officer would not fall easily into a trap.

Then he saw the lights of a car turning in the gates and went to meet it. He saw it was a police car with its red top light—coming to break the dreadful news.

The police driver had been one of those in the boat. "Just checking, Mr. Lowry. Your wife left here to go to the Ridingtown School. Have you any idea where she'd have gone from there? Any friends she might drop in on?"

"My God, that's the point. I told the lieutenant I had no idea—"

"Nobody but the cook's at the Rossiters'."

"I know that. I told 'em that."

"Is there anybody she'd be likely to meet?"

"No, no. I explained that—"

"You looked carefully for a note? They sometimes leave a note and you don't find it right away."

"Look, she left no note."

"Oh, OK, keep your shirt on. We'll find her." His radio crackled and he held up his hand. Lowry could make nothing of the gibberish coming over it. "Nothing. Bus rammed a car in Lynbrook. See you."

At twelve minutes past ten, as he stood in the doorway within arm's reach of the telephone, she arrived. He ran to the car and as she opened the door and swung her legs out, he picked her up in his arms.

"Oh God, are you all right?" She turned her mouth away as he kissed her but put her arm around his neck.

"What you mean, yes. I must get to the telephone. Put me down."

She looked exhausted but composed in the light. He followed her into the library.

"Close the door," she said picking up the telephone. "Give me the Overseas Operator." Then her voice broke and she said, "Stephen, please help me. I can't speak. Get Armas, he must come at once."

In the long wait for *Ici parle Paris, 'allo,* she told him in a torrent of emotion, sometimes in his arms, then, with the length of the room between them. Mrs. Rossiter had said it was difficult for her, she knew it was difficult for Rosalie. There was the possibility of a mistake.

"I thought it was all about the rescue. She said she knew I was born in Estonia from the children's application. I said, 'It is so that I was born in Estonia.' I hadn't said that in many years, since you told me it wasn't quite English. Then she said it all came from a newspaper account of the rescue and my picture. Then she said, 'Mrs. Lowry, have you any idea what I am going to say?' I shook my head and she said, 'I never had this experience before. Forgive me if I do it badly.' I said just to tell me what it was. She had not seen the article or the picture. A maid of the Dubosques, who have the school in Lattingtown, went to Mrs. Dubosque and showed them to her. She said it was a wonderful thing and the maid said she had shown them to their new school cook and she had said, 'It is so it is not wonderful to me. That woman is my sister.' "

"Inge?" he asked.

She nodded. "I've been there. It is Inge. She looks over sixty. I said, 'Inge, my darling, what joy to find you.' I told her about Armas and all the happiness and that I would help her pack her things and she must come with me and she said she never wanted to see me again. Oh Stephen, she is full of hatred. She said, 'I have no sister. I have no family. I don't want anyone. Go away. I have my work here with clean food.' "

"Darling, in the first surprise of seeing you it may not have been unnatural."

"It was. She wouldn't listen to anything. She looked horrible; old, some of her teeth gone, her hair thin and pulled back and she said, 'Did you ever suffer?' I tried to answer and she said, 'You look as young and beautiful as when you ran away from your mother and sister that day in Tallinn while they searched for you.' I said I had not run away. I couldn't get home. Stephen, you have to hear all she said. I'll stand here. You won't want to be near me. She said in that horrible voice of hate and contempt, in Estonian, 'How gentle they must have been when they ravished the young virgin. Or did they have to ravish you?' And she said did I want to learn what they did to my mother and her, and, oh Stephen, how many there were and that she had remembered it all these years except when she mixed it up with the day the Nazis came. And I said, 'Inge, my sister, you must try to forget. I have had to try,' and she screamed at me that she did forget with her cooking, and her clean food she kept talking about, until she saw me and how did my husband, the American businessman she read about, like sleeping with a woman who slept with her ravishers or did I 'forget' to tell you, or did you know about wars and labor camps and I said you knew and understood everything, and she said, 'Does he know what it's like when you're no longer good enough for a Nazi camp guard?' I think I'm sorriest of all for you because now I'll never be *riante* again for you and that's all there is about me you really love."

"Dear," he said calmly, "there are some other things."

"I have no right to this house and its lovely things." She looked around the room at the new things bought in America, the rug, the color of the light blue hills, got in Istanbul, two paintings, gifts from Armas and all the mirrors in which she saw herself. She had nothing now that she had had that day in Tallinn. On the sofa were some things of the children and she sat down, holding them, overwhelmed by the thought of her mother and all the tender, little things of girlhood.

"You must stop crying this way," Stephen said. "Inge is ill and we shall have her cured. You mustn't get sick. Too much depends on you."

"Everything I said about love she rejected and kept telling me the horrible things that happened to Mother and her. That last morning I saw her she was one of the most beautiful girls I've ever seen and now she's ghastly, like someone from the House of the Dead. I tried to put my arms around her. She said I had hidden from them that day and that I willingly let the Russians do it to me and that's why they let me escape. You must understand what happened, you must let me speak of it. I can't go on with it inside me any longer."

"Dearest, I knew when Nedberg translated as 'an unpleasant time' whatever you told him I didn't need—"

"But *I* need to tell it. Can't you listen?"

"Yes, of course," he said quietly.

"Do I want you to know because I want you to suffer too?"

"No, I think I was wrong. Maybe you can only forget it if you tell me." He started toward her and she shook her head, standing by the fireplace, half turned away.

"I was at the bakery three streets from the flat. We thought we had several hours yet, when their motorcycles burst into the street and farther down I saw them jumping out of their lorries and I turned and ran toward home. Then it seemed like masses of cavalry tore past at a gallop, spreading out across the square and I saw I couldn't get home and I saw a cellar door under a shop. Its shutters were up and I ran down the steps. It was dark and I crouched in a corner. And I didn't know what to do. I could hear them yelling and some firing and I was terrified more at the moment because I was afraid Mother and Inge would try to go to the bakery to find me. I had on a pretty little wrist watch Father had given me and I could see its dial in the dark and I thought of the long, long daylight that day. It would never be really dark in the streets. You could tell from the noise that the streets were full of soldiers. You cannot imagine how frightening it was or how alone I felt and wanted to be with Inge and Mother and we would each have helped the other. Late in the afternoon I could tell by glass breaking and the yelling that they were beginning to loot the shops. They thought our poor little city was the Kingdom of Heaven. I heard them breaking the shutters open over my head and then the door. It was a little dress and notions shop. Then three of them came down the other stairs in the cellar and saw me."

"My darling."

"It wasn't then. They were laughing and they weren't drunk yet, and an officer with a flashlight came in and began to question me. I was afraid to say who I was because of Father. They took me to the street. It was crowded with their horse wagons piled with every sort of thing from the shops. Three doors away there was a sort of headquarters where people were being questioned and sent off under guard to the railroad. I saw a woman I knew who whispered to me that our apartment house was full of them and Mother and Inge were arrested. I was taken before a colonel and when he saw me he ordered his aide and his orderlies out of the room and he sat on the edge of the desk, offering me a cigarette. He said I was very beautiful and that he was a man of culture. Said he could tell from my face that I was an aristocrat and I said I was a peasant. I mustn't think they were rapists. Was I afraid, he asked? I tried to say no. He took my hand and I couldn't get it away and he said that if I was nice to him, I had nothing to fear and that he would protect any women in my family too. I didn't believe him. It was a chance to save Inge and Mother, but I was afraid to tell their names. Yet I wanted somehow to gain time—Stephen, I didn't know what to do. He drew me to him. He kissed me. I didn't struggle. I was trying to think. Then he released me. It was not beastly, a bare half-minute, and I said, 'May I think a little?' and he said yes, not too long, and if I said yes I must mean it. He wanted love, real love, he said, and then he took my wrist watch off and put it in his pocket. I think I said it was mine, to give it back, he mustn't keep it and he laughed and laughed. Then a general and a lot of officers came in and soldiers marched me out to a room in the back of the place and I couldn't understand what they were saying. They left me alone to listen to them tramping up and downstairs and to the occasional firing outside. It was much later when two of them came back and I was terribly hungry, frightened as I was. It's hard to believe how quickly you get hungry at first. They were drinking and they offered me the flask. I knocked it away and the man holding it almost dropped it and he turned on me. I fought and fought. I forgot Mother and Inge and everything but myself. One of them laughed and took his coat off and put it on the floor. The other one did it first. I don't know when it was he fell asleep. The other one drank until he fell half asleep. I got up very quietly. The streets were almost quiet. The other one was by the door and when I opened it he sat up and started to pull me down beside him. I was on one knee. I managed to smile at him. I patted his cheek and made it clear I would be back in a moment. There was a bayonet in his belt and I thought if he kept me there I would manage to get it and kill him and, if not, myself. I wished I could kill the other one. I'm not sure, perhaps for a few seconds I pretended to be acquiescent. I kept whispering to him, 'In a minute, please.' And he let me go. The streets were full of patrols. I could not go near our apartment. I realized my whole family were gone, like my wrist watch. At the time I didn't want to live and yet I did, terribly, and thinking only of myself. No one else had me and each hour that I was not found I wanted more to live and escape. I knew in my bones my father was already dead and even then, as I have all these years, I tried not to think about what was happening to my mother and Inge—and now at last I can run away from it no longer because she has told me, hating me. I don't know what I shall do, except that I can't go on even with you and the children as I did. Don't pity me, be sorry for your poor self, married to me."

He went over to her. "No, no," she said, crossing her arms.

The telephone rang and he reached across the sofa to answer it. There were the seemingly interminable *pour parler's* to complete the call before he heard Armas's voice.

"Armas," he said, "Rosalie has found Inge here . . . yes . . . yes . . . no, very bitter . . . yes, very old . . . she is dead . . . can you leave tomorrow night . . . good . . . he wants to speak to you, darling." He handed the phone to Rosalie.

"Oh Armas, come quickly, she may listen to you because you were taken. I don't know. Goodbye. What? Oh what does it matter about me?"

When she hung up, he took the telephone and asked for the police and told them Mrs. Lowry had returned. That there had been trouble with the car.

She sat breathing like a spent swimmer. "Now that you know about that day and night it's almost like the stone rolled away but I don't see how you will stand being with me. I thought about telling you all the way home, I mean all the way back, and I couldn't think how we'd tell the children why we had separate rooms." In a moment she went on, almost without emotion. "Mrs. Dubosque sent me out to speak to her alone. She was looking down absorbedly at carrots she was dicing and there was an air of peace about her until she glanced up. I said in Estonian, 'Inge, my sister, what joy to see you,' and she said, 'I have no wish to see you. I have no family. I have my work. Do you want to hear how your mother died?' And when I talked to

Mrs. Dubosque before leaving, I said I hadn't been able to persuade her to come to our house, was it possible for her to keep her temporarily? She said she knows how bitter Inge was and realized how terrible it had been for us, but that I must understand that to her Inge was an individual and that if she wanted to stay with her, her conscience would not let any pressure be worked on her. She said that Inge had had a thorough medical examination, because of the school, and was entirely well. The school psychiatrist found her competent, self-reliant and adjusted to her sphere in life."

"But dear all this is very encouraging–"

"She went on to say that 'the courage and strength which had saved Mr. Hopkins's life' would not fail me. I told her that physical courage and strength are something that animals and often the lowest of people had. I wanted to tell her the men who raped me had them. I had them when I put my mother and sister out of my mind and escaped."

"Stop crying," he said sensibly. "Here, blow your nose," and he tossed a large, clean handkerchief in her lap. She obeyed, trying without success to control her tears.

"I feel as though everyone's to know my sister went through these things and is a school cook–oh Stephen, if she won't come to us, what am I to do? How am I to go on day after day with her so close, without seeing or talking to her? Suppose, like other people, she's ill in bed. Am I to leave her to Mrs. Dubosque's care? Am I to go on pretending to people that I've had the safe, normal life they have? How am I to know whether the security she has at the school is all she needs and that I might finally destroy her by breaking into it?"

"Dear, she's alive, time and love are on your side. All these other things will be solved."

He looked at her, his heart aching with love and pity for her woe. If anything, her story had been less dreadful than he had feared. It had long been a game to pretend in a dull world that life was all fun. He had never really supposed it was or that behind every happiness there was not the dark sail. He saw it was folly to be protective with her now.

"What is it," he asked directly, "that you blame yourself for? I understand the first shock of seeing Inge, changed as she is. I know that any arrangements will be very difficult. They will not be impossible. This is all very terrible, but are you glad or not that Inge's alive? Or is a dead sorrow better than a living?"

"Why do you ask such a terrible question?"

"Because I want you to be yourself, the person who has learned to live with the present so well until now. Unless you feel you're superior to the human race, you have no reason to blame yourself for what you've done. Few people, none we know, have faced the terrible choice you did that day. To me you *are* superior to everybody else. Who else you know is capable of bringing Inge back to herself? Think of the challenge to your love and wisdom. And there's something else. You must not let me down. I need your love and absolute confidence, because tomorrow Cramer may be able to force me out of the Company. There was a great blunder in the bid for the bridge in Venezuela for which I am responsible."

"Oh Stephen, my husband—"

"Now don't be guilty about me."

"No, no," she said, "I won't. I'll take care of you. I'll help you, oh darling, if it helps I'll be *riante*."

"That," he said, "is very good news. I shall now carry you up to bed. All will yet be well."

"I know," she said, as he swung her up in his arms.

As he reached the bottom of the stairs with her, Richard's head poked over the banister. He yawned prodigiously, rubbed his eyes and said, "Oh Mum's home! That's super! Goodnight, Dad, goodnight, Mum."

28

LOWRY AWOKE A LITTLE BEFORE SEVEN THE NEXT morning. Rosalie was not beside him. The room was tidy and their bathroom empty. He was so light a sleeper, she so sweetly drowsy in the morning, that for a moment he was half afraid of what might have happened.

He had gone downstairs for a sandwich and a glass of milk for her while she was getting ready for bed, and as she ate and drank he had told her the full story of the bridge and Cramer's and Hewitt's proposal to solve it. And he had also told her of the Parry matter and that he was displeased with himself in regard to it. But though all secrets were being revealed he had seen no point in telling her that Cramer had seen the tabloid stories of the rescue. She had held his hand, that sometimes most intimate of acts, as he told her.

"This may be very silly," she had said, "but I think without this, Inge and Principal Errors might have overwhelmed me. Or if you had not been able to hear the Tallinn story as you did. But now, why, I feel quite sure of us. And of myself as wife, mother and sister."

He went to the head of the stairs, hearing the boys talking in their room. The aroma of coffee was in the air and he heard the chink of table silver as a sideboard drawer was opened.

"Forks *and* knives, Mummy?" Lainvee was asking.

"Yes, darling, and spoons."

"Well, would Aunt Inge live here with us, then Mummy?"

Knowing that all was well, he called to his sons not to dawdle and went to shave and shower. When he came down, Rosalie met him at the pantry door with floury arms. Tired though she looked, he saw from the beauty and peace of her face that all was indeed well.

"Mummy's made scrumptious muffins, Daddy, and I beat the eggs. I have to turn the bacon now," Lainvee informed him.

"Dear, I thought your wife's cooking your breakfast was what you needed on a day like this. Are you all right?" she asked, opening a drawer for a napkin to cover the muffins. "I started early because I wanted to call Mrs. Dubosque, unless you think it's too terribly early, before you left. I have told Lainvee about Inge and she accepts it quite easily, so the boys will hear about it from her at breakfast. You do think I was right, don't you?"

"Oh yes," he said, "but it was startling to find you gone from bed."

"Darling," she said, kissing him, "I am not a lie-abed-till-noon just because I don't like the sunrise. I was up very early in a place called Norway, if you can remember."

Mrs. Dubosque answered her call and brushed away her apologies pleasantly, saying that as a schoolmistress she was an early riser even during vacation.

"I wanted just to ask whether my sister was there and as usual. Our brother will be here tomorrow and I thought I would make no further effort to see her before I talk to him. But if anything happens, will you call me, please? I can never tell you how grateful I am to you."

"Well first, your sister is as usual. I think, now I can't be sure, but I think in spite of everything she was glad to see you, because I felt I had better break the narcissistic shell, as the psychologists say, and speak of you this morning. And I said, 'Inge, your sister is a woman whose goodness shows in her face.' And she said, I thought just a little proudly, 'In a beautiful face.' One doesn't know, but I'll call you if there's anything, and expect to hear from you tomorrow and please don't thank me."

"Just to be sure, please don't mention my brother's coming."

"No, of course not."

Rosalie drove Stephen to the station. There she said to him, "Now, my dearest, please understand, please know down to your toes that whatever you decide to do, whatever it is, I will help. Even if somehow you *can* or want to use Armas's arrival to help you—maybe it's providential—I want you to. I think I'd better tell Paula about the book, just in case she should call you—"

"Yes, if you will," he said.

"Now one last thing. I was not born of a peasant family for nothing. I have a savings account, a hoard in a small way, but plenty to pay off the maids and still have enough for the children's first-term tuition. And I have no objection to your getting rid of the car or the station wagon. Or of anything but me and the children."

"This is all very good, my angel," he said, "but I have no intention of losing to Master Cramer."

"No, I am sure of that too. I just wanted you to know you have a sensible wife with reserves—even reserves of her love."

In asserting he was not going to lose to Cramer, Lowry had of course pretended to a greater confidence than he felt. While he was sure that Delano and the other directors would not fall in with Cramer's plan to use Daran, and that the exposure of it would greatly damage Cramer, neither of these things would help him. In the directors' places he would be inclined to say, "Well you'd both better go."

As he went through the office, he saw that Curtis was already at his desk.

"Have you heard about Venezuela?" Lowry asked him.

"Yes, I've heard," Curtis said. "I was at a meeting at Mr. Delano's when he was called out to hear it. I'm afraid it's rather a bad setback for you."

"I realize that."

"Mr. Delano is not a Rutledge. He blew his top, I believe it's called. I couldn't but think how wise you'd been in not going to him about Parry."

Curtis's voice was as cold as his words, his manner aloof as though he were making clear that he did not want to be involved in support of Lowry any more than of Parry.

"For your information," he added, "Mr. Delano will not be at his office today."

While Lowry had not expected him to say "Well, it's not your fault. It's an organization mistake and we're all in on it," he had not expected so arctic an attitude. Certainly it would be very hard to duplicate such a job as he had. And if it was lost and not quickly replaced, could they keep the house before his resources ran out? The equity was still thin. In the eight months, which had gone so quickly, he had seen almost no one, except in Ridingtown, who was not connected with C.I.C. He had done what Raymond Fosdick warned against—made it the be-all and end-all, the end in itself. He had seen fewer old friends than he had when they were in Europe. A jocular paragraph in the alumni magazine about "our newest addition to our swelling ranks of tycoons is Steve Lowry, etc., etc." had brought in a number of "friends," whom he never knew very well, to borrow a hundred bucks, to see "if you could help me get to the right man in that Foreign Aid setup, whatever you call it," or to ask "if by any chance you need an assistant. Here's my record and here's what's happened." He had done what he could, thinking that the terrors of insecurity or unemployment devastated men more than those of battle.

He began to worry about all the self-control he had been showing. He had said to Rosalie the night before, "Unless you consider yourself better than the human race. . . " Was that the feeling, in part an amused superiority, which let him repress his feelings over Principal Errors, listen outwardly without emotion to the Tallinn story, take the elder Cramer as he had, not tell Colonel Channing he needed help?

The ordinary activity of the business filled the morning. Cramer, breaking the rule of a lifetime, had his door shut, Miss Marshall reported. Lowry talked to Delano's secretary about seeing him the next day. She said she would speak to Mr. Delano on his return. Paula Hewitt telephoned. She said Rosalie had told her about the book and had said not to call him but she was so sorry, it would have meant so much to Jim to be working on something with him again, and, besides, she had another reason for calling. First, she must tell him she had had a hilarious set-to with Calvin, of which more later. Just now her chief aim was to prevent fistfights.

"Now Stephen, here's the other thought. Would you like some money for your Johnson Foundation? Something in low six figures to start with? Maybe more later."

He groaned to himself, knowing of course what would follow if he accepted this obsessed offer. A first gift and then the next, then a place for Jim in the Foundation, then why not on the Board? She would say, "If you want him with you, Dennison and Caithness won't say no. Surely, having been the agent of his downfall, the friend who was going to stand by him, you can't refuse this." And how holier-than-thou he would sound if he said, "Paula, you can't just buy his way back. He has to do something himself."

And so he said, "Paula, this is very kind of you. I'd have to talk to Mrs. Johnson and—"

"Oh, I'll talk to her," she said quickly.

"Well, let me think it over."

"But you could use the money, couldn't you?"

"Oh yes."

"Then why don't you and Jim talk it over? He can represent me. Stephen, be a lamb and say yes, it would mean so much to him."

"All right," he said, "but not this week."

"Soon?"

"Soon as I can."

"Bless you, you *are* a lamb."

He hung up with a sigh. As Tom Johnson had said sadly months ago, "A decision used to be a simple thing."

Before leaving his house the next morning he got the usual word of delayed arrival for Armas, and calling Idlewild again on reaching the office was told his flight was now expected at eleven-thirty.

He turned from his telephone call telling Rosalie that he would not be able to meet him to find Cramer beaming.

"Friend Lowry, just by chance Miss Wilkins heard the operator telling you that your brother-in-law's plane was late and I hurried in here to say how glad I am you've reconsidered my little suggestion. I want to say that there's no reason on my side why we can't clear this whole thing up on the most friendly basis. I take it Doran's on call in Paris."

"Daran is in Paris, as far as I know."

"Good. Can you spare a few minutes?"

"Yes."

"Now let's be frank. You've made mistakes, *but so have I.*" He slapped the desk with the palm of his hand as he said each of the last four words, adding hastily, "A different kind of mistake, but mistakes just the same. I've very badly misjudged a man and I may have misjudged you. I may have overdone the corrections of fundamentals here. We have made—Miss Wilkins has just given me a tabulation—changes in office-supply purchasing procedures, in payroll deduction operations, in female workers' rest periods, complete overhaul in mail distribution and postage-meter control; we have reduced and standardized office equipment, made prompter collection from the staff on personal toll or three-unit calls—I'm only skimming the surface—but all those savings in time and money do not, in my own eyes, justify mistakes I've made. I want to tell you this. After you left night before last, Calvin Hewitt and I had a long talk about the future of the Company. We had gotten to see eye to eye, so I thought, on our trip. Frankly, Hewitt had represented himself as able to acquire a large, a very large amount of stock and to pool it with me. We hadn't forgotten you. We were going to make a generous offer to your Johnson Foundation for theirs. Mr. Rutledge could have been relieved of his. Now all those plans are out the window. My good will and my confidence have been taken advantage of. Last night

Hewitt asked me to come to his apartment. He was not well, he said. I arrived to find him intoxicated. Friend Lowry, do you know why?"

"Possibly he had too much to drink."

"He had had a great deal too much. His wife has left him. That scoundrel, Peale, first puts his hands in our till and then on another man's wife. That's where she was. That's why we couldn't find her. A shocking thing but it does not justify Hewitt's condition in my eyes. I'm through with him. He told me about it and the Suydam money and then he made one of the most disgusting remarks I've ever heard." Cramer looked cautiously at the open door behind him and spoke in a whisper. "He said to me, 'D.P. you better get going because I want to get a woman in here tonight.' Now about your brother-in-law."

"His coming over is fortuitous. He's come on a family matter."

"Why won't you tell me what you intend doing? I strongly urge you to work with me. If you plan to go to Mr. Rutledge or Mr. Channing, I can tell you they carry no weight."

"I hope to see Mr. Delano if he's back."

"Do you know where he was yesterday?"

"No I don't, do you?"

"Do you feel that my proposed solution was ethically wrong?" Cramer asked, without answering.

"Well I try not to sit in judgment on people, but you must know what I think about it."

"In my desire to help perhaps I spoke too quickly, but any issue you raise on that will not cover your responsibility for the loss we're involved in."

"So you would rather I didn't mention it to Mr. Delano? You forget how often you've said to me, 'Why was I not told?' Still, this is beside the point. I have no assurance Mr. Delano will see me. You have his ear. I haven't."

"Let me say one final word. You'll need friends. You must know that Charley Curtis won't lift a finger to help you. Hewitt is gone. Are you wise in turning on me? I don't believe so. I think you'll find I'm right."

"Well, we shall just have to wait and see," Lowry replied and

Cramer left. A few moments later Lowry saw him with his hat on, leaving the office.

Shortly before noon he was surprised by a telephone call from Curtis, saying that he was at Mr. Delano's office, where Lowry was asked to be at one-thirty.

"I had better tell you that Mr. Cramer has just left, after giving us a rundown on the bridge. I'm afraid that's all I can tell you."

Lowry thanked him and buttoned his coat. He had already heard of Lainvee's arrival from Rosalie, who said that Armas was going alone after lunch to see Inge. By nightfall they should know where they stood at home and abroad.

When the receptionist at Delano's announced him, Curtis came out after a moment like a bailiff to lead him in.

Delano, behind his desk, said "Howdya do" without getting up. A third man, looking out of the window, turned around and said, "Good afternoon, Stephen." It was Rutledge.

"Before we get to this unfortunate business in Venezuela, Mr. Lowry, there are some questions I should like to ask you," Delano said. He went on to say that he had a great many interests, far too many in fact, and Lowry must realize C.I.C. was only one of them, though, because of long friendship and association on many boards with Mr. Rutledge and Mr. Johnson, by no means a small one. "In other words what I'm saying to you is that the welfare of C.I.C. is as important to me as any industry I'm connected with, but my duties at the Art Museum, New York Hospital and Grace Church do not leave me a great deal of time. With them it's arrive early and leave late." This was said as though he personally swept and dusted those edifices daily. "Now then, how do you and Mr. Cramer get along?" If, as Curtis reported, he had blown his top, he had evidently replaced it. He asked the question as though he were inquiring how Lowry liked his new house.

"All right," Lowry replied.

"Are you interfered with at every turn?"

"No."

"Did his son, that is to say his assistant, participate in the bridge bid?"

"No, sir."

"But Mr. Cramer had asked for such participation, had he not?" His tone was casual but there was now some acid in it.

"He had asked for general participation, something that was difficult to arrange in practice."

"So that he has no responsibility for this error?"

"None. And he was in Chicago when I signed the bid."

"Had he been in New York what would have happened?"

"I suppose he would have seen the final figures before they went out."

"Might he not have caught the error, had he been given the chance?"

"That is possible."

Delano stared at him for a moment and then said, "Would you mind if I had a word with Mr. Rutledge? Could you just step outside a moment?"

"Certainly."

He was waiting in the anteroom when Henry Dennison hurried through with a curt greeting and joined the others. And it was perhaps five minutes before he was called back. From a glance at the faces he got no idea how it was going. Dennison and Rutledge were standing by the window, talking in undertones and the four of them had the air of judges about to sentence a man to whom they wished to show consideration rather than sympathy.

"Henry," Delano said, turning to Dennison.

"Yes. Mr. Lowry, when you were made a vice-president of C.I.C. you presumably had already found out who the directors were and decided they were men in whom you could have confidence. Is that so?"

"Yes."

"Now these men, in whom you had confidence, after careful thought, elected Mr. Cramer to be president of C.I.C. We want you to tell us what you think of their choice and decision."

Delano, with unexpected hospitality, lifted the cover of his outsized silver cigarette box, pushed it toward Lowry and then took a cigarette himself, which Curtis lighted for him. Lowry shook his head.

"Do you regard that as an improper question, Mr. Lowry?" Delano asked.

"I think it's a very broad one."

"I'll reframe it," Dennison said. "Mr. Lowry, has a proposal for the settlement of the Venezuelan bridge been made to you which you find morally offensive? That is a simple question, pertinent to the issue."

He could not believe that Cramer had told them what he proposed, nor could he see how otherwise they had heard of it. But he was determined that he would not charge Cramer with it, above all in his absence. He would not willingly use the methods he so much disliked in Cramer. They were all watching him very closely. It was hard to find any answer that was not self-righteous. He was sick of self-righteousness and justification. On the other hand he had no intention of carrying magnanimity toward Cramer to a fantastic length.

"I'm not prepared to say that any proposal made in the excitement and the difficulty we're in is morally offensive. An idea I didn't like was put forward, possibly only to be shot at. That's all I have to say about it."

"I see," Dennison replied. "Do you mind telling us why your brother-in-law, Mr. Lainvee, came to New York so suddenly today?"

"No. My wife's sister, who disappeared when the Russians entered Estonia in nineteen-forty, has been found. I naturally telephoned my brother-in-law in Paris night before last, and he's here."

"Oh I'm delighted to hear that," Rutledge said.

"I'm sure we all are," Dennison said, "but I must put another question to you, if you'll allow me. Do you intend, in view of this happy coincidence, to use your brother-in-law yourself as was suggested?"

"The answer is no, and as emphatic as I can make it."

"Then what, Mr. Lowry, are you going to do to get us out of

this grievous loss, for which in the final analysis you are responsible?" Delano asked.

"We shall have to take the money loss. Nonperformance would involve far greater losses in reputation and prestige."

"May I ask this," Curtis said. "Have you considered the damage to our reputation and prestige which will result from our competitors' spreading the story that this was a deliberate error, made either to buy our way into a new field, or made because it suited a tax situation?"

"Does it suit a tax situation?" Delano asked quickly

"It may," Curtis replied.

"Well whether it does or not, we can't ask an easement in Caracas and we can't consult our competitors' wishes," Lowry said. "The bid had a fair margin of profit. I know we're not in business to do it for nothing, but I'm sure also that as regards the organization, our competitors, the Caracas government, we must proceed as though we still had a profit."

"We've concluded that is true, Mr. Lowry," Delano said, "but it raises two points—what lesson are we to learn from it and, to put it frankly, are we safe in entrusting another bid, or rather the future of our foreign business to you?"

"The second you must decide of course. As to the first, you may be sure that all concerned have learned a bitter lesson they will not forget."

"Before asking you to retire again for a moment, Mr. Lowry," Delano said, "you are entitled to say anything you like. As you may know, we talked to Mr. Cramer this morning. Has this come about, in any part, because of pressures and annoyances put in your way by him?"

"In no way at all."

"As you look on the matter of Jim Peale, do you feel now that you could have handled it differently?" Dennison asked.

"I shall always wish I had had more wisdom or that I had found some way to help him. But I don't see that I could have done anything different as regards the Company."

"You know where he is today?" Dennison asked.

"Yes, I do," Lowry finally replied.

"Now will you be good enough to give us a few minutes," Delano asked.

He had been waiting some time when the receptionist told him his secretary wished to speak to him.

"Mr. Lowry, I'm sorry to bother you. Mr. Cramer is looking for you and I didn't tell him where you were. He wants me to trace you, call your house and so on. What shall I do?"

"Tell him you just heard from me and that I'm here."

"Thank you. I was so afraid of lousing things up."

He went back to his chair with outward composure. He wondered if Curtis also knew Bagehot's remark that most of the evils of life arose from man's inability to sit still in a room. He was inclined to feel he had not "done well." The best he could say was that he had not been drawn into an attack on Cramer.

He heard the receptionist speaking and she came in to say, "Mr. Lowry, would you come through here? That door. Mr. Rutledge will see you in there."

Well, Lowry thought, it will at least come at the hands of a friend.

"Sit down, Stephen," Rutledge said soberly. "When we first talked New Year's Eve afternoon you said something to the effect that your job might not be such 'fun,' et cetera. Do you remember that?"

"Yes."

"It troubled me at the time. What did it mean?"

"To paraphrase Chester Barnard, I suppose it was a poor way of saying there was not enough vitality in dollars alone to make business anything but a lifeless failure."

Rutledge pondered it a moment. The words of one of the very great executives of the country were, of all men, worthy to be believed.

"I remember how you looked when you came to me about Jim. I watched you while you were being questioned now. It hasn't been fun for you, has it?"

"No, not fun," Lowry said.

"I suppose there was a quicker and easier way of telling you what we had decided. The others felt it necessary to do it this way. However you may feel about it, you have the satisfaction of knowing that each of us was deeply impressed, deeply, by the way you behaved in there and by what you would not be drawn into saying. I don't know just how to tell you this, Stephen," Rutledge said, rising and walking around the room, hands in his pockets.

"You can tell me straight out, I don't expect it to be fun," Lowry replied.

"In the first shock of Jim's tragedy, I took the easiest way out. I'm ashamed of it now. If ever a man was called on to stay and face the consequences of what was his own negligence or misjudgment I was that man—though I did not, of course, foresee Tom's breakdown. But I should have. As a consequence we put in a man who, all of us ought to have known, was utterly unfitted for the place. One of the worst aspects of it is that we were wholly unfair to Cramer. And that's not going to be easy to put right because he's going to feel he hasn't been given time to show what he can do, and if we gave him time he'd wreck the Company. I can't imagine what we were thinking of. Jim's affair was so shocking that we went to the other extreme. Harold Titcomb came out to warn me. Titcomb, the head of the mailroom, saw what none of us saw. Bill Delano thought the sun rose and set in Cramer. Well, I'll not go on, but on September first I'm resuming the presidency of C.I.C. Bill Delano will keep the chairmanship, pending some negotiations I'll tell you about. What do you think of it?"

"Well, I think it's marvelous. What happens to Mr. Cramer?"

"Oh we're sugaring the pill, you may be sure. We can use him in the Shelbyville project. He doesn't know yet. Now what about you?"

"What about me?"

"You've elected to say nothing against Cramer and I'm not going to ask more questions—"

"I'd better say this. I elected not to go into trivialities and personal matters with or about him, but I want to make clear that I was not prepared to lose to him on the large issue of the bridge."

"Henry Dennison had a call from Hewitt about Cramer's plan to use Daran and your brother-in-law and he also told Henry about his wife and Jim. With Bill and Henry, a senior warden and an elder of the kirk, you had every chance, my boy, of saying the wrong thing. Cramer said it in every instance. Well now, I'm going to have your support?"

"You want it in spite of this bridge business?"

"Most decidedly," Rutledge said and put out his hand. "Susan and I are looking forward to Rosalie's and your dining with us Saturday. The Barwicks are coming out for the weekend. I'll tell you about that. Oh, and tell Rosalie America's headed in the right direction. I saw in *Life* that the flower-growing industry is over a billion dollars. Let's see these other fellows."

"I have tried to avoid personalities, but I would like to know before we go in there, is Charley Curtis opposed to this and to me, as his manner indicates, and has, for several days?"

Rutledge smiled. "In a way Charley has brought it about. What you said to him about Parry brought him out to see me. In his quiet way he has great influence and when he told Delano that Cramer must go, or he would, the thing was settled. Bill Delano spent yesterday with me. Charley was sure you would behave as you did but he wanted Delano to see for himself. If anybody but Charley had told us you had no idea what was coming, we wouldn't have believed it. Or believed the intolerable annoyance Cramer has been to you. You know I have been terribly depressed about my responsibility for Jim—and now about Calvin—but when I consider that in our whole organization only two men without character have appeared, I don't feel too badly."

"They are not entirely without character," Lowry said. "They both missed the great builder of character."

"Which is?"

"A happy marriage."

They went through to Delano's office.

"I hope you don't feel we were too hard on you, Mr.—er, Stephen," Delano said, "and I would like you to know I never understood what advance-action cables meant, had never heard the word."

Curtis was smiling. "My wife has always felt the stage lost a great ornament in me, Steve, but it was a hard part to play. I shouldn't have blamed you if you had told them that I said to you I was too tired to fight with Cramer. I think we'd better get back to the office. Cramer's due here shortly."

"Yes, and you and I had better get out, Henry," Rutledge said.

Delano shook his head sadly and then said, "Oh Stephen, I'd like to have some men meet Mr. Lainvee at lunch or dinner, whichever suits him. I'd suggest dinner at my house at Cold Spring. Will you ask him about it and let me know?"

At a quarter past four Lowry's telephone rang and Cramer asked him if it would be convenient to come to his office, "or I can come to you." Lowry said he would be right in. Whatever his other feelings toward Cramer, pleasure in his downfall was not one of them and few things could be more distasteful than to listen to a man cover his humiliation—who knew, even his heartbreak—behind a cloak of quick-woven lies. But Cramer was standing by his desk looking like a feline who has just eaten a small yellow songbird.

"Charley's had to go out and can't join us but I didn't want to hold you up. Sit down, please. Let me say right off that what I have to tell you should not affect you. I made it a prior condition of my agreement that you are to go on, others are to go on, just the same as though I were here to look out for you. But friend Lowry, if the President of the United States appeals to the American Red Cross in some disaster, they answer the appeal, they don't shuffle their feet, and I'm no better than they are."

"You mean that you're going to do something for the Red Cross?"

"For years as you know I have been the Red Cross—in a management sense that is to say—to the Founders Trust Company or the industries represented on their board. It's never been mine to question why, but only to be used where the need was greatest. Well, I pack my grip tomorrow and head out for Shelbyville,

Kentucky. That whole setup there is, as we used to say in the war, snafu. I know what you're going to say, you're going to say I'm needed here. I realize that only too well and unfortunately I'm going to have to take Miss Wilkins and John with me. But, friend Lowry, if you'd been in my shoes today, sitting there, being asked for help by Mr. Delano, you couldn't have found it in your heart to say no, any more than I could, or you're not the man I know you are. We've had a very happy association here, you and I, and I am satisfied I've gotten the train back on the track. The results of a man's work are often not apparent until much later."

He leaned back in his chair and from every outward sign appeared to be a man entitled to a good deal of satisfaction in what he had accomplished. As he would have phrased it, Delano *had* done it in the nice way.

"This will be the seventeenth rescue or, to put it another way, the seventeenth time I have been the disaster-unit to a hard-hit business. Three times in North Carolina, textiles, twice in East Texas, sulphur, once in Virginia, aluminum foil, machinery in Indiana, Ohio, Illinois, Missouri and Michigan. What gives me the greatest satisfaction is that the first time the call has come from New York has been the time where my work has been most quickly done. I say this to you, as I wouldn't to anyone else, I wasn't sure until I tried it that I could do what I have in New York City. I thought the whole setup and the people would be very, very different than they are in the Middle West and South. Friend Lowry, they're just the same. The New Yorker, once you get inside of him, is no different from your Southerner or your Middle Westerner. There are good people all over this broad land. Well, I know you and I'll meet often, but I wanted you to know how much I value our friendship and the help you've given me." He put out his hand and Lowry shook it heartily.

"Knowing you has been a rare experience, Mr. Cramer," he said. "I wish you every possible luck."

"Thank you," Cramer said, beaming, and looked for an envelope on his desk. “Oh here are those tabloid clippings Hewitt showed me. You may want to keep them.”

“You’ve forgotten you already gave them to me,” Lowry said.

“No, these *are* the ones Hewitt showed me. The ones I gave you Miss Wilkins had cut out for me.”

29

LOWRY TELEPHONED ROSALIE FROM THE STATION, asking her to meet his regular train, telling her what had happened.

"Then my breakfast helped?" she asked gaily.

"It was indispensable. You know, for all the fact that he's a terrible fellow, I feel sorry for Cramer tonight. It must be an awful blow."

"Darling, what nonsense. He knew it wouldn't last. That's why his wife never 'came on from the West.' Armas isn't back yet."

Hopkins, fully restored, sitting next to him in the club car, looked at his grave face.

"Lost your last friend?" he asked. "Or is this just the pause in the day's occupation?"

"No, as a matter of fact that 'just one man in the office' is leaving us."

"Then why aren't you drunk?"

"I am wondering how I'd act if it had been me."

"Well, my boy, introspect that on your own. I have just bought this immoral novel, which is alleged to tell all in words the ordinary man like myself can understand. Wake me as we approach Ridingtown."

It was still hard for Stephen to take in what it meant to be free of Cramer. It was even invigorating to realize that hereafter there would be no excuse for anything he himself did, and that all his immediate associates would be men who were his equals or superiors.

As Rutledge had said, the months had not been fun, nor in prospect were those ahead likely to be. The day's work, even without the capital letters in which Cramer referred to it, blanketed his whole life. Whatever else, however personally important, he wanted to do was subject to its discipline. But he had been shown clearly today it was not the service of Mammon and there was a great company besides himself who, having been born men, were unwilling to die as grocers. And what demanded more from the talents, aspiration and energies of men than the relentless purpose still to seek and find wisdom and beauty in spite of the din of the marketplace? *Ardent the struggle, splendid the prize!*

The club car was the last on the train but after nudging Hopkins awake, Stephen was one of the first to reach the line of waiting wives, chauffeurs and parked cars, and he kissed Rosalie as though it were the first in months.

"I'm full of ideas," he said. "Another book, better than Principal Errors, trips, love under the stars, lots of business and beaucoup francs. Do you love me?"

"Oh I adore you, but we must be very humble about all these blessings."

"I know. What about Inge?"

"Armas still wasn't back when I left. I hope he hasn't been arrested. We were both so excited we forgot he had no driver's license. Oh he is very enthusiastic about Daran and says Beatriz is delightful."

Armas was soberly pacing the driveway as they turned in.

"Well," he said, "it went badly. Nothing I said seemed to be right. She was perhaps less bitter toward me—because I was captured—but she refuses help, repeats she doesn't want to see us, and my suggestion that she would be happier in Europe with me, shall I say, offended her. I suppose one mistake was to let her see how shocked I was by the change in her, but I was overcome by emotion."

Rosalie patted his hand. "Don't blame yourself. So was I."

"Yes, but you had warned me—"

"Armas, you are her brother. You're not a psychologist or a physician with a bedside manner. You behaved like a brother and I don't believe it harmed her. We must remember it is a shock to her to see us. I think we can only move step by step, but all will be well, I am sure. Now I must get dinner. The children will be back from the beach in a few minutes. You'd better have a drink inside. It's very blowy on the terrace and I think it's going to rain. The wind *is* east, isn't it, Stephen?"

"It is east and it is going to rain."

"Rosalie, do you still sing, *Wild wailing winds of misfortune and sorrow?*" Armas asked.

She sang the next line, *Wizards from Finland, ride by on the blast.* "Yes, often. I sang it to Stephen in Estonian the second day we met. And today a wicked wizard was ridden out of his life. Tell Armas, dear. Light all the lamps. It's getting very lowering."

Very shortly after dinner, Rosalie took the sleepy children and the exhausted Armas up to their beds. It was now raining heavily and the wind was wrenching at the branches of the trees and flattening the flower borders. Stephen, watching it from the darkened room, saw an apple tree, heavy with fruit, sink to the ground like a weary ballerina, her sequined skirt spread wide around her.

Rosalie came softly in, her feet in Wellingtons, as the children still called them. "Darling, I must see Inge tonight. I suddenly know what I must tell her. Will you drive me there, storm or no storm?"

"Of course, get your coat," he said.

"You'll never know, Stephen, what heaven it is to have a husband who doesn't weigh pros and cons."

They were an hour and a half reaching Lattingtown, detouring from flooded roads, moving slowly through the torrential rain, Rosalie nestled close beside him, speaking little except to direct him, until at Jericho she lost the way, and he pulled up at a police booth for directions.

Finally they saw the school's white shingle waving in the wind and turned in between the stone markers. Lights were on in the Dubosque cottage and they could see the low lines of the school adjoining. "Say a prayer," she said, getting out and steadying herself a moment before the wind. He watched through the lowered window as she ran to the vestibule and stood waiting. A light over her head snapped on and the door opened. He could see her talking to someone inside, then she shed her coat and soft felt hat, turned to wave an instant to him and went inside. He did pray that she would not have to come back with her bright hopes broken. Surely the Power which cared for the frightened and craven cared also for gallants.

It was three-quarters of an hour before the door opened again. Upstairs some lights had gone off. Rosalie stood in the vestibule alone, pulling on coat and soft hat. He leaned across the seat to open the car door and she got in with a sprinkling of rain.

"I wasn't sure until the last moment that I had succeeded, but I have. I am sure, because she wouldn't let me bring you in and she wouldn't come to the door because she didn't want you to see her as she is now."

"What did you tell her?"

"It's hard to repeat exactly. I realized today that she was someone to be proud of, not to pity and care for—that underneath her bitterness was wonderful strength and self-reliance, and that few people could survive, get to America, make their living as she was doing. I asked her to go away with me someplace for three or four weeks to a spa. I thought of White Sulphur that Jim talked about. And she asked what it would cost and I said it didn't matter. Armas and we would arrange that. And finally she said that in another month she would have saved over five hundred dollars and that if she could pay her own way, maybe she would. But that I must leave her alone to decide. Then she asked if I had a picture of you and the children and I said I hadn't brought my bag, but I could bring you in. I was sure you had pictures of them. It was then she said she wouldn't see you yet. Dear, we'd better leave. I see someone watching us from upstairs, and they must want to go to bed."

Stephen started the car, steering carefully around the winding scarcely visible driveway.

"Oh, she said also that I must not press her to live with us."

"What do you think made her change?"

"Different things. Armas's coming so quickly. He apparently quite broke down with her. And your bringing me on such a night. The terrible need even very brave people have to be wanted and loved, whatever they pretend. The feeling I had when Richard sleepily said, 'Oh Mum's home, that's super.' "

"I must remember these roads. Rutledge wants us to dine Saturday night and Delano wants me to bring Armas to a men's dinner. Would you like to stop in a diner for some coffee?" he asked as they reached the Jericho Turnpike.

"Oh darling," she said, "I want to be home. I'm not quite as composed as I sound. I'll get us some supper there." He could feel her trembling beside him and turned on the heater.

The house was quiet, snug and curtained from the storm. There were no messages by the telephone and Rosalie said, "Go up and count the children while I fix something."

They had some eggs and cocoa, washed their cups and dishes, put the pans to soak and went upstairs together.

"Are you very tired?" he asked.

She turned and gave him a little smile. "A little, not *too* tired."

He leaned back on the chaise longue, watching her as she undressed.

"I was wondering," he said, "whether I possibly had the brains to write a book about Chance and Destiny and was it always inevitable that I should volunteer for Sardine—"

"And find a herring-gutter?"

"Um. And did that bring Jim where he is and Calvin where he is? And put poor old Cramer out in Shelbyville. And Daran and Beatriz in a center of culture?"

"And save Mr. Parry's job? And show your brother-in-law Robert you were human? Oh, incidentally, never tell Armas about it."

"Oh no. But was it inevitable and did these other things happen because of it?"

"Darling, you are the most important man in the world in my eyes, but even I suspect these people all had their own destinies."

He rose and took off his coat and tie and looked down at the rain-soaked cuffs of his trousers. His clothes would need pressing, and as Hewitt had once said, he would only have to leave them over a chair.

"I must have seen you get ready for bed three or four thousand times and each time it's like seeing a New-Found-Land," he said.

"Dear, I'm too tired even to wash my face. Peasants and herring-gutters—"

"It's rain-washed. You know, I made a brilliant observation to Rutledge today. I told him something that transcends chance or destiny, business and desire, God and Mammon. Like all great truths it is quite simple."

"I listen."

"A happy marriage is the great builder of character."